CONSPIRACY OF MAGIC BOOK TWO

WOUNDED MAGIC

MEGAN CREWE

To my readers, who make the magic in these books come to life

CHAPTER ONE

Rocío

The Mages' Exam buildings didn't look like the kind of place where sixteen-year-old novices were tortured and murdered. The hallway I followed Examiner Welch down gleamed spotlessly white. A crisp, ozone-y smell hung in the artificially chilled air. Our footsteps echoed only faintly on the polished floor, despite the quiet around us. I had to suppress the urge to hug myself.

The whole space would've seemed bright and unassuming if I could have forgotten that this island used to be a prison. These buildings had been converted or rebuilt from the original structures. Who knew how much violence this hall had witnessed before the North American Confederation of Mages had taken it over and whitewashed it clean?

I'd found the history of Rikers Island unnerving even before I'd crossed its bridge five days ago. Now, after everything I'd been through since then, the setting for the Exam felt perfectly fitting. And I couldn't wait to leave it behind, even if what lay ahead might not be any more pleasant.

Examiner Welch led me past several doors, but I didn't hear a sound from behind any of them. At least nine of my fellow examinees—the nine who'd made it to the end of the Exam with me—should've been around here somewhere. The hush made me wonder if the examiners cast a muting 'chantment to keep whatever was going on in those other rooms private.

Welch stopped at one of the doors and nudged it open, beckoning me ahead of him. "All of our examinees undergo a small procedure before returning to the outside world," he said. "It'll only take a few minutes, and then you can see your parents."

The room beyond him was about the size I figured a jail cell would've been, its walls as white as the hallway's. A padded, slightly reclined chair like the ones at my dentist's office stood in the middle of the room. Another mage, a middle-aged woman in the gray uniform all the examiners wore, waited beside the chair. She gave me a mild smile.

They were going to need more than a smile to coax me into that chair. My legs balked. "What kind of procedure?"

Welch's ruddy face stayed blank, his tone measured, as if this were all completely reasonable. As if everything that had happened here was reasonable. "A 'chantment to prevent you from discussing the Exam beyond these walls. We value our confidentiality, Miss Lopez."

I bet they did. According to the official story, every year all the sixteen-year-old mages under the Confederation's domain were fairly evaluated based on skill and temperament, and then either chosen to enter the Confed's college or scheduled for Dampering: having all but a small portion of their magical ability wiped away. The Mages' Exam was one last chance offered by the powers that be for any unchosen novice to prove themselves worthy of the college.

Sure, everyone knew the trials were so brutal that not every novice even survived them. But I couldn't think of anyone who'd have guessed the examiners would send us into actual battle—that they would trick us and then force us into killing people, that in the final stage they'd encourage us to turn on the examinees who'd fought at our sides. Their most closely guarded secret, though, had to be that even those of us who "won" a spot as Champion didn't get into the college. The Exam was a recruiting and training ground for a magical special ops unit.

Everyone in our society, magical and nonmagical, would freak out if they discovered that.

Still, I hadn't been prepared for the examiners to magically enforce our silence. My back stayed rigid as I stared at the padded chair. When I'd talked to a guy from school who'd gone through the Exam a few years ago, he'd said he couldn't tell me anything. I'd assumed he'd been worried about facing punishment if he let the examiners' secrets slip, but apparently he'd meant the "couldn't" part literally.

"The 'chantment will be quick and painless," the woman by the chair said, still with that smile that I guessed she meant to be reassuring.

As if I could trust that was true, or even that the 'chantment would only do what Welch had said, after all the lies I'd already been told. I wet my lips. I'd hoped to work around my position as Champion to find a way to expose what really happened here. That was going to be a hell of a lot harder if I couldn't speak about anything I'd seen or been through.

"Is there a problem?" Examiner Welch asked.

"I wasn't expecting it," I said, scrambling to think of any excuse to get out of this. I came up pretty much blank. "Is it really necessary? I can keep quiet without any compulsion."

Somehow Welch managed to look skeptical and impassive at the same time. I'd been careful not to say anything too antagonistic about the Confed when they might hear, but after the defiant way I'd approached their trials, maybe I couldn't blame him for not taking me at my word, either.

"It's policy," he said. "You agreed to this by entering the Exam. It'll be easier to conduct the 'chantment if you accept it willingly. Can we proceed?"

It would've been nice if they'd let us read the fine print ahead of time. I dragged in a breath. The hum of energy in the air, like a faint but steady melody, wrapped around my shoulders to embrace me.

I had more than just the people harmed by the Confed's machinations to protect. The magic had reached out to me and pleaded with me to pay attention, to notice the way destructive castings hurt it as much as whatever they were destroying. I was the only one who'd felt its presence like that. If I lost my connection to the magic and it had no one else to speak up for it, it might completely die.

I had no choice here. I had to play along like a good little soldier while I watched for the right opportunities. There were ways to expose people without speaking. 'Chantments could be broken.

"All right," I said.

I forced my legs to unlock and climbed into the chair. It was more comfortable than the dentist version, the padding silky soft instead of sticky plastic. I leaned my head back, trying to ignore the thump of my pulse.

Welch shut the door, leaving me alone with the woman. A 'chantment like this, designed to permanently affect the mind in very specific ways, must take a huge amount of concentration. He wouldn't want to distract her.

"Close your eyes," the mage suggested. I did it with a clench of my jaw. She leaned over me, singing a verse under her breath.

The magic thrummed around us alongside her song. Bit by

bit, it resonated with her intent and tingled into my forehead and scalp.

The strands of magic didn't affect my thoughts in any noticeable way. She hadn't been lying about the painless part, at least. Would they be able to make the same promise to Finn when they brought him into one of these rooms to burn him out?

My fingers started to curl into my palms. I willed them to relax before they turned into fists, but the ache of anger remained.

Before I'd come here, Finn Lockwood had been just a boy I'd watched from afar in his academy's library. A boy I'd never thought I'd even talk to because of the charmed old-magic life he obviously led. But he'd given up a Chosen spot to enter the Exam and prove he actually deserved that privilege; he'd pushed himself to his limits and stood by me every step of the way.

With his bright smile and his wry honesty, he'd worked his way into my heart. If I ducked my head right now, I might still be able to catch a hint of his fresh sweet scent from our last embrace before Examiner Welch had called me away.

Finn hadn't made Champion, and anyone who failed the Exam got a fate worse than Dampering. Dampering at least left a mage able to cast a small range of spells focused around a speciality, like my father's affinity for cooking and my mother's for fabric and thread. Finn was going to have his entire ability to hearken and conduct magic burned out of him—utterly destroyed.

He might not have a strong talent, but it was *his*. No one should have been allowed to take it away from him.

"All done, Miss Lopez," the mage said. "You're ready to go."

My eyelids popped open. The woman had straightened up with another smile, but the fringe of hair along her forehead was damp with sweat from the effort of the casting.

My hand rose to my temple automatically. "That's it?" I said. No disorientation or dizziness hit me when I pushed out of the chair. Even the initial faint tingling of the 'chantment had faded. If they hadn't told me what they were doing, there'd be no way for me to know they'd cast anything at all on me.

"That's all there is to it," the mage said. "You'll find you won't be able to speak about your experiences in the Exam at all. You'll also be restricted from discussing details of your upcoming training and missions with anyone other than colleagues. It's best not to try to push past the limitations, or you may feel some side effects. The 'chantment shouldn't interfere with other conversation."

I should've figured they'd cover my activities as Champion too. Welch hadn't bothered to mention that part.

He was waiting for me in the hall. After a quick glance up and down as if he could see whether the 'chantment had worked by looking at me, he set off at a brisk pace. I hurried after him. He'd said I'd get to see my parents now. My hand jumped up to clasp the sunburst necklace Mom had given me right before I'd headed into the Exam.

They must have been so worried the last five days. Mom hadn't wanted me to declare for the Exam at all, and I couldn't imagine Dad had either, even if he'd kept quiet about his disapproval. They'd already lost one child to these trials: my older brother, Javier.

But they hadn't lost me. That was one victory won. The examiners and their old-magic prejudices hadn't managed to beat me down. All the pain I'd been through, all the pain I'd put them through, would be worth it if I could stop other families from facing the same thing.

Welch turned a corner and pushed open a door. Muggy summer heat wafted over me. I stepped out into the courtyard between the main Exam buildings, all of them as white on the outside as they were inside. The late afternoon sun seared my eyes. It wasn't even that bright, but I hadn't seen anything except artificial light in days.

A gasp and hasty footsteps reached my ears. I blinked away the natural brilliance to see my parents rushing over, so familiar the sight wrenched at my chest. I threw myself into their arms.

"Rocío!" Mom cried. "¡Gracias a Dios!" She hugged me first, swift and tight, and then Dad did, with a long squeeze. A sugary scent drifted from him. Or from the bag he was clutching, which he pushed into my hands when he stepped back.

"I didn't have time to bake anything for you myself," he said, sounding a little choked. "But I thought you might appreciate something better than whatever they've fed you here. I'll whip up a proper congratulations dinner when you're home."

The bag held one of the buttery cinnamon rolls from our favorite bakery a couple blocks from our apartment. Suddenly *I* was choking up.

"Dad…"

He wrapped his arms around me again. "We're so thankful you've come back to us, mija. Come back to us, and as Champion. You'll be able to do everything you wanted."

My throat constricted even more. They had no idea. They thought I was heading off to the college to study and develop my magic. That dream had died the moment an evaluator had marked me for Dampering, deciding my talent and my new-magic background were too big a threat for me to remain a full part of the Confed.

Mom's gaze settled on the sunburst necklace. The gold was faintly singed, one of the jagged points curved to the side where the heat of a casting had melted it. A casting that had been intended to kill me.

"Are you all right?" she said. "They told us you were, but you never know…" She made a vague gesture that managed to encompass the unpredictable authority of the Confed as represented by the buildings all around us.

"Yeah." What else could I say when they were looking at me like that? "Yeah, I'm okay." My thumb dropped to rub the little finger that the examiners' magimedics had reconstructed. I couldn't count how many cuts, bruises, and burns they'd whisked away.

I probably didn't sound enthusiastic enough. Mom frowned. "What did they put you through in there, cariño?"

Without thinking, I opened my mouth. I hadn't been going to say anything all that secret, just a couple of the less horrifying details to put off further questions, but my jaw froze. My vocal chords went still.

The 'chantment that'd just been laid on me was definitely working. My pulse stuttered as I scrambled for an answer that wouldn't activate it.

"I can't really talk about it. Lots of tests, some of them hard." *They sent monsters after us. They turned innocent people into walking bombs that we had to kill or face being killed ourselves. They crushed one of my teammates into a pulp with a mass of 'chanted vines.* I shrugged, hoping the memory of Judith's shrieks wasn't coloring my expression.

"You came out on top," Dad said. "That's what matters."

Examiner Welch strolled over to us. For the first time, I took in the rest of the courtyard. It wasn't just me and my parents here. Prisha, Finn's best friend and another of my teammates, was standing at the other end of the yard surrounded by a group I guessed were her parents and a few brothers and sisters. Her dad's deep voice rolled across the space as he declared something "brilliant!"

The four other Champions mustn't have had family who lived close enough to make it here for an immediate reunion.

Prisha and I were the only two local to New York—possibly the only two from the whole Northeast.

"You have an hour," Welch reminded us. "It's imperative that the Champions meet with their tutors and begin their transition into college life as quickly as possible."

Mom pursed her lips. I knew she was thinking that I could probably already cast my way around most of the novices the Confed had chosen for their college, but the examiners would've warned them ahead of time that this would be a short visit.

"I'm sorry," I said. "I wish we could have that dinner now." I wished I could have just one night in my bed at home before my new instructors hustled me off, not to college but to my military training.

"It's all right," Mom said, squeezing my arm. "We understand how important this is to you. Your happiness matters more to us than anything."

My happiness. So much for that. My stomach curled around itself into a massive knot.

"It's a very immersive program," Welch said. "She'll have time to visit every few weeks once the initial transition period is complete."

Dad's head snapped up. "Every few *weeks*?"

Welch offered him the same impassive expression he'd given me when I'd balked at the silencing 'chantment. "That information should have been conveyed when you were notified."

"Yes, but—I assumed in our case—we live in *Brooklyn*. The college isn't even an hour away. Can't she at least come home for weekends?"

"As I said, it's a very immersive program. She'll have the greatest success this way."

Dad looked like he was going to argue further. I touched his arm. They had to be okay with this. If they kicked up a fuss now, for all I knew the Confed would decide they were a bad influence and restrict our time together even more.

"I think it's best if I follow the usual protocols," I said. "It won't be forever."

Dad turned back to me, and his eyes softened. He nodded to Welch, who moved on.

We ended up sitting on the concrete in the shade of one of the buildings. I broke off pieces from my cinnamon roll to share with Mom and Dad, despite their protests. I had a hard enough time forcing the rest past the lump in my throat, even though the buttery, spicy dough tasted as delicious as always.

Mom told me about a new commission she'd gotten to make dance costumes for a ballroom studio, Dad did exaggerated impressions of the wackiest people he'd gotten on the line at the call center, and all three of us pretended this was just normal catching up after a vacation or something. I lost myself in the moment enough that it didn't feel like a whole hour could've passed before Welch came ambling over again.

"Time to go," he said, quiet but firm.

Mom and Dad pulled me into another round of hugs. "You show those college mages just how impressive you are," Mom said. "And don't forget how proud we are of you to have gotten there."

I swallowed hard as I smiled. The smile was a lie, but I couldn't bring myself to even hint that they might not have the whole story. How would it help them to be worrying even more about what I'd be doing now? They were so relieved that I'd made it through the Exam. I couldn't spoil that joy when they couldn't change what was ahead of me.

Someday, I'd be able to tell them. I'd get through this new ordeal and back to the people I loved, lo prometo.

Another man in Exam gray showed up to escort my parents

back over the bridge. I gave them one last wave before they passed out of sight. Welch patted me on the back.

"Let's go. You've got a plane to catch."

A weight settled in my gut as I followed him. I was about to leave Rikers Island, but I was bringing the Confed's prison with me—in the 'chantment they'd cast on me and in the lies I had to keep telling to protect everyone and everything I cared about.

CHAPTER TWO

Finn

It turned out it was a lot easier to be brave when you had someone to be brave for.

I'd thought I'd found some sort of inner Zen about my fate while the Exam's staff tidied up my various injuries until I reached a condition befitting a Lockwood. Afterward, standing in this waiting room with Rocío, holding her and knowing that she'd won as much as anyone could, and that I'd played some small part in her victory... That consolation had seemed like enough to carry me through.

As the great Virgil line went, tu ne cede malis, sed contra audentior ito. I would not give in to the evils within the Confed but fight them all the more boldly however I could.

Then one of the examiners had come to collect Rocío. Alone with a table of food I couldn't summon any interest in, the certainty of purpose that had felt so solid a moment ago started to crumble. The minutes slipped by as I waited for someone to come collect *me*, and a clammy sensation of dread seeped over my skin. I paced from one end of the room to the other, but I couldn't shake it.

They were going to burn me out: sever my connection to the magic, which had been as much a part of my life as air, as gravity, and leave me utterly deafened to it.

No more melodic whisper in the air. No more swivel of a thumb or murmur of a poetic lyric to conduct that energy to my will. I would be as dull as the Dulls.

I couldn't imagine it, and that was terrifying.

No more struggling to cast even half as well as the rest of the family, I reminded myself. No more studying until my head ached and then receiving my latest grades with a sinking heart. No more pretending I could somehow construct myself into a great mage, because I wouldn't be a mage at all, not in any tangible way.

Nausea twisted my stomach at that thought. The magic and I might have a fraught relationship, but I'd wanted to be better, not just to impress my family and peers but also because I loved what little I could do with it. There was nothing more exhilarating than weaving intent into being by working in harmony with that energy.

An examiner appeared in the doorway: Examiner Khalil, one of the three who'd remarked on my performance in the Exam and delivered their verdict. She was one of the youngest examiners I'd seen here—mid-twenties like my sister Margo, I estimated—and unlike the other two, she'd been generous enough to look a little sad.

"Mr. Lockwood," she said now. "If you'd come with me?"

My feet resisted for a second before I managed to propel myself toward her. I'd come here because I wanted my future to be defined by my actions and not my family's name. That was what I'd gotten. I could at least put a good face forward.

I fell into step beside the examiner. "Are you going to give me the standard doctor line?" I asked in the most cheerful voice I could muster. "'It won't hurt a bit'?"

Examiner Khalil's fingers twitched as she adjusted the edge of her hijab, which was the same shade of gray as her uniform. Her dark eyes were solemn.

"I don't believe there's any pain from the actual procedure," she said in her soft, clear voice. "Afterward, naturally, you'll find there's some discomfort as you adjust to the loss of magical sensation. There are mages who specialize in easing the transition. Your family should be able to connect you with one as need be."

Did they offer the same reassurance to all the novices who ended up burned out, even the ones whose families didn't have the means to pay for undoubtedly expensive therapy—which was most of them? I suspected not.

"One more adventure," I said. "It certainly has been an exciting week."

My attempt at good humor fell flat before the words were even out. I swiped my hand over my mouth, trying to think of a better follow-up, and Khalil stopped in the middle of the hall.

The examiner's gaze darted up and down the narrow, white-walled space. No one else was in sight. She leaned closer, her voice dropping.

"I don't agree with all of the policies we follow here," she said. "I—I can't do anything about the burning out. They'd notice. I *can* try to mitigate some of the rest, so you won't lose everything."

"The rest?" I repeated. A deeper chill rippled through me. "What are you talking about?"

She'd already focused her gaze on my forehead, her hands rising to either side of my head. "I had a placement under your father for a year while I was in college. From what I saw, he was a good person. From what I've seen of you, you'll be one too. But you can only exercise that goodness if you still know."

Before I could question her any further, a lilting lyric slid from her lips. The magic she wove tickled across my scalp. I hesitated, torn between wanting to know what in Hades's name she was doing and not wanting to ruin the casting by interrupting her. Everything she'd just said indicated she wanted to help me, not harm me.

The tickling crept down the back of my head as Examiner Khalil sang another line. The tap of footsteps carried from somewhere deeper in the building. Her voice wavered. She caught it and spun out a quick coda. With a jerk of her hand, she gestured for me to start walking again.

"What—?" I said, and Examiner Lancaster came around the bend up ahead. The elegant, silver-haired woman who appeared to be in charge of the Exam proceedings glanced us over with a thin smile. Khalil bobbed her head to her supervisor. She directed me to a door just a few paces from where she'd stopped me earlier.

"I'll be waiting to escort you to your parents when the procedure is finished," she said, her tone carefully even.

"Thank you," I said, as if it made any sense to be thanking her for leading me to my punishment. Perhaps I should be for whatever she'd been attempting to do a moment ago, if she'd even been successful.

On the other side of the door, two mages waited in the small room: one with a magimedic crest on her blue uniform and the other in regular Exam gray. My mouth went dry as I sat in the padded chair. I tried to smile to show I didn't blame them for what they were about to do, but I couldn't seem to work the muscles in my face quite right. I suspected it came out more like a grimace.

"We find the procedure is best done under sedation," the

magimedic said. As I nodded, she rolled her casting from her tongue. My lips parted with questions I meant to ask—and a wave of blackness swept through my mind, blotting out my consciousness.

* * *

A hollow buzzing filled my ears, as if I were underwater. My lungs heaved instinctively, sucking in air that was right there for the taking, and I blinked awake with a flinch against the chair.

The magimedic stood next to me, studying me. The other examiner was gone. I shook my head to clear it. My thoughts stayed as jumbled as if *they* were underwater—pebbles tossed by the current of a rapid stream.

The hollowness didn't leave. If anything, it expanded to completely encompass me. The numbness crept all across my skin and blanketed my tongue. My hand moved to shape the familiar rhythm that would tune me into the emotions of those around me, and my fingers stumbled.

There was nothing to apply that rhythm to—not the faintest hint of energy I could hearken in the space around me. The world had gone empty, drained of magic.

My pulse stuttered in the instant before I remembered that wasn't the case at all. The magic was still there. I simply couldn't reach the slightest strain of it. Whatever part of my mind had once responded to its harmony might as well have been ashes.

Burned out.

"Your Exam is complete," the magimedic said gently. "I'm afraid that despite your efforts, you did not meet the criteria for Champion, and so have undergone the burning out procedure."

I barely registered her words. My heart kept pounding hard. The sound of it in my ears, the thud resonating through my chest, made my surroundings feel even more vacant. A quiver ran through my limbs. I gripped the arms of the chair, fighting for some semblance of internal balance.

"Take your time," the magimedic went on. "Some disorientation is normal, but it'll pass as you settle in. My best advice is to look forward and make the most of what you have, not to dwell on what might have happened before."

What might have happened? Why was she talking as if I wasn't already aware of my "efforts" and their result? I knew precisely what had happened to bring me here. There'd been— I'd had to—

Images flitted through my memory: a hedge of razor-sharp thorns, a boy hurling a bolt of magic at another. My head ached when I tried to focus on them. I rubbed my temple and pushed myself out of the chair.

Walking made the hollowness worse too. No shifting undertone of magic twined with the tempo of my steps. I grasped the handle on the door, and a sudden, vicious urge tore up through me, the urge to throw myself at that blank surface, batter it with fists and feet until I provoked some kind of echo in answer.

I'd done something like that before. There'd been a clouded wall creating a numbing distance from the magic. Prisha's voice pierced the haze in my head: *One, two, three, go!*

That situation had been different. The wall had been a construct around me, around her, around—someone. I couldn't break through anything to get back to the magic now. *I* was broken.

A shudder of panic ran through my chest. It wound tight around my lungs as I stepped into the hall.

An examiner was waiting for me: a young woman with a hijab covering most of her wavy black hair. I'd spoken to her before—there'd been a table, they'd sat there, three of them… *A concerning disregard for the security of the Confederation.*

No, she hadn't said that bit. It'd been the other woman, the older one with the sleek silver hair. The examiner who'd appeared at the Exam's end, when I'd lain reeling on my back at the base of that barbed hedge. She'd also—a silver box. A screen with an image of a house. *Soldiers.*

The fragments jumbled even more. I frowned and gave my head another shake. What was this examiner's name again? Perhaps she hadn't introduced herself.

We started walking down the hall. I hardly noticed my legs moving. "Normally we arrange transport home," the examiner was saying. "But in your case, with your parents so nearby, of course they insisted on coming themselves."

My parents were here. The panic swept even deeper, dislodging every other discomfort. Dad and Mom knew now— they knew that I'd failed, that I was a *failure*, even more explicitly than I'd been before.

I had no time to brace myself. The examiner ushered me into another white-walled room, and there they were, standing tensed by a couple of unused sofas.

A hot flush of shame surged over my face as I fumbled for words. Before I needed any, my mother caught me in her arms with an inhalation just shy of a sob. She hugged me to her slender frame so tightly it was my eyes that heated next.

She was holding me as if she were afraid she'd never get to hug me again. I supposed she probably had been afraid of that. O gods, they hadn't even known if I'd *survive.* Perhaps the rest didn't matter all that much, at least not yet.

I hugged Mom back as I hadn't since I was a little kid. The warmth of her embrace penetrated the numbness around me just a bit.

Nevertheless, the shame returned the moment she eased back. "I'm sorry," I said. "I tried. I—"

"Finnegan," she said firmly, cutting me off. She never used my full name unless she wanted my immediate attention. Her eyes shone with a watery gleam. "You're here. You're all right. We'll figure out the rest later. But you have *nothing* to apologize for."

Dad gripped my shoulder. When I turned to look at him, his jaw was tight. He tugged me to him, clapping his other hand against my back and giving my shoulder a squeeze.

I'd declared for the Exam and refused to rescind that declaration against his very adamant protests, but when he spoke, the rawness of his voice wasn't remotely angry.

"It's good to have you back," he said. "Please tell me you're done proving yourself for at least a little while?"

The half-hearted joke made me choke on laughter, but it also reminded me that I wasn't done, not at all. I'd been going to tell them—they needed to know what really happened in the Exam, all the lies we'd been fed, all the ways the Confed's military division was using people. I'd promised her. I'd promised—

I stiffened as the memories jarred in my mind. I could see her perfectly: those dark brown eyes that could be fierce and tender at turns, the stubbornly sharp point of her chin, the waves of her hair tossed in a breeze. I could *feel* the shape of her in my arms when I'd held her not more than a few hours ago. Why couldn't I remember exactly what I'd said to her?

Why couldn't I put a name to that face?

"Finn," Dad said, but my thoughts were whirling too swiftly for me to answer. Someone had said something—someone had stopped me in the hall—

So you won't lose everything.

The way the magimedic had spoken to me, as if I wouldn't know where I was or why, made sudden, sickening sense. They hadn't just taken my connection to the magic. They'd meant to take my memories of the Exam too—and they'd nearly succeeded. As it was, all I had left were those ragged fragments.

The girl who'd led our way through the Exam, the girl my heart squeezed at the thought of, the girl I'd meant to do whatever I could to stay by—I'd lost her name.

CHAPTER THREE

Rocío

On our first morning of training, I found myself in a room that reminded me a lot of the gym in my old high school. The ceiling loomed high overhead, and the running shoes I'd been handed along with the sweats I was now wearing squeaked on the waxed wooden floor. The air smelled faintly rubbery. A basketball hoop was even fixed to the wall at the far end, but I wondered whether anyone who trained here under the Confed ever used that or if it was leftover from whatever this building had been before they'd taken it over.

Many of my Dull classmates had used that high school gym to take turns "accidentally" bumping and elbowing me, seeing if they could piss me off enough that I'd retaliate with a casting. I was pretty sure I'd have to get through whatever challenges waited for me here the same way: head low, mouth shut, focused on coming out the other side.

The examiners had said they'd been impressed by how I'd tackled the Exam's trials. That they wanted me to help them find more "effective" strategies for their military missions. No one had said anything about that since I'd been passed into the National Defense division's custody yesterday evening, so I guessed I'd have to bring it up myself.

A cool draft blew through the room, and I rubbed my arms. How much damage had the magic already suffered in the three decades of fighting between our mages and the magical insurgent groups that had risen up after our Unveiling? It was desperate enough to have reached out to me. We had to get started on healing it soon.

Over by a door labeled *Equipment Room*, Desmond, one of my teammates from the Exam, flashed a grin at Leonie, the old-magic girl from New Orleans who'd joined up with us in the final stages. He sidled a little closer as he said something that made her laugh. His tall, skinny frame looked almost relaxed in his standard-issue sweats. Of course, he'd talked as if this training were an extension of the sci-fi books and movies he liked to quote from, so maybe he wasn't as nervous as I was.

Our other teammate to make Champion, Prisha, was leaning against the wall near me. She didn't come across as half as polished in those sweats as she had in her blouse and slacks when I'd seen her at the beginning of the Exam, but even though she was way more new-magic than me, she still held herself with Academy girl airs. From what Finn had said, she was the first in her whole family to show a talent—just rich enough to buy her way into the right circles.

And then she'd sold her loyalty to the examiners for reasons I didn't know. She'd had inside information. Finn had blamed her for at least one of our teammates' deaths. They'd seemed to reach some kind of understanding by the end of the Exam, but that didn't mean I could trust her.

A pang ran through my chest at the thought of Finn. He'd be burned out by now. How was he coping? I wasn't even sure what country I was in, but it'd been a long flight. I felt the distance between us, an ocean and more of separation, like a scrape down the center of me.

My parents were just as distant. I had no one nearby I really knew, other than the magic with its ever-present hum.

A brawny man strode into the room with two more figures in tow. I tensed at the sight of the girl with the ragged brown hair. Just two days ago in the Exam, I'd watched her slam a hatchet into the back of a boy's head. The wiry guy who walked in next to her I'd seen attack a teammate he'd been fighting beside a moment before. After that, the two of them had banded together with a couple of the other examinees to kill the rest of us. These two were the only ones from their group who'd made Champion.

And now we were colleagues.

The brawny man spun on his heel at the front of the room, facing us with a clap of his broad hands. A few flecks of gray shone in his tawny buzzcut, and a narrow scar below his right cheek pulled the corner of his mouth down in a perpetual grimace.

"All right, Champions," he said in a terse but resonant voice. "Come on over here, and we'll get started."

We moved to form a semi-circle around him, the four of us who preferred not to murder people keeping a healthy distance from the other two Champions. The brawny guy took us all in.

"I'm Mitchell Hamlin, and I'll be overseeing your training here," he said. "I've read all your files from the Exam and from your academies and tutorials before then. The one thing you all have in common is the strength of will to not just survive the Exam but come out on top. It's because of that strength that you're here today, about to take on one of the most important jobs in National Defense."

I hoped my expression wasn't too skeptical. I'd gotten the impression that the Confed used the Champions for their special ops squads because we were the dregs of mage society—the old-magic kids who'd disappointed their families, the new-magic kids who'd never had much hope of getting recognized in the first place. People who could be whisked off across the ocean to fight the Confed's most dangerous battles without anyone raising much of a stink.

"Why lie about it, then?" Leonie asked, tossing back her burgundy dreadlocks. "Doesn't anyone care that we went into the Exam because we wanted to go to the college, not become some kind of secret soldiers?"

Hamlin gave her a stern look. "Our enemies have spies and hackers trying to uncover our weaknesses. The secrecy protects you and your families—and our operations here. If the enemies of the Confederation have their way, there won't *be* any college for anyone to attend."

"So why don't the people who got to go there defend it?" the wiry boy muttered.

"You entered the Exam because you wanted to earn the right to keep your magic," Hamlin said. "This is the final stage in that process. You'll receive a thorough magical education, where you'll learn techniques no one in the college even considers. You were given the choice to back out halfway through your Exam. You can still back out now."

"And be burned out," the ragged-haired girl said flatly. Exactly. It wasn't much of a choice when that was the alternative.

Hamlin spread his hands. "Billions of Dulls manage to survive without magic. You can choose security, or you can fight back against the forces that would destroy our safety. It's up to you."

Prisha shifted restlessly on her feet, but no one asked to leave. Hamlin nodded.

"Make no mistake," he said. "What I'm going to train you for *is* the most important work you could be doing. There are rogue mage groups throughout the world who are right now attempting to bring chaos and violence to our home. The governments of the countries where they operate rely on our robust magical coalition for support, and our service is a key component in maintaining positive relations between the Confederation and our own Dull government. Your squads will be taking on mage combatants that Dull soldiers can't handle and regular National Defense forces don't have the flexibility to effectively pursue."

He started to pace in front of us with measured strides. "The people you'll be going up against spread lies and confusion. They kill innocents to advance their agenda of terror. In the Exam, the six of you were competing against each other. Now you need to band together against an even greater trial, where the stakes are life or death—not just for you, but for millions of others under threat. I expect to find you up to that challenge."

When he aimed his penetrating gaze at us again, the two Champions across from me visibly straightened their posture. I guessed that kind of rhetoric appealed to them—or they were just looking forward to fighting some more. But even Desmond had raised his chin, his eyes bright against his dark brown skin.

Well, we all had to make the best of the situation we'd found ourselves in, didn't we? I couldn't help imagining what Javi would've said, though. *The people up top, they decide that what's good for them will just have to be good for everybody else too. The worst thing is how they've convinced people to believe they're working for us, even while they're walking all over us.*

And those they didn't convince sometimes ended up dead. The examiners might have arranged Javi's death in the Exam because of opinions like that.

"How long is the training?" Prisha asked, her tone unreadable. Was she hoping she'd still find some loophole to get out of this mess before we had to go into actual combat?

"That depends on you," Hamlin said. "We'd like to get you

into the field as quickly as possible. We've been at a standstill too long—neither the Circle nor the Dull government is happy about that. But I won't send you out there underprepared."

From what Finn had told me, the pressure to defend the country was mostly coming from the Dulls. The only reason the nonmagical authorities kept their fears about magic in check was that we fought on their behalf instead of against them.

"Usually I can get a new group of Champions in good enough shape to take on a support role in about a month," Hamlin went on. "When we've finished that initial round, you'll be stationed at one of the local bases within the territories seeing the most insurgent activity, and you'll continue training there in between operations. Your ten-year contract with National Defense starts then."

"Ten-year contract?" Desmond repeated.

Hamlin inclined his head. "When it's over, you can choose another career path if you'd like."

Ten years. No one had mentioned a definite end point at all, but one that far off didn't make me feel a whole lot better. I had to find a way to expose the Confed's lies sooner than that.

"The Exam was designed to test you under the worst possible circumstances you might find yourselves in," Hamlin said. "You should be relieved to hear that most of your missions won't be anywhere near as intense. You'll be gathering intel, detecting and disarming malicious 'chantments, bringing in mage targets for questioning, that sort of thing. This is a long, slow war we're fighting. I'm going to do my best to ensure you make it back to your base after each mission. All I need from you is that you listen hard and work harder."

"And in a month we'll be out there battling terrorists?" Leonie said, sounding doubtful.

To my surprise, something like a smile curled Hamlin's lips in defiance of his scar. "You know, when I was first assigned to this position after serving in the regular National Defense stream, I balked because the Champions weren't 'real' soldiers. In the years since then, I've come to realize that's exactly why you're an asset. You wouldn't be here if you weren't adaptable, with on-the-spot smarts and the ability to maneuver. Everything you need is already in there." He tapped his chest. "All I do is help you find it."

The words were stirring, even though finding the ability to tangle with terrorists wasn't anything I'd ever wanted. I crossed my arms over my chest as if I could shield myself from his attempts at inspiration.

"Enough talk," Hamlin said. "We'll get into your informational lessons and the higher order magical techniques later. No matter what mission you're on, there'll always be enemy forces nearby. We want you in excellent physical condition to match your magical precision."

He ordered us through a set of exercises that felt way too much like my old gym classes, just ramped up to ten times the intensity. Sprints, push-ups, sit-ups, pull-ups—on and on, until my muscles were burning and sweat stung my eyes. Next to me, Prisha swiped at her damp bangs.

Hamlin must have decided we needed a break. "Time to switch things up," he said, motioning us to the other side of the gym where a black panel stretched along the wall. Hamlin detached a remote from its holder and pressed a few buttons.

The panel shimmered. Six humanoid forms appeared in a row on the digital screen, glowing green against the black.

"The targets can detect magical pressure." Hamlin gestured with the remote, and red spots gleamed here and there on the figures. "Since it's your first day, we'll keep this simple. Hit your target with magic on any of those key points. Use whatever technique you're most comfortable with. The harder and more focused the impact, the better."

With a clenching of my gut, I studied the figure across from me. The flow of energy around me jittered faintly against my skin, as I'd known it would. These targets might not be real, but our intent was what conducted the magic. And the intent to do harm, to destroy, weakened the magic's inherent harmony.

Hamlin's gaze weighed on me. He'd seen our records from the Exam—how much detail had the examiners included? Did he know why I hesitated?

It *was* just a picture. If I wanted to make a difference here, I couldn't give them any reason to doubt me.

I made myself draw a lyric into my throat. As I sang out the line in Spanish, I focused my intent around the magic with the words, shaping the rhythms of energy in the air into a little conjured spear. With the last syllable of the lyric, I sent that bolt flinging across the room. It struck the red dot on my target's throat right in the center. The screen chimed, and a score appeared over the figure.

The magic quivered again, making me queasy. This wasn't right.

I tuned out the niggling of distress as well as I could, but when Hamlin called the exercise to a halt, I'd only thrown a few more castings. "All right," he said. "Twenty laps around the gym. Go!"

As the others set off, I walked over to him. "Can I talk to you for a minute?" I said.

"What is it, Lopez?" he asked.

"I—" Was he just playing dumb, or did he really not know what the examiners had told me? What could I say around that maldito silencing 'chantment that would make sense? I wet my lips.

"I was told… I've noticed that destructive castings like the ones we were just practicing disrupt the magic. I got the impression that once I got out here, National Defense wanted me to look into ways to run operations so they don't weaken it."

Before I'd even finished, Hamlin was grimacing from more than just his scar. "Kid, we're pushing back against militants who'll kill you first chance they get. You've got to be just as forceful, or you'll all end up dead."

"But if it's hurting the magic—"

"There's been magic for thousands of years, and no doubt there will be for thousands of years more. Worry about making sure you and your squad don't get hurt." He gave me a brisk pat on the shoulder. "Listen, I don't know exactly what they told you, but the examiners will say all kinds of crap if they think it'll get a potential Champion on board. I'm sorry if they misled you. You've got a real talent. There are all kinds of other ways you'll be able to help out here."

He was trying to reassure me, but his words did the opposite. I'd known Examiner Lancaster might have been placating me, but I hadn't wanted to believe it. How could the Confed not care if we were wearing away the magic?

How many of the officials even knew about the depletion? I'd never suspected anything, never dreamed the magic had some kind of consciousness, until the Exam, and I was the only one there who'd felt it. But I couldn't even explain that to Hamlin when I couldn't talk about anything that had happened in those five days. I gritted my teeth against my frustration.

"All these missions, all the fighting—I know it's having a huge effect," I said. "We might be *killing* the magic we're supposed to be working with."

Hamlin got the same expression that Finn and the others had when I'd claimed the magic might be alive—like I'd suggested we were all actually on Mars. "Look," he said, in a tone that was kind but unyielding, "if something like that is going on, the commanders will be taking it into account. Warfare is all about calculated risks and temporary sacrifices. If you see a specific reason for concern during a mission, you can always bring it to your mission leader's attention."

He wasn't going to believe me. My spirits sank as that certainty hit me. My only option was to refuse to continue—and then they'd burn me out, and that helped no one.

The other Champions jogged by. Prisha shot a concerned look in my direction. I squared my shoulders, gathering my resolve to push back the chill inside me.

There were other people here who knew what I'd felt, who'd been with me and believed me. I was just going to have to make people in the special ops contingent see it too. Show them, talk to them, convince them. If I could get enough of them on my side, we could push to change the standard strategies. The higher-ups like Hamlin would have to listen.

Protect the magic, and then expose the Confed's treachery. One thing at a time. I'd been ready to play a long game.

Because if I couldn't manage that, soon there might be no magic left for any purpose, good or evil.

I ducked my head. "Okay," I said. "I just—what they said—I was confused."

"No harm done." Hamlin waved me off. "Now get on with your laps."

No way was I catching up with the others, but I ran until my calves were outright throbbing and my breaths felt raw in my throat. I let my mind slip back to my last moments with Finn, to his crooked smile and the glint of determination in his bright green eyes, the warmth of his cheek against mine. *We've made it this far. Just let them try to stop us now.*

I wouldn't let the Confed's authorities stop me, no matter how hard things got. The magic, Finn, my parents, everyone—they needed me too much.

CHAPTER FOUR

Finn

I used to think that suffering people's disappointment in me was the worst feeling in the world. That was before I discovered pity.

The pity mostly came in the looks I received whenever I ventured out of my family's brownstone. 81ˢᵗ Street had been a haven for mages since long before the Unveiling, and almost all of my neighbors were magical. By now, nearing the end of September, most of them knew that the youngest Lockwood had been severed from magic, even before they glimpsed the little curved X marked on my temple like a four-legged spider. I could thank gossip for preceding me.

People who used to shoot me a casual greeting now offered solemn bobs of their heads or pained half-smiles. I didn't need supersonic hearing to decipher the murmurs after I'd passed by. *The poor boy, whatever is he going to do with himself now? Can you imagine how his parents must feel? Such an unfortunate situation.*

I knew because I'd heard the same murmurs about other Burnouts, novices from this or that middling old-magic family who'd come out of the Exam similarly marked. If anything, the tongues would be wagging harder for me. I was a Lockwood: grandnephew of a member of the Circle, son of two of the most respected mages in the city. Things like this weren't supposed to happen to novices like me.

No, I was supposed to have my place in the college handed to me on a silver platter regardless of how little I deserved it.

My family was handling the situation as well as I could have hoped. My parents were giving me a wide berth while I sorted my head out, but when I talked with them, other than occasional tentative pauses, the conversations flowed almost as well as they used to. They were concerned about me, obviously, but they seemed to have decided not to lay those concerns at my feet while I was grappling with the immediate consequences of my failure.

My older sister Margo showed up for brunch on a Sunday morning three weeks after I'd emerged from Rikers Island. She wrinkled her nose at the Burnout mark, declared it "awfully barbaric," and proceeded to tease me throughout the meal in that fond way she'd always had, as if I couldn't be all that fragile. For moments here and there, I almost forgot anything was different. I started to wish she didn't have to leave.

After the dishes had been cleared, the two of us ended up in the back garden on our own. Margo flopped onto one of the padded birch-wood benches and stretched her lanky legs out over the stone tiles. I sat across from her next to one of the granite planters. The warm early-autumn breeze carried the scent of our next-door neighbors' rose bushes through the high wooden fence that surrounded this pocket of privacy. A 'chantment on that fence muffled our voices to anyone who might have attempted to eavesdrop.

Margo ran her fingers through the flyaway strands of her ash-brown hair and rested her arm along the back of the bench. She glanced over at me, and for the first time since she'd turned up, her dark blue eyes looked completely serious. My thumb itched to spin with my habitual casting to get a deeper read on her mood—a casting that now wouldn't touch the magic I could no longer hearken.

"There's no shame in it, you know," Margo said. "Six Champions out of, what? Sixty or so who tried for it? That's a lot more in your position than in theirs."

It was generous of her to say that when she'd pulled out every stop to convince me to back out of the Exam and I'd refused to listen. She'd warned me it would be brutal. I didn't think she knew even the half of it.

"I know," I said. "It's okay. You don't need to try to console me."

"Are *you* okay?" she asked softly.

At least a couple dozen people had asked me that question in the last three weeks, but Margo said it differently. She meant it differently. It wasn't about whether I could continue being a contributing member of mage society or whether I could navigate the world without having some sort of breakdown, but how I was faring, in and of myself.

My chest tightened. Her courtesy made me want to be honest in a way I hadn't really attempted with anyone else. What could I tell her, though?

I had nightmares every night—one if I was lucky, two or three if I wasn't. In them, my former classmate Callum shoved Prisha over the edge of a high platform to tumble to her death. Blood streamed over my hands after I left a gaping ruin in Callum's leg. The panicked eyes of an innocent man stared back at me in the seconds before I struck the target the examiners had painted on him, thinking I was killing him.

During my waking hours, fear and anger bubbled in tandem beneath the surface of my thoughts. Prisha and the girl—the girl

whose name I'd racked my brain for and still hadn't turned up—
were out there somewhere, being thrown into the line of fire with
our enemies. The Circle sat by not knowing or not caring...
Probably a little of both. The examiners were preparing to push
the same horrors on a new crop of novices next year.

All that was true, and I couldn't do one bloody thing
about it.

I couldn't even talk about it—not with Margo, not with
anyone. I'd found that out too, within the first minute after I'd
climbed into the car with my parents on the way home from the
Exam. When the examiners had tried to steal all my memories of
the Exam, the memories that woman who'd stopped me in the
hall must have helped me retain, they'd also stolen my ability to
speak of what had happened there.

The silencing 'chantment was a failsafe, I assumed, in case
any of those memories resurfaced. They wouldn't want us
Burnouts telling anyone they'd taken our memories in the first
place.

Even if I could have talked about the Exam, they'd taken
enough that I didn't have anything all that concrete to say. I'd
have sounded like a lunatic babbling about monsters and torture
devices. I had impressions, feelings, images, but the pertinent
details... What had been the names of the examiners, or that boy
in our group who'd been fried to a crisp, or the girl who'd been
crushed by the vines? Where was that house we'd stormed, and
whose house had it been?

What thoughts had I shared with that girl, my Dragon-
Tamer, and what had she shared with me? I'd held on to
moments of her clear voice, her wary gaze warming, the
answering warmth of awe wrapping around my heart, but only
snippets of our actual conversations remained.

Everything that should have been sharp was blurred. I'd
meant to rally against the entire Exam system in every way I

could. The examiners had left me none. They'd been smarter than I'd given them credit for.

I worked my jaw, turning all that truth over in my head, feeling my throat lock against it. "You weren't wrong," I said finally, meeting my sister's gaze. She'd know what I meant by that. "It's going to stay with me. But I don't regret having declared."

The corner of Margo's mouth twitched upward, forming a bittersweet smile. "I suppose that's the best I could ask for. Have you come up with any ideas for what you'd like to do next?"

Fates save me, I'd been asked *that* more than enough too. I must have started to grimace in spite of myself, because Margo gave a quick laugh and said, "If you'd rather not get into that subject—"

"No," I said. "It's fine. I just— Granduncle Raymond came by the day after I got back, insisting Dad find some convenient spot to slot me into for appearances' sake. Dad told him to take a hike, that I needed time to regain my bearings, but I know Granduncle's still hassling him on a regular basis."

"Of course he is," Margo said. "I think that's all Granduncle Raymond knows how to do. From the fuss he made about me moving to that place in Tribeca, you'd think I'd uprooted to the Everglades or somewhere."

"I remember those rants." I shrugged. "I'm still considering my options. There's no point in rushing into anything if I don't have to, right? From what I've gathered, the options for nonmagical work within the Confed are limited. I want to make sure whatever I commit myself to is the right thing. And I'm still getting used to— It feels so strange."

My hand rose to my temple automatically. I yanked it back, my fingers clenching. I could have talked about that, but I didn't have much desire to. I was used to the numbness around me now, the muted sensation of the air, but the loss of the magic still ached.

"You should take your time," Margo agreed. "After you've been through—whatever you've been through—it's best not to make hasty decisions."

"Yeah." I did want to find *something*, a job where I could be at least somewhat productive. If I could find a placement meaningful enough to wipe the concern from my parents' glances, then perhaps all the pitying murmurs would stop too. I could still contribute in my own way.

I hoped.

"You know," Margo said, leaning forward, "just to add to the options you're considering, there are government positions you shouldn't need magic for. Liaison for the nonmagical departments, or a similar role—someone to bridge the divide between the Confederation and the Dull system. I'm scheduled down in Washington for the next few days; I could always put out feelers."

"Would those politicians really want to deal with someone who's hardly even a mage anymore?" I asked.

Margo's mouth tightened. "You're still a mage," she said emphatically. "And anyway, a lot of the Dulls in Washington still aren't all that keen on magic. I don't think a day goes by when I don't hear someone complaining about how we in the Confederation are only looking out for ourselves and not contributing to the country as much as we should." She rolled her eyes. "As if we would have exposed our talents to the world just for the joy of lording it over the Dulls. They'd feel safer dealing with someone who couldn't possibly 'chant them."

I cocked my head. "All right. But even if the Dull politicians prefer someone who can't cast, would the Circle really want to send out a representative sporting this?" I motioned to the Burnout mark.

Margo looked as if she were going to argue, but then she simply sighed. "You might have a point there. I'll still keep my ears perked."

"Thanks," I said.

She leaned over farther and grasped my hand, fixing me with that keen gaze of hers. "If you need *anything*, Finn, you can always come to me. Call, or drop in if I'm in town. I'll do whatever I can."

Emotion swelled in my chest. "Thank you," I said. "Really. I appreciate that." It was more generosity than I would have taken for granted. It was more than I ever wanted to take advantage of.

I had to find my own way back onto my feet, or I really would be nothing more than a failure.

* * *

The next morning, my parents left for work and most of the mages around my age headed off to either the Manhattan Academy of Aspiring Mages or the college. I waited until there would be minimal eyes on the street to produce further gossip, and then I called for a taxi.

I studied the map on my phone while I waited for it to arrive. The girl, my girl, had conjured a dragon into the sky the weekend before the Exam. The closest thing to a name I'd been able to uncarth was that fond nickname: *Dragon-Tamer*.

She'd been new magic—that much I was sure of—and she'd lived close enough for me to see her conjuring. There were two tutorials for mages who couldn't make it to or afford the Manhattan Academy: Manhattan-Bronx and Brooklyn-Queens. Her dragon had soared among the clouds to the south of here, so down across the Brooklyn Bridge I went again, directing the driver to a landmark near my most recent wanderings.

When I got out, I didn't linger. I meandered along the

streets, glancing through shop windows, taking in every face I passed. I didn't really expect to run into my Dragon-Tamer here. Most likely, National Defense had already shipped her out to wherever they were running their special missions. She might be fending off magical attacks meant to murder her right now...

My stomach lurched, and I braced myself against that worry. She'd held her own through the Exam. I had to believe she'd make it through whatever other horrors they sent her into.

There was a small chance I might pass by her, though, and a slightly larger chance I might run into someone whose features were similar enough to peg them as a relative. What I'd do if the latter happened, I hadn't entirely worked out. Mostly I just wanted her name. If I had her name, I could reach out to her, instead of failing in my last promise to her too.

On a few of the streets I wandered down, mine was the palest face around. The looks I got were curious, although a few of the locals jerked their eyes away when they caught sight of the Burnout mark on my temple, as if that somehow made me a more dangerous mage, rather than a neutered one. I supposed in the eyes of the ruling powers, it did, and that was why they marked us. It was a symbol of reckless incompetence.

I wove back to one of the more commercial areas, debating where to grab lunch. I was just passing a club, its black walls splattered with a dappling of neon paint, when my gaze caught on a bright yellow piece of paper tacked beside its door. My feet froze in place.

The curved X I saw every time I looked in the mirror stared back at me from the flyer.

I eased closer, so I could read the words that were printed around the Burnout mark.

Burnout? Dampered? Want to do more? Meet us in Newark.

The message was followed by a time and a date—this Friday —and an address.

My pulse thudded faster as I pulled out my phone to snap a picture of the flyer. It could be simply a support group or the like, but the vagueness of the message left room for possibility. I made myself walk on, but the words kept worming through my head. Suddenly my step had a little more spring than had been there before.

Want to do more? By Jove, yes, I did.

CHAPTER FIVE

Rocío

The ballistic vest weighed down my chest as I strapped it over my shirt. I adjusted my sunburst necklace against my skin so the charm's points didn't pinch me. The equipment guy had told us that standard vests were heavier. Ours were 'chanted to reduce the need for padding—and to ward off conjured projectiles as well as bullets.

I pulled on the similarly 'chanted hoodie next, leaving the hood down for now, and zipped it over the vest. Prisha tapped her foot against the floor as she sat on the edge of her bed, across from mine.

"First real mission," she said. "Very exciting." Her voice had more trepidation in it than anything else.

"Yeah," I said, with similar feeling. "At least it shouldn't be anything too intense."

"Let's hope Hamlin knows what he's talking about," Prisha said. Her first field mission was scheduled for tomorrow night.

I took one last look around the dorm room we shared, trying to avoid the thought that I might not see it again. We'd only arrived at our assigned base in Estonia three days ago, but this space felt a lot more like a home than the sparse four-bed setup we'd had during basic training. The beds came with actual wooden frames and comforters that were more cozy than lumpy. We each had a matching bedside table with a lamp that gave off a warm amber light.

My skeptical side wondered if the special ops officials kept the accommodations unappealing during training so that we'd have to appreciate our new quarters when we got here.

The whole base, or at least the part of it we'd had access to so far, had a similar vibe. Like an oversized ski chalet, I'd thought when I first walked through—based on seeing ski chalets in movies and stuff, not ever having actually been to one. The broad hall I walked down to reach the briefing room had wood-paneled walls that gave off a piney scent. Dense maroon carpeting absorbed my footsteps. Light glowed from sconces beneath the ceiling beams.

The only thing it lacked were windows. Windows were hard to defend.

My gaze snagged on the phone alcove as I passed it. In a few more days we newbie operatives would be allowed our first call home. I didn't know which I felt more—eagerness to hear Mom and Dad's voices again, or dread at the thought of trying to figure out what to say to them. Most of what I'd been up to in the last month I *couldn't* say.

"Hey." Desmond caught up with me, dressed in the same uniform. He and Leonie had been sent here too, while the other two Champions had been assigned to a base in Syria. I doubted any of us had been sorry to see them go—which was probably why Hamlin had suggested the split.

It must have been obvious where I'd been looking, even to Desmond's limited eyesight. "At least they'll let us reach out every now and then," he said.

"Because they know that people back home would go bonkers if they stopped hearing from us completely," I said.

"'Tell no one where we've gone until we've returned,'" Desmond said in his quoting tone, with a pained smile. Then he added, more casually, "Are you going to talk to Finn?"

The question made my throat tighten. Finn and I hadn't exactly announced our relationship during the Exam, but it mustn't have been too hard for the others to notice. "I can't," I said. "I don't have his phone number."

Not that I hadn't thought about trying to find it out. But would it be a good idea to talk to him over the base's phone line anyway? I didn't know what the examiners had made of whatever closeness they'd witnessed during the Exam. The Confed might not like the idea of one of their golden boys, Burnout or not, continuing to associate with a street-magic girl they'd once considered a threat... and maybe still did.

He had to be struggling enough right now without me bringing more scrutiny down on him. I'd have my leave in another few weeks, and then I could see him in person.

My heart leapt at that thought, as if it could spring across time straight to the moment when I could look Finn in the eyes again.

"That sucks," Desmond said. "The not knowing what's going on back there is killer, isn't it? Heck, even the TV shows I'm missing..." He elbowed me gently. "Kidding, kidding. Obviously not the same deal."

"I guess it could be worse," I said. "He could be *here*." About to set off on a mission to fight violent militants who reveled in illegal magic.

Desmond's sympathetic grimace confirmed what I'd thought I'd seen developing between him and Leonie over the last few weeks. "Yeah. That sucks too. I've wondered what's worse— knowing someone you care about is in horrible danger, but at least you know—versus having no real clue what they're going through. I've come to the conclusion that I'd prefer neither."

A hollow chuckle tumbled out of me. "Too bad they didn't give us that option."

"At least it sounds like they've got an actual job for me," Desmond said as we reached the briefing room. "No way did I want to be stuck in some little room like an invalid while the rest of you were off putting your necks on the line."

The briefing room held a long oak desk and two rows of wooden chairs. I couldn't help checking the poster on the wall as I slipped by it. The green column listed attacks thwarted; the red, the ones our unit had failed to stop. Right now, the green column was a smidge longer. *We're never going to catch every plot,* Hamlin had said when he'd pointed the poster out to us, *but if we can keep the balance on that side, we're doing all right.*

Hamlin was standing behind the desk now, with the base's head, Commander Revett, at his right, and the Estonian government official who acted as our consultant, Mr. Ilves, at his left. Four other figures sat in the rows of chairs. I recognized three of them from earlier introductions: Samak Rojanwan, one of the mission leaders, who'd said straight off with a flash of a smile, "Call me Sam"; Tonya Sekibo, a senior operative with wary eyes who specialized in monitoring; and a junior operative with a perpetually clenched jaw who'd only offered his name as "Brandt." The young woman sitting off to the side I guessed was this mission's translator.

"Right on time," Hamlin said with his usual clap for attention as Desmond and I sat down. "Let's get started. This should be a relatively tame night—we don't want to throw Powell and Lopez into the deep end on their first time out. We've received a bit of intel via the official channels." He glanced at Ilves.

The Estonian consultant stepped up to the desk, his narrow

jaw working for a second while he gathered his words. He hadn't looked very comfortable when I'd first met him yesterday, and he didn't now either. I'd gathered the Estonian government was still iffy about the idea of employing mages at all—they didn't have their own magical military branch. Whether they'd called for our help to fill that gap or because our government had bullied them into it, I wasn't totally sure.

Ilves pointed to a map on the large computer monitor atop the desk. "Reports have come in from locals in this town near the border, where there's a significant Russian population," he said in his thinly accented voice. "Two men we believe were involved in the recent train bombing by the Borci have been seen coming and going from a particular house multiple times over the last few months, most recently five days ago."

My stomach knotted. We'd seen footage of that bombing during training—the cars thrown off the rails, some of them collapsed and smoking. Dozens dead, hundreds injured, because of a magical explosive on the tracks. The Borci Za Spravedlivost, which apparently loosely translated as "Warriors for Justice," had left their mark.

The Borci were a militant mage group based primarily in Russia but operating throughout the countries that had once been part of that empire. *The Kremlin and their official mage association have publicly denounced the attacks,* Hamlin had explained during training, *but evidence suggests they're pulling the strings behind the scenes. Conveniently, more often than not the Borci chooses targets the government would want to intimidate.*

The train bombing had happened just a few days after Estonia had refused the terms of a major trade deal with Russia.

The politics made my head spin. The situation sounded complicated enough without us shoving ourselves into the mix. But the Borci had also targeted US ambassadors and European branches of American companies, and the nonmagical militants they associated with were waging their own kind of digital war on us over the internet. I could see why our Dull government was taking action.

Hamlin ran his hand over his buzzcut. "We have no reason to believe these men will be on the premises tonight. You'll go in, question the inhabitants to determine if they have any useful intel or are sympathizers themselves, search the premises for illegal magical items, and then get back out. Rojanwan?"

Sam stood up at his name. He was only a couple inches taller than me, and his frame was slim, but you could tell just from that motion how strong those lean muscles were. He managed to smile even now, but his expression was tighter than yesterday.

"Lopez, you'll be going in with me and Brand," he said. "You can shadow one of us the whole time. Powell, you'll stay with Sekibo in the chopper, taking care of monitoring and communications."

"There's our team," Hamlin said. He looked at each of us, his gaze coming to a stop on me. He tipped his head slightly, and I remembered his sort-of pep talk yesterday when he'd told me I was ready for my first field mission. *You've got the skills. It's been a pleasure training you, and I'm looking forward to seeing how far you can go. So keep your head on straight out there. I don't want to lose my best student, all right?*

It was kind of nice knowing someone in charge cared whether I survived, even if he thought I was slightly delusional.

"Take it slow and steady," he added now. "Maybe we're not going to catch these killers tonight, but you can get us one step closer to shutting them down. Work together like you've trained, watch each other's backs, and make us proud."

At his gesture, we all stood up. My pulse rattled through my ears as I followed Sam out the door.

It was really happening. I was about to set off on an actual

military mission, like a soldier. No, not just like. I was a soldier
now.

What would my parents have thought seeing me hustle
toward the waiting chopper? What would Javi have said? This
wasn't the future they'd ever have wanted for me. It wasn't what
I'd wanted for myself, Dios lo sabe.

As we jogged across the dark concrete yard, I dug my hands
deep into my pockets and turned to the mantra I'd been
repeating since the first days of training.

I could be more than a soldier. I could be more than a
magical talent the Confed used for its own purposes.

This was my first chance to really interact with anyone in the
division other than the other new Champions and Hamlin.
Maybe tonight I could start winning support for *my* purpose.

* * *

Our shoes rasped against the sidewalk in the quiet of the street.
The yellow light from the streetlamps glanced off the dark
windows and pastel clapboard of the houses we were striding
past, none of them more than two stories tall. Not much
nightlife in this little town.

A chilly breeze licked over me, and I tugged the zipper of my
hoodie the last few notches up to my chin. I had the hood pulled
low, the thick fabric providing a helm of magical protection. But
if the concealment 'chantments we'd cast on ourselves did their
work, no one should notice us passing by at all.

Sam, Brandt, and our translator marched ahead of me
without hesitation. A loose shingle rattled somewhere across the
street, and it took all my self-control not to flinch.

"No unusual activity so far," Desmond said through my
earpiece. "It looks as still as Hoth out there."

He and Tonya were monitoring the area via satellite feed and also periodic magical scans. I guessed it made sense the commanders would assign him that job. With all his practice monitoring his surroundings with magic to supplement his vision, he was probably more experienced at those kinds of castings than a lot of the senior operatives were.

Sam pointed to a house near the corner, blue paint flaking around the windows. "We always do a close scan before entry," he murmured. "You conduct your own, Lopez, and we'll compare results."

He sang out a brief line under his breath in a language I didn't recognize. The magic coursing through the air around us quivered in a way that amped up my nerves. I closed my eyes and drew in a breath, letting that energy flood over my tongue before I shaped it to my intent.

The casting we'd learned in training was a much more focused version of the scans Desmond and Tonya would be conducting. It should pick up pretty much any trace of magic, but even checking a single building took a fair bit of effort. I stretched out the syllables of the lyric I'd picked, raising and lowering my pitch in a controlled rhythm, waiting until the magic around me resonated in harmony. Then I sang faster, making the rhythm turn staccato.

The energy flowed out toward the house. It quivered through my thoughts at the same time, sparking a vague impression of a hollow space expanding behind my eyes. Nothing in the three rooms on the ground floor. Nothing at the front of the second floor. Then a glimmer shone against the emptiness as my conjured wave washed over the back rooms. Just a faint flicker before I lost it again. The wave washed away, and my eyes popped open, taking in the outside of the house again.

Sam was watching me. He must have conducted scans like that so many times it barely took any thought at all.

"There's something 'chanted or conjured," I said. "Small, not much power to it—I only barely caught it—in the room at the back of the second floor. The rest of the house looked clear."

Sam's eyebrows twitched upward for an instant before he caught them. "Back room on the second floor," he said. "Are you sure?"

Hadn't he noticed it? "I definitely felt something," I said. "I've got no idea what it was."

He made a humming sound. "We'll have a look, then."

It'd been impossible not to realize during training that my magical ability went way beyond any of the other new Champions. I hadn't thought about whether that might extend to the older operatives. But almost everyone who entered the Exam had been rejected by the college for having too weak a talent, not too strong. Specialized practice would have gotten my senior operatives pretty far, but I might outpace them quickly too.

I didn't completely like that idea, but I clung to the little boost of confidence that came with it. If I impressed Sam and the others with my connection to the magic, they'd be more likely to believe me when I shared what else I'd learned about it.

Sam stepped up to the house and rapped on the door, calling out a request in Estonian and then Russian to cover all the bases. This town, like many near the border, had a large Russian population.

After a moment, he knocked again, louder. A woman's voice carried through the door. She sounded both groggy and worried. Sam said something in an even voice and motioned to the translator to add a few comments. The door swung open.

As we filed in, the family we were intruding on assembled in their living room around the worn but sturdy-looking furniture. The scent of roast meat lingered, I assumed from their dinner earlier. The husband and wife looked a little older than my parents, a faint spidering of wrinkles lining the corners of their eyes and mouths. Those creases deepened as Sam flashed his ID. They didn't look guilty, only frightened.

Their shoulders tensed even more when their teenaged son tramped downstairs. I pegged him as thirteen or fourteen, but the dark scowl he aimed at us wasn't at all childish. A bruise colored his cheek purple around a freshly scabbed scrape.

"There are two men who've been seen coming and going from your house," Sam said, with our translator echoing him. He held out a photo of the men. "You're not in any trouble. We're just trying to find out their current location and anything else you might be able to tell us about their regular whereabouts or plans."

The husband and wife exchanged a look. Their son bristled. As his father shot a glower his way, his mother started to speak in a wavering voice.

"She doesn't know anything about what those men do," the translator said. "She and her husband don't ask. They *would* get into trouble if they interfere. They'd rather be left in peace, but they don't have much choice."

That response didn't seem to surprise any of my colleagues. They hadn't expected these people to be terrorist sympathizers. They were just victims we'd barged in on in the middle of the night. I shifted my weight from one foot to the other, not sure what I could contribute here or whether I even wanted to.

"You haven't overheard anything at all?" Sam said to the wife. "If we find them, we can make sure they don't bother you anymore."

When she shook her head with another apology, he turned to her son. "What about you? Have you talked with them?"

The boy's chin jutted out. "You don't belong here," he said in stilted English. "Why don't you go?"

His father clamped a hand on his shoulder with a hushing sound. Sam's calm tone didn't falter.

"We have an agreement with your government to help them investigate potential criminals," he said.

The boy looked uncertain until he got the translation. Obviously his English wasn't that great. Once he had it, he wrinkled his nose at us and spat out a string of Russian.

"He says they're not his government," the translator said, with a hint of exasperation. "This place should be for Russia."

"Well, we're not here to debate international politics," Sam said. "We just want to catch some killers."

"The kid's obviously the one who's been encouraging these guys to come around," Brandt said. "We can't let him off the hook."

Our mission leader gave the blunt-nosed guy a mild glance. "I don't think badgering him is going to convert him to our cause." He turned to the parents. "We'd like to do a quick search of the house to make sure these men haven't left anything unsafe behind."

At the translation, the husband nodded wearily. I wondered if we would have let him refuse if he'd tried to.

Sam motioned for me to follow him. "You keep an eye on the family," he said to Brandt. "Maybe we'll turn up something we can use to encourage the kid to open up."

Brandt let out a huff of breath, but he didn't argue.

Sam and I moved through the dining room and kitchen, and then upstairs to the bedrooms, starting at the front. We opened and closed cupboards, checked dresser drawers and closets, even peeked under the mattress in the master bedroom. Sam moved with a deliberate care, leaving the rooms no messier than we'd found them. That fact only made me a little less uncomfortable.

As we headed to the last bedroom, the one at the back where I'd sensed some sort of minor magic, a thump and a curse carried up the stairs. Sam froze, but before he had to call down, Brandt's brusque voice traveled to us.

"Everything's under control. I get the impression there's something up there the kid doesn't want you to find."

A jitter rippled around me with a pinch of discomfort. Brandt had conducted a casting the magic wasn't all that happy about.

We'd already searched the bedroom that must have been the boy's: an unmade twin bed with the smell of stale sweat on sheets that hadn't been washed in a while, band posters tacked over the desk. Sam caught my eye outside the last bedroom. He gripped the doorknob, but it jammed. Locked.

Sam inhaled, and I could sense the shape of the casting he was about to draw forth—a punch of pressure to snap the lock. The energy in the air cringed.

"Wait!" I said. "I can open it as fast as breaking it."

"We don't have time for—"

I'd just have to prove it. My mouth dry, I barreled into my own casting. To loosen, to open. "Que se abra la puerta…"

I directed the magic into the keyhole against the dips and ridges that could turn the tumbler. With a few last forceful words, I flipped it over.

"Lopez!" Sam said, his voice low but severe. "I'm your mission leader here. What I say goes."

I'd never seen him look even remotely stern before. I jerked back from the door, my hands dropping to my sides. Mierda. The last thing I wanted was for him to be pissed off at me.

"Sorry," I said, a flush spreading over my face. "I thought the point was to unlock the door. I wasn't trying to go against your orders."

Sam tested the knob, and the door squeaked open. For a second, he just blinked at it. His expression started to soften. "I've never seen anyone work that kind of casting that fast."

"I just figured, since I could…"

He set his hand on my shoulder, and in that moment, the

genuine concern in his dark brown eyes brought back an echo of Javi's presence. "Look, I get it. This time, a few seconds didn't make a difference. But sometimes even one second matters. Locks can be fixed. Lots of other things can't. Like this, for example." He knuckled the side of my head above my ear in a way that only intensified the brotherly impression. "Let's see what we've got in here."

I wasn't sure if I'd made any progress at all with him, but at least he hadn't completely chewed me out. And I'd proven I *could* make an alternate, nondestructive casting work.

We entered the room more cautiously than the others, but it looked pretty ordinary: a bed, this one neatly made except where it looked as if a couple people had sat on the edge, a bare desk and chair in the corner, and a matching wardrobe. A few scraps of paper remained on the desk. Sam checked them, frowning, and took photos of them with his phone. "Just in case," he said.

I murmured to the magic, a wisp of my earlier scan. The energy shivered when I directed it toward the bed. I knelt to peer underneath and fished out a notebook with a creased cover.

Sam and I flipped through it together. Nothing about the pages looked menacing to me. They held little pen sketches, rough patterns and pictures. Then Sam pressed his thumb next to one, and the lines twitched and jumped with a faint 'chantment. Oh.

"Is that some kind of code?" I asked.

The mission leader shook his head. "I've seen this kind of thing before—practice exercises to focus the mind. Looks like the kid is trying to develop a talent."

"You think *he* 'chanted these pictures?"

Sam gave me a crooked smile. "That's how these groups often rope in new recruits. The kid probably didn't know much about what he could do. No opportunities here to grow a talent. These guys take notice and start treating him like he's important.

Teaching him, earning his loyalty." He dropped the notebook onto the bed. "And then they'll order him to use his talent to destroy anyone who stands in the way of their goals, whatever those happen to be that day."

He snapped pictures of the sketches and tucked the notebook back under the bed where I'd found it.

"That's it," I said. "That must be the bit of magic I sensed. There's nothing else here?"

"It looks that way," Sam said. "That happens a lot. Things like that notebook are why we can't jump to conclusions from an outside scan. At least half of the time we don't turn up anything we can use, and the rest, what we do turn up isn't very conclusive. But the missions are worth it for the times when we hit on something good. We can keep a closer eye on the son, and that might lead us somewhere. He might even end up volunteering information if we play things right."

He led the way back downstairs. The couple was still standing where we'd left them, tensed and worried, in the middle of the living room. The translator was talking with them in a soft voice. Brandt stood next to the son, who was sitting very stiffly in the armchair.

It only took a glance and a taste of the uneasiness in the room's energy for me to figure out what had happened. The boy had made some kind of move, and Brandt had magically bound him to the chair.

"We'll talk to their son alone for a few minutes," Sam said to the translator. "Tell them he isn't being arrested or anything."

The father's face tightened, and the mother's eyes widened, but they moved into the kitchen after a few brief comments back and forth. The translator came to join us.

Sam caught Brandt's eye and cocked his head. The younger officer released the 'chantment with a mutter under his breath. Latin, it sounded like—he must have been an Academy graduate.

The boy started to spring up, but Sam held up his hand, and the kid paused. He met the mission leader's eyes with a defiant gleam in his. Sam bent so their faces were level.

"We found your notebook upstairs," he said quietly. "You have a talent—you can work with the magic. You don't want your parents to know?"

The boy paled a little as the translation came, but his mouth stayed clamped shut. Every country had its tensions between mages and the nonmagical, prejudices that could go as far as violence, and Estonia obviously wasn't one of the more relaxed ones.

"We won't tell them," Sam went on. "But if you want to learn, there are ways you can do it without tying yourself to criminals. Those men, they've hurt people—killed people. I don't think you really want to be a part of that. If you reach out to the Confederation's magical forces, we can help you and teach you without asking anything in return. Here's the number. You can call it any time. Say Samak gave it to you."

He held out a card. The boy stared at it sullenly. Then he snatched it and shoved it into his pocket. I couldn't tell whether he was actually listening or he just wanted to get it out of his sight so we'd leave.

Sam wasn't even telling the complete truth, was he? We would ask something in return: information. Observations, at the very least.

Restlessness gripped me as I stood there. I was supposed to be proving myself—winning over my senior operatives as much as Sam was trying to win over this kid. If my mission leader was anything like my older brother, I knew what kind of gesture he'd appreciate.

Or maybe I was just making excuses to do what felt like the right thing. I was okay with that.

I tapped my cheek and pointed to the boy's with its scrape.

"Did they do that—the men who've come? I can seal it up, so it'll heal faster." We'd learned some strategies in training to supplement the basic magimedical first aid tips we'd all gotten in elementary school.

"Hold on," Brandt started.

Sam elbowed him. "Let the newbie get in there. She's not going to hurt anything." But he was watching me intently, as if this had suddenly become an even bigger test.

The boy's eyes shot to me when the translator finished. He snapped out something in Russian. She replied before she reported back.

"He wanted to know if it'll hurt. I told him you're trained. It'll make the cut feel better."

I nodded to confirm what she'd said. The boy's shoulders came down maybe half an inch. He wavered for a moment longer, and then he gave a sharp jerk of his chin before turning his face to the side.

I'd already drawn the lyric I wanted onto my tongue, a soothing verse from one of my abuela's old lullabies. One I remembered Javi using to soothe the pain when I'd scraped my knee, ages ago. I drew it out slow and soft, my fingers hovering beside the boy's cheek.

The skin sealed over the raw spots around the forming scabs, pink but whole. The bruise faded to half its previous color.

When I dropped my hand, the boy raised his, testing the wound. He gave me a startled glance, as if he hadn't really believed I could do what I'd offered. The magic that drifted between us thrummed happily.

Sam wasn't looking at me anymore, but I thought I caught a glint of approval in his eyes. He straightened up, his gaze on the boy. "Remember what I said."

The boy shrugged and slumped back in the chair. The translator called the parents back in to tell them we were leaving. As I turned to go, the boy muttered two words: "Thank you."

My heart leapt, but I didn't let myself turn back and make a big deal out of it. That reaction seemed more likely to scare him off than to reassure him. Still, as we marched back out into the cool of the night, a hint of a smile crossed my face.

I'd followed my orders, and I'd followed what I believed in too. I might not have won over any minds tonight, but I could get there. Slow and steady.

CHAPTER SIX

Finn

L ying to my parents hadn't felt like all that large a betrayal until I'd seen how overjoyed they were. Their smiles and the relieved looks they kept sharing as I pulled on my jacket made me want to dig a hole and bury myself with guilt. Despite the massively important international conference Dad was in the process of organizing, he'd come out of his study to see me off. "If you're not sure about the taxis out there, you can always call us," he said. "I'll keep my phone on and nearby."

"I'm sure it'll be fine," I said, my cheeks starting to ache from holding up my own smile. "It's just a concert. There'll be tons of transportation options around."

"Exactly. Don't worry about that right now." Mom patted me on the shoulder. "You just have fun—and say hello to Prisha from us!"

The sentiments behind their enthusiasm might as well have been blaring through the front hall. *He's getting out of the house! Doing normal teenager things! He must be starting to adjust after all.*

It was the first night since the Exam that I'd gone out, supposedly with friends.

There really was a concert by the Bleeding Beats, a hot new indie rock band that many of my classmates at the Academy had adored, at Radio City Music Hall tonight, but I wasn't going there. It'd made the perfect cover for my venture out to Newark. I doubted my parents would have been half as pleased if they'd known this excursion wasn't about moving on from my burning out but rather delving deeper into that aspect of my life.

They didn't need to know. There were a lot of things they didn't know about me now.

Thankfully, their happiness had meant that Dad had backed down when I'd said I'd rather make my own way to the concert hall than have him drive me. I hopped in the cab outside and told the driver to head to Penn Station.

The train I caught rumbled over the short distance to Newark, a route a lot of Dulls who traveled for business must have made on the regular, since the airport was just a little farther down the line. Half of the people who'd gotten on with me were lugging suitcases. I tucked myself away in a corner and watched the city lights slide by through the deepening evening outside the window. My foot bobbed impatiently.

I had no idea what to expect from this meeting. It could be just a handful of Dampered mages and Burnouts looking to grumble about their situation. There might be no one at all there, a failed attempt at a gathering.

No matter how many times I told myself that in order to keep my hopes in check, the words from the flyer stuck with me. *Want to do more?*

When the train pulled into the main Newark station, I slipped past the suitcases and found the taxi stand outside. The driver gave me an odd look when I told him the address, but he pulled away from the curb without comment.

We cruised through a neighborhood of abandoned industrial buildings, foreboding in the hazy glow of the streetlamps. They gave way to a stretch of low-rise concrete apartment buildings. The taxi driver parked at the next corner, outside a brick church with a steepled roof and tower.

"Here you go."

The sign outside the place had the same address the flyer had given, but the arched windows were dark. I hesitated and then pushed myself onward, handing the driver a twenty.

Somewhere out there, my Dragon-Tamer was being forced to battle our most vicious enemies. I couldn't be afraid of a little uncertainty, especially when it might get me closer to paving a way home for her.

I circled the building and spotted a glow from a lower window next to a side door. A couple of figures were ducking inside. With a leap of my pulse, I hurried after them.

A stout guy who looked to be around thirty was standing just inside the door. He gave me a once-over. "You're new. Hold on."

As I stopped, he murmured a lyric with a small motion of his hand. The skin beneath my Burnout mark prickled, and then he gave me a brisk nod. "Come on in. Good to have you joining us."

Had he been testing to make sure the mark was real? If he was Dampered, his remaining affinity could have been for illusions or something similar. What were these people up to that made them worried someone might sneak in under false pretenses?

I headed down a drab hall and through another set of doors that led into a large room. Dozens and dozens of people were already milling around—more than a hundred, I estimated at a glance. A few had seized plastic-backed chairs from the stacks along the walls and sat in small groups, but most were on their feet. Their voices bounced off the high ceiling, melding into an undulating warble.

The left end of the room held a small stage. A woman there was tugging a podium into place, front and center. The smell of coffee and sugar wafted from a table set against the wall opposite the door, where several attendees were picking over a few platters of donuts and pastries.

I shifted to the side as more people came in. My skin was starting to feel tight. The guy at the front had welcomed me, and I did have a Burnout mark, but looking at the figures around me, it was difficult to believe I belonged here. The clothes they wore, the way they held themselves... I'd met more new-magic mages in the five days of the Exam than I'd spent time with in my entire life up until then, and based on that experience I judged that most of the people in this room had come via tutorials rather than the academies.

What were they making of *me*, standing here in my tailored shirt and slacks with old-magic airs I wasn't even totally conscious of? How would they welcome me if they knew I was related to one of the men who'd decided their fates?

That question sent an uneasy quiver down my back. My gaze darted through the room. Was there anyone here who'd know me from the Manhattan Academy? I didn't recognize any of the faces around me. Plenty sported a Burnout mark, perhaps half those in the room. The rest I had to assume were Dampered. The Confed didn't brand those who accepted the Circle's judgment.

A girl with a dark brown pixie cut sidled over to me, her skinny arms crossed over her blouse, which looked a little fancier than what most of the others were wearing. "Hey," she said. "Is this your first time? You look kind of lost."

Possibly she was old magic too. She didn't show any sign of recognizing me, though. I relaxed slightly. "There've been a lot of firsts in the last month," I said, with a gesture to my mark.

"Fresh out of the Mages' Exam? Geez." She gave a little shudder. "I don't know much about it, but I've talked to other mages who went through it, and it's pretty impressive that you're here at all this soon after. I'm Noemi, by the way. Resident fantasy fanatic and far too curious for my own good—at least, that's what I'm told."

She gave me an unassuming grin and her hand for a brisk shake.

"Finn," I said in return, and motioned to the room. "Is this — What exactly do we do here?"

"They always wait a little while to make sure everyone's had time to arrive, and then people have a chance to speak their piece. Sometimes we organize smaller activity groups—writing letters or planning calls... The last few meetings there's been some prep for a more overt protest, but I'm not sure when that's going to get off the ground." She laughed. "I sound like I've been doing this for ages, but this is actually only my fifth time here. I was lucky I connected with Luis at all."

"Luis?"

"You'll see," she said, her smile turning rather dreamy. I suspected she liked this Luis for more than just getting her involved in his get-togethers.

I was going to ask if she was from around here—she didn't look more than a couple of years older than me, but I didn't recall ever passing her in the halls of the Academy—when a guy ambling past us caught my eye. He had a blue mohawk about an inch tall jutting down the center of his stubbled scalp.

I knew *him*, and not from the Academy.

"Hey," I said automatically, raising my hand to get his attention, and then fumbled when his name didn't swim up from my head as it normally would have.

Of course it hadn't. I could picture him standing in the courtyard outside the gleaming white Exam buildings with a

mohawk five times as high, could hear him making some
muttered comment about not making friends when our group
had gathered in the dorm the first night, but as with every other
factual detail from those five days, I'd lost his name. I had the
impression I'd known where he was from, too, and that it wasn't
New York, but the specifics escaped me.

The guy considered me with puzzled wariness. "I don't think
I know you," he said. His Burnout mark stood out as starkly as
mine against his pale skin—skin that was faintly mottled here
and there with pink scars. Another fragment of memory rose up:
every inch of him raw and blistered, groans wrenching from his
lips as we'd tried to hustle him down a vast, black hallway.

The magimedics hadn't been able to perfectly heal the
wounds he'd received.

I hadn't known he'd even survived. Relief washed through me
even as I groped for a response.

I couldn't tell him I knew him from the Exam. The
'chantment on me prevented it. The examiners must have wiped
his memories completely, judging from the way he was eyeing
me. He didn't know me at all.

"When was yours?" I said, tapping my temple. Nothing
stopped me from *asking*.

"This year's," he said, and paused as if he wasn't sure he
wanted to continue the conversation. "You?"

"The same. I had a feeling."

He studied me more intently then, but not a hint of
recognition crossed his face. A chill tickled down my back. I'd
have looked at him the same way if that one examiner hadn't
interfered. I'd have lost everything.

Of course, from the bits and pieces I recalled of this guy's
bitterness toward old-magic types, it might be for the best that
he had no idea who precisely I was.

"I can't talk about it," he said, and I understood what he

meant by that "can't" in a way only a fellow former examinee could.

"I know," I said. "Anyway, er, I like your hair."

He brushed a hand over his mohawk with an expression that was somewhere between pride and embarrassment. "It used to be better. Bigger. I'm growing it back. Anyway, I'd better grab a donut before they're all gone."

The squeal of electric feedback carried from the stage. A guy there—early twenties, broad-shouldered and fit, with bronze-brown skin and black hair that curled beneath his ears—tapped the microphone he'd set up at the podium. Noemi bobbed on her feet at the sight, her face brightening.

"Hello, everyone!" the guy said in a smooth, warm voice. "It's great to see so many of you ready to share your stories and maybe take some action tonight."

"Hi, Luis!" a chorus of voices hollered back from the crowd. Ah, so this was the guy Noemi had hinted was in charge.

"We're going to get started," he said. "I've got some people here eager to have their voices heard. But first I'd like to welcome everyone who's made it out to the Freedom of Magic League for the first time tonight. We're open to anyone—Dampered, Burnout, Dull—who's been excluded from the full possibilities of this magical world by the leaders of the Confederation. When I first started organizing these meetings four years ago, it was just to find a space where a handful of us could talk. It's amazing to see how much this group has grown, both in numbers and in enthusiasm."

Applause and a few cheers rippled through his audience. Everyone had turned toward the stage, watching avidly.

"Get comfortable, enjoy the refreshments, and keep open ears and an open mind," he added. "That's all we ask. If you've got something to say too, you can approach me any time. I'll make room for you."

He stepped back to offer the podium to a chubby white guy. "We all know the reasons the Confed gives us for Dampering," the new guy began, his determined tenor carrying through the room. "And we also know that they're full of crap."

Several people around me whooped in agreement. The guy went on, pointing out examples where Chosen mages had caused harm and where Dampered mages had managed to accomplish a lot of good but could have done more with their full connection to the magic. I might have missed the whispering melody around me, but a different sort of energy was flowing through the room, full of passionate resolve.

My pulse thumped faster. The policies this guy was disparaging had been written by people like my great-grandfather and Granduncle Raymond. I'd heard my own parents support Dampering. I had no idea what anyone in my family would have made of this speech or the fact that I'd come out here to listen to it. Yet despite the pinch of my nerves, I found myself grinning.

Jupiter, Mars, and Venus, these were just the people I needed if I was going to take on the Circle, the Exam, and everything those institutions stood for. They saw the same corruption I did, even if they hadn't been through it or couldn't remember it directly.

After the Dampered guy, Luis offered the mic to a young woman named Ary, whose Burnout mark was visible on her olive-brown skin just under the fringe of her pink-streaked hair. Her talk was more of a rant, complaining about the secrecy of the Exam and how the examinees were treated afterward, but I couldn't deny that her anger resonated inside me. Then, to my surprise, Noemi walked onto the stage.

"I'm so glad you all have welcomed me since I started coming here," she said, her voice wavering a bit as she clutched the microphone. "I know a lot of mages think people without magic have no place getting involved in your community, and with the way we 'Dulls' have treated you, I can't really blame them. But I feel like there's so much we could learn from you—and really, that's what I'd most like to do. I grew up on stories of witches and wizards, and I'd love to find out just how the reality compares. You don't have to use magic to study it. If the Confederation would open up even a few spots for nonmagical academics to do research in their libraries, to run tests and experiments so we can *all* understand this phenomenon better, I think that would benefit everyone."

I stared at her as she laid out the rest of her reasoning and recounted her attempts to convince the Confed officials that she was serious and devoted to her study of magic. She was *Dull?*

I shouldn't have been shocked. Luis had mentioned Dulls in his opening remarks. It wasn't as if there'd have been any way to tell by looking at her. I simply, well...

It was silly to presume anything about Dulls when I'd never spoken to anyone nonmagical outside of ordering food in the occasional Dull restaurant or telling a cabbie where to take me. I'd still been thinking they were somehow distinctly different from us, even though the only difference was the connection to the magic which many of us here had been stripped of anyway.

To hear Noemi talk, she clearly loved the concept of magic every bit as much as I'd loved the experience of it.

When she finished, a middle-aged Black woman took the podium. "All right, folks," she said. "All talk and no action doesn't get us anywhere. I'd like to continue our discussion about possible targets for protest action. Who's ready to move forward? Come huddle with me by the donut table."

My legs locked as I watched a significant portion of the crowd shift toward the table. My family was an obvious target for protest. As giddy as the atmosphere was making me feel, I wasn't sure it'd be wise to hang myself out quite that blatantly yet.

I could at least listen to the suggestions and see if I had

anything useful I could add without exposing my ties to the people they saw as the enemy. What had I come here for if not to do *something*?

I dragged in a breath and marched over to where a swarm of bright-eyed volunteers was gathering.

CHAPTER SEVEN

Rocío

"Damn, there are even more boxes back here," Sam said, accompanied by the rasp of tarp heaved aside. "Come on, let's get this out of here."

Brandt was already hauling one of the crates of guns packed in straw out of the garage. I hustled over to Sam next to one of the more junior operatives, a girl named Joselin who couldn't have been more than a couple years older than me. With a swish of her chestnut-brown ponytail, she grabbed one of the boxes and bounded out.

Our unit had located this stash of magically enhanced weapons thanks to a tip and some careful scanning. 'Chanting weapons was illegal under international law, but I guessed that was exactly why the Borci Za Spravedlivost figured they could give their nonmagical militant allies an edge that way.

At least no one would get to use the weapons now. We were taking them back to the base for neutralizing. But seeing the stark black muzzles and egg-shaped grenades in the dim light of the electric lantern made me shiver at the thought of how many stashes there might be that we *hadn't* found yet—and who those insurgent groups might be planning on using them against.

"Careful," Sam reminded me as I lifted the box next to him. "Keep hearkening the magic in them as you go. If anything shifts in a direction that feels bad, drop it and cover yourself."

"Got it," I said. I'd run ten missions in the last two weeks, with more training and debriefing filling the rest of my waking hours, but tension still wound through my muscles as I hefted the crate of weaponry. No bulletproof vest, 'chanted or not, was going to save me if all this ammunition exploded.

The cold nipped at my cheeks as I carried the box over the cracked concrete of an alley to the gravel parking lot where we'd landed the helicopter. This far north, Sam had said we might start seeing snow as soon as next month. From inside the chopper, lit by its interior lights, Desmond gave me a quick nod where he was perched at the communications array. His face was tight with concentration, his lips moving with a near-silent casting.

I shoved the crate into the back of the chopper and jogged back to the garage. I tramped inside just in time to hear Joselin say, "What the heck is this?"

She'd tugged a dirt-stained paper out from under one of the boxes. Her thick eyebrows drew together as she squinted at it. "Crap. That's a schematic for an explosive 'chantment, isn't it?"

Sam leaned over with a frown. "It is. There's an address in the instructions." He tapped some writing in Cyrillic near the top of the page. "If it's nearby, we'd better take a look and see if they planted the 'chantment there and if it's still active." His hand rose to press the button on the mic clipped to his hoodie. "Powell, we need you to look up an address. I'll send you the image."

"On it," Desmond said over my earpiece. A minute after Sam had snapped the photo, his voice returned. "Five blocks north and two east. A tall stone place with a red roof. Do you want me to direct my scans to that area now?"

"I think you'd better. And call back to the base to see if they've got any idea why that building would've been targeted." Sam turned to the rest of us. "Brandt, Lopez, inspect the building. If you find the 'chantment, deal with it if you can, or call it in if you need backup."

Brandt motioned for me to follow him with a jerk of his hand, his gaze even more steely than usual. We set off at a lope down the street, past the grimy clapboard faces in this desolate part of town.

A couple blocks along, the road widened with freshly patched pavement, and the houses got a little bigger. A sedan growled around a corner up ahead, and I swerved my path closer to the walls.

Brandt glanced at me with an expression that might have been approving of my caution or accusing me of cowardice. Sometimes I had trouble telling whether he had any emotions other than anger and frustration, especially in the intermittent lamp glow that deepened the shadows around his blunt features and made the dark blond spikes of his short-cropped hair look like little knives.

Desmond's voice crackled into our ears again just as a narrow stone house with a red-shingled roof came into view in the dimness ahead of us. "The house belongs to the cousin of an Estonian government minister—one who's voted against Russian-friendly policies. Either they're trying to punish her by going after her family, or they're hoping they can take her out if she pops in for a visit."

"It doesn't look like anything has already been detonated here," Brandt said into his mic. He slowed coming up on the house.

An off-key twang of energy prickled over my skin. My gaze darted along the trail I sensed.

"The front step," I said with a shiver. "The explosive 'chantment is there."

Brandt's brow furrowed as he rattled off a scanning casting. His jaw clenched even tighter. "The 'chantment is active," he reported into his mic. "We can get rid of it."

The impression of the explosive made my stomach churn. The 'chantment seemed to be churning too, an erratic whirl of magic I could hearken embedded in the concrete step. I made myself step closer despite my uneasiness. It didn't feel all that *big*, at least.

Movement in a window across the street caught my eye. The lamplight glanced off the pale form of a girl not much older than me leaning close to the glass. Her fawn-brown hair was yanked back from her face, and her arms were crossed over what looked like a scruffy jean jacket. Our concealment 'chantments must have been wearing thin, because she was staring right at us.

"What?" Brandt said, jerking around to follow my gaze. The girl had already vanished into the darkness beyond the window.

"Nothing," I said. "Just a neighbor looking out to see what's going on."

"Half of them probably think the bomb was a great idea," he muttered.

The locals might not be any more enthusiastic about us than he was about them. What would they make of our sudden appearance here? Did they see welcome helpers or unwanted intruders? A crawling sensation ran up my arms, almost as unpleasant as the twang of the explosive 'chantment. I had the urge to run all the way back to the warm lights of the base. As if I even could have if I'd let myself.

I had my own mission here, and it'd been slow going so far. I knew I'd gained at least a little of Sam's respect during my missions under him. Brandt still seemed skeptical. Turning tail and fleeing wasn't going to earn me any points with him, that was for sure.

"How do you want to handle it?" I asked. The strategies we'd learned for neutralizing magical bombs flitted through my head. This was the first time I'd encountered one in the field.

Brandt circled around to the opposite side of the steps. "Either no one's home or they're all asleep. No point in causing a commotion. We conjure a shield around it together, solid as we can make it, and then I'll detonate the explosion inside that."

The instant he said the word "detonate," the magic humming around me flinched. I winced inwardly. But this was a chance to convince him. Did I dare to hope he might feel for himself the magic's relief if we handled this more peacefully?

"We don't have to set it off to stop it from hurting anyone," I said. "It'll ruin part of the house like that. Why don't we diffuse it?"

He made a scoffing sound. "Because that'll take tons more time and energy? The government will pay them back for the damage."

It couldn't pay back the magic for the harm done there. I didn't think I could talk about that yet without sounding crazy, though.

"It won't take me that long," I said, dropping to my knees by the steps. "I'll show you." My fingers curled into my palms for a second before I extended them. I didn't want him to see my hands shake.

Even Hamlin had said that a lot of the time just detonating an explosive was safest unless the casting was incredibly simple. But if I couldn't do this, I might as well be some Confed drone.

"Lopez," Brandt started, and I decided I couldn't give him any more time to argue. With his few years of seniority, he could technically order me around, but he hadn't told me directly not to try yet.

"Make your shield," I said quickly. "We'll want to be safe about it either way." Then I launched into the soft strains of a soothing melody.

Brandt cursed, even though I wasn't really casting yet. He probably couldn't tell. As he started conducting his conjuring in poetic Latin, I let my intent simply flow through the energy around me. The erratic cadence of the explosive 'chantment niggled at me even more unnervingly. All I wanted to do right now was test the rhythms of the casting's structure, hearken how those whirling threads had been woven together.

I'd watched Finn dispel a malicious 'chantment of his own during the Exam. His casting had worked very differently from the one placed here, but he'd unraveled the tangles of magic bit by bit. I should be able to manage the same.

The magic tickled at my senses as if nudging my attention. Yes, that faint whine of a note felt a little loose to my hearkening. And it threaded right through the hot crackling center of the 'chantment. If I could tease it out, ever so slowly…

I murmured a lyric about unwinding and slipping apart, narrowing my focus to that one piece of the 'chantment. It clung in place for a second, and then it rippled away, taking a shred of the sense of heat with it.

My pulse pounded against my skull. I turned my attention to a different wavering thread within the ball of contained power. My lips moved again: cool it, relax it, ease it apart.

The crackling sensation ebbed. I tugged at the tangle with the roll of a lyric off my tongue, and the rest of the 'chantment disintegrated.

My shoulders sagged as I released my focus, every muscle trembling. That work had taken more out of me than I'd realized. But I'd done it. That was what mattered. I pressed my hand to the ground to steady myself, just for a second, and then shoved myself upright, willing my legs not to wobble.

"The explosive is diffused," I said into my mic.

Brandt smacked my hand away from my collar. "What the hell was that?" he demanded.

I stared at him, any words I might have said catching in my throat. His face had turned red in the dim light, his mouth twisted with an emotion it didn't take any special insight to read. He was furious.

"It's done," I said. "It didn't take very long." We wouldn't get into how much the process had drained me.

"How much time have you spent around explosive casting, newbie? You could've blown it up in our faces."

"But I didn't," I said. "I knew I could handle it. We had—"

"It doesn't matter!" Brandt burst out. He forced his voice lower. His hand jabbed toward the houses around us. "You know what matters? Just us. Our unit. These people don't like us any more than the damned Borci Za Spravedlivost do. We get in, we do what we have to so the commanders will be happy, and then we get the hell out. You don't take risks to protect somebody's front step."

Was that the way he saw things—we were only looking out for ourselves? Nobody else, not even the locals the militants were targeting? I didn't know how to argue about that. But I did feel the grateful embrace of the magic slipping around my shoulders like a shawl made out of warm silk.

"What if that's not the only thing I was protecting?" I said. My throat tried to constrict around the words, but I made myself keep going. I had to try. "Can't you feel it? The way the—"

Desmond's voice blared through my earpiece. "All operatives, back to the chopper. We got a distress signal from the base. There's some kind of attack—they say they need all the assistance they can get. Hurry!"

My stomach flipped over. Brandt's eyes widened. We took off for the helicopter without a thought given to the argument we'd been in the middle of.

Our feet thundered down the streets so loudly I wouldn't have been surprised if the whole town could hear us passing. The helicopter's blades were already whirring when we reached the parking lot. Sam wheeled his arm, urging us faster.

The chopper lurched into the air the second Brandt and I scrambled on. My back thumped against the window. I sank onto the bench, my lungs burning from both the run and the casting I'd done to diffuse the bomb.

I was tired. How much fight did I have in me now?

How big a risk had diffusing that 'chantment really been?

"Do we know anything about the attack?" I asked. No one had ever mentioned any concern the base might be hit. The officials kept it so tightly secure, I couldn't even have said exactly where the compound was on a map, and the outer walls tingled with magical defenses. Had our enemies not only tracked us down but broken through those wards?

Desmond was tapping away at his computer controls. "They weren't able to say a whole lot. I think everyone there is busy defending the place. All tonight's squads have been called back."

Prisha and Leonie had been out on missions of their own with other groups of more experienced operatives. They'd be flying into the line of fire right now too.

"We'll hurl those pricks right back to where they came from," Brandt said, but his knuckles were white where he was gripping the bench. The bravado was a front.

"How did they find us?" Joselin asked, her boots drumming against the floor.

No one had an answer to that.

I could tell we were almost at the base when the magic started twitching around me, tugging and releasing my joints with an increasingly urgent frequency. *I'm on my way*, I thought at it. *This is as fast as I can come.*

But what was I going to do once we arrived? Even at well-rested, I wouldn't have been able to stop a whole army of insurgents from hurling destructive castings.

The magic was counting on me. I was the only one who even understood how much it was hurting. I swallowed hard.

"They've breached the base walls," Desmond reported, his voice strained. "Commander Revett says to get in there and push them back, any way we can."

The helicopter landed with a jolt in the yard outside the domed building. Its lights revealed scorch marks around a wide crack down the middle of the concrete wall. An image glowed beside it like magical graffiti: a ghostly face with round eyes and lips drawn back in what could have been a scream or a battle cry. That was the Borci Za Spravedlivost's calling card when they wanted to make sure they got credit for their crimes.

That was all I had time to notice before a few figures darted past, wearing glowing white masks with the same anguished grimace. They threw a wave of searing heat toward us. I spat out an instinctive lyric to shield, to chill, with a rush of gratitude for all the drills Hamlin had pushed us through. My voice merged with others all around me.

Sam hollered something. Light flashed in the distance, followed by the grunt of a fallen attacker. "Go on, go on," he said. "I'll cover the rest of you. You focus on securing the base."

We ran. I jerked my gaze away from the bodies of two of the base's soldiers sprawled nearby, and my heart lurched at the sight of the door they'd been guarding wrenched halfway off its hinges. How the hell could we secure *that*?

A bolt sizzled past me, clipping the back of my hood. Despite the protective 'chantment, pain shot down my spine. I dove into the hallway.

The magic flailed around us. More burnt streaks marked the wood-paneled walls, the spongy carpet. An almost chemical tang hung in the air. Our pseudo-chalet didn't feel so cozy anymore.

Commander Revett's voice leapt from my earpiece.

"A few of us are blocked in the communications room. We need immediate assistance."

Two masked figures burst from a room down the hall. With a shouted lyric, they whipped a hail of razor-sharp shards our way. Joselin and I belted out words to deflect the attack, an ache seeping across my scalp as I did. Brandt yelled a line with a smack of his hands against his chest and a stomp of his feet: the shockwave technique we'd learned in training.

His casting propelled its energy down the hall, and the magic wrenched at me, yanking my breath from my lungs. One of our assailants toppled, blood splattering from a head wound. The other dodged around a corner up ahead.

Brandt charged after the fleeing figure, Joselin on his heels. I raced after them, veering right toward the communications room. Desmond's feet thumped right behind me.

The magic felt as if it were tearing at my arms, my hair. *I don't know what to do*, I thought at it. I'd practiced adapting the new techniques we'd learned—in secret, not under Hamlin's watch—but I'd never tried them on an actual assailant. My breath was coming shakily, my head throbbing. What if I couldn't pull it off?

We hurtled past another limp body—one of our translators, I realized with a swallowed sob—and around a corner. Three more masked figures were poised outside the communications room door.

All my training took hold. I didn't let myself think, just threw myself into the same casting I'd just watched Brandt do.

I'm sorry. They'll *keep hurting you if I don't stop them somehow.*

Desmond stomped his feet in time. Our combined blast

knocked the figures right over. Two of them slumped, and Desmond nodded to me as if acknowledging the success of our collaboration. But even though I'd watched bodies crumple hundreds of times in simulations over the last several weeks, the reality socked me in the gut.

This wasn't who I wanted to be.

The other insurgent heaved himself back to his feet. The magic clamped around me with a frantic pressure, and I groped for all the strength I could find through my horror.

Dios mío, let this work. I called out the other lyric I'd picked, setting my feet at a slightly different rhythm, and hurled all the energy I could conduct at the final attacker.

It walloped the masked man flat against the floor, pinning him in place, but his groan told me I hadn't killed him. The magic's grip loosened around me with a whiff of relief. I dashed to the doors without time to enjoy it. I didn't know how long my conjured vice would hold.

I yanked open the door to the communications room. "If the goddamned Dull president would just *listen*," Hamlin was rasping. His voice cut off at the squeak of the hinges. He, Commander Revett, one of the other senior officers, and two combat soldiers were braced in a row inside.

"The hall's clear!" Desmond shouted from behind me.

The officials rushed to join us. Our reprieve only lasted a few more seconds. Another barrage of castings shrieked toward us from down the hall. The magic jerked around me in a spasm and smashed into the wall, denting the wood.

Hamlin leapt in front of me and Desmond to shield us from the worst of the attack. I choked out a defensive casting. The mages around me were singing out lyrics in the languages they each turned to. At my right, Commander Revett thrust out her knobby hand with a hasty line in Ancient Greek—and the magic barely shifted at her command.

Just ahead of me, Hamlin was hollering too, but his castings wavered as they flew to meet the enemy. Had the attackers damaged their connection to the magic somehow?

I conducted more barriers into being with my hoarsening voice. Yells echoed off distant walls. "Reinforcements are arriving," Sam announced through my earpiece.

The magical attacks ebbed as our assailants must have shifted their focus in the other direction. Commander Revett strode forward with no sign of distress at the possible loss of her magic, only determination. Had she not even realized she'd been weakened?

I mumbled a quiet verse as Desmond and I hurried along with them. With the melody, I reached my awareness toward Revett's head and then Hamlin's, hearkening for that glowing spot where their minds were attuned to the magic. The spot where, in the last desperate moments of the Exam, I could have burned out one of my fellow examinees if I hadn't caught myself.

The energy I conducted quivered against that glow. I didn't sense any 'chantment clouding it. But in both Revett and Hamlin, the pulse of the energy felt tenuous and tattered. Not what I'd have expected from one harsh blow; it was more as if their ability had been worn down by a gradual battering. When I turned my attention to the other official, who looked to be in his forties, I felt the same thing.

The fraying was worst in Revett, who had to be at least ten years older than the others. Her connection was stripped down to a trembling thread.

Age made a difference, then? But I'd never heard of a talent declining as a mage got older. From what my parents had said, their Dampered abilities had been the same since they were teens.

My gaze tripped back down the hall to the spot where the

magic had bashed the wall like a wild creature. My mouth went dry.

I'd felt the way it tore at me in its anguish. What if it struck out even more directly at the mages who repeatedly cast the spells it hated? Lashing back at them, wearing down their ability to call on it at all?

"Last combatant down," a voice said through my earpiece. "Other units report."

"We're clear here," Sam said.

"No continuing activity in the east wing," Commander Revett said into her mic, her pace slowing.

I couldn't help staring at her for a second before I yanked my eyes away. My understanding of the world had just tipped in a familiar way. Like the first time one of my Dull classmates had tripped me and spat the slur "bruja-ratera" at my back, and I'd realized my kindergarten teacher didn't have the power or the will to do anything but chide weakly and flutter her hands—and then look the other way when it happened again.

Our victory weighed on me. We'd won mainly by slaughtering our foes exactly the same way they'd meant to slaughter us. And the magic—I'd never felt it so frenzied. What if it had hit one of us with the same force with which it'd smacked the wall? What if next time it broke completely?

Slow and steady wasn't enough. I had to get through to the other operatives soon.

But even as that realization shot through me, a tiny spark of hope penetrated my queasy exhaustion, very different from that hopeless moment years ago.

Diffusing the explosive 'chantment had tired me out, but I'd still managed to fend off at least one of our attackers without destroying his life in the process. Fighting while protecting the magic *was* possible. And if what I'd noticed about the senior officials was true across all the senior National Defense officers...

If using the magic to do harm had hindered, over time, their ability to cast... then the young recruits like us had an edge none of us would've imagined.

I didn't need to convince the high command to change tactics. Getting people like Sam and Brandt to understand what was happening to the magic could be more than just the first step in a long process—it could be a real victory right there.

Once I had enough of my fellow operatives on my side, it didn't matter what the officials believed. If we had to, we could force them to listen.

CHAPTER EIGHT

Finn

My whole life, the one thing I'd been able to count on was that my family name would bring me advantages—often ones I hadn't asked for or wanted. I hadn't realized just how much of a cushion that was until I'd entered in this new life, where most of the people around me would have flinched away if I'd properly introduced myself.

To some extent, though, presenting myself just as plain old Finn was freeing. Like Odysseus returning home in disguise to take stock incognito, I drew no special attention in the more worn clothes I'd picked for my fourth meeting with the League. I moved through the crowded room, catching up in brief snatches of conversation with various members I'd talked to over the last few weeks, and no one saw me as anything other than a fellow reject of the Confed's system. No one expected anything all that great from me, but no one expected villainy either.

Even the guy with the mohawk, who'd sneered at old-magic types during the Exam, gravitated toward me as if we were friends. I'd like to think we were becoming that. I might not have had his name—Mark—until our second meeting, but I knew how adamantly he would stand by his principles, even if his attitude wasn't the most welcoming.

"I need to get a better bed," he muttered, rolling his shoulders where we'd come to a stop near the refreshments table. "Crashing on an air mattress in my aunt's basement is no way to live."

He'd told me before that he'd decided to stay on in New York rather than head back to his mom in San Diego because there were things he still wanted to do. I supposed the main thing was finding answers about his brother, who'd made Champion some time ago. I shouldn't have been able to remember that, though, and I wasn't going to push Mark to open up more if he wasn't ready to. In any case, he was making do here on very limited funds.

"Any luck with the job search?" I asked.

"Still stuck with the overnight janitor gig, and they won't give me more than three shifts a week. So far, any place else takes one look at my mark and my hair and gets all edgy." He grimaced and bit into the blueberry danish he'd taken from a platter on the table. His eyebrows jumped up. "Wow, this is a step up from the usual grub."

"You think so?" I said, keeping my expression neutral. Over the past three meetings, I'd gathered that Luis and a few of the other longtime League members grabbed the desserts for these get-togethers at a major discount for being on the verge of staleness. Tonight I'd stopped at my favorite bakery on my way over and picked up a spread I'd ordered in advance.

We were working on important matters here—we deserved a good snack now and then. Why shouldn't I contribute what I could?

I didn't want to emphasize those monetary-based contributions, though. I'd gotten here early so that only a handful of people had seen me bringing in the tray. It was easier to enjoy Mark's enjoyment without questions about how I had the means to make that donation.

"They are good," Noemi said from where she'd come up by my other side. She licked the remnants of icing from her thumb and returned to Mark's unemployment conundrum. "Isn't there a law against discrimination based on magical status? I read that the Confederation pushed to have one passed just a little while after the Unveiling."

"It's not like they *tell* me that's the problem," Mark said. "They say I'm not a good fit or what-the-hell-ever. But I see the way they look at me."

Tamara, the middle-aged Dampered mage who'd been spearheading the movement toward a full-out protest, was ambling by. She stopped and gave Mark a tight but sympathetic smile.

"Getting rid of the Burnout marks is one of the issues we need to push the Circle on. There's no reason for it except to shame people—for what? Wanting to keep their bond with the magic? What's so shameful about that?" She shook her head, the wooden beads at the ends of her tightly braided hair clicking.

"They want everyone who looks at us to have a constant reminder of the consequences of refusing their judgment," I said. It gave them an easy way to identify those inclined toward resistance as well.

Tamara hummed. "And isn't it convenient that none of the relatives of anyone in the Circle are ever anything but Chosen? The bias couldn't be more obvious, and it means they've got no personal stake where we could apply pressure."

My pulse hitched. It was because of that assumption that no one here would ever guess I was the grandnephew of Raymond Lockwood. Not that my situation made Tamara's comment any less true. Granduncle Raymond didn't give a flying toga what happened to *me*; he only cared about how I affected family appearances.

"There are other ways of making the issue personal," I pointed out. "I was going through some old records"—a scrapbook of my mother's, actually—"and it looks like Jacqueline Allerton was heavily involved in the early integration efforts. I'll dig up as much as I can, but appealing to her activist side might get us somewhere."

"That's something, anyway." Tamara looked around the room. "If we can ever get a proper protest off the ground. I think a lot of people wish this was still just a support group where all we did was vent and then go home."

As if on cue, a voice crackled from the microphone on the stage. "Freedom of Magic people! Enough chatting. We've got big things to discuss today."

I wasn't all that surprised that the speaker hadn't waited for introductions when I saw who it was. Ary, the skinny, sharp-eyed young woman who'd ranted against burning out during my first meeting here, had a temper I could only call irrepressible. Today the streaks in her long black hair were a deep blood-red that seemed to fit her mood better than her previous pink. Luis was leaning against the wall at the side of the stage, watching her, so he mustn't have minded her taking the lead.

Ary's hair swung against her back as she paced on the stage. "The first-year placement exams are coming up at the college. All those Chosen mages are looking forward to finding out what cushy careers they can get started on while we're here begging for whatever scraps the Confederation will give us. Does anyone here actually think that's *right*?"

"Hell, no!" someone hollered from the crowd, and a little cheer went up around him.

"So, let's remind them that we exist. Let's remind them who they're stepping over to get those placements. Let's bash through the Confed's whole damn system! If we don't get a chance at that kind of future, why should they have it handed to them? We have to get out there and strike a real blow. If you're too afraid of the Circle to even try to stand up for yourself, what the hell are you doing here?"

She knew how to rouse an audience—that was for sure. Even Mark had perked up, his expression avid as his gaze followed her. Still, even though I agreed in essence with everything she'd said, something about her words sent a tremor of uneasiness through me.

"What did you have in mind?" Luis asked from the sidelines, loud enough that his voice carried over the rising murmurs in the auditorium.

"I have a few ideas," Ary said with a smirk. "How about we march down there right when the college opens that morning, barricade the doors while we douse the place with gasoline, and on our way out, light it up? If we can get by without a college, they can too, don't you think?"

She made the act of burning one of the Confed's oldest institutions to the ground sound perfectly reasonable. When she painted that picture, just for a moment, some small part of even my spirit leapt at the thought of watching all that unearned privilege go up in flames. It was only a small part, though. The rest of me rocked with a wave of horror.

The voices echoing through the room mostly sounded eager, but I obviously wasn't the only one unnerved. "What if there are other people in the building?" someone called toward the stage. "They'll have security guards, won't they?"

Ary shrugged. "I think there are enough of us that we can deal with them. And if they don't want to be lit up too, they'll just have to get the hell out."

She winked as if to keep that sentiment playful, but the piercing light in her eyes made me wonder if she wouldn't rather a few Confed employees go up along with the building. I'd seen that ferocity during the Exam on more faces than I liked to remember—usually right before that person went for the kill.

"We'd lose the whole college library," Noemi said beside me, her body tensed. If Ary wasn't much concerned about loss of life, I doubted the loss of some books would mean much to her. Those texts were part of the Confed's legacy too.

Ary came to a stop at the podium and gripped its sides as she leaned toward us. "The Confed's leaders think they have all the power here. They don't care how many letters we write or phone calls we make. If we show them just how much power we can wield too, then they'll *have* to listen to us. Hit them hard enough, just once, and we've got them."

"I'm in!" a girl shouted from the other end of the room. More voices rose in agreement.

No. Every bone in my body balked. Possibly Ary was right... or possibly her plan would backfire catastrophically. She couldn't remember the brutality of the Exam, the lengths some members of the Confed went to in order to get their way. She hadn't seen how fiercely people like my granduncle would defend their standing in the eyes of the rest of the Confed and the world at large.

The Circle wouldn't go easy on us if we barged into the college. They'd shut us down as swiftly and completely as they could. How many of the people here might be burned or bleeding by the end of it?

My mouth moved before I had a chance to second-guess myself. "Hold on! If we take that approach, we could ruin everything."

Ary's eyes narrowed as they found me in the audience. "If you're too scared to join in, no one's going to force you."

Suddenly everyone around me was looking my way. Sweat broke out on the back of my neck, but I managed to keep control of my tongue. "It's not about being scared. I just don't think this kind of move is going to get us the results we want."

"And who are you to judge that?" Ary asked with an edge in her voice.

That was the question I least wanted to answer. Before I had to, Luis stepped forward, holding up his hand. He caught my gaze and tipped his head toward the stage.

"If you've got other ideas, why don't you come up here and share them, Finn?"

A shiver that was both excitement and nerves ran over my skin when he said my name. Noemi had introduced me to the de facto head of the League a couple of meetings ago, but I wouldn't have expected him to remember me among all the people here. Apparently he'd taken note.

I didn't want to go up there. I'd come here to support people I agreed with, not to try to sway the room with my opinions.

As I hesitated, Ary raised the microphone to her lips again, still glowering at me. A jolt that was more panic than anything else unglued my feet. I pushed through the crowd, and Luis held out his hand for the mic. Ary passed it over and stalked off to perch at the corner of the stage.

The crowd in the room looked even larger from behind the podium. Luis handed me the microphone, and my fingers clamped around it. For a second, my throat was too tight for me to speak.

I didn't have to say much about myself. I could leave my family history out of this. Just make a logical argument. It shouldn't be that hard.

"The Confed's leaders make most of their decisions based on what they see as potential threats." I pointed to my Burnout mark. "They mark us so they know who challenged their rulings. They Damper new-magic mages because they don't trust them to stay loyal. They restrict the number of mages who go to the college every year to prove to the Dull government that they're keeping control, that the Dulls have nothing to fear—no reason to condemn us."

"So?" a guy near the stage said.

"So, if we do something as destructive as burning down a major Confed building, we'll be proving the Circle *right* about us. When they only thought we *might* be a threat, all they did was take away our magic. What do you think they'll do to us if we start acting like actual criminals? They won't sit down and listen to our demands. They'll raze all of us to the ground."

Ary snorted. "The Circle is a bunch of bluster and not much action. You've bought into their posturing too much. When push comes to shove, they'll back down."

The murmurs that followed sounded like agreement. The faces turned toward me were skeptical. I passed the mic from one clammy hand to the other, my stomach knotting.

They weren't listening. They didn't believe me.

I had to give them a good reason to, or I was about to be shouted off the stage.

I inhaled deeply, bracing myself against my doubts. Imagine *she* was in the audience, I told myself. The girl who conjured dragons, the girl who'd resisted the Confed's intentions with every shred of her being, without raising a hand against anyone.

I knew what she'd have wanted me to say. Perhaps I should stop worrying about what was easiest for me and be her mouthpiece while she wasn't here. There was a lot more than pastries I could offer if I let myself. No one else here knew as much about the inner workings of the Confed as I did.

I drew myself up as straight as I could. "Look," I said to the hundreds of figures peering up at me, letting that conviction flow through me, "I'm not making guesses here. I'm speaking from experience. I—I come from old magic. I've been around the people we're trying to influence; I've talked with them; I've seen how they work with my own eyes."

Ary sucked a breath through her teeth with a faint hiss. "Sounds like you're a spy, then, not a supporter."

"No!" I barreled onward before her suggestion could take root with the crowd. "I'm not going to lie. I've had a lot of advantages that I know other people haven't—through luck and not because I earned them. But I obviously also know what it's like to be judged and deemed unworthy; I know what it's like to lose your magic. Growing up the way I did, I always knew I didn't measure up. I worked so hard *trying* to be good enough, turning to every damnable exercise and meditation technique that was supposed to bolster a talent... but it was never enough. I hate that it was never enough. I hate that any of us has been made to feel we weren't worthy of the talents we were born with."

I had their attention now. I could see it in the gazes fixed on me, feel it in the silence that had settled over the room.

"I want to change all that," I went on. "The Dampering, the wretched Exam—they shouldn't happen. I want to put a stop to both as quickly as we can."

"All right," hollered a guy with a sheen of white-blond hair, whom I'd seen hanging around Ary before. "So why don't we go with Ary's plan and get on with it?"

"Because it won't work," I said. "Not the way we want it to. If we make ourselves look dangerous, the Circle and those who stand with them *will* crush us, every way they can, in the name of protecting the rest of the community. And if we go so far that we tear them down completely, do you really think the Dull government will just stand by? A lot of them are looking for an excuse to crush us themselves."

"What would you suggest instead, then?" Luis said at my right. I'd gotten so caught up in my speech I'd almost forgotten he was there.

I reached for the ideas that had been gradually forming in my head over the last several weeks. "I don't know what all the answers are," I said. "But my parents and my grandparents were part of the early efforts leading up to the Unveiling. My whole life, I've listened to them talk about how the tide shifted. The thing that made the biggest difference was showing how much *good* we could do—good that the current policies were preventing.

"So... if we want to get more people on our side, I think it needs to be totally clear that *we're* the good guys and the Confed's leaders are the ones in the wrong. You know, during the integration, a lot of mages played down their power and let the Dull authorities bully them because that got them sympathy. It made them look human to people who might have been scared of them otherwise. Perhaps there's some way we can use that kind of tactic."

A familiar voice rose up from the middle of the crowd. "We could work with that." Tamara gave me a nod. "Sometimes brute force can get the job done, but often your best bet is playing the game to sway public opinion. We can use the placement exams, but we don't have to burn the place down. Blockade it and stop all those new mages from getting on with their careers. Let the Confed try to shut us down. Make them use force on us while we're just trying to raise awareness. We could get a lot of people —mages and maybe even Dulls—considering our side."

"Yes," I said with a grateful smile. "I think that plan would get us a lot closer to our goals."

More people were murmuring in the audience, but the tenor had shifted. Had my appeal gotten through to them?

Luis joined me by the podium again, and I happily relinquished the microphone.

"We've heard a lot of passionate commentary tonight," he said. "Ary and Tamara have both suggested concrete actions we could take—and Finn clearly has insights we don't want to ignore. I suggest the three of them work *together* organizing this protest at the college. All in favor?"

A cheer carried through the crowd. I glanced toward Ary and cringed inwardly at her expression. She'd schooled her face blank, but the tightness of her mouth radiated resentment.

"I believe we have a couple more people who'd like to speak on other topics," Luis went on. "And then we can get down to the planning. Thank you for sharing, Finn."

I bobbed my head awkwardly and scrambled down from the stage. As I eased my way back to Noemi and Mark, several people patted my shoulder, my arm, with quick words of support in passing. It was difficult to feel too nervous, looking at all those sympathetic eyes. Perhaps I'd been wrong to think my background would be that much of an issue—at least, the nonspecific version of it. They knew I was with them regardless of where I'd come from.

My pulse had mostly settled into its usual rhythm by the time I reached my friends. "That was awesome!" Noemi said, grinning. "I didn't know you had that in you."

"Not a bad speech," was Mark's much more restrained assessment.

"And what was that bit you said about exercises to improve your magic?" Noemi's eyes had lit with curiosity.

"There are a bunch of different strategies that are supposed to strengthen a mage's connection to the magic," I said. "Developing concentration, rhythm, everything associated with casting. I'm not sure how well they worked, but I think they did at least a little for me."

A guy was just starting to speak on the stage. Noemi tapped my elbow with hers. "I want to hear more about that later."

* * *

When the taxi dropped me off outside my family's brownstone, I was still buzzing from the meeting and the tentative plan we'd started to build for the protest at the college. That must have been why I didn't notice the car parked one house over until a gravelly baritone voice broke the quiet of the street.

"Finnegan."

I jerked around. The taxi was already leaving, the growl of its engine fading as it turned the corner onto Madison Avenue. Granduncle Raymond was leaning against the side of his Lexus in the deeper shadows between the jaundiced light of the streetlamps. He tapped the end of his cane against the sidewalk.

"Granduncle," I said, in as even a voice as I could manage. What in Hades's name was he doing lurking on the street at this hour?

He pushed his stout frame off the car. "Your father said you were out with friends." His gaze took in my clothes and returned to my face. "Not your usual friends, I'm guessing. What have you been up to, Finnegan?"

He didn't sound as if he knew anything definite. "I'm not sure what you're talking about," I said lightly. "What other friends do I have?"

He waved his cane at me. "Don't give me that nonsense. I know the look of someone who's getting ideas too large for his head. You're not settling down. You're getting riled up."

A spark of anger lit inside me. Who was *he* to lecture me on what I could and couldn't believe? As if one of the Circle members—who chose to look the other way, to stay blissfully ignorant of the torture the examiners inflicted on so many novices because the results were convenient for them—was in a position to judge anyone else.

"I don't know where you're going with this, but I do know it's none of your business what ideas I have in my head or how I feel about them," I returned.

Granduncle Raymond blinked. He hesitated before he spoke again, as if he hadn't expected a reply like that. I wasn't sure I'd ever talked back to him so directly before. Up until the Exam, I'd always been striving to earn his good favor or at least offset his obvious disappointment.

"It's my business to protect the people I was appointed to serve," he said. "And not to let the careless passions of a few undermine the security we've managed to establish. You haven't been alive long enough to know how lucky you are to have as much as you do. Believe me, you wouldn't want to go back to the days of riots and unchecked Dull-on-mage violence. Work out your frustrations if you must, but make sure you stay on the right side."

Would he be talking to me like that if he knew how much mage-on-mage violence I might have averted tonight? I couldn't restrain a retort, though I kept my tone level. "Whatever you're accusing me of, I can assure you I've got no part in it," I said. "Can you say the same? Ignoring evils that happen under your watch doesn't erase their existence. 'Cui prodest scelus is fecit,' if I need to remind you of your Seneca."

My granduncle's expression shuttered. "You—"

"Have nothing else to say to you. Good night, Granduncle."

I strode up to the door without a backward glance, and he didn't call me back.

CHAPTER NINE

Rocío

The whir of the helicopter's blades had become so familiar that I could've nodded off to it if my nerves hadn't been on high alert. I shifted on the bench next to Sam, clasping my hands in front of me to hold them from fidgeting. The magic niggled at the back of my neck and my inner arms as if it knew exactly where I'd find it hardest to ignore. It hadn't completely settled since the attack on the base four nights ago.

The few enemy combatants we'd taken prisoner—the ones who hadn't died in the skirmish—had provided a little intel. Our first two leads had only turned up one minor player in the Borci network, a guy who'd managed to get his hands on some specs for the base and sold them. Commander Revett had made it clear she wasn't satisfied with our progress.

We need to make a decisive strike, she'd said in an operations meeting a couple days ago. *This petty back and forth has gone on long enough. I want this terrorist force so hobbled that they couldn't dream of assaulting one of our bases again.*

My gut clenched just remembering the furor in her voice.

Somehow I didn't think the kind of "decisive strike" she was talking about would differentiate between the actual killers who'd slaughtered six of our people in that one night and the locals who weren't much more than regular civilians on the fringes of the conflict, like the guy with the specs or the boy I'd met on my first mission. Maybe I could believe those masked figures who'd wrecked our base deserved to be destroyed in turn, but the others? Shouldn't we care who got caught in the crossfire?

And really, when it came down to it... how were even the terrorists all that different from the examiners who'd hurt and killed novices like me before forcing some of us into their war?

I rubbed my forehead, and Sam glanced over at me. "Everything okay, Lopez?"

Across the cabin from us, Brandt's gaze jerked to me, a little more eagerly than I liked. I'd felt him watching me warily during our last mission, like he was just waiting for me to make a mistake he could call me on. Still sore that he hadn't gotten to really lay into me about the way I'd handled the bomb, I guessed.

Next to him, Joselin had her earbuds in as always, her ponytail bobbing lightly in time with whatever she was listening to. She liked to get herself pumped up before we hit the ground. Prisha and our translator were talking in hushed voices. Desmond was monitoring the area ahead of us at his terminal, the screen zooming in at a twitch of his fingers when his limited sight needed a closer view.

I had potential support here. And I had to work my way up to the subject I really wanted to talk about somehow. This might be a decent place to start.

Still, I held the question in my throat for a few heartbeats before I let myself ask, "What do you think about the way Commander Revett has been talking? Is this really the first time a base has been attacked? She seems to think the situation has gotten so much worse than it used to be, that we've got to get so much more aggressive to push back."

Sam shrugged. "I'm not high up enough to be in on all the behind-the-scenes conversations, but from what I have picked up, there's been increasing pressure from the Dull government to get 'real' results. Their military division is pretty nervous about ours in general, you know. The only thing scarier than magical soldiers across the ocean who might try to kill you, like the Borci, are magical soldiers right in your backyard who could decide to do the same, right?"

The Dull government. Finn had talked about those pressures, and Hamlin had alluded to them in our training—the idea that our service here helped keep the peace between mages and the nonmagical back home. Hamlin had been venting about something to do with the Dull president during the attack on the base. But our commanders made the ultimate decisions about what missions we ran. We couldn't just let them off the hook.

"It's not as if the Dull military has been able to shut down any of the terrorist groups they're fighting," Brandt muttered. "Every time they chop off one head, another one sprouts in its place. They should focus on their own failures."

"I don't recommend you point that out to them the next time one of the Dull officials comes by," Sam said mildly, and turned back to me. "I think we've been at a standstill with most of these insurgent groups for a long time. The longer we keep this holding pattern, the more likely it is someone will figure out a way to deal a catastrophic blow to us. The commanders are getting more and more concerned about dealing that blow to our enemies first."

I guessed that made sense, even if I knew any kind of catastrophic blow dealt with magic would probably end up being a catastrophe for all of us.

"Has the pressure to make that kind of strike increased a lot since you started?" I asked. "How long have you been part of the special ops unit anyway?"

"A little over eleven years," Sam said. "And yeah, I'd say there's been more and more talk about 'big results' and that sort of thing."

"Eleven years?" I blurted out. "I thought we were allowed out after ten. That's what Hamlin told us."

Sam gave me a crooked smile. "A lot of us former Champions—the ones who make it through the first ten years— end up staying longer. When you've got a decade of your life you can't really talk about, and all the baggage that comes with this kind of work... I'm not really sure what else I'd do. It's hard for you to imagine it now, but you have your first leave this weekend. Wait 'til you see how you feel back home."

I'd already been having trouble sleeping, trying to figure out how I was going to talk to Mom and Dad during those few days or how it might be when I saw Finn again after all this time. The five days we'd spent fighting our way through the Exam together had felt like an eternity at the time, but the last two months had stretched way longer. A niggling murmur in the back of my head kept popping up to ask how often he'd have been thinking about me.

I rubbed my arms, pushing aside those thoughts. I had other things I needed to talk about right now. My throat constricted for a moment, but I might not get another opening like this. And I was running out of time.

"What if hurting the terrorist groups like that would end up hurting us just as much, or more?" I said tentatively.

Sam's eyebrows rose, but he didn't dismiss me outright. "What makes you think that?"

"I just..." I hadn't realized how hard it would be, trying to explain what I'd sensed from the magic, after all this time keeping it to myself. Squaring my shoulders, I forced myself to keep going. "I think the magic is alive. I don't know exactly how, but I can hearken a sort of intent from it sometimes, as if it has things that it wants or even needs. And any casting that hurts things, breaks things, makes it… upset. Like it's been hurt too. Like we're wounding it."

Joselin had taken out her earbuds at some point during our conversation. Now she stiffened. "You think the castings we use are breaking down the magic somehow?"

Brandt guffawed. "That's the stupidest thing I've ever heard. The magic is just magic, like electricity in the wires or *gravity*."

I trained my gaze on him. "I can feel it. I knew where that explosive 'chantment was without even casting a scan. You've seen me pick up on things no one else has."

Prisha shifted on the bench. "I haven't hearkened the same things Rocío has, but…" Her mouth tensed. She couldn't talk about our experiences during the Exam any more than I could. "I think she's probably right," she said. "And I wouldn't buy into that kind of theory without a good reason."

I hadn't known for sure if she'd speak up on my behalf. A startled smile tugged at my lips, and she returned it with a small one of her own.

"I've got to buy into Rocío's theories too, at this point," Desmond put in. "Don't you ever feel that way when you cast? Like you're having a conversation with the magic, asking it to work with you, not just maneuvering an inanimate substance?"

Joselin was nodding, but Brandt rolled his eyes. "Sure," he said. "And centuries ago, people thought the sun and the moon and trees and stuff had spirits in them too. They 'felt' all kinds of nonsense. Why the hell should we worry about making the magic upset? With the terrorists cutting us down and the Dulls shoving us around, we've got to look out for each other."

"I think it's an interesting idea," Sam said, with a glance at the junior officer that looked like a warning. "Maybe I need to pay a little more attention to exactly what I can hearken."

Even the examiners know, I wanted to say. *They admitted it right to my face.* But that secret was locked away behind the silencing 'chantment. No wonder they'd pretended to care. They'd known I wouldn't be able to call them on their false promises.

At least not yet.

For now, I took Sam's openness to the idea as progress. "That's why I try to avoid destructive castings on the missions," I said. "I think we could change our approach so that we defend ourselves without damaging the magic in the process." Or maybe we could back out of the conflict completely and focus on healing the damage that had already been done. But that was probably too much to propose at this point.

"I'm fine with you using whatever strategies work best for you, as long as they do *work*," Sam said as the helicopter started to descend. "*Never* breaking or hurting anything... That's not going to be possible in every situation. But if you have a new idea, and there's room for us to implement it, go ahead and share it. Then we can all draw our own conclusions."

Brandt made a skeptical sound, but I decided que me vale what he thought. If I won Sam over, he was senior enough and respected enough that other operatives would follow his lead.

The chopper landed in an empty parking lot between several looming concrete apartment buildings. We'd been sent to a city this time—according to the mission briefing, a militant who'd helped plan the attack on the base might be living here. We were to bring him in by force if we found him and gather any information we could if we didn't.

"The housing unit we're supposed to check out is on that street," Desmond said, pointing without even looking. His other hand was drumming out a faint rhythm on his knee as he cast. "Just a quarter mile from here. I don't hearken any major magic being worked in the area or any other suspicious movements, but there are quite a few people in the building. If one of them does make a move, I might not be able to sound the warning before they're on you."

"Keep a close eye from here, and we'll be cautious out there," Sam said, giving Desmond's shoulder a quick pat.

"Thanks," I murmured as I passed my old teammate. He shot me a quick grin and a thumbs-up before turning back to his enlarged screen. Sometimes I got the impression he actually kind of *enjoyed* the work he was doing. It must be easier to focus on the skills and not the meaning of what we were doing when you could stay at more of a distance from the actual people involved.

We all hopped out onto the cracked asphalt. The street Desmond had pointed to was completely dark, only a gleam of a streetlamp at least a block in the distance. The sour smell of days-old garbage laced the chilly air. The kind of people we went looking for never lurked in the nice parts of town.

We hustled down the street with quick but wary steps. I winced when broken glass crunched under my boots. Sam had murmured his distraction 'chantment to keep attention off of us, but it wasn't going to protect us from anyone in the building we were about to breach.

The housing unit we arrived at was a smaller version of one of those concrete apartment buildings, only three stories tall. We couldn't give the courtesy of a knock when we were hoping to catch one of the occupants by surprise. I braced myself as Sam stepped up to the door. He sang softly to the lock—not breaking it, just unlocking it, like I had on our first time out, I realized with a flicker of satisfaction—and shoved the door open.

He strode into the hall on the other side, shouting out a few phrases in Estonian and then Russian: a call for everyone to come out and present themselves. A tired family spilled out of one door: grandparents, parents, and three young kids. Two couples emerged from the other, rubbing sleep from their eyes. None of them matched the description or photos we'd been given.

Sam motioned Brandt and me toward the stairs and back door at the far end of the hall. "Check all the apartments; don't let anyone leave." Joselin and Prisha hung back with him as he started questioning the inhabitants with our translator's help.

Brandt and I were halfway to the stairs when two figures bolted down them with a scrabble of hard soles against rough concrete. Brandt snapped out a casting that heaved the first figure into the wall so hard that the woman dropped to her knees, her hands shielding her scraped face. The magic shuddered around me.

I flung out my own casting: the same vice-like blanket of energy I'd conjured during the attack on the base. It smacked into the second figure just as the guy reached for the doorknob and pinned him to the floor.

"What have we got here?" Sam said, coming up behind us. He took in the woman with her now-bleeding nose and the guy I'd captured without injury. Neither of them was our mission's target either.

"They must have something to hide," Brandt said. "They were running like bats out of hell."

"Check the upper floors for the target, and then we'll question them," Sam said, and paused. "And if they're just running, not attacking, let's try not to batter them around. Lopez's technique is sound." He tipped his head to me. "You should show the rest of us exactly how you cast that conjuring when we're back on the base."

The flicker of satisfaction danced higher in my chest. Brandt grimaced but didn't argue. He charged up the stairs ahead of me.

No one else ran, but no one else we called out of their

apartments—which looked to be made up of no more than a shabby room or two—matched the guy we'd been hoping to catch. We asked all the residents to come downstairs, checking each room as they left. Then we returned to guard the back door while Sam and the translator continued their interviews.

The residents shifted in the now-crowded first-floor hall, their faces pinched with worry and exhaustion. My uncertainties crept back in. Who the hell were we to come into a country that wasn't even ours and drag all these people out of their beds to interrogate them? Didn't the Confed interfere with enough lives back home?

A face caught my eye as I scanned the crowd—pale and snub-nosed, with fawn-brown hair pulled into a tight braid and the collar of a scuffed jean jacket turned up to the base of her jaw.

It was the girl who'd been watching Brandt and me tackle the explosive 'chantment a few days ago. What was she doing here? The town where I'd seen her was a hundred miles away.

What were the chances she'd been both right by the explosive site *and* here simply by coincidence?

Our gazes met. She eased through the crowd toward me, stopping by the two runners we'd stopped, who were now magically bound to chairs against the wall. I went to join her, a lyric ready on the tip of my tongue.

"That one you did," she said, pointing to the guy. Her accent wasn't as thick as the boy we'd questioned my first night out. "The spell—it doesn't hurt him?"

I'd meant to question *her*, but I couldn't see why I shouldn't give her an answer first. "No," I said. "That's not what I'm here to do. If I had things my way, no one would get hurt."

The girl gave a faint snort. "Never works like that when you people come in, does it?"

I wasn't sure if she meant specifically the special ops team, or all of National Defense, or any Americans at all. I offered a tight smile. "I try. I'll keep trying."

"I know. I've seen you," she said, in a tone that made me wonder how often she'd watched and I hadn't noticed. She grimaced. "So many people wanting to hurt and not caring much whether they hit the ones who deserve it. On your side and right here. Sometimes I think from here is worse. They should care more, but they don't seem to."

"Do you know something about the people here?" I said delicately. "You can tell me. I know you're just trying to help."

She studied me for a long moment. "I am," she said. "I don't want more getting hurt. Maybe you can help with that. Please."

She reached into her pocket. I stiffened automatically, but all she pulled out was a small digital recorder. She pressed it into my hand in one swift motion and then darted between two other figures in the crowd, pushing into one of the apartments.

"Hey!" Brandt said from where he'd stayed by the back door. He barged over, and I leapt after the girl instinctively. I dashed into the apartment in time to see her clambering through an open window.

In that moment, in the space of a breath, I could have stopped her. I could have cast to knock her to the floor and locked her in place like a criminal. But her *please* and the look in her eyes when she'd handed me the recorder were still resonating through me.

She'd trusted me. She'd asked me to do right by her and everyone else here. One quick casting could shatter that trust forever.

Brandt barged in just as the tip of her braid vanished beyond the glass. He pounded past me to the window, but I could tell from his face when he peered out into the night that she was gone.

"You let her go!" he said, spinning around.

Sam appeared in the doorway. "What's going on?"

"There was a girl," Brandt said, his face flushed with the same anger that colored his voice. "She gave something to Lopez and ran for it. And Lopez just stood here."

"I came after her," I protested. That much, at least, was true. "I wasn't fast enough." Which was also true, as long as I didn't explain that it'd been my thoughts and not my feet that had slowed me down.

Sam looked between the two of us. He grasped Brandt's shoulder. "Whatever happened, she's gone now. Keep holding the back door." As Brandt hustled off with a frown, our mission leader turned to me. "What have you got, Lopez?"

I handed the recorder to him. "She said she wanted to help us stop… well, she wasn't totally clear about who, but it sounded like she meant the Borci or people like them. I don't think she's on their side."

"It still would've been good for us to question her now to see what else she might know," Sam said. From his expression, I could tell he suspected I might not have put every possible effort into stopping her. "I'm not going to write this up, since you were attempting to follow orders—but next time run a little faster?"

I hoped my cheeks didn't show the heat that had risen in them. "Got it."

"All right. Now let's see what we've got here."

Sam leaned out into the hall and motioned our translator into the apartment. He pressed the play button on the recorder. The translator leaned close.

A voice trickled from the speaker, mid-sentence and partly muffled. Maybe the recorder had been hidden in a pocket or under a jacket when it'd caught this conversation. I'd been on this assignment long enough to recognize the words as Russian.

Then a thin voice piped up—speaking a different language,

one I didn't know at all. The translator went rigid. Sam's eyebrows drew together, his shoulders tensing too.

A third voice said something in the same unfamiliar language, and the thin voice from before seemed to pick up the thread in Russian. Going back and forth, like our translators always did between English and Russian or Estonian when we questioned people.

Oh. Because that middle voice must be a translator too.

"That's a member of the Borci Za Spravedlivost talking with a representative from the Bonded Worthy—the insurgent network that's been launching attacks throughout the Middle East and Asia," our translator said, her face pale. "They're discussing a possible temporary alliance—as a way to take down the Confederation."

CHAPTER TEN

Finn

I'd never felt all that connected to my parents' stories of pushing forward the Unveiling. Those had been tales from another time before I or even my older siblings had been born, when there'd been clear injustices to rally against. I'd imagined that any conflict that called for heroics on my part would involve enemies from abroad. I'd gone so long without realizing how many injustices still existed right here at home, waiting for me to rally too.

Right now, rallying consisted of a meeting in a café in Queens, where we were nailing down the details of the more vigorous rallying to come five days' time.

"Along with the three obvious entrances to the college, there's a fourth one for maintenance here." Tamara pointed to the markings on the blueprint she'd set on the café table. Her fourteen-year-old son had a knack for combining magic with computers, two elements I hadn't thought would ever bond, and he'd managed to dig up some records we could consult. "No unexpected access points that I can see. We'd want to be in place at each entrance before any students arrive."

"The college officially opens at seven in the morning," I said, gulping my now-lukewarm coffee. The bitter flavor jolted me even more alert. I glanced at Floyd, a Dampered guy in his early twenties who'd joined our little planning group. "What did you see from the security patrols?"

He smiled eagerly. "Their last patrol of the morning is around five-thirty."

"Then I think we'd want to get in place around six-thirty. Early enough to get there ahead of the students, but not so early someone might sound the alarm and remove us before we have a chance to make our point."

"How many of our Dampered members think they could help hold off security?" Mark asked beside me.

I checked my notes on my phone. I'd spent part of our last meeting circulating and chatting up every Dampered mage in the church rec room. "Eight have volunteered so far who feel their remaining talent will make at least a small difference. There's a guy with an affinity for shielding, and a woman who can work temperatures—not that I think we should try to burn them, but she could make getting close to us uncomfortable. That sort of thing."

"With eight we can place two of them at each door," Tamara said. "One stronger and one weaker at each, so we don't leave any entrance poorly defended. If anyone new comes forward in the next few days, that's a bonus."

"There are ways we can make it harder for them to move us that don't take any magic, right?" Noemi said, leaning her elbows on the table. "Digging in our heels, if you know what I mean?"

Tamara smiled. "Both of my grandfathers were very active in protests that had nothing to do with magic, back in the day. I've heard all their stories—I've got plenty of ideas there. We can have a little teaching session at the meeting before the protest." She turned to me with a click of her beaded braids. "Any word from Ary?"

I shook my head. Ary had taken a few of her friends to supposedly do some additional scoping out of the college building. It might have been an excuse not to have to work directly with us. She'd agreed to approach this protest Tamara's way, but with a frenetic enthusiasm and a sharp little smirk that seemed to suggest she was simply waiting to crow when the protest failed and we saw how wrong we'd been to argue with her.

"She hasn't messaged me," I said. "I'm not sure how much she'd want to share any information she came across, anyway."

"She'd better get with the program," Tamara said. "What we need more than anything is a united front—she's got to accept that most of us aren't ready to tear the whole Confederation down just yet. There'll be plenty of time for that later if moderate measures don't gain us any ground."

Noemi winced, and I suspected she was thinking of that library again—burned down before she had a chance to delve into its books. "I don't think that will be necessary," I said quickly.

"Force has its place. But I'm hoping we won't have to go there." Tamara reached to fold up the blueprint.

"What should we be focusing on until the meeting tomorrow?" Floyd asked, his gaze on me. Tamara was technically taking the lead here—her experience trumped anything I could offer—so I glanced toward the older mage to show I deferred to her opinion if it differed from mine. Even so, it gave me a little flush of pride that many of the League members had started turning to me for input.

"I'm thinking recruitment is key right now," I said. "We've got a few more days to reach out to friends, family, neighbors, colleagues—any Dampered or Burnout mages who might be willing to stand up to the status quo—and encourage them to show up at the meeting. Strength in numbers?"

"Dulls too," Tamara said with a tip of her head toward Noemi. "They can clearly be an asset. And we all know the Dull government can put pressure on the Confed themselves if they're getting hassled by their constituents. I'll be calling the major news channels to see if I can spark some interest in covering the protest."

"Is your family going to get involved?" Noemi asked her as we got up from the table.

The wince Tamara tried to suppress suggested that was a painful subject. "My son and husband, yes, and maybe some of the in-laws. My younger brother-in-law took his own life a decade ago, and we all know his depression came on at least in part because of his Dampering, so feelings run pretty strong there... They're just also a little cautious. My folks, you won't see at all."

"They want to stay out of it?" Mark said, his tone suggesting he had experience with that sort of attitude.

"They don't even want to hear about it, most of the time." She sighed. "It's funny how fighting one type of prejudice doesn't make you immune to participating in other kinds. My parents aren't so keen on the whole magic situation, even though, for all we know, they might have tested magical if they'd been young enough for the Confed to bother checking in the Unveiling."

That didn't seem likely to me. After all, the whole reason the Confed had only tested those sixteen and under back then was that anyone who could hearken magic generally showed it before they reached puberty. These days, the Confed simply tested every newborn for potential, to have them already on record and so those with a talent could start training early.

I didn't see the need to point any of that out, though. I just made a face in sympathy. "I hope they come around eventually." She shrugged. "It'll be what it is. I'll touch base with Luis and fill him in on where we're at. If you do hear from Ary, keep me in the loop, all right?"

"Of course."

The five of us stepped outside the café into a crisp but gray November day. Mark and Floyd headed off on foot—we'd met in Queens because it was the most convenient neighborhood for them and Tamara. Noemi waved down a cab. Tamara touched my arm to hold me back for a moment.

"Is everything okay?" I asked. What would she have wanted to say without the others here? Had I put my foot in it somehow? It wouldn't be the first time.

She gave me a wry smile. "I think so. Mostly I wanted to thank you for stepping up the way you did last week. I know it can't have been easy to put yourself out there. You've had some useful things to contribute—and you know how to talk to people, which is half the battle right there. I'm glad to have you on our side because of that, and because, even young as you are, the old-magic crowd is going to listen to someone who's one of them before anyone else."

My face heated up. "I didn't want to— I mean, I don't think I—"

"Hey," she said, holding up her hand. "It's okay. I don't mean it as criticism; it's just a fact. I can tell you mean well. Which is why I also wanted to remind you, just for the future, because who knows where it'll take us: make sure you keep listening to the people you're speaking up for. You've got to listen, and to listen well, if your intention is to boost everyone's voices and not just your own."

"That makes sense," I said, my cheeks still burning—but I welcomed that discomfort if it meant her words stuck with me.

"I definitely didn't get involved with the League just to benefit me."

"I didn't think you did, Finn," she said, waving me off as she started ambling away. "You're a good kid. Stay that way, all right?"

I stood there in front of the café for a moment longer, the brisk breeze cooling my face. My parents expected me to be out at least a couple more hours. Perhaps the walk to the nearest subway station would do me good.

The exhilaration of the meeting, feeling the pieces of this protest come together, had faded in the wake of an anxiety that had nothing to do with Tamara's cautioning. Well, other than the fact that it tied directly into my being an old-magic kid.

I had to join the others at the college for the sit-in. I couldn't put myself forward as one of the organizers of the rally and then abandon the effort at the most crucial moment. What were the chances that one of my former Academy classmates *wouldn't* spot me and make some sort of comment, though? Nearly nil, I suspected.

It wouldn't be awful to simply be recognized in front of the others, since anyone could have guessed I'd gone to the Academy after what I'd shared, but I couldn't count on keeping that one last awful detail—my family name—secret. The League members had accepted me as an old-magic failure. I wasn't certain they'd ever accept a Lockwood, not while there was another Lockwood among the ten in the Circle.

Even if they did accept me, Ary and her supporters would probably jump at the chance to leverage my personal ties by whatever means they could.

No, it was better that I stayed partly anonymous, for both the League and my family. I could help more like this. If I stayed at the back of the crowd with my head low, perhaps I could escape much notice.

I paused at a corner, deciding which direction to go from there. A voice whispered past my ear, so familiar my heart flipped over.

"*Finn.*"

I whirled around. A couple meandering by gave me an odd look. No one else was near me. How— What—

"Finn," the whisper came again. "Cross the street and head east. The convenience store with the papered window."

That was magic carrying her voice to me. I nearly tripped over my feet as I hurried to the opposite sidewalk. I spotted the store toward the end of that block—newspaper sheets over the display window, the yellow sign cracked down the middle. When I was just a few steps away, the grimy door eased open. The face that had featured in so many of my fractured memories emerged from the shadows.

She was here. She was really *here*. The girl from my memories, the girl I'd spent so many days searching for. Her deep brown gaze rested on me, as watchful as ever, but a cautious smile curled her lips. The sunburst necklace she'd held onto through the exam glinted below the collar of her maroon sweater.

She stepped back to make room for me to come in. My legs propelled me forward with no instruction required from my brain. My thoughts were spinning. Then I was standing there amid the dusty display shelves, right in front of her.

"Dragon-Tamer," I said. Really it was more of a croak. I'd had some idea, when I'd imagined finding her again, that I'd stay warm but collected, as strong as she'd always been. All that went out the window.

I reached for her and she moved to meet me, and it took all my self-control not to cling to her even more tightly than she was hugging me. My head bowed next to hers, a ragged breath escaping me. The freshly sweet smell of her dark hair filled my lungs.

She was back. She was here. She was *okay*. Nothing out there, wherever the National Defense division had sent her, had broken her.

"Sorry for the subterfuge," she murmured against my shoulder. The fact that she didn't seem any more eager to let go of me than I was to release her absolved me of any embarrassment. "I'm not sure how much I'm being monitored— I didn't know how anyone might feel about us seeing each other."

"It's fine," I said. "I'm just glad to see you. You have no idea. I was worried about you, but I didn't know how to get in contact—"

"I know," she said. "It's hard when there's so much you can't talk about, isn't it? I wish I'd— I could've—" She drew back slightly with a noise of frustration that echoed the emotions I'd felt so many times before. I knew without her saying anything else that she couldn't talk about her experiences as Champion any more than I could discuss the details of the Exam.

"Yes," I said. "Exactly. But I—I'm so relieved to see you're okay."

She smiled up at me, touching my cheek, and with the Fates as my witness, if I looked at nothing else for the rest of my life, I'd be perfectly fine with that. The impulse raced through me to lower my mouth to hers, to bring into vivid reality the kisses I could only recall vague fragments of. To have one whole memory to carry with me after this.

Someone coughed passing by the papered window, and the girl flinched. She gestured toward the door with a quick Spanish verse sung sotto voce. The lock snapped into place.

"We might not be able to talk all that freely, but at least we can talk in private," she said. "This place hasn't been used in a while. I made sure no one was following me."

It occurred to me that she must have 'chanted the lock open to get in to begin with. Dodging potential surveillance, jimmying locks—those were useful skills for running covert missions, no doubt. She seemed so matter-of-fact about it that I had to stop myself from staring at her.

The people she worked for now might not have broken her, but they'd started to reshape her in just two short months.

"How did you find me?" I found myself asking.

"I've learned things…" She gestured in an offhand way that managed to indicate some distant training I could only attempt to imagine. I'd studied tracking techniques back when I still hoped to work for National Defense myself. For a mage of her skill, it couldn't have been all that difficult to narrow down my location within the city. "It took longer than I expected," she added. "I searched all over Manhattan first. What are you doing out here?"

That one thing I could talk about. "Doing the work I can to change things," I said. "There's a group—Dampered and Burnouts and Dulls—we're putting together a protest—I think we have a good chance of making progress if we keep at it."

"That's great," the girl said, but her voice had softened. Her gaze and then her hand rose to my temple, her fingers hovering by my Burnout mark. "Are *you* okay?" she asked, her eyes so solemn that a lump rose in my throat.

"Oh, you know me—I'm nothing if not adaptable," I said. "It's almost a relief. No magic, no pressure to work it well."

She didn't look as if she completely believed that answer, but, fair enough, neither did I.

A knot formed in my stomach as I looked back at her. I was overjoyed to see her, but it felt so wrong to be missing such a basic element of who she was.

"This is going to sound strange," I said, "but could you tell me your name?"

The girl knit her brow. "My name? Why—what's going on, Finn?"

How could I explain when I couldn't talk about what the examiners had done? I fumbled for the right words. "There aren't just things I can't talk about. There's... I know you're the girl I called 'Dragon-Tamer.' I know *you*."

"But you don't know my name."

The vaguest of phrases managed to form on my tongue. "I've lost things. Things were taken. Bits and pieces."

The girl went completely still. Then she let her hand come to rest on the side of my head, near my mark. Anger sparked in her eyes. In that moment, I could see that no matter what she'd been through and how it might have altered her, she was still every bit the girl I'd fallen for.

"They messed with your *memories*?" she bit out. "It's Rocío. Rocío Lopez. And I'm the girl who's going to make them wish they only had to deal with dragons."

CHAPTER ELEVEN

Rocío

Finn's shoulders sagged as if the sound of my name had given him some kind of release. I tugged him to me again, absorbing the warmth from his lean body, the solidness of his presence. I'd searched for him torn between excitement at the thought of seeing him again and terror that something would have changed. But nothing had changed at all about the way he looked at me, the way he felt in my arms, or the wry tone he used to play down his problems.

He hadn't been able to suppress the crack in his voice when he'd mentioned the memories he'd lost.

"How much did they take?" I said against his shirt, and then, when his muscles started to tense, "No, sorry, of course you can't say that. Um. Possibilities, not things that actually happened. That's one way to talk around it. What do you think they did to the other novices they burned out?"

"I think the examiners wiped them completely," Finn said. "Everything from after we crossed the bridge. I've talked to Mark

—he's still here in the city. He didn't remember he'd ever seen me before."

But Finn had still known me, obviously. I breathed in the softly fresh smell of fabric softener clinging to his shirt, which I'd somehow been missing too, and shaped another careful question. "Why do you think the other Burnouts would've held on to less than you did?"

"They didn't have anyone who was willing to help them," Finn said without hesitation.

Someone *had* helped him, he was saying. But not enough for him to remember everything. Not enough for him to keep my name.

The anger that had seared up through my chest earlier simmered higher. If the examiners had gotten their way, he'd have forgotten me completely. Forgotten everything we'd shared. Forgotten the promise we'd made to each other to fight back.

Forgotten what he'd even wanted to fight back against.

The examiners covered their tracks so thoroughly. Thinking about all the Burnout novices who had no idea what they'd been forced to do or what had been done to them made me queasy. They'd been stripped not just of their magic but their understanding of how they'd lost it. My hands clenched against Finn's back.

"I wish it wasn't this hard to talk," Finn said. "There's so much I want to ask you, but I know you probably can't give me many answers. Can you say—what are you doing in the city now?"

"We get a break for three days once a month, now that we're 'settled in'," I said. "Mine started last night. I get phone time once a week, though. After I'm back… at the college… if we decided it was safe, or if I needed to talk to you enough that safety didn't matter anymore, I could get in touch between visits that way."

"You just need my number," Finn filled in with a raw chuckle. "Do you have your phone on you?"

"No." It'd been sitting in my bedroom at home since the morning I'd left for the Exam. After all those weeks without it, I'd gotten out of the habit of carrying it. "I wouldn't be able to use it anyway." No way would National Defense let us bring private communication devices out to the base.

Finn nodded and looked around the vacant shop as if for something to write on. My gaze followed his over the dusty shelves and counter, noting every detail, my lips starting to form a scanning casting instinctively before I caught myself.

This wasn't a mission. I had to shake the new habits I'd picked up in the field. My mind slipped back to Sam's casual comment about how hard it was to come back to the regular world.

No. I wasn't going to let the Confed take over the whole rest of my life like that.

I wasn't sure I could take *anything* back to our new base with me. I touched Finn's arm. "Just tell me. I can memorize the number. I'm getting very good at retaining important information quickly." Lots of practice. At least that habit could come in handy.

Finn made a face as if he were imagining dangerous missions where I'd needed that skill, but he recited the number to me. I repeated it to myself a few times like a casting, forming the string into a picture in my head.

He watched me with the same clear awe as when he'd watched me actually cast during the Exam. His expression sent a tingle over my skin.

I'd been nervous in general coming back here—bracing myself for how differently I might feel, how differently everyone might treat me. My parents had been overjoyed to see me but a little puzzled, especially by my hesitations as I figured out what to say to them about my time at the "college." A distance had opened up between us from the moment I'd stepped onto the bridge to Rikers Island, and I wasn't sure if I'd ever make it all the way back.

But Finn looked at me as if I were the same person I'd always been. I hadn't known how much I needed that confirmation until this moment.

"We can talk more in a minute," I said. "First…"

I bobbed up on my toes to kiss him, gripping the front of his shirt with one hand. Finn's arm slid around me again as he kissed me back. Heat spiked through me at the tender eagerness of his mouth, drowning out the dim, dirty store and the rumble of Saturday traffic outside.

Why couldn't we do this forever? Why couldn't the rest of the world just go away?

Once we'd started kissing, I didn't want to stop. One kiss bled into another and then another. I pulled Finn even closer, my lips parting against his, a heady shiver rippling through me at the pleased sound that worked its way from his throat.

Being with Finn like this was the exact opposite of everything I wanted to escape. Like a salve, inside and out, over all the parts of me that had been scraped raw by the things I'd seen, the missions I'd run, on the other side of the ocean from him. Part of me longed to fall right into him, and from the way he was holding me, he needed me just as much.

A month. After I went back, it'd be a whole month before I'd be able to see him again. I wanted to absorb every bit of him I could to carry with me.

The thought of how much catching up we still had to do now, how little time we might have to do it in, gave me enough motivation to ease back. Finn's face was flushed and his eyes bright in a way that made me want to kiss him all over again. I resisted that urge, reaching into my pocket instead.

"I got you something," I said. "For your birthday. It was a few weeks ago, right? Since I couldn't be here for that…"

I handed him the small box I'd carefully wrapped this morning and then had to stuff my hands back into my pockets to stop them from fidgeting. Finn stared at the present and then at me.

"You didn't have to—"

"I wanted to. I wasn't sure what you'd even like, but I saw something—maybe it's silly. Just open it, okay?"

The corner of his mouth curled up at a soft angle. He opened the foil wrapping paper with a tug of his thumb and slid out the tan cardboard box. I rocked on my feet a couple times as he reached for the lid.

Finn's hand fell to his side with the lid. His Adam's apple bobbed in this throat with an audible swallow.

"It's not silly at all," he said. "It's perfect. My Dragon-Tamer brought me a dragon."

Nestled on the foam padding was a dragon figurine about the length of my forefinger—a serpentine dragon with scales in rich greens, blues, and purples that had made me think of the dragon illusion I'd conjured, the one that had impressed Finn before he'd even known me. I'd hoped it would remind him of how strong we could be, both together and apart. I'd had no idea at the time that my dragon might be the only clear memory he had left that connected to me.

"It's a keychain," I said, unable to keep myself from beaming at his reaction. "I figured it wouldn't look too odd for you to carry it around—but of course if you don't want to—"

"I want to," he said firmly, catching my gaze. "It's— Hades take me, should I know when *your* birthday is?"

How much had he lost of that frantic conversation in the tunnel when we'd been drowning out a hostile 'chantment? "It's not until April," I said. "Nothing to worry about."

He made a sound of consternation. "Well, I'll remember it now." With a practiced gesture, he fished out his keys and removed the leather fob with the Academy's crest on it. "About time I got rid of this anyway," he said in a lighter tone. "Is there anything I should know about this dragon? Special 'chantments, secret catches?"

I shook my head. "Just a keychain."

His bright green eyes didn't waver for a second. "There's nothing 'just' about it."

I didn't think he was talking only about the gift. A weird shyness came over me. I groped for something to say or do as he worked the keys on and tucked them away. Finally, I settled for taking his hand and walking over to the store's bare counter. We might as well rest our feet while we talked.

The laminate surface was as dusty as everything else in the room, but I'd dealt with a hell of a lot more dirt than this recently. This was nothing.

I hopped up onto the edge, and Finn joined me, sitting with his shoulder resting against mine. Our hands stayed twined together. He tapped his free fingers against the counter's edge, and my heart leapt at the sudden thought that maybe he hadn't lost all his magic after all.

"If someone stopped them from taking all of your memories, did they manage to deflect some of the burning out too?" I had to ask.

Finn's jaw tightened. "I'm burned out," he said. "It's all gone. Just..." He held his hand out in front of him and closed it around the air. "Empty. Numb. Dull." He let out a short, rough laugh. The pain of that loss tensed the corners of his eyes.

My previous anger twisted into a ball of resolve. I was going to expose the Confed for what they were doing—and if any way existed to bring the magic back to Finn, I'd find it.

"Can I…?" I said quietly, touching the side of his head by the soft fall of his golden-blond hair.

He shrugged with an arch of his eyebrow. "You're a great mage, but I don't think even you can un-burnout someone. You're welcome to try, though."

"We'll see," I muttered. I sang a few words from a pop song I'd loved as a kid, and my attention narrowed to the whirl of energy around Finn's head.

The spot where he should have hearkened from wasn't just frayed. I sensed nothing at all—a vacant space. I swallowed hard. "Burned out" was a pretty accurate description for what it felt like. Could that piece of him be healed?

The magic I conducted toward him just quivered away from the spot, none of it taking hold. I hadn't really expected to solve that problem right now, but the failure gnawed at me anyway.

"It really is okay," Finn said. "I'm finding other ways to be useful. Not all that difficult, considering I hardly made myself very useful with my casting even before."

The self-deprecation of that comment bothered me as much as similar ones in the past had, but I decided to focus on the positive. "Tell me some more about this group you've found and the protests they're doing." He could talk about everything he'd been up to since the Exam without the silencing 'chantment getting in the way.

A smile crossed Finn's face that told me more clearly than words how energized he was by his new purpose. Even as my spirits lifted seeing that, a pinch of jealousy tugged at my gut.

The emotion was silly. But I couldn't help thinking of how strong we'd been together. I wanted to be working with Finn, not on the other side of the world from him.

"The group has been meeting for a few years," he said. "Working up to more of an active resistance gradually. This is the first major action they've planned. Everyone there thinks

Dampering and burning out and the Exam—all of it—are unjust and should be stopped. It's just a matter of getting that message out, making more people aware of the problems, without looking like a problem ourselves."

"What exactly is this 'major action'?" I asked, any jealousy I'd felt disappearing under a twinge of fear. Was he going to be putting himself in the Confed's sights? His family hadn't been able to prevent his burning out—I wasn't sure how much they could protect him.

"Basic nonviolent protest. Shutting down the college on placement-exam day for as long as we can. I doubt it's going to change the whole system in one go, but it's a start."

I squeezed his hand. "Just be careful, all right? I've... I've gotten the sense that the Confed leaders are especially stressed right now."

The corner of Finn's lips quirked up. "All the better for us to get their attention and put the pressure on." He bumped his shoulder against mine at my grimace. "I know, I know. Believe me, I've been getting plenty of practice at being careful already. Do you think I've been able to tell my family what I'm up to?"

"Do the people in this group know who your family is?" I said.

He ducked his head. "No. I don't think— It could get weird, with my granduncle being in the Circle, and..."

"Hey," I said, tipping my cheek to his shoulder when he didn't seem to know how to continue. "You don't have to justify yourself to me. If you think it's better to keep that detail to yourself, then you're probably right. You're a good judge of people. I'm pretty sure no one could burn out *that* talent."

Finn's smile came back, sheepish this time. "Let's hope not." He shifted closer to me, letting go of my hand, but only to tuck his arm around my waist. "Is there anything at all you can tell me about where you've been, what you've been doing?

How careful have *you* needed to be? You're the one off…
you know."

I drew in a breath. "Well…" I had so many things I wished I
could tell him but couldn't. A different kind of fear wound
around my lungs. No one on the base had known what to make
of the recording that girl had given me. If two of our most
powerful enemies struck at the Confed's forces together… I
wasn't sure any amount of careful was going to protect us—or
the magic.

"Hmm, let's try that possibilities thing again," Finn
suggested. "What do you think Prisha has probably been doing?"

I couldn't answer that, since it wouldn't be a guess. "I
can't say."

"Oh. She's still in the same unit or whatever with you? That's
good. I haven't heard from her—without her phone on her, she
probably doesn't know my number either." He chuckled lightly.
"How do you think she's holding up?"

That question I could make a little headway with. "Not
too badly."

"Still all in one piece then, I hope. Er, let's see, Desmond?"

I started to smile. Maybe what I couldn't voice told him just
as much as what I could. "I can't say."

He grinned at me. "The same crew still together, as many of
you made it. That's something." Then his expression turned more
serious. "How do you feel about what you've been doing?"

Ah. The silencing 'chantment didn't hold me back there. "I
hate it," I said, with more vehemence than even I'd been
prepared for. I swiped at my mouth, gathering myself. "But I'm a
little hopeful that I—if I—" A growl escaped me. I switched
back to more general terms. "The magic is hurting. I'm trying to
get other people to see. Nothing else is going to matter if it dies."

"You won't let that happen. It couldn't have asked for a better
Champion."

Finn's voice was so confident that my next breath came easier. He understood what I was trying to accomplish, how much it meant to me. He'd have stood beside me out there just like he had in the Exam, without a single doubt. Even though I couldn't bring him across the ocean with me—and wouldn't have wanted to—that knowledge was such a relief it brought unexpected tears to my eyes.

I blinked hard. "Yeah. I think I'm getting somewhere. So I've felt a little good, here and there. And... I've only been scared for my life a few times."

"Only a few," Finn said. "It should be *no* times."

I glanced up at him. "That's what we're both working toward, right? Like we meant to."

His eyes softened. He leaned in to kiss me, and for a little while, talking didn't seem important at all.

*　*　*

I had to go sooner than I'd have liked. "I want to see you again before my break is over," I said as we meandered reluctantly to the door. "My parents are planning a big family get-together with my grandparents and aunts and uncles and everyone tomorrow, but maybe the next morning... I'll text you when I know."

"I understand if you can't," Finn said. "I mean, I don't expect to get more priority than your *family*, and you haven't seen them in a long time too. You really don't have to—"

"Finn," I broke in, grasping his arm just as we reached the door and turning him toward me. My gaze searched his. "You're important to me. So important. You're a big part of what makes everything less scary than it could be. I want to come back to *you*. And I will, te lo prometo con todo mi corazón"

I hadn't known if that would be the right thing to say, or enough, but Finn seemed to understand the sentiment without any translation. Maybe the look on my face said it for me. Something in his posture relaxed.

He dipped his head down to steal one last kiss, this one so gentle it left my heart aching. "I want you to come back to me too," he said softly. "You're my inspiration, Rocío. If I can be half as brave as you are, I'll have really gotten somewhere."

A blush warmed my cheeks. I hugged him, hard, and then I forced myself to unlock the door.

Finn waited with me at the stop for the bus until it showed up. When I climbed on, moving away from him, the ache in my chest rose to fill my throat as well. He waved to me as the bus lurched away from the curb, his gaze following my window until I couldn't see him anymore.

I was just coming to the front steps to the walk-up that was still technically my home when a black jeep jerked to a halt by the sidewalk just ahead of me. Two men leapt out of the back with military precision. My hands flew up defensively even as I registered the Confed's crest on the collars of their jackets. One man muttered a quick line that brought a crackle of magic into the air around me—holding in any casting I might have made.

"Rocío Lopez," the other said in a gruff voice. "You need to come with us, now, on the orders of National Defense."

CHAPTER TWELVE

Finn

Growing up, there had never been anyone in my whole life whom I'd wanted to be like more than my father and his father before him. I would have given anything to crusade against injustice, whatever the odds, and win, as they had. If only I could cast a little better, I'd thought, perhaps I could contribute something similar to our world.

It was a strange feeling, then, to look up from my desk to where Dad had appeared in my bedroom doorway and realize there was nothing at all I could tell him about the day I'd just had. I was far closer to making a real difference in our society than I'd ever been before, and somehow that had taken me farther from him at the same time. The understanding sank heavy in my stomach.

"Is this a good time to talk?" Dad asked. His light brown hair gleamed a little more silver than I thought it'd been a few months ago. I hoped I wasn't the cause of that graying.

"Sure," I said, typing a few more words in my final text to Mark and then turning off my phone. I swiveled as Dad ambled into the room. Even against the smooth leather padding of my chair, staying relaxed was quite a feat when he looked that serious.

He propped himself against the edge of the desk in a stance that would have looked more casual if his mouth hadn't been slanted at such an awkward angle.

"Hard day at work?" I asked in my best bright yet sympathetic voice.

His lips tipped into something more closely resembling a smile, but no less grim. "You could say that. Our international conference is only a few weeks away, and the Dull government is still balking at approving representatives from the mage societies in a few of the countries I was hoping to include."

"It's the Confed's conference," I said. "What should it even matter to them?"

"It's politically powerful mages arriving on their home ground," Dad said. "They always see the threat before the benefit of international goodwill. I'll handle it; I just want to avoid us taking a hit with them in other ways. They've already been pushing back against the plans for next year's Unveiling Day parade too—apparently one of the vocal anti-magic groups has been complaining about the last one." He rubbed his hand over his face. "But enough about work. That's not what I wanted to talk with you about."

"No?" I hadn't really thought it was, but the redirection had been worth a try.

"It's been two months now. I thought it was time we touched base about your future plans."

I opened my mouth and found I had no ready answers. I wasn't going to fill him in on the plans involving shutting down the college for a day. In truth, I hadn't given much thought to my future outside of the Freedom of Magic League since I'd started going to those meetings.

The League couldn't be my whole life, though. I had to stand on my own two feet at some point—making my own money, cultivating my own resources. My accomplishments weren't truly mine while I was sponging off my parents.

Even if I was a figure of pity in many of our neighbors' eyes, I could still build a life my family would be able to look at with some small measure of pride. Ut desint vires, tamen est laudanda voluntas.

"I'm still contemplating what would be the best path for me," I said cautiously. "I don't want to jump in until I'm sure. I know once I get on a track it'll be hard to shift directions. If you have suggestions, though, I'm all ears."

"You seem to be adjusting well," Dad said. "You've been going out to see friends and entertain yourself regularly. I understand why you don't want to commit to any career track right away, but perhaps we could look into possible volunteer placements, so you can get a taste of different work environments?"

There was certainly time in my days for that. "Absolutely," I said, with enthusiasm I didn't need to feign. "I'd like that. I think I'd still prefer to work on something practical in the field— whatever field I end up in—if at all possible. Even if I can't be hands-on with magic, there's got to be a way I can offer more than pushing paper around in some office."

Dad's smile warmed. "You're too much like me, you know. Wanting to get out there and grab hold of whatever you can. I'll see what I can find."

I was *too* much like him? Did he say that because he saw his natural inclinations as a flaw or because I hadn't been bestowed with the magical ability to see the same passion through?

A twinge of the shame I'd nearly put behind me rippled through my gut, but his words emboldened me at the same time. Dad *had* crusaded. If anyone in the Confed could understand what I was doing now, it should be him. Tamara had been right that we needed as many people as possible on our side—and that old-magic voices would be heard first. If I could get through to him somehow...

"I also—" I started, and then paused. It didn't feel safe to start with what *I* was doing. Dad had crusaded once, but I'd seen him support the Circle's party line far too recently. How much did he actually know about the Exam and what happened after?

"Dad, after I declared, you made some comments about the responsibilities the Champions have and how complex the situation is... What did you mean by all that, specifically?"

Dad stiffened slightly. As Chair of the Confed's International Relations board, he wasn't directly involved in the Exam or National Defense, but if the Champions were out there fighting in other countries, he couldn't be totally unaware of the negotiations around that subject.

He didn't know the full extent of how the examinees were treated. He never would have let me go in if he had—he'd have found some way to stop me, regardless of my protests, if he'd realized my only options were burning out or being forced to become a soldier on the front lines of our international conflicts. He'd seen enough to determine the Exam wasn't a simple ticket to the college for anyone, though.

"Don't you think it's better if we leave that subject behind us?" he said, shifting his weight against the desk. "Focus on the future."

"Well, the future still has the Exam," I said. "More people burned out. More Champions. More dead. Do you really believe everything about that system is above criticism?"

Dad grimaced. "It's not my area. And the situation *is* complicated, far more than I'd imagine even I've been able to follow. I'm not in a place to make judgments. Finn—"

"Dad." I looked at him until he met my gaze again. "When

you were only a little older than me, you broke all sorts of rules saving those people out in Washington—using your magic when the volcano erupted, even though Dulls would see you and you were supposed to be keeping it secret. You didn't know everything there was to know about the decisions the Circle had made then. You just knew what was happening wasn't right, and that was enough."

"The thing is, it wasn't really enough." Dad hesitated. "There's part of that story I've always left out, Finn. Perhaps I shouldn't have, but it's not something I'm proud of, and, well…" He exhaled in a rush. "While I was deciding what to do about Mount St. Helens, I met a girl. A girl from a family who had no idea about magic, but she had just enough talent that a mage like me could notice her inadvertently disrupting the energies around her."

I leaned forward. He hadn't said anything at all about a girl before. "What happened with her?"

"I decided that it wasn't right for her to live without understanding magic. So I took it upon myself, despite all the policies in place, to tell her about magic and to start teaching her how to hone her talent."

"Of course that was the right thing to do," I said.

Dad shook his head. "I didn't really know what I was doing. The way she hearkened the magic, once I taught her the exercises to make her more aware of it—she wasn't prepared. It was unnerving for her. And her abilities could have ruined her relationships with her family, with all the friends she had… There was no scaffolding in place to ease a transition like that back then. I was more concerned with being a hero than what was actually good for her."

The strain in his voice made my stomach tighten. "Did she get through it okay?"

"The Circle found out what I'd done," Dad said. "They

arranged for her memory to be wiped of anything to do with me or magic. I was furious at the time, but honestly… I think it was probably for the best. Her abilities never emerged enough for her to seek out the Confederation after the Unveiling. None of her kids have shown potential during the testing."

His smile came back, wry this time. "I check on her every year or two, because I feel a little responsible for her. She's happily working as a nurse in Albany now."

Her memory loss was probably for the best, he said. I caught my hands before they could clench. He didn't have any idea that *my* memory had nearly been wiped as well, did he? Would he be furious about that if he knew, or just shrug it off?

Dad reached to squeeze my shoulder. "All I'm trying to say is… Right and wrong are a lot more complicated than they often seem when you're seventeen. And you have to pick your battles. Do I agree with every choice the Circle makes? No. But now that I've had so many dealings with the Dull leadership myself, I understand much better why your granduncle is so cautious. If the Dulls ever turned on us en masse… There are tens of thousands more of them than there are of us. I fought for us to expose our differences to the wider world so we could help those outside our community, and you know that transition left your grandfather dead and hurt or killed dozens of other mages. The last thing I want is for that movement to lead to the end of us."

I'd heard fellow mages talk about the need for caution when it came to the Dulls many times before, but after everything I'd seen in the last few months, it'd become difficult to imagine them being more of a threat to us than our own leaders. I studied his face. "Do you *really* think the Dulls would try to wipe us out?"

"If there's one thing humans have in abundance, it's the ability to fear that which they don't understand and to turn that fear into violence," Dad said. "You know I push back against any policies I disagree with, Finn. But I believe that any uncomfortable decisions the Circle makes, they make with the security of our entire community in mind. We can't undermine that when we don't have enough information to fully understand the fallout that might result."

I had that information, at least when it came to the Champions. I just couldn't give it to him. The 'chantment gripped my tongue until I let go of the urge to propel the secret out. Instead, I motioned to my Burnout mark. "What good reason could they have for branding people like me like this?"

He brushed his fingers over my hair in an affectionate gesture. "I'm sure there are fears tied up in it to do with dissidence and uncertain loyalties," he said. "But, you know, it also claims you as one of us. You'd have no way to prove to anyone who didn't know you that you're a mage by demonstrating magic. The mark proves you had magic once."

I hadn't thought about it that way before. I wasn't sure I liked thinking about it that way, as if it were some sort of feeble replacement for what they'd taken from me. Was there some positive spin the Circle would have used to justify the Exam, their special ops teams, and all the rest of it?

Even if they *could* justify it, just a smidgen, with an appeal to the security of our community, was it right even then to force mages like Rocío to make that sacrifice for the rest of us?

"I want you to stand up for what you believe in, Finn," Dad added. "I just don't want you to rush into any battles so quickly that someone gets hurt despite your best intentions. Especially when that someone could be you. Remember, *est modus in rebus.*"

There is a middle ground, he meant. Under his scrutiny, I had to nod. He couldn't have called the League's activities simple teenage rebellion. Most of the members weren't even teenagers anymore. It was clear, though, that Dad valued caution over passion these days. Perhaps if I could have told him everything I knew, he'd have stood up with me... but I couldn't.

My hand dropped to my thigh, my thumb tracing the line of my new keychain through the fabric of my jeans. A different question wriggled its way out of my belly. Rocío had been worried there'd be backlash against our relationship. The least I could do was discover if any would come from within my own home.

"I met a girl too," I said. "Not Dull—not by a long shot—but new magic. Is *that* going to be a problem?"

Dad blinked. "Of course not," he said. "Even if she *were* Dull, it wouldn't matter now—you'd be able to share who you are with her. When do we get to meet this girl?"

A little of the tension inside me dissipated. "I don't know," I said. "She doesn't have much time for family dinners or whatever at the moment. She made Champion."

A shadow crossed Dad's face, there and then gone, and again I wondered exactly what information he did have. Still, the fond expression he summoned afterward looked genuine enough. "Well, I look forward to getting to know her. Whenever she is free from her responsibilities, whenever you're ready, you should invite her over."

Imagining Rocío in our vast polished dining room brought a flutter of pleasure into my chest that I hadn't expected. The girl could conjure dragons with scales like jewels. She belonged here as much as she did anywhere else.

"I'll do that," I said. "And let me know if you turn up any volunteer possibilities that look promising. I'll keep my ears perked too."

Dad gave me one last pat on the shoulder and stood up. I waited until I heard the faint creaking of old hardwood as he descended the stairs. Then I scooted my chair over to the bookshelf against the wall by my desk.

His admission had stirred up another idea he probably hadn't intended. He'd once taught a nonmagical girl magic when she wasn't even supposed to know it existed. Compared to that, what I'd like to do wasn't anywhere near as scandalous.

* * *

"It's barbaric," Luis said to the reporter. The voices of the crowd still milling on the street outside the college warbled around us, but not loudly enough to diminish our leader's confident tone. Only a couple of the news outlets Tamara had reached out to had arrived to cover the protest, but Luis was making the most of what chance he had for the public's ear. I hung back behind several of the other members, close enough to hear the interview but beyond the range of the camera.

"We're talking about government-sanctioned mutilation here," Luis went on. "Would we accept officials cutting out a teenager's *eyes* because they didn't meet some arbitrary standard of skill? Slicing out their tongue? Of course not. Maybe only a small percentage of human beings have the ability to hearken magic, but for those of us who do, it's as much a part of us as any other sense. So why do we allow the practices of Dampering and burning out to continue?"

"Exactly," Tamara put in where she was standing beside him. "The lucky ones come here to the college to put their magical ability to use, picking their career paths and dreaming of great futures, while the rest of us are left with only a shadow, if any, of the talent that used to be ours. It's time to address that huge injustice."

"And to remind them we've still got some power," Ary murmured from where she was standing behind Tamara, just quietly enough for the reporter to miss her words.

She might have resented that we hadn't demonstrated our

defiance her way, but our first show of opposition had gone better than I could have hoped, negligible media presence notwithstanding. The two hundred or so of us who'd shown up early this morning had held the college's entrances until almost noon before the security team had managed to displace us.

The cold November wind had given me ample excuse to keep my hat pulled low and my coat's collar high, and I hadn't heard a single former classmate shout my name, though I'd caught a glimpse of a few I recognized meandering aimlessly along the sidewalk. A fair number of Dull spectators had stopped to observe us by the time we'd been ousted too.

Mark squeezed through the crowd on the sidewalk and knuckled my upper arm. "We really pulled it off, huh?" he said.

"Yeah." A smile split my face. Change seemed to hum in the air, as potent as the magic had once been to me, and I'd been a part of conjuring it. "And this is just our opening move."

"It figures you'd already be planning our next project when the first one isn't even done." Mark shook his head, his mohawk swaying with the movement, but he was smiling a little too.

As the news crew headed back to their van, the protestors and our audience began to disperse. Floyd and a few of the other League members I'd been sitting near this morning walked by, a couple of them pausing to salute me. I glanced around, my fingers closing around the strap of my shoulder bag. Noemi hadn't left yet, had she? I'd wanted to wait until after the protest to pass on my somewhat delicate cargo.

There she was, wolfing down a hot dog from the stand across the street. I clapped Mark on the back and headed over to her.

"Hey," I said, motioning for her to follow me farther away from the others. "I brought something I thought you might like to borrow for a bit. You just have to promise me you won't tell *anyone* about it—not even Luis—and keep it out of sight. All right?"

Noemi wrinkled her nose at me in mock-dismay at my prohibiting Luis, but her dark eyebrows had leapt up to the fringe of her pixie cut. She swallowed the rest of her hotdog and wiped her hands with a paper napkin. "With a pitch like that, how can I say no? I won't get you into trouble. Believe me, my parents don't know half the stuff I've been up to. I can keep a secret."

I trusted that she could, or I wouldn't have been doing this. I fished the leather-bound volume out of my bag and passed it to her quickly. An almost reverent look came over her face as she grabbed it and tucked it into her purse before anyone else could notice the exchange.

"What is it?" she asked.

"One of the most renowned texts on mental exercises to develop a mage's connection to the magic," I said. "We learn the basic methods in the academies, but this one goes far beyond that. I think it's the one that helped me the most, as much as any of them did. You mentioned you were curious about those strategies... Technically it belongs to my parents, though. Very limited edition."

"And they wouldn't be happy about you lending it to some Dull?" Noemi said dryly.

She sounded as if she were making fun of the idea, but that basically summed it up. If I'd passed the book on to Prisha or one of my other classmates a year ago, Dad and Mom would have made some noise about making sure we got it back for the family collection—I knew they'd gone to some expense to track down a private copy for my use—but they wouldn't have minded otherwise. If they found out I was sharing it with someone who wasn't even part of the mage community...

They'd pretend they were only concerned about proper care being taken, but really, the idea of someone nonmagical reading our texts would make even them twitchy. If Granduncle

Raymond ever found out, I might as well head straight to Tartarus, the way he'd come down on me.

None of them would know, though, because Noemi *would* take care. Possibly we'd have made a lot more progress building friendly relations with nonmagical folk if we'd been more open to letting them study alongside us from the start.

"That's the gist of it," I said.

Noemi patted her purse. "Well, thank you. Tons. You have no idea how much I've been dying to pore over *any* of the mage writings. I promise I'll return it in pristine condition." She did a brief but giddy little dance on the sidewalk. "Oh my God!"

I had to grin at her excitement. "Let me know if you see anything in there you think is particularly intriguing," I said. "It can't hurt those of us in the know to get a fresh perspective."

CHAPTER THIRTEEN

Rocío

I forced myself to sit still in the small white room, even though my skin crawled with the urge to move. To get out of here somehow. The blank white walls and the sparse furniture—the hard-backed chair I sat on and the two matching ones on the other side of the glossy white table—reminded me too much of the Exam building. The faint drone of the air filtration system didn't exactly improve the atmosphere.

I knew the Confed wasn't going to send me into more trials. That wouldn't make any sense at all. But the totally illogical fear scrabbled at the back of my mind, insisting they might toss me back into that maze of barbed hedges at any moment.

The men who'd grabbed me off the street outside my apartment had escorted me straight here without a word, staying quiet through all my questions about why they wanted me and what might have gone wrong. They'd led me to this room and left me in it, locking the door behind them. At least an hour must have passed, but no one else had come.

I was debating getting up and pounding on the door to see if that would bring someone, when the lock clicked over. Even though I'd been waiting for just that, I tensed. I didn't delude myself that I was here for a friendly chat.

A burly man and a hook-nosed woman stepped inside, both of them looking to be in their fifties and both wearing the same black-trimmed moss-green uniforms that Commander Revett and a couple of the other higher officials usually wore. The jacket had the Confed's crest at the collar, but also another on the right shoulder: an image like two feathered wings embracing a yellow spiral. *Magic swift and concealed*, Hamlin had told us during training. It was the emblem of the special ops division.

"Operative Lopez," the man said. "It seems we need to have a talk."

"Great," I said. "Here I am."

I'd tried to keep my tone even, but a little snarkiness must have slipped in anyway. The woman gave me a sharp look before she and her colleague took the chairs across from me. They sat in silence for long enough that I started to squirm inwardly.

"You've been with the Confederation's Special Operations Force for nine weeks now," the woman said, as if she were consulting an invisible personnel file in front of her. "Four weeks of basic training and five of active duty."

Was that a question? When her pause stretched, I said, "That's true. Can you tell me what this is about? I have no idea why I'm here. I'm supposed to be getting my leave now, and I only—"

The man held up his hand. I shut my mouth, my fingers curling around the edge of my seat.

"Your leave has been interrupted due to a matter of international security," he said. "A report from one of your fellow operatives led us to assess your performance in the field. We'd like to review several incidents with you."

A report from a fellow operative. I gritted my teeth. Brandt —it had to be. Not that I was best friends with every other soldier and officer on the base, but he was the only one I'd really clashed with. He'd probably been itching for my first leave to come so he could report me without feeling like he was betraying me right to my face.

How much could he have told them, really? I couldn't think of anything that mutinous I'd done, in his presence or not.

"Go ahead," I said.

The woman clasped her hands on the tabletop. "Let's start with your first time in the field and move forward. Is it true that you delayed the completion of a mission to tend to a pre-existing superficial wound for an associate of the Borci Za Spravedlivost?"

The word "associate" threw me for a few seconds before I figured out what she was talking about. "He was only a kid," I said. "Younger than me. Scared. I thought if I did something kind for him, he'd be more likely to turn away from their group if they started pushing for his allegiance."

"So, you acknowledge that you took that action, beyond the scope of your orders?" the man said in the same flat tone as before.

"I healed a scrape on his cheek," I said. "It took less than a minute. My mission leader gave me the go-ahead."

They were already moving on as if nothing I said about it mattered. "Your fourth mission, in Orava," the woman said. "Your mission leader ordered the squad to quickly clear out a building. You delayed while talking to a man there. Is that also correct?"

Again, the moment had seemed so innocuous at the time that I didn't recognize what she meant at first. "He tripped and fell down," I said. "I just asked if he was okay." But I did remember Brandt yelling for us to hurry up. "Would you really want—"

"Is. That. Correct?" she interrupted.

I bit back a grimace. "Yes, it is."

"A couple of weeks later, you ignored the direct instructions of a more senior colleague about how you would handle an explosive 'chantment."

"Our orders were to get rid of it," I said. "I did that. And when I started diffusing it, he hadn't even told me not to."

The man took over. "Your last mission before your leave, you let a young woman who had a clear connection to the insurgents escape."

I had to bristle at that accusation. It might have been true, but Brandt didn't even know that for sure—he'd just assumed I'd gone against orders. "I did go after her," I said, using the same answer I'd given Sam. "She made it out of the building before I managed to stop her. Besides, she was trying to help *us*, not them. Do you really think she'd ever help us again if we tackled her like some kind of criminal?"

The woman sighed. "It isn't your place to question the tactics we employ. When you accepted the role of Champion, you agreed to serve the Confederation and your country with your skills. That includes following the orders you're given. I've seen a disturbing pattern of defiance and collusion with the enemy."

Collusion? Because I'd healed a kid's scrape and didn't batter the locals around like Brandt did? ¡Por el amor de Dios! Had he also told them I was loca for the things I'd said about the magic?

"When I accepted the role of Champion, I—" My throat closed around the next words I'd meant to say. I did grimace then. "You know I can't even talk about things from back then to explain myself." There were other ways I could address that point, though—not specific events but my general impressions.

"Every time we perform castings that destroy things, hurt people, disrupt the natural harmony of the energy we're using, it hurts the magic too," I said. "All I've tried to do is find ways to avoid that damage where I can and to not piss off the people we're supposedly trying to help. If we destroy the magic, how the hell do you think we're going to fight at all?"

"Operative Lopez," the man said. "Those considerations are for your senior officers. You don't have the experience or the training to make the clearest decisions."

By what standard? I was the one the magic had reached out to. I was the only one who seemed to be paying enough attention. Most of my senior officers probably couldn't hearken it well enough to follow its patterns even if they tried.

"I *thought* I was being accepted as Champion specifically so I could help with that," I said, not that I thought the protest would do me any more good here than it had with Hamlin. *That's what they told me. Just one more of the examiners' lies.* I could've thrown my most recent discovery in their face. How did these senior officials feel about the diminishing of their magical ability?

But from the stony expressions facing me, I didn't think that revelation would get me anywhere. They might feel even more threatened that I'd figured it out.

The woman obviously still had some ability left. She murmured one verse and then another in Latin, and the energy around my neck vibrated along with the rhythm of her words. When she asked the next question, her voice had a singsong quality that echoed her casting.

"Do you have any sympathies for the insurgents we're fighting?"

The 'chantment gripped my throat in a different way from the silencing one. My answer spilled out automatically. "The ones who've killed people? No. I want to stop them. Just not the way we've been doing it."

She was using a truth-compulsion 'chantment. Those were complicated castings. A chill washed over me. They must have been really worried about my loyalties. I didn't think they could ask me anything that I couldn't answer truthfully without getting myself into major trouble, but how could I know for sure?

"Do you have any intention of assisting the insurgents?" the woman asked.

"No, I never would."

"Why have you gone against your orders?"

"I don't think I really have," I said honestly. "But when I picked a different tactic, it's always been to try to spare the magic more distress."

The woman leaned forward, her gaze intent. "Where did you go in the city today after you left your home?"

Oh, so they had been trying to track me. And I *had* slipped their attempts to do it. I might have laughed if my mouth hadn't already been forming my answer. "To see Finn."

For the first time, the sternness of the woman's expression softened just a tad, with what looked like... amusement? "Do you mean Finnegan Lockwood?"

"Yes," I said, because I had to. So much for keeping our continuing relationship secret.

"Is that the only thing you did before you were brought here?"

"Yes."

"What did you want to see him for?"

"Just to see him," I said, my voice going terse. "To hear his voice. I missed him, and I care about him. I didn't get any orders about that."

The pressure at my throat was fading. The woman didn't renew the 'chantment, only leaned back in her chair.

"How did he react to seeing you?" she asked, and I remembered with a jolt that Finn wasn't supposed to have remembered me at all.

At least from the Exam. The waning 'chantment gave me just enough room to put together a story that was true enough—and that would give us room to see each other again without raising more questions.

"There were things we couldn't talk about, of course," I said. "But I knew him from before, when I used to study in the library at the Manhattan Academy, so it wasn't totally awkward."

Thankfully, the officials didn't ask whether Finn had known *me* back then. The woman drew her hands back into her lap. "Thank you for answering our questions."

Did they believe me? They had to know I wasn't a traitor after my answers under the truth compulsion, didn't they? "So, what happens now?" I asked.

The two officials exchanged a glance.

"Your concern for the magic is commendable," the woman said in a gentler tone. "But we cannot have our special ops members breaking protocol and ignoring their seniors to follow their own inclinations. You're a skilled mage, Operative Lopez. We very much want your talent on our side. You've seen with your own eyes the destruction our enemies are capable of. Don't you want to stop *that* destruction?"

If I'd still been under compulsion, I'd have had to spit out an emphatic *No*. Even if I'd agreed with all the Confed's strategies, I would never really *want* to be out there in the field carrying them out. Thankfully I could dodge answering. "I think protecting the magic is more important."

"More important than the actual human lives you're saving?" the man asked. "More important than the lives of your squad-mates? Do you really want to be responsible for their deaths for some small adjustment that may not make any difference at all?"

It does make a difference, I wanted to say, but my throat

tightened of its own accord. How much of a difference *had* my attempts really made so far?

What he was saying wasn't untrue. If I really gave the military service my all, I probably could save lives in a much more tangible way than I'd been able to defend, let alone heal, the magic. Was I being selfish by refusing?

This was just more of the same rhetoric they'd been giving us all along, wasn't it? But my thoughts were all jumbled now. I could say one thing for sure: "If someone's life is at stake, I'll do whatever it takes to help them." I had before, during the attack on the base. I had blood on my hands.

"We need to know we can count on your loyalty," the woman said. "As great a contribution as you could make to the fight against those who want to spread chaos, there's no room for loose cannons in our ranks. Are you going to stand with us?"

What choice did I have? To instead be as burned out as Finn was, helping no one at all?

Say what they need to hear so you can get where you need to go, Javi would've told me. *They lie to our faces all the time. Why should they expect anything else from us? All we can do is look out for ourselves out there.*

"I will," I said. "I still want to be a Champion." More than I wanted the alternative, anyway.

The man gave me a measured look. "We're grateful for your service. Remember how many lives and livelihoods may be riding on the actions you take, Operative Lopez. Not just those abroad, but your parents, the Lockwood boy... Every action or inaction can have wide-sweeping consequences."

My back went rigid. Was that a threat? He could have meant that if we didn't restrain the terrorist networks enough, the insurgents might hurt people here too... but he'd purposely left his wording vague. The hard glint in his eyes made my heartbeat stutter.

What would happen to Mom and Dad, to Finn, if the Confed decided I was a traitor after all?

"I understand," I said in a tight voice. "I know what side I'm on."

"All right then." He pushed back his chair to stand up, and the woman followed suit. "Because it appears you could benefit from additional time in training, we're cutting your leave short by one day. You still have the rest of today and tomorrow with your family. Make the most of it."

* * *

The little transport plane shuddered with the air currents outside. I curled deeper into my padded seat, both looking forward to and dreading the moment when it would land at the base.

I should have squeezed every ounce of joy I could out of my last day with my parents, but even the big family get-together had barely managed to distract me from the implied threat hanging over me. I was backed into a corner.

I didn't even completely understand what I was fighting so hard for.

The magic thrummed around me up here as it did everywhere. I'd picked a seat with a little space from the five other soldiers joining me on this flight. Now, I shut the window shade against the bright sunlight we were flying into and closed my eyes. Dragging in a breath, I clasped my fingers around my sunburst necklace and reached out to the energy that had called to me so often. That had made me its champion before the Confed had ever stuck that label on me.

The magic tingled over my tongue with its familiar melody, the lilting rhythm it fell into naturally when we weren't conducting it to our will. I whispered lyrics from a dance song

Dad had liked to listen to while he cooked, years ago. "¿Por qué me llamas? ¿Por qué me hablas?"

Why have you called out to me? I thought as I tried to speak to the magic. *What are you trying to say? What do you need me to do? Please.* I needed to understand better than I did. If it could express something to me that would help me decide where to go from here, maybe I'd be able to sleep tonight.

Tingling wisps grazed my scalp and sank through my skin. The magic wrapped around my head like thin gauze. Images burst in my mind like film from a stuttering projector.

A conjured blast smashed a stone wall, shattering the bonds that had melded the particles of its structure—and shattering the threads of harmony all through the magic in and around it at the same time. A man jerked as a 'chantment strangled him, the energy shuddering out of tune with each spasm of his body as his own life energy snuffed out. Discordant notes jarred against each other, their distress echoing farther and farther through the atmosphere, as streaks of magical fire hailed down on a city block, searing the very oxygen from the air.

The horror of those moments radiated through my chest. For a few seconds, it felt as if my own ribs would be torn apart, my limbs twisted from my core, my entire being mangled in a mess of—

My eyes snapped open, my lungs heaving with a gasp for air. One of the soldiers in a seat across the aisle frowned at me, and I quickly jerked my gaze away. A sweat had broken over my skin, thick enough to paste my sleeves to my arms. My pulse was hiccupping in my ears.

The magic hadn't shown me anything I hadn't already suspected. But I felt it now, down to my bones—the agony that wrenched through it when mages pushed it to batter the rhythms of substance and energy that held our world together.

Its presence was clinging to me now, clutching my shoulders

in a desperate embrace. *Why me?* I thought. *Why only me?* But I
didn't think it could answer that.

I was one of the strongest mages of my generation. Maybe it
had seen something in me that had told it I would care. Maybe it
had needed a novice who'd be in the closed environment of the
Exam to make those initial observations. And now that it had
deepened the connection between us, I only hearkened it more
strongly than ever.

But I was still just one mage. A mage who had too many
factors to weigh, too many people whose lives might hang on my
decisions out here. *Remember how many lives and livelihoods may
be riding on the actions you take, Operative Lopez. Your parents, the
Lockwood boy…*

I didn't have much more time to dwell on my uncertainties.
My ears popped as the plane soared down toward the ground. I
braced myself for the jolt of the landing and for the building
waiting for me once I stepped outside.

We hadn't been able to stay in the old base after the attack. It
wasn't safe now that the militants knew that location.
Commander Revett had moved our unit to an older base that, as
far as I could tell, hadn't been used by the Confed since at least
the '90s. Fixing up the place hadn't been a priority after we'd
moved in last week.

I tugged my hoodie closer around me as I headed down the
hallway with its dingy beige walls. One of the light panels
overhead sputtered, its glass cover cracked. The others cast a stark
glow that made every face look a little ghastly.

This base was smaller too. Prisha and I were sharing a dorm
room with Leonie and Joselin here. At least we'd managed to
bring the soft, thick comforters from our beds with us. I could
snuggle up under that blanket and let it blot out the rest of this
place for at least a few hours.

A man I didn't recognize stepped out of a room up ahead—

the one Hamlin had taken over for an office. This guy looked about ten years younger, his face all sharp angles and his tan scalp completely shaved. He eyed me. "Lopez?"

I gave him a quick salute, and he nodded. "I understand you're supposed to resume training immediately. Get changed and meet me in the gym."

He strode off, leaving me staring after him. ¿Cómo? Who was this guy? I peeked into Hamlin's office, but our usual trainer wasn't there.

Desmond ambled out of the cafeteria with a sleepy expression, Tonya, the communications and monitoring senior operative who'd mentored him on his first few missions, right behind him.

"Welcome back?" he said.

Tonya cut her dark gaze from us to the office and back. "Hamlin's gone." She jerked her thumb toward the outer walls.

My heart hitched. "Was there another attack? Did he—"

Tonya was shaking her head, sending the short, coiled twists of her hair swaying. "Not that kind of gone. Fired. Apparently, an order came down from the Dull government that he didn't agree with, so he made up his own plan, and they got pissed off." She motioned in the direction the new trainer had gone. "The new guy showed up with a Dull rep who's going to be 'supervising' operations for a while. Lucky us." Her tone couldn't have been more bitter.

Hamlin had defied government orders? I swallowed hard. I'd heard him complaining about the president that one time, but he'd also encouraged us to be proud of proving our value to the Dulls. What had they asked him to do?

"It's too bad," Desmond said. "I kind of liked him."

"Yeah," I had to admit. "Me too." He'd been the only one of the senior officials who'd acted as if he saw us as people and not just tools.

Had all my attempts to adjust standard procedure ended up tripping him up somehow too? I'd never know. And now I'd have not just the Confed's officials but also a Dull one breathing down my neck.

Lucky us.

CHAPTER FOURTEEN

Finn

One of my favorite teachers at the Academy used to remind us, *What you don't say can matter as much as what you do. When you cast, you must keep in mind both the words you choose to reflect your intent—and the gaps you leave that the magic may respond to as well.*

I'd appreciated the sentiment at the time, but it seemed even more meaningful now, applied to a great deal more than just casting. When you had a 'chantment literally dictating what you could and couldn't say, even silence spoke volumes. The quick text Rocío had sent me a week ago, letting me know her leave had been cut short, had been so vague I'd been left worrying about what lay in the gaps.

My phone rang with an actual call for the first time since then while I was sitting in the back of a cab that smelled like pastrami, on my way to a Freedom of Magic League meeting. The call display listed the number as unknown.

"Hello?" I said.

"Hey, Finn."

My heart flipped over with relief at the sound of Rocío's voice. "Is everything all right?" I asked before she could say anything else. She was alive and well enough to talk to me, which calmed the deepest of my fears, but I had plenty of lesser anxieties clamoring for attention.

"Yes," she said, with a pause that I read more into. "Are *you* okay?"

It was a strange question from someone who was literally going to war to someone who was safely back home on the relatively peaceful streets of Manhattan. "Of course. I'm not doing anything dangerous. You don't have to worry about me, Dragon-Tamer."

"I think maybe I do," she said in a careful voice that made me twice as alert.

I sat up straighter against the worn leather seat. "Did something happen?" I wasn't sure if I should press any further than that. How private was this call?

"No," she said. Her tone shifted again, artificially casual. "I got some questions about seeing you. Had to tell them about how we met in the Academy library."

The Academy library? Oh. That was one shred of memory from the Exam I'd kept: the two of us huddled near each other on a hard floor, a tingle of excitement shooting through me when she'd mentioned seeing me, *noticing* me, back then.

Then the full implications clicked into place. If someone who knew about the Exam's procedures found out the two of us had talked, they might wonder why I'd talked at all with a girl I shouldn't have remembered. Unless they believed we'd known each other already. A surge of gratitude for Rocío's wits swept through me.

"Did you bore them with all the details?" I asked. How much had she needed to make up?

"No, they were happy enough with the gist."

Not much then. She paused. "Anyway, I— Just look after yourself, okay? I'm going to do my best to make sure everything's good the next time we see each other."

The sense prickled down my back that she was protecting me again, like she had so often in the Exam, only this time from some threat she couldn't even tell me about. She should have been focusing on keeping *herself* safe.

"If I get into any trouble, I'll just have to talk my way out of it," I said brightly. "I'm told I can be very persuasive."

That comment got me a laugh, genuine enough that I could smile in turn. "Are you trying to put that talent to use on me now?" Rocío teased. "I'm going to worry about you the whole time we can't see each other. You'll just have to deal with it."

"I suppose that's fair, since I'll be worrying about you too." I leaned back in the seat, my gaze following the arc of posts along the edge of the bridge the cab was cruising over. The untarnished spots on the metal glinted in the stark noon sun. What time was it where she was right now? She wouldn't even be able to tell me that, since it would mean admitting she *wasn't* at the college.

"I can't talk much longer. Our phone time is pretty limited, and I already used some to call my parents." She sighed. A thread of longing crept into her voice. "I wish we could've had more time together last week. I just wasn't…"

She trailed off as if she didn't think it wise to finish that sentence. What *had* cut her visit short—or had she simply been debating whether it was safe to see me at all? I supposed this call meant she'd weighed the risk in favor of staying in contact.

I'd held on to those new, sharply clear memories of her like a touchstone ever since that afternoon. "Me too," I said. I could at least offer her some small token of my commitment. "You know —I told my dad about you. Just a little, but, well, he knows you exist."

Rocío laughed again, but it sounded a little nervous this time. "And what did he say about that?"

"I think he's got the idea that you being Champion may cause some complications, in general. But he's already invited you over for dinner whenever we want to take that step."

"Oh." Her voice was surprised but pleased. "Um. Maybe that'll have to wait until I can actually talk coherently about more than five percent of my current life. But I'm glad. You could… When I have time off again, I'm sure my parents would be happy to have you over, if you'd want to. I mean, it's kind of awkward even there, but considering… Am I supposed to be calling you my boyfriend now?"

My lips leapt into a grin I couldn't have suppressed if I'd wanted to. "I suppose you can call me whatever you want. But that does seem to be the usual term for a male person you spend a significant amount of time kissing."

"Okay. Boyfriend." Suddenly she sounded a little shy. "I've never had one before, so I guess I'm a little out of touch. And it almost seems too ordinary after… after everything, doesn't it?"

"It does." A warm shiver passed through my chest, affection and the ache of missing her and the rawness of all the horrors we'd been through together condensing together. "But it works, since that's what we've got. Girlfriend."

She snorted and then muttered a curse in Spanish. "My time's up. I'll talk to you again next week. I promise."

I wished she could make that promise and actually know nothing could stop her from fulfilling it.

"Next week," I said.

The bittersweet ache stayed with me as the taxi growled along the highway into Newark. I held the sensation and connection it gave me to Rocío until we pulled up outside the church. I handed the driver his cash and yanked my mind back to the present with the chilly blast of wind that hit me on the sidewalk.

It was our first get-together since last week's protest, and the meeting room was buzzing with more energy than I could remember it ever having before. Not all of that energy was cheery, though.

"I can't believe they buried the story on page fifteen," one of the girls near the doorway was saying.

I ambled over to join her little cluster. "Hey. What's going on?"

"The reporter that interviewed Luis and Tamara," another girl said, making a face. "We only got some tiny article where they made it sound like we're spoiled jerks wanting special treatment."

"*What?*" I'd never gotten in the habit of checking the Dull papers—something I obviously needed to change. "Didn't they take some film of the interview?"

"Noemi said she saw a clip the first night," the first girl said. "But it was blink-and-you-miss-it. They just didn't see it as a big deal."

The guy next to her scowled. "I guess a couple hundred people getting upset about something doesn't seem like that much in a city this large."

That was all our efforts had amounted to in the eyes of the outside world? I didn't let my disappointment color my tone. "We're just getting started," I said, catching each of their gazes so they could tell how much I believed what I was saying. "We'll build up our numbers. We'll grab more attention. It took two *years* from the time the Confed first started seriously discussing the Unveiling to it actually happening. But we still got there."

"Right," the first girl said, her face brightening a little. "Of course we're not going to fix everything all in one go."

I left that group feeling I'd done something right and offered similar encouraging words to the other League members who looked downcast. The next time I turned around, I found myself standing next to Luis.

He gave me a welcoming nod, his hands slung in his pockets in a relaxed pose, but there was a bit of tension in his broad shoulders, which I got the impression he was trying to hide. I was so used to watching him from something of a distance, his confident voice ringing out from the stage, that I kept forgetting our leader wasn't *that* much older than I was. I'd never heard an official number, but up close it was difficult to imagine he was much past drinking age.

"Nice to see you keeping everyone's spirits up, Finn," he said.

"I think we've got a lot to feel good about," I said, and found I wasn't sure what else to say to the guy who'd brought us all together. "I— Thank you for giving me the chance to pitch in. In general, I mean. I really appreciate the chance to take on some responsibilities and contribute."

He flashed me a grin. "Don't be so quick to thank me. The responsibilities can pile up faster than you think."

"I really do want to help any way I can," I said quickly, though he'd sounded like he was joking. "It's amazing how you've gotten so many people involved."

"It is," he agreed, still smiling, as he turned his gaze back to the crowd around us. He ran his hand over this thick black hair. "You know, I never meant to create some big activist group. I had a lot of friends in the Newark tutorial, and it was awful seeing how those bonds just fell apart after most of us were Dampered. I thought maybe we just needed a real space to vent about everything we were going through, where we made it clear it was *okay* to talk about that stuff. Five of us came the first time, but then more and more people heard, and, well…" He gestured to the room, which was teeming with figures now.

"Oh," I said, unable to stop my eyes from widening. "Wow."

"You never know when an idea's going to snowball, I guess," he said. "A lot of people needed something like this, and if they needed it, I wasn't going to tell them there was no more room. We just found bigger rooms. I like that we have so many voices pitching in, trying to figure out how to get to someplace better. But keeping things on track can be a little overwhelming."

The guy who'd been watching the new arrivals shut the door to the room. He motioned to Luis, who tipped his head to me and wove through the crowd to bound onto the stage.

"Let's get started!" he said, the words resonating through the room with no trace of the vulnerability he'd given me a glimpse of. A hush fell over the crowd as everyone turned to look at him. "I know a lot of us are riled up about the way the Dulls reported on our protest, but let's not forget the gains we've made. We've gotten a bunch of new people interested in joining us. First order of business tonight, I'd like to come up with a plan for keeping our group and the discussions here secure in case the Confed decides to interfere. Anyone with suggestions, please come up to the front."

I ambled closer to the stage to hear what other members would offer.

"I think we should switch up meeting spots," one woman was saying. "A different place every time, or at least mix it up some. It's too easy to figure out when a meeting's happening just by watching this place. The Confed authorities have probably already pegged this location."

"Maybe we need more subtle ways of passing on the word too," Floyd put in. "Anyone can see those flyers—people will start to be on the lookout for them. Could we set up a protected group to communicate over the internet?"

"Yeah, I think it's time we got online," Tamara said. "I'll talk to Daniel and see if he has any bright ideas for keeping it on the down-low."

Luis assigned a few volunteers to scope out possible meeting spots. Ary hopped onto the stage and stalked over to him, her long black hair swaying, its streaks an electric purple today. She leaned close to say something in his ear. He stepped to the side of the podium.

"Next, Ary has a new proposal."

Ary raised her hand in the air with a fierce smile, and I know down to my gut that I wasn't going to like whatever she was going to say.

"Freedom of Magic people!" she called out. "We made a smash last week, didn't we? Let's hear it for us!"

A cheer rose up, one I had to join in on, even if I was wary of the person expressing that sentiment. She'd suddenly decided that Tamara's plan had been a wonderful success?

"We can learn from the parts that didn't go so well," she went on. "It's obvious the Dull media isn't going to give us the time of day. Fine! We don't need them. We've got to keep pushing while we've got a bit of the Circle's attention—another protest, bigger and more powerful than the last one, and this time focusing on messing with the Confed's bigwigs directly. Don't *let* them look the other way. Show them we're a real force to be reckoned with."

"Yeah!" Mark hollered from where he was standing not far from me, and a chorus of agreement followed.

Ary's smile widened. "There are a bunch of head honchos from mage organizations around the world coming to town later this month for some sort of conference with the Confed. I say we find out when and where they're coming in, and we blockade them. The Confed's leaders shouldn't get to speak to them on our behalf when they never listen to us."

My stomach had clenched into a ball as murmurs of approval carried around me. She was talking about the conference Dad had been stressing over for the last several weeks—the one he was in charge of organizing. He'd said he was already having trouble with the Dull government over some of the representatives from our more tentative allies. How would they react if the event turned into chaos?

It was easier to speak up today than it had been the first time. "International relations are a very sensitive area for the Confed right now," I said, pitching my voice to carry. "There are other ways we could get the Circle's attention."

"The fact that it's a sensitive area for the Confed is *exactly* why we should target that conference," Ary said, giving me a baleful look. "The Circle isn't going to pay attention unless they don't like the consequences of ignoring us."

"I've got to agree with Ary," Tamara said at the base of the stage. "This conference is happening now. We won't get many opportunities like that."

I suddenly felt the weight of a plethora of gazes turned my way. I'd swayed people in the direction I'd wanted before. They were waiting for my next argument, to see if I'd do it again.

Did I actually have a good one?

If I forgot who I was and who I thought Ary was, I couldn't deny that I'd have made the same assessment Tamara had. Disrupting the international conference would force the Circle and other major figures in the Confed to take notice. When the representatives from the less strict mage organizations abroad heard us standing up for the right to keep our magic, they might even encourage their home countries to put pressure on the Confed too.

If my father hadn't been involved, would I have hesitated even for a second? No. I knew that, the truth of it filling my mouth with a bitter flavor.

I hadn't planned to go directly against my parents, but then, Luis hadn't planned to find himself leading a group like this at all. He'd stuck with it because people needed it. Quite possibly we needed this protest too.

I was either in this or I wasn't. Handing over a book to one Dull girl, sitting on the steps outside the College with my hat pulled low—those things were nothing. I'd wanted to take a stand... and Dad was part of the system we were standing against.

My throat clenched for a second, but I forced the words out, louder than the thudding of my pulse. "You know what? You're absolutely right. Let's target that conference."

"Anyone else have objections to raise?" Luis called out. When no one spoke, he smiled. "Then it looks like we have our next project. All those who want to be involved in organizing, join Ary to the right of the stage."

With feet heavy but chin raised, I set off to plan the greatest failure of my father's career.

CHAPTER FIFTEEN

Rocío

A thin layer of snow coated the rooftop I was perched on—just enough for the chill to start to seep through the soles of my boots. Next to me, Joselin blew her breath into her cupped hands to warm her face. We'd been stationed there, overlooking the stone-block building we were waiting to storm, for a few hours now.

One of our mission's targets was inside. According to our intel, the other should be joining him sometime tonight. She was the one the senior officials were pretty sure had orchestrated the conjuring of several monstrous creatures that had sliced and gouged their way through the employees in a bunch of government buildings a few days ago.

Twenty-four people dead. More than a hundred injured. With all the uncertainties still twisted tight inside me, I focused on the small bit of satisfaction I could take in knowing we might save more people this mage would have hurt in the future.

If we didn't end up hurting the magic a whole lot more in our efforts to grab her and her associate.

How much was I risking if I tried to offset that damage? Brandt was here too, poised on the tiled rooftop on the other side of the target building. If he saw me—if Joselin decided to report some adjustment I made to our planned strategy...

I glanced over at her. She hadn't laughed at me when I'd mentioned my theories about the magic before. But the decisions I made affected not just me and the people I cared about back home, but everyone here on my team too. Every time we went out here like this, we were putting our lives in each other's hands.

It would be so much easier if I only thought about the staying alive part in the middle of a mission. Easier and maybe safer for everyone... except the magic.

The pressure of all those conflicting responsibilities sat like a boulder on my gut. I wasn't getting any closer to sorting out my thoughts by just stewing in them.

"Sin que los oyera nadie," I sang under my breath, bolstering the sound-shielding 'chantment I'd cast around us when we'd first gotten into place. It still felt unnerving to speak up in the stillness that hung over this part of town so late at night. Music occasionally trickled to us from a bar open late a few blocks away, but otherwise, the neighborhood seemed to be asleep.

"This could be a pretty rough one," I said to Joselin quietly.

The other girl shifted her weight, tucking her gloved hands deeper into the sleeves of her jacket. Beneath its hood, the heavy brown fringe of her bangs fell across her forehead to her eyebrows.

"Yeah," she murmured. "The stuff this lady thought up..." She gave a shudder. Her gaze rose to meet mine. "I guess you've got other reasons to be upset about how she casts—from the things you were saying about the magic and all."

Her comment wasn't exactly a question, but the look in her eyes was. And this was the reaction I'd wanted to judge.

"Yeah, I do," I said. "Even with this mission, it's hard to see how our side isn't going to end up hurt one way or another."

"You don't think we could take these two down without disrupting the magic?"

"I don't know. I don't know how easy it's going to be to try."

She bowed her head. "How sure are you about all those things you said—about destructive spells damaging the magic? What have you really hearkened?"

My thoughts tripped back to the night two weeks ago now when I'd asked the magic for guidance—to the anguish it had sent wrenching through me with those impressions of devastation. Even remembering that world of torment sent horror resonating through my bones.

The magic's pain and panic were so vast, and I was only one mage. Could *any* one mage be enough to champion it?

It had reached out to me... but maybe it was asking for more than I could give, no matter how much I wanted to.

I pulled myself away from those doubts. "Completely sure," I said. "There's... kind of a natural energy in everything, right? When we push the magic to shatter the harmony that's keeping a body alive, or a wall intact, or whatever, there's a rebound effect. The magic's energy gets weaker, shakier, harder to conduct. At least, that's the best way I can explain it, from what I've hearkened so far. I haven't had much of an opportunity to figure it all out."

"I've never felt anything like that," Joselin said. "I've never heard anyone talk about it, even at the Seattle Academy. Why wouldn't someone have noticed before?"

"I don't know," I said. "I think probably a few people have, but it's been too inconvenient for them to want to really tackle the problem. But mostly... how many times would an ordinary mage be using magic to kill or destroy something? Even doing it on a small scale isn't going to have much impact on all the magic in the world. It was only… in an enclosed setting, where there were a lot of awful things going on all at once…"

Joselin's mouth tightened. She nodded, and I could tell without either of us trying to break the silencing 'chantment that she knew I was talking about the Exam.

"I've always had a strong connection to the magic," I added. "And once I started noticing the effect, it got harder and harder to ignore, even outside of that place. It's like I'm tuned in now to a frequency I had to learn how to hear."

Also, the magic seems to have purposefully reached out to me for help and badgered me into listening. You'd just think I was really crazy if I told you that part.

"You got into trouble for the way you were handling the missions, didn't you?" Joselin said after a moment. "That's why they took you off duty."

I'd spent my whole first week after my leave back in training with the guy who'd replaced Hamlin. Then I'd been let out of the base for a few low-key missions, ones they'd figured I couldn't screw up much, just to see how I handled myself. I didn't think the commander had stuck me with operatives I hadn't worked with much before—other than Brandt, who'd been along for each one—by coincidence. The higher-ups liked that he kept an eye on me.

This was the first major mission I'd been assigned to since the interrogation. The first one where I'd be called on to compel the magic to harm, maybe even to kill.

"They were concerned about my loyalties," I said. "I guess they figured I might have been trying to help the Borci, not just the magic. I just figure, why destroy something if you can just disarm it? Why hurt someone if you can stop them without that? Especially if it hurts the magic in turn. I don't want to lose *it*."

"Gods, no." Joselin shuffled her feet again, looking down into the shadows of the alley below us before raising her eyes to me. "Sometimes we don't have much of a choice what we cast, right? When it's down to the wire... But I get what you're saying."

She fell silent for a long moment, her jaw working. Then she inhaled sharply. "Before the Exam, I thought I was a pretty good person, you know? But in there, to make it through... I think about the decisions I made, and honestly, it scares me. I had no idea I could be that selfish, or that vicious. I hate what came out of me."

Regret had turned her voice raw. It stirred a twinge of sympathy in my chest. "I bet most of us feel that way. They *wanted* to push us to those limits."

"Yeah, but still..." She tugged at her bangs. "Sometimes I feel like I deserve to be here instead of at the college. Like I'm doing a kind of penance. Running missions isn't even so bad if I think about how the lives I might be saving balance out the people I hurt. But if I'm wrecking the magic while I'm saving them, how does that solve anything? I'd rather be a part of saving it too, is all I'm saying."

Hearing those words didn't fix even half of my problem, but they were more than I'd had a few minutes ago. I was about to thank her for at least trying to believe me when our mission leader's voice crackled out of our earpieces.

"There's a car approaching from the east. Looks like the right one. All operatives prepare for engagement."

Joselin and I leaned forward automatically. We had no room left for conversation, for anything other than the job ahead of us. I braced my hands against my knees and drew the lyric I'd practiced onto my tongue.

The plan we'd discussed in our briefing was to pierce through the protective magical barrier around the house in one swift blow and get in there before the inhabitants had a chance to heave us back. The team on the ground would grab the woman in the car.

The four of us—me and Joselin on this side and Brandt and Leonie on the other—had to find and capture the guy inside. We weren't totally sure how many other mages he might have around to guard him.

"And... engage!" the mission leader called.

Tires screeched on the road beyond our view. I twisted my tongue around the lyric, gathering the magic around my intent as the words tumbled out.

I had to break *something* to fulfill my role in this mission, but I'd made my casting as nonviolent as I could. My awareness stretched toward the thrum of the barrier in front of me, and I yanked at a piece of it with a lift of my voice, imagining that fragment was a stray thread in a massive woven structure. Not smashing it, just unraveling it.

Joselin spat out her casting at the same time. The energy in the air shuddered and released. I trained my attention on the window I'd been eyeing and sang out another verse to transport me from the roof to the room beyond that pane.

With a lurch and a flash of darkness, I was landed in a shadowed study. A crisp birch-wood scent laced the air from the bookshelves and desk I could barely make out. My arms had jerked up defensively, and another lyric was poised on my tongue, but I was the only one in the room.

Shouts were already carrying from somewhere deeper in the house. I dashed for the closed door. A thump and a groan radiated through the wall, and the magic flinched against my skin.

Brandt's voice blared through my earpiece. "We've got him! Target down and secure. Two guards subdued."

Dead, I was sure he meant, as the magic seized my shoulders with what felt like fingers digging straight into my muscles. My awareness of it had gotten even stronger since I'd opened myself up to it so freely the other night. *I can't do anything about him*, I thought at it, but the bottom dropped out of my stomach anyway.

And yet, at the same time, some of the tightness in my chest faded. I hadn't needed to make a choice. Part of me was *glad* Brandt had killed those guards so that it hadn't come down to me. Dios mío, how selfish was I?

"Bring him in," the mission leader said. "Lopez, Stravos, now that the barrier is down, I'm detecting a 'chanted object with a lot of power somewhere on the third floor. Locate it and report back."

I drew my back straight where I'd stopped by the door. The mission wasn't over yet.

At the quick casting I murmured, the magic quavered around me and offered up a condensed hum from close by on my right. The 'chanted object was here in the study with me. Over... there.

Joselin burst into the room as I yanked open the deep lower drawer on the desk. She must have done a scan of her own.

"I found it," I said into my mic, clicking on my flashlight to peer at the knobby metallic device inside the drawer. The energy roiling off it sent a tendril of queasiness through me. I recognized the shape of the thing from training. "It's one of those disorientation devices. Not activated."

The pattern of bends in the metal bits that were soldered together amplified the 'chantment cast on the device. If set off, it'd release a blast of energy that would hit everyone in range with the equivalent of an emergency-grade migraine. Give it a minute, and you'd start bleeding from your ears.

"There could be a long-distance activation point anywhere," the mission leader said. "Demolish and move out."

The magic tremored at his words. I swallowed hard. Joselin stood still, watching to see what I would do.

The safe thing would be to burn the device up with one

quick casting. No one could fault me for that. That was what my mission leader had meant. What most of the operatives would've done.

Follow my orders. Keep everyone depending on me safe. Cripple the magic a little more.

The magic that was clinging to me right now like a hysterical child.

I closed my eyes for a second, and a memory of my brother swam up unbidden—sitting on the floor together in our bedroom, Javi beaming with awe and pride at some new casting I'd eagerly demonstrated for him.

You are going to be a marvel, Ro. I can't wait to see you put all those Confed pendejos to shame.

He'd never gotten to see me dazzle anyone. He'd died trying to win a future full of magic for me.

What had it all been for? The sacrifice he'd made—the pain I'd put my parents through, that they'd borne in the name of my happiness—the lives I'd taken and the people I'd failed to save in the Exam—what had any of it been for if I helped destroy the thing I'd fought so hard to keep?

The only one I'd put to shame was myself.

I might be just one mage, but I was a mage to be reckoned with. I owed it to them and to the magic not to give up.

I looked at Joselin, my hands clenching. She gave me a small smile. The resolve I'd found expanded through my chest with a blazing glow.

"I can detach the 'chantment in less than a minute and then smash the device," I said. "That's demolishing."

A conspiratorial glint lit in my squad-mate's eyes. "Yeah," she said. "Of course it is. I want to see this."

She stepped closer as I bent over the drawer. I didn't want to risk even touching this thing. I trained my attention on the strands of the casting in the device, the caustic melody designed to scatter people's thoughts and shred their nerves. The verse I brought to my lips to test against it was soft and soothing. Where was the trigger point?

I hearkened a spot like a deeper pulse amid the tangled notes. With a shift in the pitch of my voice, I teased the magic I was conducting around the trigger. Pluck a strand free here with a hitching rhythm; loosen another one there with a quavering dip. The process was a more delicate, more precise unraveling.

Sweat trickled down my back even though the room was cool. I called one last thread of the 'chantment away, and the rest disintegrated with a ripple through the air. Joselin let out her breath. The magic around us calmed.

I scooped up the now-vacant device and tossed it on the floor. "Want to do the honors?"

Joselin grinned and stomped down her heel. The contraption burst apart with a chatter of metal bits.

My legs wobbled under me as we made for the ground floor, but the shakiness felt weirdly euphoric, as if my upper body wasn't totally connected to my lower half. I'd been warned and threatened, I'd defied the Confed's authorities anyway, and here I was, still standing.

"Lopez and I are heading out," Joselin said into her mic. We hustled to the front door our squad-mates had left open, toward the whir of the helicopter our pilot had brought around.

We were just bounding down the front steps when a figure flew at Joselin, seemingly from out of nowhere.

It was a woman, stringy-limbed, with pale, tangled hair. A conjured shard of glowing light gleamed in one of her thin hands —a makeshift weapon. It couldn't have been a carefully planned assault, only a moment of desperate opportunity. A short phrase I couldn't translate wrenched from her mouth in a cry.

Joselin's hands shot up with the instincts hammered into us in training. The words Hamlin had made me drill into my head

during my own practice sessions sprang to my lips. Joselin was
sputtering out her own hasty casting at the same time.

Hers struck the woman in the middle of the chest with a
searing hiss. The conjured weapon nicked my squad-mate's
throat as the woman crumpled. My casting, an instant later, only
clipped her shoulder now that she was falling. I'd been aiming at
her heart.

The magic tore at my arms. The woman slumped lifeless on
the ground. Joselin inhaled with a shudder and rubbed her
elbows, fear still stark in her eyes. She glanced back at me, and
her expression tensed.

"Good reflexes, Stravos," our mission leader said in our ears.
"Now get over here before any more crazies come out of the
woodwork."

My heart was racing as if I'd been the one almost assaulted.
The magic's frantic energy kept nipping at my skin. *I'm sorry*, I
thought at it. *I'm so sorry.*

But what else could we have done? Sam had said it all the
way back during my first mission: *Locks can be fixed. Lots of other
things can't.* Like Joselin's life. With all the skill I had, I wasn't
sure I could've cast anything that would have deflected that
attack in time while sparing her attacker.

I could champion the magic all I wanted, but as long as we
were out here, we were soldiers too.

Bile filled my throat, but I managed to nod to Joselin. "I'm
glad you're okay."

The tension left her face. We loped the rest of the way to the
helicopter together. I dropped into my seat still feeling sick, not
sure whether today had been more of a victory or a defeat.

I had to work better, work faster. So much and so many
depended on me. I wouldn't let them down.

CHAPTER SIXTEEN

Finn

Where was the line between courage and cowardice? I must have toed it many times in the last few months, but I still couldn't determine the answer.

Was I bold for risking even more of my parents' disappointment by stealing some of Dad's confidential work information to help the League with our protest—or was I pathetic because I'd made sure I stayed invisible during that protest, staked out in a hotel room overlooking the crowd we'd assembled? I'd like to think it was more the former than the latter, but the niggling sensation in my gut wasn't so sure.

"How're things looking from the west side?" Tamara asked through the phone I had pressed to my ear. She'd found an observation point across and farther down the street from mine.

"As far as I can tell, everything's going smoothly," I said. The five hundred or so people who'd come out to rally were now swarming around the cars that had been carrying the international mage representatives to the conference center. I'd been able to tell everyone when to gather and where to wait, thanks to the documents on Dad's work laptop that I'd snuck a peek at.

We'd been holding our ground for nearly an hour. The crowd was mostly still, waving posters we'd spent our last meeting writing up and shouting requests for fair treatment. Luis and a couple of his close colleagues circulated through the mass of figures. He'd just interrupted a couple of guys who'd started to pound on one of the cars.

We're doing this as much to grab international attention as the Confed's, he'd said at our last meeting. *Those representatives need to see the Confed is committing violence against us, not the other way around.* The consensus had been to keep this gathering immovable but peaceful.

Not all of us had been enthusiastic about that decision. "I think we can step this up a notch," Ary said, the third voice in our conference call. She was stationed in a fifth-floor restaurant by the north end of the street, though I suspected she'd rather have been down in the crowd yelling at the cars than observing. She just didn't want Tamara and me to be the only ones advising Luis.

Luis, the fourth and final voice, had to holler for us to hear him over the racket around him on the ground. "I don't see any need to push harder when we're accomplishing our goals. We're making our point here. And if we hold back a little now, we'll have more chance of surprising the Confed next time."

"Hey, it looks like there might be a few people on the verge of a fight over at the southeast edge of the crowd," I said, frowning. It was difficult to make out a lot of detail from my seventh-floor room, but a couple of our protesters had turned away from the main mass of bodies to talk to some of the spectators who'd stopped around the fringes. From the way one girl was jabbing her hand, it didn't look like a friendly conversation.

"On it," Luis said. He must have made a gesture, because Mark, easy to identify from his blue hair, broke from the crowd and loped over. My frown fell away as I watched him ease into the argument and redirect our people back to the protest.

In my memories from the Exam, he hadn't been much of a peacemaker. Perhaps the League had inspired him to find a new calling.

"We can't get complacent," Ary said. "The Confed's not just going to sit back and take this. We'd better be prepared for whatever they try next."

The security people inside the cars had already made a couple of attempts to open up the blockade around them, but we'd been ready to deflect both. Dad's plan for the conference arrivals had included a list of defensive protocols—ones I imagined had been worked out in case of a possible terrorist threat, not in anticipation of any local demonstration.

A number of Dull police officers had turned up as well, but they'd hung back around the edges of the crowd. I suspected they were hesitant to get involved in a conflict where magic could come into play. For the most part, the Dull authorities saw it as the Confed's responsibility to police its own, which was a policy *our* authorities generally encouraged.

"The Circle will have called in the Confed's primary security force, I'm sure," Tamara said. "We'll just have to watch what tactics they decide to take when they get involved."

"Weren't you supposed to have all the inside intel to get us through this, Finn?" Ary said, a hint of snark creeping into her voice.

I didn't let myself bristle. There'd been a little contention over the fact that I hadn't revealed the source of my information or given the files over to anyone else to look through—I might be willing to use Dad's position to help the League, but I intended to stay in control of how far we used it—and that was fair enough. Luis and the others had taken my advisement into account, which was all that mattered.

"I know they'll call in Security," I said. "That's common sense. The specific tactics, they can't have planned in advance. They had no reason to anticipate this situation."

"The Confed hasn't needed to deal with any large-scale disruptions since before you three were born, I bet," Tamara said. "This will be interesting."

My gaze lingered on the dark sedans that held our international visitors. What *were* they making of this protest? Some of them came from national mage organizations that were more lenient than the Confed, but others had even stricter Dampering policies than ours.

"Hey!" Ary said. "There's movement heading this way at my end. A bunch of cars and some people on foot—definitely security types."

I peered to the north, my pulse thumping faster. Our first clash with the Confed's security force could be the deciding factor in the protest's success.

In a moment, the cars and a few lines of jogging figures came into my view. They paused several feet from the nearest spectators. More security officers spilled out of the cars, several of them motioning for the spectators to move out of the way.

It'd taken them a while to remove us from the College, but we'd been able to put walls at our backs there, and we'd only had small areas to guard. Here, if they managed to break even a slight gap through the mass of bodies below, the whole blockade would fall apart.

I studied the officers' movements as they assembled at the edge of the crowd.

"Stand steady!" Luis was calling to the protesters. "Be ready to link up like we did before."

The mouths of the security officers started to move. They

raised their arms, ready to make a sweeping motion, a pose that jarred me with recognition.

I'd read every book in existence on defensive magic strategies back when I'd still hoped I might join National Defense someday. Perhaps I couldn't hearken the magic anymore, but I could sense the technique they were about to implement with every particle in my being.

"Luis!" I said. "Get everyone moving. Find a rhythm— stomping feet, pumping arms, twisting from side to side—as much as you all can. Now!"

"What the hell?" Ary said, but Luis's voice echoed through the phone as he hollered my instructions to the people around him.

The security force had already launched into the main thrust of their casting. The mages at the front of their team sliced their hands through the air in time with the lyrics they must have been chanting, and several stragglers jerked away from the edge of the crowd on their own two feet. They stumbled and swiveled like puppets guided by an unsteady puppeteer.

The rest of the mass on the street had begun moving with a ripple that spread from the point where Luis was standing. Hands waved, heads bobbed, and signs flapped. Even though many of the people down there couldn't reach out to the magic directly, a large enough clamor could still interfere with the reach of a complex casting.

The security force must have been aiming to part a path through the crowd with that one effort, but the magic couldn't catch hold when so many of the protesters were thumping out their own clashing rhythms. No one else budged. The mages' postures stiffened as they drew themselves up to try again.

"Keep at it," I said. "As long as you can. Don't give them a chance to grab you with the 'chantment."

"People are going to start getting tired," Tamara added. "As long as Security is working on us, we should get a rotation going —people who are stronger or fresher moving to the outer edge, letting others come toward the middle when they need a break. The commotion should stop the casting from reaching the center."

"Putting that idea into action now," Luis said.

The crowd churned like dancers in a huge street party. When a second casting had no effect, the security force huddled to confer. A smile crossed my lips even as a twinge ran through me that I wasn't down there in the midst of that mass of motion.

"How did you know that would work, Finn?" Ary said. Did she sound... suspicious?

It wasn't as if it hurt me to be honest with her. "I've wanted to go into National Defense since I was a kid," I said. "I studied up on their techniques, everything I could get access to, because I thought that would improve my chances. I've read about that casting before."

It wouldn't have mattered to me that I was a mediocre mage in general if I'd managed to be good at that one thing. Of course, now I wasn't a mage in practice at all.

For the first time, that thought didn't arrive with a mournful twinge of its own. Non omnia possumus omnest. None of the ancient lines I'd memorized in my Academy days could have rung more true, but I'd done something useful here today without any magic at all. No one had been harmed. I hadn't compromised my family beyond what was required for the protest to succeed.

Looking down at all those people who'd risen up in support of this cause, I couldn't help thinking we might fix the horrors within the Confed sooner than I'd dared to imagine.

If only Rocío could have been here with me to witness it.

* * *

"And here's to Finn!" someone shouted in the crowded rec center room, and everyone raised their pop cans and water bottles—since Luis had a strict "No Alcohol" policy—with another cheer. Warmth crept across my face, but I raised my own cola with a grin.

Voices rang loud and merry all through the space where we'd convened after the protest had broken up. Nothing definite had changed yet, but the energy resonating between us reverberated with hope.

"I can't believe we managed to hold them off for *eight* hours," Mark was saying with a grin of his own, unexpected on his usually stern face.

"Next time we'll have to set a new record and make it a whole day!" Noemi said. "What's coming up on the agenda, Finn?" She shot an amused smile my way.

"I think it's Luis you'll have to be asking," I said. "I just offer support when I can."

"Yeah, yeah. Says the guy who got us in the right place *and* saved the day."

"I can't wait to hear the Confed's official response." Mark chuckled. "Let's see them try to downplay this." He paused, and in place of both his usual gruffness and his current cheerful enthusiasm, his expression softened. "You know, when I woke up burned out and knew I hadn't made it, I was really scared I'd lost my one chance to take on the Confed. My brother—if he sees this... Even if he doesn't, we'll force some answers out of them."

That was the first time he'd mentioned his brother to me at all, that he remembered. I didn't want him to regret the brief openness. "More than that," I said firmly. "We'll force them to give us better ones."

"Yeah," he said, his grin coming back.

"Hey, who's hungry?" someone called from the direction of the kitchen area. "The first batch of burgers is done!"

My mouth watered at the smell trickling through the air, but I hung back as Mark headed over. I'd ordered hotel room service from my lookout spot—some people here hadn't eaten much all day.

"That new book you lent me is *awesome*," Noemi said. "Is it okay if I keep it for another week?"

"Sure," I said. It was the third I'd passed on to her from the assortment I'd been keeping in my room. If my parents hadn't worried about them being missing from the family library this long, they weren't likely to come hunting for them any time soon. "But I want to hear all about what you're making of that material at some point."

"Oh, I'm coming up with all kinds of theories I'll want to share." She made a face. "You must think I'm a total dork. It's okay. Pretty much everyone who knows me does. There's a reason the League stuff is basically my entire social life."

I waved off her remarks. "Noemi, I spent my whole life practically obsessed with getting as close to the magic as I could. Believe me, I have no trouble understanding wanting to be a part of it."

She'd been speaking in a joking tone, but her eyes brightened at my response as if she'd needed to hear something like that. Then her gaze slid toward the other end of the room, and her smile turned a bit sly. "I think I'm going to go see if Luis could use any help with... anything."

I laughed. "Go for it."

She gave me a thumbs-up before moving off through the crowd.

I turned, feeling buoyant on my feet, just as the guy who usually acted as a bouncer for our meetings appeared in the doorway. "I've got some newbies looking to join in," he called over to Luis. "They check out."

A few figures trickled in from behind him at his gesture: a

young woman who looked about my sister Margo's age, a slightly grizzled man with a pair of oval glasses—and a gangly guy sporting a shock of ruddy hair.

My whole body froze. Callum Geary—my neighbor, my former classmate, and the guy who'd gleefully tried to kill us all during the Exam—glanced around the room with a hesitant expression. The Burnout mark stood out starkly against his pale, freckled skin. He looked skinnier than before, his over-wide shoulders more angular.

I hadn't seen him since the last day of the Exam, when I'd stopped him from leading an assault on me and Rocío and the rest of our little group. I'd stopped him by disintegrating a large portion of his thigh with a magical weapon. He shouldn't remember that, not if the examiners had done their job successfully. He'd sure as Hades know who I was, though, and he'd never been any friend of mine.

I stepped back, ready to duck away. In that moment, his eyes caught mine and narrowed.

CHAPTER SEVENTEEN

Rocío

A shake of my arm wrenched me out of sleep. Someone was bending over me in the dorm room, gripping my shoulder.

"Lopez," the someone said in a low voice, and my still half-asleep brain registered her as one of the senior operatives who'd led a couple of the missions I'd been on. "You're needed. Suit up and let's go."

She waited with her arms folded over her chest as I fumbled my way into my current uniform of cargo pants, thermal long-sleeved tee, ballistic vest, and hooded jacket. Prisha stirred on the neighboring bed. Her gaze caught mine in the darkness with a questioning glint.

I gave a nod to say that I was okay, even though I didn't really know that—but it wasn't as if she could've done anything to help if I hadn't been. Prisha tipped her head in return and burrowed it back into her pillow. Knowing she'd noticed my leaving and cared made me feel a little more okay, somehow.

The woman who'd come to collect me ushered me through the dim halls of the base to the operations room. Even a few weeks after we'd moved here, the place still didn't feel broken in. Dust lingered on the baseboards, and a stale smell hung in the air as if at least a few of the filters needed changing. I'd take this over staying somewhere the insurgents had painted a target on, though.

The bright fluorescents of the operations room stung my eyes as I walked in. I blinked hard, taking in the long rectangular table where we planned our missions. Commander Revett, Tonya Sekibo, and Colonel Alcido were standing there. Alcido, the sharp-jawed Dull military representative who'd turned up when Hamlin had been booted out, had his thin lips twisted into an expression even more sour than his usual one. I guessed this late-night meeting hadn't been his idea.

"Operative Lopez," Commander Revett said. "It seems we need you in the field."

"Right now?" I said. I hadn't been scheduled for a mission tonight—if I had, I never would've gone to bed. And this was way later in the night than missions usually left. I rubbed my temple, still feeling groggy from my interrupted sleep.

"One of tonight's squads encountered a young woman who appears to have some sort of information. She's saying there's only one person she'll talk to, and from what she's said and the fact that she matches the description of the local who gave you that recorder, we have to assume she means you."

The girl who'd given us that tip—she was asking for me, somewhere out there? My mind snapped more alert in an instant.

"Did you instruct her to come specifically to you?" Alcido asked, his nasal voice even more abrupt than Revett's.

What? "No," I said. "I didn't instruct her to do anything."

"Colonel," Revett said.

Alcido ignored her like he usually did. He seemed to think he got to call the shots now... and from the way the senior Confed officials acted, maybe he was right.

"So you don't know what this is about?" he said.

I stared at him. Did I *look* like I'd been expecting this wake-up call? "I didn't even know anything was happening until a minute ago."

"The squad is waiting," Revett said, her tone annoyed but resigned.

Alcido made a humming sound, but he turned away from me. "The mission leader knows I expect this entire interview to be recorded?"

"Of course," Revett said. "I've already relayed that order." She motioned to me. "You'll fly out with Officer Sekibo, who'll fill you in on what we know so far. The less time we dally on this, the better."

Tonya was already striding toward the door. I nodded to the commander and the colonel and hustled after the senior operative.

A helicopter was waiting in the yard, the blades just starting to whir as we emerged from the building. We jumped in, and it took off with a lurch.

Tonya sat down in her usual spot at the communications array. "Here's the story," she said in a tight voice. I got the impression she wasn't too happy about her interrupted sleep either. "Rojanwan had a mission to one of the border towns. This girl approached him but then tried to take off, I guess because she saw you weren't with him. The squad restrained her, but she insisted she'd only talk with you. So here we are."

Sam was leading the squad—at least I'd see one reasonably friendly face out there. "What was the mission for?" I asked. "What do they think she could tell us?"

Tonya shook her head. "I don't know. I've only got what Revett reported to me while they were getting you up. You can ask the squad when we get there."

I leaned my head back against the vibrating wall of the helicopter and suppressed a yawn. "This wasn't my idea, you know."

The downward curl of her lips suggested she was blaming me anyway. We hadn't been on many missions together, so I wasn't sure why she would dislike me, but I had seen her chatting with Brandt during meals more than once. Maybe he'd been telling her tales about my supposed insubordination too.

"You gave this girl the impression that you're better than the rest of us," she said after a moment. "Nicer." That last word came with a bit of a sneer. "Don't be too nice. It looks like she's awfully tangled up with the enemy."

The girl had helped us. She wasn't going to keep doing that if we treated her like an enemy. I didn't think Tonya was interested in hearing any arguments from me, though.

I might have dozed a little despite my best efforts. It felt like way too soon that the helicopter dipped down toward the ground. I braced my feet against the floor as we landed.

Tonya led me through the night, down a short road to a wide, squat brick building lit by a single streetlamp. It looked like some kind of office space—one that hadn't been used in a while, based on the film on the windows.

Just inside, in a room that might have once been a reception area, a few chairs had been shoved into a jumble by one wall. An electric lantern was perched on one, casting an eerie glow through the space. Sam, Brandt, Joselin, Leonie, and their translator stood around another chair in the middle of the room, where the girl with the scuffed jean jacket was sitting.

Sam nodded to me as we came in, and the girl's head jerked

WOUNDED MAGIC   185

up. Her fawn-brown hair hung loose today, falling just past her shoulders. She looked younger than I remembered—she might not have been any older than me after all. Her dark blue eyes were stormy. Her pose and the quavering in the magic between us told me she was bound to her seat.

She shifted in the chair against the magical restraints I couldn't see, and the pained slant of her mouth sent a jab of discomfort through me. I'd arrived too late. They'd already treated her like a criminal. Was she going to talk even to me at this point?

"You were looking for me?" I said, stepping closer.

The girl's gaze held mine for a long moment. She wet her lips. "I want to help. Not hurt anyone. But I don't help *them*." She spat the last word, with a twitch of her head toward the rest of the squad.

"I can be a go-between," the translator said. "If she'd be more comfortable speaking in Russian or Estonian." She repeated the same offer to the girl in another language.

"No," the girl snapped. "I speak enough English. No one twists my words like you people do so much. Stay away from me. I only want to talk to her." Her gaze shot back to me.

Sam gestured for the others to back up to the walls. I took another step so I stood just a couple feet from the girl's chair. The conjured bindings tied her calves to its legs, her shoulders to its back, her wrists together in her lap. The magic around me jittered uneasily.

"I'm sorry," I said. "They were worried you knew something really important, and that if they didn't stop you, we wouldn't find out what."

Brandt snorted at my apology. The girl glared at me as if she didn't think much of it either. "You would have done this too?"

"No." But why the hell would she believe me? I hesitated,

feeling the gazes of the squad on me. None of them had anywhere near as strong a connection to the magic as I did. They couldn't hearken from several feet away how well her bindings were holding. They wouldn't notice a subtle casting, I didn't think. I could reassure her and the magic.

Unless the girl betrayed me. If I'd misjudged her, if she was more dangerous than I thought, who knew how she might lash out after the way the squad had handled her?

I swallowed hard. One more dilemma I had to face alone. They kept piling up.

I balled my hands at my sides and gathered myself. I trusted my instincts. I trusted my skill. If this situation went sideways, I could get it back under control, couldn't I?

Relaxing the fingers of my right hand, I pattered out a faint rhythm against my thigh where none of our spectators could see it. Casting without words to focus my intent was hard—a wave of respect for Desmond passed through me when I thought of how he managed these wordless castings all the time—but I found a pattern of beats that resonated. With a brief drumming, the bonds around the girl's limbs relaxed.

They weren't gone, but now she could slip them in an instant if she wanted to.

The girl's expression softened. To my relief, she kept herself in exactly the same position, as if she were still clamped to the chair. I bobbed my head slightly in acknowledgment. We were in this together.

What did I say next? Launching straight into a demand for information she wasn't volunteering didn't seem like the best way to keep her trust.

How would Finn have talked to her? He was always so good at warming up the atmosphere, making people feel at ease.

My thoughts slipped back to that first evening in the Exam

when he'd suggested we all introduce ourselves. Of course. How could I be allies with someone when we didn't know even the most basic fact about each other?

"I'm Rocío," I said. "What's your name?"

"For fu—" Brandt started to mutter. From the corner of my eye, I saw Sam swat him quiet.

"Polina," the girl said. "This is a strange way to meet."

I almost laughed. "Yes, it is. Ah, part of the reason my colleagues aren't sure how to act with you is they're wondering how you got the recorder you gave me last time. Were you there when those people were talking?"

"Am I friends with those people, you mean," she said.

"Yeah. It's— People have died, right? There've been so many attacks. We're just trying to be careful."

Polina didn't look as if she totally accepted that excuse, but she sighed. "For a while, I was... together? With a guy who is friends with them. Sometimes I go along when they talk. They think maybe I will help too. But I was not sure, the way they act. I don't like Americans being here, but those people, they are not good guys either. They push us around too; they take things from us; they... After some time, I think they are worse. So..."

She made the closest thing to a shrug she should've been able to manage if her shoulders had still been clamped to the chair.

The starkness of her wan face in the thin light jolted me back through time to another girl, slim and pale but tough as nails when she'd been pushed to the brink. Lacey. She'd seemed way more victim than villain when we'd started the Exam, but by the end, she'd gone wild with fury at how she'd been treated—by the examiners, by the boyfriend who'd dragged her into the Exam in the first place, by the rest of us on her team. She'd said, right up until the end when she'd nearly killed Finn, that she just wanted to stop being pushed around.

I'd screwed up with Lacey. I hadn't realized how far she might go, I hadn't found the right way to show we were on her side, and I'd ended up pushing her too.

But Polina wasn't Lacey. She'd already trusted me. And I knew better now—I could do better. I could make sure the Confed didn't grind her down with its machinations like it had so many in the Exam.

She didn't want to hurt anyone. All I had to do was make sure she never felt she needed to. Keep her on our side, find out what I could from her to stop coming attacks, and I'd be protecting the magic too.

Lacey's rage hadn't started with the Confed, though, not directly. It had started with her boyfriend, the one who'd left finger-shaped bruises on her arms. I kept my voice as even as I could. "Are you still 'together' with this guy?"

"No. He was getting too pushy too." Polina's jaw worked. "But I still must be careful. If he—his friends—if they found out I am speaking to you, there will be trouble for me. A lot of trouble."

"I understand," I said. "Why don't we finish here quickly then? You came to the squad—you wanted to speak to me. Was there something specific you wanted to tell me?"

"Yes." Polina paused again, and I started to think she might not tell me after all. Then she wrinkled her nose. "I heard there is another meeting, like I recorded. More details to talk about. In Uzbekistan. They mentioned Qarshi. I'm not sure when, but soon. Maybe a few days?"

By the wall, Sam murmured into his mic. A tip like that, we'd want everyone to know about ASAP.

"Thank you," I said. "Is that all the information you have?"

"I am lucky to hear even that much," she said. "I don't like the sound of how they are talking. What they will do... I know if your people get angry, it will not just be bad guys they hit back at. We all suffer. No. Better if you can stop them."

"I'm sure we will." I wished I could guarantee that, for both her sake and the magic's. As long as she was willing to keep helping us, we had a much better chance of that. I glanced over at Sam. "Can we let her go now? I think she's telling the truth that that's all she knows."

"She's in with these terrorists," Brandt protested. "We can't just leave it like that. What's she going to go tell them about *us* now?"

Polina twisted her head around to scowl at him. "I have nothing for them."

"Hey!" I said, holding up my hand. If he kept shooting his mouth off, he'd unravel whatever progress I'd made here. "We've got no reason to think she'd act against us. And as long as you haven't been spilling important secrets, I don't know what you think she could tell."

"Hold on." Sam tugged his mic closer to his mouth. I bet he was speaking directly to Commander Revett now. After a minute, he lowered his arm and came over to join me.

"You're not a prisoner," he said to Polina. "We have no reason to believe you've assisted with any crime, and you've shown us good faith in bringing this information to us. If you hear anything else, there's an easier way you can reach out. We can arrange for Rocío to be the one who talks to you if you call this number."

He sang a few words to release the bindings he couldn't tell I'd loosened. As Polina got up, rubbing her arms, he offered her a card.

"I can't have this," she said. "Let me see it." She peered at the number, her lips moving as she recited it to herself. After several times, she nodded. "I think I will remember."

"Thank you," Sam said. "You're free to go now."

Polina darted out of the building without a backward glance. The rest of us tramped out a moment later. "We're all heading back together," Sam told Tonya. "The base called your chopper back."

"Lots of company," she said with a grimace. "Sounds like fun."

No one said anything else until we were loaded onto the helicopter and it had lifted into the air.

"That's it?" Brandt burst out the moment no one on the ground could have overheard us. "She's got intel like that, and we just let her go? And what the hell is this weird obsession she has with Lopez?"

"The data people back at the base have been scanning for any connection between her and the Borci—or any other insurgent group—since we got the recorder," Sam said. "They haven't found evidence of involvement with any attack. Her story checks out." He gave the younger officer a baleful look. "And I wasn't going to *tell* her, obviously, but I put a tracking 'chantment on her when we first grabbed her. We'll be able to watch where she goes. If she's more mixed up with the Borci than she said, she'll lead us right to them."

My stomach dropped. "They might detect the 'chantment on her. If they think she let us track her, what'll they do to her?"

"What the hell does it matter?" Brandt said. "You heard her. She's just looking out for herself and whoever she thinks her people are. We look out for ours. That's how it's supposed to work, if you don't have your head up your ass."

"Brandt," Sam said firmly. The other guy frowned but looked away. Sam turned back to me. "I used a light touch. Even if someone does notice, it's not the kind of 'chantment you'd see on someone volunteering."

Right, because these insurgents were such levelheaded people that they'd take that into account. Even the slight trust

Polina had offered the Confed might already have sealed her doom.

At my expression, Sam leaned forward on the bench across from me. "I get why you're worried about her. And it's impressive that you've been able to gain her trust like that. We need those kinds of relationships if we're going to come out on top. You did good work there."

"Good work," Tonya repeated in a mutter. "Now we'll be off to Uzbekistan to deal with Lord knows what garbage. I've been almost blown up enough times this year already, thank you."

"Are they going to send *us* out there?" Joselin asked. "Isn't there a base down in Afghanistan or somewhere that'd be closer?"

"They'll probably send a squad from both here and somewhere closer to Bonded Worthy territory," Sam said. "Since we're dealing with multiple groups."

Brandt rubbed his hand over his face with a weary look. "And multiply the crossfire too. But hey, if it makes Alcido and the rest of the Dulls happy, what does anyone care about us?"

"It's our job," Sam reminded us. "And it's not as if the commanders *want* us to be in danger. We already lost Hamlin. Can you imagine how the Dull government would come down on the Confed officials if they found out we *didn't* follow up on a lead like this? They'd probably label all mages traitors and round us up."

Next to him, Leonie shuddered.

Joselin flopped back against the wall. "It isn't right that they get to call the shots."

It also wasn't right that National Defense pretty much forced us Champions to do their dirty work, but I kept my mouth shut about that, considering the guy who'd already tattled on me once was three feet away from me. I didn't exactly like having Alcido breathing down our necks either.

"There isn't a whole lot we can do about it, is there?" I said.

Tonya sucked a breath through her teeth. "We'll see about that."

My gaze jerked to her.

"What does *that* mean?" Sam said, his voice light but his eyes serious.

The other officer shook her head. "Nothing. Just saying."

But it hadn't sounded like nothing to me.

CHAPTER EIGHTEEN

Finn

I t was amazing, in a maleficent sort of way that I'd rather have never experienced, how the presence of one person in a room full of friends and allies could turn the atmosphere foreboding in an instant. The arrival of a would-be—and possibly actual—murderer in the League's midst might as well have burned out all the exhilaration I'd been feeling from the crowd around me.

Of course, nothing had changed for anyone else. To my collaborators, Callum was simply another Burnout novice joining us because of the League's newfound publicity. A moment after our eyes had met, he was swept away by a bunch of older members who appeared to be directing him toward the refreshments table. Words of good cheer continued to bounce off the high ceiling as my peers proceeded with their victory celebration.

Callum's red hair made him easy to track even in the throng. I sipped my cola, exchanged more chatter with my comrades, and finally swung around to grab myself a hamburger when the line diminished, but most of my attention was trained on that starkly crimson head. At any moment, he might comment on the Lockwood in attendance. At any moment, a ring of shocked faces might ripple out toward me from his spot in the crowd.

It wasn't even a question. It was only a matter of time.

The hamburger was perfectly charbroiled, but each bite stuck in my throat. My cheeks started to ache with the effort I was putting into my smile. I didn't hear Noemi saying my name until what must have been the third or fourth time, given the exasperation in her tone. "*Finn!*"

I jerked my gaze to her with another tight flash of a smile.

She raised an eyebrow at me. "Are you all right? You don't seem like you're all here."

Oh, I was here, just mostly on the other side of the room at the moment. I let out a chuckle I hoped was convincing. "It's been a long day. I'm wondering how the Circle will respond, what our next steps should be—it's difficult not to think ahead."

"Maybe you should get some rest before you get into all that."

Mark had ambled back over too. "It looks like people are starting to head out," he said.

Luis jumped up on a chair near the door where we could all see him. "It's been an amazing day, Freedom of Magic League!" he hollered over the din. "But we need to recuperate so we can come back even stronger. Keep your eyes open for opportunities you'd want to present to the group, and we'll see each other in a few days."

I traced Callum's path from the corner of my eye as I meandered toward the exit and managed to contrive to leave the building just ahead of him. My chest clenched around my thumping heart.

My usual policy had been to avoid the guy as much as possible. The last thing I wanted to do was speak with him. I couldn't leave him floating around in the League like a ticking time bomb, though. If there was anything for us to hash out, we'd better hash it out now, or I'd be in an even worse spot before I knew it.

As I reached the sidewalk outside the rec center, I glanced back and caught his gaze. "We might as well share a cab since we're going to nearly the same place, don't you think?"

Callum considered me warily. Then his mouth curved with a smirk. "If you're paying."

If I hadn't wanted to keep this conversation as peaceful as possible, I might have rolled my eyes. The Gearys didn't have quite the fortune the Lockwoods had amassed over the generations, but they were hardly badly off. Still, it was a reasonable gesture of goodwill.

"Simpler than splitting," I said evenly.

Most of the League members were streaming off toward the nearest public transit stops. I ambled around the corner to the busier street there and hailed the first taxi that cruised by. Callum stood a few feet away from me as we waited for it to maneuver over to the curb, his shoulders slouched and his hands shoved in the pockets of his loose jeans. The bite of the wind was turning his ear-tips nearly as red as his hair. He didn't speak.

I slid into the cab first and gave the driver Callum's address while he followed me in. For the first minute of the drive, we sat in silence. I cycled through a thousand things I could say and rejected all of them. I'd been sort of hoping he might broach the subject himself and save me the trouble of settling on an appropriate opening.

In the end, I went with a bald, "Do you think you'll come to another meeting?"

Callum turned his head toward me with one of his typical narrow looks. "I can if I want, can't I? You're not running the show."

"I wasn't trying to say you couldn't," I said quickly. "I just wondered if it met your expectations."

"It's something," Callum said, his gaze drifting away again. "Not where I expected to see *you*, that's for sure. The Academy's golden boy hanging out with a bunch of ruckus-raisers. What do they make of the fact that your granduncle is at the top of the pyramid they're trying to topple?"

I opened my mouth but hesitated for a second too long. Callum blinked at me, and understanding momentarily lit his face. "They don't know, do they? *That's* what this ride is all about. You're afraid I'm going to spill your little secret."

A flush crept up my neck. "It's common practice for everyone in the League to stay relatively anonymous."

"But everyone else there would be worried about people like your granduncle coming down on them." His lips pulled into a sneer. "Are you some kind of mole for the Circle? I *should*—"

"No!" I interrupted. "For gods' sake, I'd sooner be reporting back to Hades himself. My granduncle hasn't got a clue I'm involved with them. I want to change things just as much as everyone else there does—I just don't know if they'd give me the chance to keep helping if they found out."

Callum studied me. "I heard," he said slowly, "that you were Chosen. Like anyone would've figured you would be. Everyone says there's never been a Lockwood who wasn't. But you declared anyway."

I couldn't tell whether that possibility impressed or annoyed him. "That's true," I said. "I could have gone to the college. But I hadn't earned it. You know that—do you think I didn't?" Even if I hadn't realized quite how much my abilities had ranked below my peers' until the Exam had brought me into brutal awareness, I'd known enough. "I only wanted to go if I'd proven I belonged there."

"What a brainless decision that was, huh?" Callum said, with such bitterness my pulse skipped. Did he remember what had happened in the Exam after all—what we'd learned about the true "prize" the Champions earned?

He slumped lower in his seat. "Both of us now with nothing to show for it. I should've taken the Dampering."

Ah. He didn't remember—he simply regretted making the attempt at all. He couldn't know how close he'd come to making Champion.

He couldn't know how large a role I'd played in ensuring he hadn't. Had the examiners' magimedics managed to fully reconstruct the muscles in his thigh? The thumb I'd lost during the testing and then regained thanks to their hasty casting still twinged oddly every now and then.

I'd seen Callum a lot of ways over the years we'd been classmates: raging and sulky and brash. I'd never seen him look defeated the way he did right now. Even before the Exam, his parents had treated him like a stray dog they couldn't quite convince to leave them alone. He'd spent almost our entire Academy career at the bottom of the ranks. Somehow I doubted they'd become more supportive now that he'd returned without any magic to speak of.

"It's tough," I ventured.

"Yeah. I bet your parents are just thrilled to have a dud on their hands too, huh?"

It seemed wisest not to mention that Dad and Mom had been quite considerate about the situation. "I'd gotten used to being a disappointment," I said, which was true enough.

"Well." He sat there in uneasy silence for a few minutes. Then he said, "I don't give a monkey's ass if you want to get in on some rebellion. I don't want anything to do with you. You want a truce? I'll keep my mouth shut about your family, and you keep yours shut about any opinions you have about me. I know you've never liked me either."

That was a rather skewed observation from someone who'd gone out of his way to harass and outright injure me every chance he'd had for as long as I could recall. I could let that biased take slide, though, if he kept his side of the bargain.

"If you'd prefer, we can pretend we've never met, so there's nothing to say in the first place," I said.

The corner of Callum's mouth twitched upward. "That works for me." The cab slowed as it reached his house, and he gave me one last glance with an ironic little wave. "Here's to pretending we're not seeing each other around, neighbor."

* * *

Stepping out into the underground parking lot of my mother's office building, I couldn't help exhaling with a rush of relief into the damp, dim space. Thank Jove that day was over with.

"Well," I said as I climbed into Mom's car. "I'd have to say that was a mismatch of epic proportions. Clearly, Hugh got all the financial affinity you had to impart."

Mom gave me a wry smile. "Sorry. I wasn't sure what they'd come up with as a suitable placement."

"No harm done, as long as they're not so horrified by my inadequacies that they shun you from the business achievement gala. Perhaps I should've come in *after* the ceremony next week."

That remark won me a laugh. The BMW's engine purred as Mom eased toward the exit. The breezy floral scent of the freshening 'chantment on the car's interior tickled my nose.

"I don't think my or Hugh's standing with that organization is in any doubt," she said. "Oh, well. It was worth a try, wasn't it?"

"Absolutely. I may as well cast my net wide." It was the third potential volunteer placement I'd gone to see about, this one with Mom's investment firm. Their idea of an ideal role for a

Burnout had been to shove me into a little basement room to re-sort computer files—by myself, where no one had to see me or interact with me. After a couple of hours, I'd been ready to bash my head against the monitor. "I just need to find a path that plays to my strengths. Such as they might be."

"You have plenty of strengths, Finn," Mom said, as a mother was supposed to, but she managed to sound as if she meant it, so I'd take the compliment. "You're going into the Media division tomorrow afternoon, aren't you? That sounds like it should be a better fit."

"Can't be much worse!" I said with a grin, but the truth was today's experience had left me with a knot in my stomach. I might be making a name for myself with the League, insomuch as they knew my name, but I had to find a way to do more than ride on my family's coattails in regular mage society too. Eventually, even my parents might start to regret the leeway they were granting me.

The lump was compounded by a twist of guilt. On balance, in the last week I'd done more to actively hurt my family's reputation than to contribute to it.

"The Circle isn't blaming Dad for that holdup with the conference, is it?" I said as we pulled out into the fading autumn afternoon sunlight. "It's not as if anyone could have anticipated what happened."

Dad hadn't said much about the protest and the disruption it had caused, but he hadn't been around much since to talk about it. He'd spent the whole weekend at the conference hall and most of the past couple days going straight from work to his home office, always with a somewhat harried look.

"There are frustrations being aired, but he got the talks back on track as quickly as anyone could have," Mom said. "It'll all be sorted out. You don't need to worry about that."

She wouldn't have said that if she'd known how much of a hand I'd had in the disruption.

My phone rang, and I fished it out of my pocket. One look at the screen made my heart hiccup, all those dark thoughts retreating. I couldn't afford not to take this call, even if it wasn't the most opportune time.

"Hey," I said, willing my voice not to change too much. Mom glanced over at me anyway.

"Hey," Rocío said on the other end. "I know this isn't the usual time—things are kind of chaotic here right now. I can only talk for a minute. But I have another 'break' this weekend."

There was nothing in Tartarus that could have held back the smile that stretched across my face at hearing that news, spoken by her voice, as strong and clear as ever. "That's wonderful."

"Yeah. So. Um. You know how we were talking about family dinners a little while back? I was thinking it'd be great if you could come over Saturday evening. My parents have okayed it. They want to meet you. Actually, I think if I hadn't suggested it, they might have insisted. They're nice, really! Just, er, not used to me having a boyfriend."

I couldn't think of any conflicting plans I had for Saturday, but even if I'd been booked for dinner with the queen of England, I would have rescheduled that. "No insisting necessary. Of course I'll be there."

"All right. Good." She laughed a little nervously. "I'll text you the address that morning when I'm home. And—"

A muffled voice said something near her. "Just a second," she protested to whoever that was, and then came back to me. "Sorry. I have to go already. I— Everything's still okay with you, right?"

"I can make no complaints," I said. "As long as you keep looking after yourself. I'll see you soon."

My smile may have stretched even wider by the time I set

down the phone. I tried to tamp it down, but Mom's expression had turned amused. "Am I allowed to ask who that was?"

"A friend," I said automatically—but then, I'd all but told Dad, and the chances he hadn't mentioned that conversation to Mom were essentially nil. "A girl. You could say my girlfriend. She's getting time off from Champion work this weekend."

I wasn't sure what reaction to expect, but Mom just laughed. "Well, if she makes you look like that, then I already like her." She stepped on the brake at a stop sign, and a shadow crossed her face. "Finn, I went for a walk a few nights ago when you were out, and I saw you come back in a taxi with Callum Geary."

I managed to catch myself before I stiffened. If she'd realized what I'd been up to that day, I doubted Callum would have been the thing she focused on. "He ended up joining the group of friends I was meeting," I said. "It seemed silly to take separate cabs home when we're just down the street from each other. Why?"

"Have you gotten friendly with him?" Mom asked. "It seems to me, from what I remember you saying when you were younger—and the other impressions I've gotten since then—that he was always something of a bully."

"And no doubt he still is," I said, although I felt a weird sense I was betraying Callum saying that after he'd admitted at least a modicum of regret to me that night. It wasn't as if he hadn't still been an ass about everything else—and a near-murderer to boot, even if he couldn't recall it. "It was a coincidence. I don't plan to spend much time with him." I planned to give him as wide a berth as possible, even when we were in the same room.

Mom let out a breath. "All right. I only mentioned it because — Well, really none of the Gearys has the most positive reputation. I wouldn't want you to feel you have to rely on the company of only those mages in the same situation as you. You are still seeing some of your friends who went on to the College, aren't you?"

I'd told her and Dad that I had been, but the question made me tense up all the same. Did she have any idea how my friends who'd gone on to the College would probably feel about *me*? I couldn't imagine how many of them had resented the generosity with which our teachers at the Academy had graded me, the praise I'd gotten here and there that I hadn't deserved.

I was a symbol of failure now—a sign that even a mighty Lockwood could fall. None of my old classmates had made any attempt to catch up with me since the Exam. They were too busy moving on with their lives along with the other Chosen. I'd rather not reach out and discover precisely what lengths they might to go in order to avoid my misfortune rubbing off on them.

How could I say any of that to my mother, though? "Of course," I said, which wasn't even a lie if we went by the official story, since officially Rocío and Prisha were enrolled in the college. "And don't worry about Callum. That cab ride only confirmed how little we enjoy each other's company."

"Good," Mom said, with so much relief it prickled.

Callum was an ass and a bully, and yeah, his family had struck me as horrid too. I still wouldn't have expected Mom to outright warn me away from any fellow mage on the basis of their social standing.

For a second, I missed the glorious ignorance I'd dwelled in a few months ago. Everywhere I looked, I seemed to find new divisions within our community. How the hell was the Confed going to weather any sort of revolution without completely fracturing apart?

CHAPTER NINETEEN

Rocío

The chilly air nipped at my cheeks as I sat on the front steps outside my family's walk-up, but I stayed put. I wanted to meet Finn out here so we had a few moments, just the two of us, before we added my parents to the mix.

I scooted farther forward on the cold concrete, wishing my jacket was long enough that it'd cover my butt, and tucked my gloved hands in my pockets. Part of me missed the compact warmth of my military jacket, as if this were a mission and not me simply waiting for my boyfriend. As much as I tried to shake my newly honed instincts, I couldn't stop myself from evaluating the street with a critical eye because of all those weeks of training and fieldwork—and because of who I was meeting.

I'd always thought we had a pretty nice spot. The neighbors might not have been super friendly toward the family of mages in their midst, but the voices that carried up to our windows from the street were happy a lot more often than they were angry. People kept their yards tidy. Trees sprouted here and there, giving a little shade on summer days.

Now, my gaze caught on every tiny flaw. An empty chip bag skittering along the sidewalk in the breeze. The paint peeling around the windows of a house three doors down. The fallen leaves that had collected in the gutters and were now turning into mulch. This was Brooklyn, not the Upper East Side. Even the nicest neighborhood here wasn't going to look anything like Finn's.

He wouldn't care, I told myself, tugging my collar higher. Finn wasn't like that. But I couldn't know for sure how he'd react, could I?

I'd spent most of the last two months on missions where I risked my life, but my nerves were jumping almost as much now as then. Although I wasn't just nervous about Finn, but about things I'd learned during those missions too. The thick, gray clouds overhead bulged ominously. The threat of hostile castings had never felt quite so close to home.

The cab pulled up right on time. Finn's pale cheeks were already flushed when he hopped out, even before the cool air had a chance to touch them. He looked up at the building behind me and then met my eyes with his usual grin. "Well, I can see I made it to the right place."

His tone was light, but I knew him well enough now to see the tension in his stance even through his gray wool coat. He hesitated at the base of the steps as if he wasn't sure whether it'd be too forward for him to come right up, and I realized he was nervous too. As if we might find some flaw in him.

My own nerves faded behind a wave of affection. I stopped on the bottom step where we were about the same height and kissed him hello. Finn's hands came up to my face, but when our lips eased apart, he wrapped his arms around me in a tight hug.

"You have no idea how good it is to be able to see with my own eyes that you're still okay," he said.

"I plan on staying that way," I said, as if I'd have much choice in the matter if things got bad out in the field. But the thought of Finn waiting, worrying, between each of our brief weekly phone conversations brought a pang into my chest. Right then, I had a hard time deciding which was worse: my parents' vaguely concerned puzzlement at how restricted my time was at "college" or Finn's much more accurate fears.

"I suppose we'd better go up, before your parents give me demerits for tardiness," Finn said. "Also, you're cold."

"You're helping with that," I pointed out, and he made a sound that was amused but pleased, and by the time we made it up the steps my lips were even warmer than before.

Mom and Dad were waiting in the apartment: Mom puttering around the living room and Dad poking at the last pot involved in the dinner he'd made, both of them trying to look casual and not like they were on pins and needles to evaluate the first boy I'd ever brought home. I was pretty sure Mom had already straightened the couch pillow she was tweaking at least five times before I'd gone down.

"You must be Finn," she said, hustling over as I shut the door behind us. "It's wonderful to meet you. Let me get your coat."

"Oh, thank you." He shrugged it off and let her take it from him to hang up. His gaze took in the apartment, a soft smile crossing his face. It wasn't much to look at—an L of a couch and love seat around a little flat-screen TV, our four-person dining table at the other end of the room by the open kitchen. A rich, peppery smell wafted from that direction. The table was done up with a lacy tablecloth and brightly patterned serving dishes I didn't think I'd seen since Mom and Dad's twentieth wedding anniversary, but I doubted they were any nicer than whatever Finn was used to on a daily basis. Finn looked nothing but happy to be here, though.

"It's great to meet both of you too," he said. "You've got a lovely home. And whatever you're cooking smells *amazing*." He tipped his head to my dad, peering at the pot.

He couldn't have picked a faster way to win my dad over.

Dad beamed and motioned with his spoon for us to head to the table. "It's just about ready—and best to eat it while it's hot. I cook to a lot of different tastes, but I thought for a special dinner like this, I might as well go traditional. These frijoles rancheros is based on a recipe of my father's, from Mexico. The tamales, well, that's just genetic."

He shot me a wink, and I gave him a pointed look in return. Sticking a bunch of authentic Mexican food in front of my one-hundred-percent gringo boyfriend was totally Dad's little test.

Dad brought over the serving bowl with his special blend of beans, pork, and peppers, and Mom started doling out the tamales. Dad *had* outdone himself. The steam rising off the food had the perfect mix of savory and spicy, leaving my mouth watering even though my nerves were still twitching around my stomach.

When we sat, Mom bowed her head to say a quick grace, which I guessed was her version of a test, since normally we just dug in. Finn waited quietly until I picked up my fork before doing the same.

"Wow," he said to Dad after a couple bites. "That has a good kick. My compliments to you and your father."

Dad looked like he was about to start preening. I figured I might as well throw in a little extra buttering up. "Dad's affinity is for food," I said. "You'll never get anything from a Dull chef like that."

"It's fantastic." Finn closed his eyes with a blissful expression as he chewed his first mouthful of Dad's famous rice, and then glanced over at him again. "Do you cook for a living? I have to think any restaurant serving food like this would have people lined up around the block."

Dad's mouth tightened slightly. "The legislation around the use of magic in food preparation makes that kind of work difficult to come by," he said. "Not many managers want to go through the hassle. And opening your own restaurant is quite a risk. If I'm ever in a position to do so, that's definitely the dream."

Finn hesitated for a second, as if he wasn't sure how to respond. I let my knee brush his under the table in an effort to reassure him.

"I hope you get there," he said in a more serious tone. "It's a shame more people aren't getting to experience this."

"What sort of work do your parents do?" Dad asked.

"Well, my father, er, heads the Confed's International Relations division," Finn said. "And my mother is with an investment firm that caters mostly to mage clients. Possibly that talent is genetic, because my older brother went a similar route."

"You just have the one sibling?"

"Oh, no, there's my sister Margo—also older—who I suppose takes after my dad. She's all tied up in politics too, just on the nonmagical side. She's assistant to the Director of the Joint Staff. I gather they do something important with military advising or some such." His gaze twitched at that last comment, as if he'd restrained himself from looking to me at the thought of the military.

"How are you occupying yourself these days?" Mom said gently. "I understand you're not at the college."

"Difficult to miss that, isn't it?" Finn said with a wry chuckle, gesturing with his fork toward his Burnout mark. "I have to admit I'm still sorting out my future plans. It's been… an interesting transition. But I've been looking into possible placements that could lead to a career down the line. I had quite a promising visit with a branch of the Confed's Media division a couple of days ago. It seems there are rather a lot of Dull news sources that want to cover Confederation-related news but aren't entirely comfortable talking to an actual mage."

"You're still a mage," I said automatically.

He gave me a fond smile. "Not in the ways that count to them. If being burned out can give me an advantage somewhere, I might as well make use of that."

"It's admirable that you had the conviction to attempt the Exam, even if it didn't work out in your favor," Mom said, and the last bit of tension left Finn's posture.

"As proud as we are of Rocío, we wish her new schedule as Champion wasn't so strict," Dad put in. "Or has she managed to find more time to see her boyfriend than her parents?" A teasing glint lit in his eyes.

Finn matched his tone. "If she had, I think I'd be duty-bound to deny it." He grinned at me, but his high spirits faded a moment later. "Sadly, that's not the case. They do keep her awfully busy, don't they? I take what I can get."

My throat tightened. "Okay, okay," I said with forced cheer. "You'd all like to see me more. I get it. I don't decide the rules of the Champion program. New subject, please!"

Finn laughed and commented on a Christmas display he'd noticed on his ride in. Mom told a story about the kids' pageant she'd just finished making the costumes for, and Dad asked Finn about his family's holiday meal traditions. For several minutes, we ate and chatted as if it really were a totally normal family dinner.

I wished I could get completely wrapped up in that normalcy. Let it wash away all thought of anything beyond these walls. But I couldn't forget the main reason I'd pushed for this get-together to happen now.

When we'd plowed through the food, and the conversation trailed off for a moment, I leaned forward.

"I'm really glad we did this," I said. "Especially because—I wanted you all to know each other. In case anything happens that I'm not around for. You're the most important people in the world to me, and I hope you'll help each other if any of you needs it."

Mom's face fell. "What are you talking about, Rocío? Why would you be thinking about that?"

My hands twisted together under the table, echoing the tangle of all the things I couldn't say. The vague threat from that senior official. The plot we were unraveling overseas way too slowly.

I wasn't totally convinced I'd be able to fix what we were up against, but I could make sure the people I cared about could turn to each other, at least. It was the only other way I could think of to protect them.

"I just... I've been hearing a lot at the college about international tensions," I said. "It seems like things have been getting worse, so it's hard not to worry."

"I don't think you have anything to worry about, mija," Dad said, so calmly, despite his confused expression, that I could have cried. If he had any idea what I'd been dragged into, he wouldn't have sounded that sure. "But of course, if there's ever a situation where Finn needs help we can offer, we'd be happy to do whatever we can."

Finn didn't need to ask what I meant. His mouth had slanted at a crooked angle. He reached out to me under the table and squeezed the hand I offered him. "And the same for me." He glanced at my parents. "If you're ever in any trouble, don't hesitate to reach out."

Mom and Dad still looked bewildered. Sam's words popped into my head—his comments about all the baggage that came with our work, the way it pushed you apart from the people back home. It happened so quickly.

I scrambled to recover the conversation. "Okay. Thank you. It might sound silly, but it means a lot to me to hear that."

"It's not silly to want to look after the people who matter to you, cariño," Mom said.

I got up to clear the dishes, and Finn leapt to help, which probably earned him about ten more points in an instant. When I moved to start filling the sink with water, Dad made a shooing motion.

"You only have a few days off, and you're working hard enough the rest of the time. I made the mess; I can take care of it." A little of his previous good humor came back into his voice.

I stepped back. Mom and Dad would probably be weird if Finn and I went into my bedroom, and besides, other than the cramped bunk bed, the only decent seating was the chair at my desk. But I did want to have a little more time alone with him. After having my last visit cut short, I wasn't going to take even one minute for granted.

"Why don't we go for a little walk before the evening gets any colder," I said to Finn. "There's a park near here that's pretty even at this time of year."

"Sure," Finn said, while Mom shot me a knowing look. But she didn't raise any protest, especially after he thanked her and Dad again for their hospitality. I wasn't sure anymore why I'd been nervous. If Finn was good at anything, it was endearing himself to people. He'd worked his way into my heart despite my best efforts at keeping up my walls, hadn't he?

The early December breeze licked over our hair as I led the way to the park. Streetlamps gleamed along the paths between the bare trees. I spotted a free bench near the entrance and nabbed it, scooting close to Finn the second he sat down. He slung his arm around my shoulders, and I nestled my head against the crook of his neck, not minding the faint itch of the wool of his coat. It just made his presence even more real.

"I got the impression that went well," Finn said. "Although, admittedly, I have only a small amount of meeting-the-parents experience to compare it to."

"It was good," I said. "I think they liked you. I'm sure I'll get the full report after you head home."

"They didn't seem bothered about…" He gestured to his mark.

Had he been worried about that? I traced my thumb over the back of his hand. "They wouldn't be. They know how the Confed works—they know the system isn't fair."

He was quiet for a moment, and I thought he might say, like he had before, that in his case the judgment had been fair, that he hadn't done enough or *been* enough. I braced myself to argue. Instead he tugged me closer and said, "Is there really something coming that we need to be afraid of?"

I opened my mouth and closed it again, struggling to find the right words—words that I could actually say. "I don't know. I just feel better now that you know them and they know you. Just in case."

He nodded. "If things get bad, will you be able to say so over the phone, or are they keeping too close an eye on you?"

"I'm sure they monitor those conversations." But I'd been pondering that problem too. "I think, if there were something really important I needed to tell you that they wouldn't want me to, I have a casting that would shield the conversation. If I did that a lot, they might catch on, though, so otherwise we'll still have to be careful." I paused. "Maybe we should come up with some way for you to signal that you need to tell *me* something they shouldn't know."

"Like a secret code word?" Finn said with a grin.

"Don't laugh," I said. "I'm serious."

"I know." He rubbed my arm. "Something natural sounding, but specific enough that I wouldn't say it by accident—and nothing to do with the Exam or your real job... Ah. I'll say I've been thinking about the dragon you conjured on the Day of Letters."

"Perfect." My embrace tightened around him. "Let's hope you never need to use that code."

"In pace ut sapiens aptarit idonea bello," he said in lilting Latin that sounded almost like a casting. "During the good times you're wise to prepare for the worst." I heard him swallow as he tipped his head next to mine. "I'd rather *you* never needed to face the worst. How long do you have until your 'break' is over?"

"A couple days." I didn't want to think about that. "Let's focus on enjoying the time we have."

His smile came back, a shade mischievous. "What did you have in mind?"

I made a face at him that lasted all of two seconds and then tipped my head for a kiss. For a little while, the warmth we created between us seemed to ward off every distant danger.

CHAPTER TWENTY

Finn

How did you judge a lifetime of friendship against one act of betrayal, especially when you couldn't even talk about the circumstances of it? I still hadn't figured that out. The best strategy I'd found for coping with the revelations about my best friend during the Exam was to pretend her indiscretion had never happened.

"Is it weird that I love the Christmas displays even though my family doesn't celebrate?" Prisha said as we strolled along Fifth Avenue. A jangling melody carried from a doorway we passed before the brisk morning breeze whisked it away.

"What's not to love?" I said cheerfully. "The garish colors? The incessantly repetitive music? The crass consumerism?"

She wrinkled her nose. "Now you're making fun of me."

"Would I do that?" I asked her, but the truth was, my teasing felt a little stiff to me, so perhaps it wasn't coming across as fond as I'd meant it to.

The *full* truth was, Prisha had gone into the Exam as a spy for the examiners and had hidden that from me until I'd stumbled on proof. She might very well be responsible for the faint scars the magimedics hadn't managed to erase from Mark's skin, and for the screams of the girl whose name I might never get back, who'd probably died in those horrible vines.

The truth was also that, in the finale, when it had mattered, she'd stood by me and helped Rocío and me put an end to the violence the best way she could.

I might pretend it hadn't happened, but I couldn't forget any of it, even if my memories of that time were hazy thanks to the examiners' attempt to erase them.

I wasn't even sure I'd rather Prisha hadn't taken their deal. Her other options had been Dampering or, once she'd made the initial commitment, burning out. The Exam's overlords might very well have arranged *her* death to ensure she could never tell anyone about their treachery.

Most of all, I wanted to believe that all the years before then, when we'd stood by each other and had each other's backs, counted for something.

"Ah, I like Christmas too," I said, peering through one brightly lit store window. "Although I think I'd like it better if it started in December. When you're hearing carols since the second Halloween is over, by the time you get to the right month, it's not that special."

"True," Prisha said. She tugged her fluffy scarf up to her ears. It was difficult to read the effects of the cold on her brown skin, but I thought she was getting a little pink. "What do you say we duck inside somewhere and grab a hot chocolate?"

"I'd say I'm easily persuaded by warmth and sweet beverages."

We found a little table in the back of a café on the corner. Prisha leaned over her mug and inhaled the steam as if she were planning to drink the cocoa through osmosis. A dreamy smile came over her face.

"It's so pathetic. I get… I get on break and all I want to do is *eat* all the things I haven't had in weeks."

"Champions don't get a very extensive menu in the college cafeteria?" I asked, my tone turning wry. We could talk about what she'd been doing as long as we followed the official story—and didn't get too close to any real details.

"Not much in the way of desserts, anyway," Prisha said. "You wouldn't think that's the sort of thing you'd fixate on, with the kind of work… and everything going on, but, well, maybe I'm just frivolous."

That last comment sounded more serious than the mood we'd been keeping up. That, and the thought of the "everything" she and Rocío and the rest of the Champions went through every time they headed back overseas, hit me like a jab in the gut.

"No, you're not," I said. "Food is comforting. Why wouldn't you think about that when you're off doing what you're doing?"

She shrugged, but she let herself drift back into the worship of her hot chocolate. She'd arrived for her "break" the day after Rocío had departed and tomorrow was heading back to wherever they were stationed.

For what might have been the hundredth time in a week, I found myself designing wild schemes to whisk them away where National Defense's special ops unit could never find them. None of those schemes had stood up to reality so far.

"How has your family been handling your absences?" I said instead.

Prisha made a sour face. "Daksh is still angling for my room. Technically, I suppose he should have it. I have no idea what sort of salary is in my future. My parents are just happy I apparently won some prestigious position, and they certainly wouldn't want to jeopardize that by fussing about my time away from home."

For the Mathurs, the family business came before any other priority. Prisha's parents assigned the best bedrooms in their brownstone to her and her older siblings based on who'd contributed the most in any given year. With the rest of the family Dull, magic had made Prisha special there. She hadn't known what kind of a place she could make for herself without it.

That sense of never quite fitting in had been part of what cemented our friendship. It was also at least half of the reason she'd taken the examiners' offer.

Something Callum had said swam up in my mind. I hesitated and then asked, "Would you do it again?"

Prisha's gaze jerked back to me. She frowned. "Do what?"

"The Exam," I said. "If you could go back, before you had to make any decision, but knowing how it would turn out—would you still declare? Or would you have gone for Dampering?"

She cocked her head as she considered the question. "You know, I've wondered that a few times. I don't even know. I'm not happy being Champion, but I wouldn't have been happy Dampered either, so…" Her voice dropped. "I'd have pushed back harder. Negotiated better. I went along too easily. You have to know I never—the things that happened—I had no idea, and I wouldn't ever have wanted—"

I touched her arm before she had to stumble on any further. A lump had risen in my throat. This was the only time she had at home, away from the wars she'd been roped into fighting. I'd meant for this to be a more upbeat visit than it was turning into.

"I know," I said. "I'm not angry anymore, in case that wasn't already clear. I have a lot of different feelings, but more than anything I'm glad we got through in one piece. You're still my best friend, Pree."

"Okay," she said, with a small smile. She shifted her arm so she could grip my hand for a second. "You've never stopped being mine. It means a lot that you've been able to at least sort of understand. I was worried… Well." She shook her head, but I could imagine what she might have said. She'd expressed some of those doubts when we'd talked in the Exam, about how I might react to the choice she made.

As much as we could relate to each other when it came to failure to meet outside expectations, my old-magic insider life had been so different from hers that I could hardly imagine what that situation had been like for her. She might as well have been stuck between Scylla and Charybdis while I'd never even needed to enter the sea. In that way, I couldn't judge at all.

Prisha gulped more hot chocolate, and her smile dipped. "It'd be nice if we had more time to enjoy the fact that we're okay, wouldn't it?"

"We'll make the best of what we do have," I said. "What else is there to do?"

After we'd finished our drinks, we wandered around one of the bustling department stores. I bought a cashmere scarf in Mom's favorite color for her Christmas present, and Prisha gifted herself with a new pair of lambskin gloves. A girl with a wavy black ponytail ambled by. My pulse skipped for a second before my double take confirmed that of course it wasn't Rocío. Most likely she was an ocean away from me by now.

Prisha followed my gaze. She'd always been able to read me like a book.

"You and Rocío are still… a thing, right?" she said as we headed out onto the street.

"Yes," I said, perhaps a little sharply. My hand slipped into my pocket instinctively as if to confirm my keychain was still there. I ran my finger over the dragon's tiny polished scales.

Prisha hadn't quite approved of my growing feelings for Rocío. Not out of jealousy or anything that petty—Pree was solely interested in girls, herself, when it came to romance—but because she'd known the examiners had an especially close eye on

Rocío, and she'd worried I'd get caught up in any punishment they rained down on her.

If Rocío hadn't been so careful, it might even have been Prisha calling down that punishment.

My best friend scuffed her boot against the sidewalk. "She's —well, I guess I can admit at this point that she's really something. I just hope she doesn't do anything too stupid while she's making her stand."

I hadn't told Prisha about the stands I'd been taking. Possibly because I had the sneaking suspicion she wouldn't approve of the League either. She'd call my involvement with them putting myself too close to the line of fire.

As if I'd be anywhere near as close as she and Rocío must on a near-daily basis.

"You'll watch out for her as much as you can, won't you?" I said. "I know she'll do the same for you."

"More because she knows you'd be sad if anything happened to me than because she likes me so much," Prisha said, without any bitterness. "Yeah. I'll keep an eye out for her—for you." She bumped her elbow against mine.

"I don't suppose you've had time to chase after any girls at 'college'?" I asked, arching my eyebrows.

She grinned. "The pickings are a little slim in my 'classes.' But I am hitting the clubs tonight. Making the most of the time I have, like you said."

Prisha was supposed to meet her grandparents for lunch, so we parted ways a short time later. I'd only walked past a few more stores when footsteps thumped behind me. I looked up to see a familiar blue mohawk.

"Hey," Mark said. "I saw you walking by. Out Christmas shopping too?" He held up a Macy's bag. "I figured I'd better get something good for my aunt to thank her for putting up with me so long."

"'Tis the season," I said with a smile, trying to ignore the prickle that had shot up my spine. It wasn't as if Pree would have revealed anything I didn't want shared, but it was still a tad unnerving to find myself face-to-face with a fellow League member on my usual turf.

As if he'd sensed my apprehension, Mark glanced the way Prisha had gone. "Who was that girl you were with? She looked like a total old-magic Academy type." The last words came with a note of derision. He didn't remember Prisha from our team in the Exam, of course.

"*I* went to the Academy," I reminded him. "I still keep in touch with some of my old friends." I did with that one, anyway.

His gaze rose to my Burnout mark, and his mouth twisted. "From what I hear, you're lucky they still consider themselves your friends. I guess *you* can win just about anyone over." He paused. "What do you make of this new plan of Ary's?"

I stopped dead in my tracks and turned toward him. "What new plan?" She hadn't pitched any ideas at our last meeting. I definitely hadn't been looped into any conversations about some new protest action.

"There's a mage business ceremony, some big annual thing, at a historic building over there." Mark waved his hand vaguely to the east. "Tomorrow morning. Ary's got a Dampered guy with her who's going to mess with the building. I think she's hoping to crush a few people."

My stomach flipped over. "The Recognition of Mages in Business ceremony?"

"Yeah, that sounds right."

Callum, I thought instinctively. The ceremony Mark was talking about was the one my mother and Hugh had been named for. Mom had gotten the honor every year for two decades straight—Callum would know that. He must have pointed Ary to the event. After his talk about a truce, he'd found a way to screw me over the first chance he'd gotten.

"When is Ary going to set it up?" I asked.

"They're out there now," Mark said. "That's how I know. I saw them—overheard them talking—I assumed she must have at least taken it up with Luis."

I wouldn't count on that—and I didn't care if she'd taken the matter up with Zeus himself. Half of my immediate family was going to be at that building tomorrow.

"I've got to go," I said, spinning on my heel, and dashed off toward the ceremony building before Mark could say another word.

CHAPTER TWENTY-ONE

Rocío

The old man outside the clothing shop gave me a sour look as he muttered something in Uzbek to my translator. The other guy turned to me, his tone apologetic. "He says he has no idea about any of this."

"All right," I said. "That's fine." I bobbed my head to the man. "Thank you for answering my questions."

Not that he really had. So far everyone we'd talked to in this strip of Qarshi had been wary and tight-lipped. I couldn't really blame them, though. *I* didn't love going up to the locals and badgering them when they were just going about their business in this little shopping area.

A couple times, I didn't think their hesitation had been only about me. I'd seen gazes dart to bits of paint on a wall or a telephone pole. The Bonded Worthy had left their mark—a red sigil designed with stylized script that I knew from our special ops training said, *Prove you are worthy.* They changed the writing to fit the dominant language of each country they branched out into, just like they adapted their call to arms to the culture of every small terrorist group they absorbed, but the design was always recognizable.

The BOW, as they liked to shorten their English name, had a habit of brutally murdering those they considered *un*worthy. Even if one of the locals had seen something and wanted the militants stopped, would they take that risk with a bunch of foreigners?

With each frown and tensed stance as I approached, I wondered what right we even had to be here as representatives of the Confed. To blend in, we'd dressed in civilian clothes rather than our usual uniforms, but anyone could tell where I was from as soon as I opened my mouth. One of our targets had been spotted on this street yesterday. We were hoping one of the storekeepers or their regular customers might give us a lead.

A consultant from the Uzbekistan government had joined our briefing this morning, along with representatives from Iran and Thailand, two of the countries with the most experience tackling the various groups that had merged into the Bonded Worthy. All three had talked about the value of our support in rooting out the terrorists, but at the same time, the Uzbek consultant had given off an uneasy vibe that had sent the magic twitching against my skin.

If he and his colleagues really wanted us to go home and let them take care of their own, would they have felt comfortable saying that?

"Hey!" With a wave, Sam called the translator over to where he'd been exchanging a few basic formalities with a couple of younger locals. I wandered toward them with another scan of the street. A thick, tangy smell drifted from a street food stand where meat was sizzling on a grill. All around me, people chattering or calling out in a language I wasn't even passingly familiar with.

In Estonia, I'd made some headway. I'd connected with

people like Polina at least a little. Here, despite the time I'd spent talking to people, I still felt completely out of place.

And in the week since we'd gotten Polina's tip, we hadn't managed to catch the meeting she'd told us about. With each day we didn't turn up any new information, the threat loomed larger over me, made up of too many pieces I couldn't control.

No. Thinking that way wasn't going to get me anywhere. I paused by the food stand and took a moment to simply breathe.

The haze overhead made the buildings around me look as gray as the sky, but it was nice to be out during the day for once anyway. This was the first time in a month I'd been outside and not cold. I soaked in the atmosphere, shoring up my confidence.

I could do this. International politics aside, we were all in trouble if the negotiating insurgent groups launched a joint magical attack on the scale they seemed to be planning. I didn't know how it might affect the magic if we didn't stop them... so we just had to stop them.

I *had* managed to connect with locals in Estonia. Maybe if I could offer to help someone here, to show my intentions were good...

A woman was limping along on the other side of the street. I was about to go to her when Desmond's voice leapt from my earpiece.

"I'm seeing some strange activity here. It looks like there's a bunch of people heading toward the chopper, using magic to conceal themselves... I've got a bad feeling about this."

I caught Sam's eye between the passersby. He motioned to me and the other two operatives in our squad, pressing the button on his mic with his other hand. "We're heading back. Keep me updated and initiate defensive strategies."

"Already on it," Desmond said.

The four of us hustled through the streets toward the vacant lot where we'd touched down. Desmond and our pilot had cast a concealing 'chantment and a conjured shield around the helicopter. No one should've noticed it—unless they'd been seeking it out by magic. If they had it shouldn't have been an easy target.

Any insurgents still active in the area might have noticed us asking questions today or on an earlier intel-gathering mission and been on the lookout for our arrival. How worried were they that we'd tracked their movements all the way here? How far would they go to strike back? My stomach balled as I picked up my pace to come up beside Sam.

We rounded the corner to the lot—and a blaze of magical fire seared across the dimpled asphalt toward the helicopter.

Desmond's shout blared through my earpiece. The magic jerked and clenched around me as I bolted forward with the squad. Several figures shimmered into view around the chopper, a few of them wearing the ghostly masks of the Borci, a couple with blood-red cloth tied across their faces—members of the Bonded Worthy. More magic warbled across the shield our colleagues inside would be reinforcing. For now, it held.

Sam snapped out a casting that bowled over two of the attackers. Brandt, at his other side, roared a lyric that sent a blast straight into one guy's head, cracking it open with a burst of blood.

The magic yanked at my scalp back and forth as erratic as the thud of my pulse. The first words I summoned caught a woman insurgent across the back of her knees. As she stumbled, I hurled one of my conjured vices at her. It slammed her into the ground face-first.

We had to try to capture at least one of them. Not just for the sake of the magic, but because they might have information we needed to stop whatever their groups had planned. But the energy in the air flailed around me with each new attack. It gripped hold of my chest, squeezing so tightly that for a second I couldn't breathe. My vision swam.

Give me space. I can't think—can't do anything—when you're grabbing at me like that.

I sucked in air, groping for another lyric. Didn't the magic see? If I screwed up, if I made one misstep and lost whatever support Sam and the others had already given me, who else was there who could fight for it?

In that moment, as I caught my balance, the two remaining insurgents turned and darted away. One of them yelled a final casting over his shoulder with a jab of his hand behind him. A pulsing spear of light shot straight through the shield, piercing it like a needle, and tossed Desmond back from where he'd been perched by the doorway.

"Desmond!" I threw myself toward the chopper, dodging a sprawled body. The pilot had scrambled around to help. Desmond sprawled across the floor of the helicopter, a bruise blooming so starkly purple it showed against the dark skin of his forehead. His body shuddered and clenched.

"Go!" Sam shouted to the pilot. "Get us out of here, back to the base. Tell the magimedics to be ready." He crouched over Desmond, murmuring a verse he was forming into a first aid 'chantment.

I knelt across from him, grasping my friend's hand—not that Desmond looked like he could feel that contact right now. A lyric spilled from my lips to test his breathing, his heart, even though Sam was no doubt already doing the same. I had to offer something.

Desmond's pulse thumped rapidly but steadily. Other than a slight hitch in his breath, that seemed fine too. But the magic around us shuddered like he had, as if still pained.

His magic. The bruise was forming right on the same spot

where Finn's Burnout mark was. On an impulse, I sang a lyric under my breath to reach my awareness toward that spot.

The threads of my casting slipped over Desmond's head. My body went rigid.

Nothing resonated inside his skull in reply. The place in his brain where he should have hearkened the magic was seared through, as dulled as in any Burnout.

* * *

The magic still hadn't settled. After I'd choked down some breakfast, I paced along the dingy hall that held our dorms, the cafeteria, and the training rooms while the energy in the air quaked against my skin. I could almost taste its agitation, a faintly burnt flavor on my tongue.

We hadn't gotten any word about Desmond since we'd made it back to the base yesterday evening. Other than a brief and restless sleep, I couldn't say I'd been able to relax any more than the magic could.

Commander Revett strode out of one of the rooms farther down the hall. She hesitated when she saw me, with a purse of her lips that might have been sympathetic or just irritated.

The magic rippled across the space between us. I could've sworn I saw it outright tug at the hem of her pant leg.

"Did you feel that?" I said, stopping dead.

Revett's mouth dipped into a frown. "Feel what, Lopez?"

No, she couldn't hearken it. I didn't know how much I was helped by my natural talent, by all the time I'd spent building my awareness of the magic, or by the way it was making a special effort to reach out to me, but no one else here had even half the sense I did that something was wrong.

Right now, the thought of even trying to explain it, trying to convince her, made me feel like curling up in a ball. "Never mind," I said, shaking my head.

"You look like you need to go back to bed," she said, her voice brisk. "Running yourself ragged doesn't help Powell, you know."

Sam was already out on another mission with Tonya, Brandt, and a couple of the others. I didn't know if that was how the senior officials had already scheduled us or if they'd decided I'd be too distracted to operate in the field.

"I know," I said. "Okay."

I made myself walk back to my dorm room. Flopping on my bed didn't make me feel any less wound up. I pulled my blanket over me and buried my head in my pillow, but after a few minutes, I pushed myself back upright. At least when I was moving around, I could distance myself from a few of my worries.

As I stood up, Prisha came in, dressed in jeans and a loose silk blouse. I blinked at her for a second before remembering she must be just returning from her leave.

She looked me over, and her mouth slanted. "How are you doing?" she said. "They told me what happened as soon as I got in."

"*I'm* fine," I said. "It's Desmond who's in trouble. The magimedics haven't updated us on how he's doing since we got here."

Prisha made a face. "Open communication doesn't seem to be a priority here, does it?"

"That doesn't mean I have to like it." I paced to the other end of the room and back. Prisha was blocking the doorway. She folded her arms over her chest.

"The magimedics *are* working on him," she said. "They patched me up fine after that assault on the base. It doesn't sound like he was hit very hard."

"You weren't there," I muttered. She didn't know how he'd been hit. I wasn't sure anyone except the magimedics would've realized what the conjured bolt had done to him, but I didn't feel like revealing my knack for judging other people's hearkening ability. Prisha had told the examiners things—who was to say she wouldn't tell the commanders things too, if she thought it would earn her points with them?

"Maybe not," she said, "but I know you well enough to be certain you did everything you could to help him."

"That doesn't do him any good if he's still injured," I said. Without his magic, Desmond would lose even more than the rest of us would. Not just all the usual castings, but the techniques he'd developed to augment his limited sight. Plenty of nonmagical people were legally blind and got by just fine, but they'd found nonmagical ways to adapt. Desmond would have to start over from scratch.

"Rocío," Prisha said, and then sighed. "Would you sit down for a second?"

My shoulders tensed, but the urgency in her voice got through to me. I dropped onto the edge of the bed, clamping my hands together in front of me to stop them from fidgeting.

"What?" I said.

Prisha sank onto her bed across from me. She looked at her own hands and then at me. "I don't know how much Finn told you about what happened during the Exam. About... the role I was playing."

"He hasn't really told me anything," I said. "I mean, he can't now, right? And before—" While we were in the Exam, he'd been grappling with whatever it was Prisha had done, unsure how much it'd be fair to say about his friend, I guessed. "He didn't want to throw you under the bus," I said. "And I didn't push him about it. But I could figure out some from the way you two talked in front of me."

"Okay," she said, her stance relaxing a little. "Well, I can't talk about it either. But if you've got the gist of it... My point is just that what I'm about to say, I'm in a position to know. Because there's not a single thing Finn could have done to change the choices I made, no matter how much he'd have wanted to."

She leaned toward me, her dark eyes intent as she held my gaze. "You can't control everything, no matter how much you care about people. They're going to do what they're going to do, and things will happen to them that you don't like, and you can't let yourself feel responsible for any of that."

I knit my brow. "What are you talking about?"

"You really—" She shook her head with a short laugh. "We've been working together for three months now. We were— in the Exam—" She let that forbidden topic die. "You're *always* trying to look out for everyone, to make sure no one gets hurt, no one goes in the wrong direction. It's going to wear you down. It already is, from the looks of things."

I couldn't help bristling a little. "So, you're saying I should just not care and look the other way?" She had no idea—all the people, all the things depending on me...

"No." Prisha combed her fingers through her sleek hair. "I'm sorry; I'm making a hash of this. All I mean is that people who stretch themselves too far end up making mistakes. Okay? Not just in situations like this. I've seen it in my family's business dealings, I've seen it at the Academy... If you want to keep your own head above water, you've got to focus on what you can control and do the best you can with that. When something happens or someone does something that's not in your plan? You have to roll with it, or you'll end up getting bowled over. You can't help anyone if you drown."

What she was saying clashed with everything I wanted to

believe. I leaned back against the wall, closing my eyes for a second, wishing it didn't also make a certain kind of sense.

The thing was, if I didn't keep going like I was, if I didn't keep hoping and fighting every way I could, I might get bowled over by this situation anyway. We all might.

"Why are you telling me all this?" I asked after a minute, with honest curiosity.

"Well, we *have* been working together for a while now. I figure it might not be a bad thing to watch out for each other a little more. Feel free to give me a kick in the arse if you ever think I'm missing something important."

Before I could decide how to respond to that comment, the door burst open. "Desmond's out!" Leonie said. "He's okay."

I scrambled to my feet, and the three of us hurried toward the medical rooms. Prisha's posh civilian shoes clattered against the tiled floor twice as loud as my and Leonie's sneakers.

Desmond was just emerging from one of the doorways, a magimedic walking beside him but not supporting him. His steps looked steady, his expression unpained. But that wasn't what I was really worried about.

"Hey," I said as Leonie grabbed his hand and squeezed it. "It's good to see you up."

"They say there's no permanent damage," he said with a grin. "I guess waking up as RoboCop was a little too much to hope for."

I hesitated. "So, everything is fine? You can—you can cast like usual and everything?"

His eyebrows rose, but he murmured a quick line and wiggled the fingers of his free hand. A ball of light formed between them in an instant. "I appear to be fully functional," he said.

"Operative Powell was stunned by the magical blow and took some superficial damage, but with rest, he shouldn't see any lingering ill effects," the magimedic said. She patted his shoulder and ducked back into her workroom.

I stared after her for a few seconds before turning to follow the others down the hall, my thoughts whirling.

Desmond *had* been burned out, or close to it. I'd hearkened the void so clearly. And the magimedics obviously wouldn't have needed to keep him overnight just to heal some "superficial" damage.

The woman might not have wanted to reveal it, but they'd restored his connection to the magic somehow. It was possible.

I'd been hoping I'd find a way to heal what the examiners had done to Finn. Apparently someone right here on this base knew what it was. A way to bring back the magic to him... and to everyone else who'd ever been Dampered or burned out.

CHAPTER TWENTY-TWO

Finn

The Christmas rush was definitely not an ideal time for a race to prevent an impending catastrophe.

I dodged shopping bags and parcels, weaving along the crowded streets. Someone muttered a snarky remark as I squeezed past a group of friends. I couldn't say I really cared about politeness in that moment.

Threatening my father's work reputation was one thing. Ary might get Mom and Hugh *killed*.

Finally, I reached a side street that wasn't entirely packed. I dashed down it, trying to remember the exact location of the building where the Recognition of Mages in Business ceremony was usually held. I'd gone to the gala once when it was Hugh's first time getting a nod. They always put it on in the same place: a historic office building that still housed a few prominent mage-led companies on its upper floors, not far from the college. Mom's voice rose up in my head, a stray comment from a year or two ago: *The little dessert shop tucked around the back has the best crème brûlée I've ever tasted.*

I stopped at an intersection, made a quick calculation, and headed right. A few blocks later, I swerved left—and spotted the stone face of the building, its arch protruding over wide front steps where the recognized mages always gathered to have their photo taken.

No one was nearby except for a couple of pedestrians wandering along. I jogged over, scanning the tall limestone and brick office-fronts around it. A sugary smell tickled my nose— from that dessert shop Mom loved, I supposed. Another time, I might have followed my senses to it.

Mark had said he'd bumped into Ary and her friends. Had they finished the job and left already?

Then Ary's impassioned voice reached me from the other side of the building, where a driveway led to the parking lot. "We need it almost but not quite there. Just enough that it'll need one more quick nudge at the right time tomorrow. If it falls too early, we get nothing."

I slowed down just enough to gather my composure, the cold air stinging my throat, and strode around the side of the building.

Ary's head jerked up at my footsteps. Most of her head was covered by a playful-looking pink hat with a pom-pom on top, but the twee attire didn't diminish her hard stare when she saw me. A few other Burnouts I recognized from the group that usually gathered around her at the meetings stood beside her, along with a guy who looked only vaguely familiar.

There was no sign of Callum, but that didn't mean he wasn't involved. It'd have been easy enough for him to point Ary in the right direction and then pull back so he didn't look guilty. I could start with her.

"Sorry I'm late," I said, tossing out the first decent-sounding remark that popped into my head. I'd been so focused on getting here swiftly that I hadn't thought of how I'd handle the situation once I arrived. "I wouldn't want to miss out on what's clearly a vital mission for the League."

"Why don't you piss off, Academy boy?" Ary said. "This has nothing to do with you."

Her voice was so caustic it gave me pause. She was full-out glaring at me now. I knew she wasn't fond of me, but I'd always thought it was simply because I'd interfered with her ideas for the League. Now, I was struck by the understanding that she *loathed* me. I supposed she didn't see any need to feign interest in cooperating when we had no one but her friends as witness.

"Funny," I said, managing to keep up the same glib tone as before. "I was under the impression that we were deciding League activities by group consensus. Where's Luis? Tamara? If you haven't had a chance to let them weigh in, I'd be happy to give them a call."

I reached into my pocket. The guy I suspected was Ary's boyfriend—stout and muscular, with a white-blond sheen on his head—took a menacing step forward.

Ary rolled her eyes. "You don't have a clue what we're even doing, do you? I don't know who tipped you off, but this isn't League business. It's *my* business. It will be good for the whole League when we're done here, though."

I crossed my arms. "Why don't you tell me what you're doing, then? Convince me it's a good thing."

"She doesn't have to convince you of *squat*," her boyfriend said, but I kept my gaze on Ary. She had to know that if she didn't convince me, I'd be talking to Luis in a moment. Her pinched expression told me she'd come up with this plan without his approval. No matter what she said, she'd want to be able to call on the League's manpower and resources later. She wasn't going to stage much of a rebellion with just these four lackeys.

"The Confed still hasn't made any concessions," she said, tempering her resentment. "If we're going to get anywhere, we have to keep pushing—we have to hit them hard. Luis is worried about getting his hands too dirty, so I'll take this on. He'll be happy when we get results."

"Results from *what*?" I pressed. I needed her to admit what she was doing, to spell it out in so many words. Perhaps it was easier to set a trap to kill someone if you never thought through the killing part out loud.

Ary raised her chin. "They're not scared enough yet. They want to celebrate their rich-ass Circle-linked mages while they steal our magic from us? We should steal that spotlight from them. Dominick here has an affinity for stone-work left after his Dampering." She tapped her elbow against the new guy's arm.

Stone-work. Like another novice from the Exam, another girl whose name I'd lost. The idea brought to mind an image of a stone spire toppling, shards protruding from the stump like knives.

"Great," I said, wrenching my mind back to the present. "What stone is he going to work, and how?"

She edged toward the foot of the driveway and tipped her head to the front of the building. "We just weaken that archway a little. Spread a few cracks, and then give them a jolt so it crashes down on those self-important heads while they're smiling for their stupid photo. Let's see them ignore *that*."

"Oh, yeah," I said. "They'll take notice—by sending National Defense to arrest the whole League." I turned to the new guy, Dominick. "Do you want to be a murderer? Because that's what she's talking about here. What do you *think* happens when you drop a ton of limestone on someone's head?"

He paled a little, but his jaw clenched. "We're not trying to hurt them *that* badly. Just enough to scare them."

"Is your control really that good? You can be totally sure of how much rock is going to fall and where? One slip and it could bash people's skulls in. Do you really want to take that chance?"

"Hey!" Ary said, her earlier glare returning. "What the hell do you even care, Academy boy? Those people stole your magic too. Do you honestly think they deserve to go around patting themselves on the back when they're doing *this* to us?" She flicked her fingers toward her Burnout mark.

"I care because I don't think anyone deserves to die over this," I said. "Not us. Not them. After what I've seen... I don't want *anyone* else dying."

If the new-magic mages had gone through their schooling with Greek tragedies drilled into their heads, perhaps they'd have seen this differently. Murders out of vengeance led to more murders to avenge those, on and on until everyone ended up dead or grieving. I'd rather not see any of our lives take that route.

Dominick shifted his weight, his expression torn, but I wouldn't put it past Ary to dig up some other stone-worker somewhere if he backed down. The other four pairs of eyes aimed at me didn't waver.

I switched tacks. "Even if you don't mind if someone dies, I meant what I said before. I know these people, remember? If we get blood on our hands like that, the Circle will pay attention, absolutely. They'll put all their attention into rooting us out and making us pay. How does that help any of us?"

The girl at Ary's left rubbed her mouth and glanced at her friend. "He might be right," she said. "We can't be sure they won't know which of us did it. I don't want to go to prison on top of everything else."

"You can't listen to him," Ary said, grabbing her arm. "He's practically one of them." She spun on me. "What's your grand plan now? We stand around with our thumbs up our asses hoping the Confed leaders take some kindness into their hearts?"

My shoulders stiffened. "Of course not. I was right there during the college protest—I dug up that information so we could pull off the one during the international conference. We push back like that. Or, gods, maybe we do some things your way. But not like this, not with you going off on your own."

Ary's stance was still tense, as if she saw me as an enemy. Why wouldn't she, though? I'd argued against every plan she'd put forward, even the one I'd agreed to in the end. When had I really tried to see her side? It wasn't as if we had nothing in common.

I dragged in a breath. "I understand why you're angry," I said. "I'm angry with the Circle, and the Exam committee, and—" Hades take me, I couldn't think of anyone in this city I *wasn't* at least a little angry with outside of the League—including my parents and my siblings. "There's a lot to be angry about. People I know have done horrible things or looked the other way while someone else screwed us over. Sometimes I do want to tear it all down."

"But you're too comfy where you are," Ary said, but her sneer didn't have as much edge to it. She was watching me now as if she actually wanted to hear what I'd say next. The others stayed silent.

"Maybe a little," I acknowledged. "But it's mainly that I don't want to stoop to their level. I want to be better than them. Don't you? Don't you think *you're* better than those assholes?"

"Of course I am," Ary snapped.

I held her gaze. "Then don't do this, not right now. It doesn't matter if you say it isn't a League thing. You know they'll tie it back to the rest of us. The Circle takes so many of our decisions away from us with the Dampering and the Exam. If you make a choice that could hurt all of us, without even giving us the chance to talk about it first, you're doing the exact same thing."

Those last words tipped the balance. Even her boyfriend's expression twitched. Ary set her hands on her hips, but I could read accession in her eyes.

"Are you telling me that if I pitch something like this at the next meeting, you're not going to shout me down?" she asked.

"I'll argue if I disagree with you, and then people will decide whose arguments they agree with more," I said. "Like always. I did end up supporting you on the conference protest. I'm simply asking that we have that discussion properly, with everyone. If you don't think this idea is sound enough that the rest of the League will agree to it, then how is it right to go ahead with it anyway and then pin us with the responsibility?"

Ary's gloved hands balled into fists, and her boyfriend bared his teeth with his scowl. Dominick turned and hurried away, his posture defensive, as if he were afraid someone might chase after him.

No one did. The other four were all focused on me.

"All right," Ary said. "Have it your way, Mr. Bleeding Heart. Just watch. People *want* to take real action. I've seen it in them. Soon they're going to get tired of waiting for some change that never comes, and then the Confed should watch out."

She jammed her hands into her coat pockets and motioned for the others to follow her out of the driveway with a tip of her head. The tension inside me drained away as I meandered after them to the sidewalk. My lungs ached when I exhaled.

Crisis averted. No stony hail would be raining down on my family tomorrow, at least.

"Hey!" a voice rang out from across the street. "Hey, Finn!"

My head jerked up. A guy in a trim overcoat was waving to me on the opposite sidewalk. It was one of my old classmates from the Academy: Bradley Chamberlain. We'd never been close, but he'd know me, all right.

My pulse stuttered, but it was too late to pretend I hadn't heard him. He was loping across the road now. Ary had glanced over at us.

Perhaps they'd keep walking. Perhaps he wouldn't say

anything that mattered. I halted, forcing my mouth into a smile and searching for an excuse to usher him in the other direction.

"Hey, Bradley," I said, hoping I didn't sound too stiff. "It's been a while."

"No kidding. Man, it feels like ages." He stopped on my sidewalk, his gaze traveling straight to my Burnout mark, which couldn't have been more than partly visible by the edge of my hat. His attention lingered there for a few beats.

At the edge of my vision, Ary and her friends had turned to watch our conversation. Fine. Just keep it easy and boring, and either he or they would leave without my two worlds completely colliding.

"Damn shame about the Exam, isn't it?" Bradley said. "You'll figure it out, though. Are the tests as bad as everyone figures?"

I wasn't sure I'd ever been more glad to say, "I can't talk about it. Sorry."

"Right, of course. Code of secrecy and all. Wouldn't want to get you into trouble." He made a gesture as if zipping his mouth. "Imagine you having to go in there at all."

"It's done now," I said quickly. "How are things at the college?"

"Oh, you know." He made a face. "Lectures, studying, the usual. It really is more dull without you around."

"Well, thanks for saying so," I said, relief starting to trickle through me. I wasn't sure he'd actually stopped for more than just to rubberneck at my misfortune, but I couldn't say I blamed him. I'd been morbidly curious about those who were burned out too. We'd exchanged niceties. Now I could get out of here.

I opened my mouth to make some excuse, and Bradley cuffed my arm. "Still can't believe you didn't make it. Finn Lockwood—I figured you were a shoo-in."

I nearly choked on my tongue. My heart was suddenly

hammering at my ears, but not loud enough to drown out Ary's disbelieving voice.

"Finn *Lockwood?*"

"The one and only," Bradley said with a pleased smile, as if he'd just done me a favor. "Your granduncle must be sorting something out for you, yeah?"

"Something like that," I said weakly.

He glanced at his watch. "Well, I've got to run, but it was good to see you."

That should have been my line. It was too late for me to use it now. Just like that, he was off again, leaving me stranded next to the last people on Earth I'd have wanted present for that conversation. I turned from his retreating back toward the cataclysm he'd just created.

Ary stalked closer as Bradley disappeared around the corner. Her trio of friends flanked her.

"You're a Lockwood," she said, her narrowed eyes all but burning a hole in my forehead. Her voice was seething. "One of *the* Lockwoods. All that 'oh, I'm angry too, I just don't want to be like those assholes,' and you *are* one of them."

I held up my hands. "Ary—"

"No wonder he was so worried about our plan," she interrupted, glancing back at her friends. "He wasn't looking out for the League. How much do you want to bet there's going to be a Lockwood on those steps tomorrow? Not to mention the one in the Circle who's 'sorting' everything out for him." Her gaze snapped back to me. "That's who that guy was talking about when he mentioned your granduncle, right?"

"Yeah," I said. "But it's not—he isn't helping me. We hardly see eye-to-eye on anything. I only wanted—"

"You *wanted* to spy on us," Ary spat out. Rage and indignation radiated from her voice, her posture. "I *knew* there was something off about you. I bet you've been reporting back to the Circle the whole time. You two-faced prick."

She swung at me, so swift and sudden I didn't have the wherewithal to dodge. Her knuckles slammed into my cheekbone. Pain burst through my face as I stumbled backward.

Her boyfriend came at me with a knee to the gut. The other girl stomped at my shin. An elbow clocked me across the temple. My head spun, blood seeping over my tongue with a metallic edge from where I'd bitten the inside of my cheek.

"Who put the rest of us in danger, huh?" Ary said, throwing another punch that glanced off my ribs. "You'd better regret the second you thought about screwing us over! We can show the Circle what we think of their kind right now."

In that moment, with my head throbbing and blows falling from all sides, it seemed like a real possibility that they might kill *me* as some sort of statement. They certainly weren't asking for my side of the story. My Academy training served me only so far as offering up a melancholic line: Stat sua cuique dies.

My last day would not be today. My feet skidded on the concrete, spinning me around. I shoved myself away from them and bolted. I just had to get back to Fifth Avenue, where more people were around...

Ary's voice carried after me. "That's right. Run like a rat! Wait 'til Luis hears about *this*."

CHAPTER TWENTY-THREE

Rocío

Polina's jean jacket looked way too thin for the cold December night. She hunched her shoulders inside it as we stood at the edge of the dark alley that looked out onto the back of the abandoned movie theater. The bitter wind tossed the strands of her hair that had slipped free from her usual braid.

When she'd insisted on escorting us to the meeting place she'd heard about rather than just telling us the address, I wasn't sure if she'd assumed we'd be taking her inside. Sam might have appreciated her intel, but he was still cautious of her. So the two of us had been stuck out here keeping an eye on the two young men who were standing guard in the thin light from the fixture over the arched back door. The rest of the squad had slipped inside through a window under the cover of 'chantments to spy on the meeting.

The guards were chatting, not looking all that on guard, really. Only a ten-foot stretch of concrete courtyard lay between them and our alley, but the bubble of shadow and silence I'd cast around us had kept us undetected. From what Polina had said, the local gang of mages who'd affiliated themselves with the Borci was on the fringes of the movement.

But she'd heard hints that they might be called in to help with a big plan—maybe the big plan they were coordinating with the Bonded Worthy. Commander Revett was hoping we'd get more details on that tonight. The squad was going to bug the theater so we could listen in on future meetings too.

Polina shifted her weight from one foot to the other. The magic stirred around me, equally restless, but it pretty much never felt calm these days. I wished I could tell Polina that she could take off if she wanted, that she'd done enough, but now that she was here, Sam had wanted her around for further questioning after the meeting. She wasn't bound to a chair, but the Confed was restraining her all over again.

The wind blew harder. Polina brought her hands to her face. I was about to offer to add a little warmth to our conjured bubble when she murmured in singsong Russian and patted her palms together. A wisp of heat grazed my face from where it had bloomed between her hands. My jaw went slack for a second before I could catch it.

Why was I surprised that she was a mage? She'd been hanging out with mages, had dated one. Back home, mages and the nonmagical didn't mix very much. I just hadn't thought about it.

I didn't really know much at all about her, did I?

The guard on the left—the taller guy, with blond hair slicked to the side—threw back his head to laugh at something his companion had said.

Polina grimaced. "That one," she said quietly. "He's the one I was with. He thinks he's so special, being a tough guy, but they don't even want him in the meeting. Just stick him out here."

"He doesn't look too worried that anyone might try to sneak in," I said.

She shrugged. "No one would have tried before."

Sam's voice carried through my earpiece. "Everything stable out there, Lopez?"

I ducked my mouth closer to my mic and pressed the button. "All's well. How's it going in there?"

"From what we've heard so far, the meeting is almost over. You might not be out in the cold long. They're talking, but it's hard to follow without having heard what they were discussing before. We're taking it all down, though."

Great. Another excuse for Brandt to mutter about how Polina's tips hadn't delivered any terrorists right into our laps. I rubbed my arms.

"I'm surviving. No need to rush back."

Polina's ex and the other guard might have been standing out here for a while, then. I guessed I couldn't blame them for getting restless. Anyway, if they'd gotten complacent, then better for us.

Their voices rose again, the shorter guy ribbing Polina's ex with a teasing tone. The blond guy waved him off with a scoff and said something that made Polina wince. They tossed a few more comments back and forth, and her ex moved his hands through the air, tracing an hourglass shape.

Polina was frowning furiously now. The magic in our little bubble jittered, even though as far as I could tell, neither of us had cast. The hairs on the back of my neck stood up.

"What are they talking about?" I ventured, even though I could make a stab at the answer. Maybe she'd feel better if she could vent a little.

"They are joking about me," Polina said tightly. "He is saying I was only good for—for—" She gritted her teeth. "He wasn't good for *anything*. So, who should be laughing?"

"Sounds like he's a jerk," I said. "It's a good thing you broke up with him."

"Best thing I ever did," she grumbled. She didn't look any calmer than she had before I'd asked. Her hands were clenched in front of her chest. The magic twitched against my scalp, and I thought of Lacey again—of Lacey with her eyes flashing as she hurled a wave of vicious electricity toward the rest of us on her team.

The signs that Lacey was getting erratic had been there for a while. I just hadn't recognized them or done enough in time.

She'd been pushed to her breaking point by the Confed— and now she was lost, a Burnout sent back to the little town where the guy who'd bruised her was waiting. What would happen to Polina if we kept pushing her around?

"He played sweet when we first met," Polina said, her gaze still fixed on the blond guy. "I should have known better. He cares about nobody except himself and impressing these..." She waved her hand toward the building as if indicating everyone inside it.

"You got out," I said. "That's what matters."

She made a rough noise in her throat. Then a haunted look came over her pale face, something pained and vulnerable. The magic quivered around me.

"I never told anyone," she said in a whisper. "But you won't tell anyone who knows me. There was... We must have made a mistake. I was going to..." One of her hands dropped to her belly. "That was what let me decide. To have a child with him— it was too awful. I took care of it, and I left him."

Her eyes jerked to me as if daring me to judge her. I didn't have a clue what to say. Dios mío, somehow I'd ended up in a total minefield. My mouth opened and closed and opened again. She shouldn't have to hear his jokes. We were torturing her, making her stand here and listen to him.

"I'm sorry," I said, meaning it. "That you had to go through that." What could I add? I'd have liked to radio Sam and ask if

Polina could wait for us somewhere farther away, but I didn't think he'd go for it. And I didn't really want to explain that request in front of Polina. I knew from experience that saying a person was reacting badly was only going to make them more upset.

She looked away, her expression hardening again. "It is over. Maybe he will be over soon. The way he treats people—everyone —I hope he gets blasted to pieces by one of your spells."

Her vehemence unnerved me and seemed to upset the magic too. It wriggled distractingly around the collar of my jacket and nipped at my jaw.

"I don't think that's likely to happen," I said, as gently as I could manage. "I wouldn't blast someone unless it was the only way to save someone else."

"Hmm. Could save a lot of people a lot of trouble."

I had no answer at all for that.

We stood there in silence for another few minutes. Polina hugged herself and then released her arms to tug at her braid. The magic kept jabbing at me as if it couldn't handle her apparent frustration. A weight settled in my stomach.

Was there something I'd missed that I should've said to her? Should I go against Sam's orders and tell her to just get out of here? But he'd already warned me the last time I'd let her go. If he reported that infraction to the senior officials, it might be all the evidence they needed to conclude I was a traitor after all.

A yawn tugged at my jaw. I hadn't slept well since I'd gotten back—too many worries, too much whirling in my head. For a second, my head felt hazy.

I snapped back to sharper alertness when the guards started laughing again. Polina stiffened. A harsh phrase fell from her lips.

"What?" I couldn't help asking.

"He's bragging about how he cheated some of the shops

around here out of money," Polina said. "I know those people—they're good people. He thinks he can take whatever he wants."

The magic flinched between us. Then the two-way radio on the blond guy's belt crackled. He raised it to his ear.

At the same moment, Sam spoke through my earpiece. "It looks like they're about to move out, Lopez. Hang tight where you are. We'll need a few minutes to finish setting up the surveillance equipment."

"Got it," I said.

Polina leaned forward as her ex hooked the radio back on his belt. He clapped the other guy on the shoulder in what looked like a farewell gesture, and that guy disappeared into the shadows. The blond guy took one last look around before heading in the other direction around the theater.

Polina's lips moved, her fingers curling. The energy in the air clamped around me with a frantic yank. My heart flip-flopped, and her hand shot up.

"No!" I said, smacking her arm down before the verse had finished leaving her mouth.

Polina whipped around. "What are you doing? Why did you stop me?"

The magic was upset, I thought, and also, *Who will you be if you hurt him?* My tongue stumbled. I wasn't totally sure who I'd been trying to protect. "You can't— It doesn't matter what he did. There are other ways to stop him. You can't just…"

Her cheeks flushed red. "What did you think I was going to do to him? It was just a trick, to take him down from his high horse a little. You think I would—what… Attack him? *Kill* him? Like I am a criminal too?"

"No," I said, but my guilt must have shown on my face. I had thought she was about to attack him somehow. "Polina—"

She jabbed her finger at me. "After I helped you so much… That is what you see. A criminal. Maybe the people in there are a little bit right. Maybe none of you Americans can look at us except from *your* high horses."

She pushed herself away from me and took off down the alley. Out of the sphere of silence I'd conjured, the thudding of her footsteps echoed through the night.

Before I could decide whether to chase after her or stay put, more footsteps thumped back toward us from the other direction. The blond guy burst into the courtyard, his head swiveling as he scanned the area. "Who's there?" he hollered in Russian, one of the phrases I could now recognize. He snatched up his radio.

¡Mierda! I hurled out a casting, my vice to pin him to the ground. The radio clattered from his hand, inactivated. But just then a woman appeared in the doorway on her way out. She saw the guy falling and stumbled backward with a cry.

I clutched my mic. "Rojanwan, they know something's wrong. Get out of there!"

Before I'd even finished my warning, shouts and a crackle that made the magic flail against me filtered through the walls. A pained yelp pierced the night, but no answer came from Sam.

They were fighting. I bobbed on my feet, now unsure whether I should ignore his orders.

He'd given them before the rest of the squad had come under attack. I clenched my jaw and dashed toward the theater.

A flash of magical light seared my vision. A thump sounded, like a body hitting a wall. I wrenched open the door to see Brandt staggering toward me down the back hall. He had Joselin with him—had the taller girl's arm slung over his shoulder. Her head hung as limp as her ponytail, her feet dragging on the ground more than they were supporting her weight. A streak of blood dribbled from the corner of her mouth.

"Rojanwan's coming," Brandt barked at me. "Help me get her to the chopper."

With my pulse rapping out a painful beat against my ribs, I grasped Joselin's other shoulder and fled toward our landing spot.

* * *

They didn't bother with the men in the jeep or the locked white room this time. I was just shaken awake from another unsettled sleep by Tonya, who scowled at me without speaking as she led me down the hall to one of the base's smaller conference rooms. The moment I saw Commander Revett, Colonel Alcido, and one of the officials who'd interrogated me last time sitting in a row at the table inside, any hope I'd held onto fell away.

"Is Joselin—Stravos—okay?" I asked as Tonya left. The door thudded shut in her wake.

Joselin hadn't been breathing when we'd made it back to the base last night, despite Sam's best efforts at first aid. The staff on site had rushed her to the magimedical ward and sent the rest of us to our dorms.

"I'm sorry to say that Operative Stravos succumbed to her injuries," Commander Revett said in a weary voice. She motioned to the chair across from them. "We'd like to ascertain what circumstances led to last night's unfortunate events. Would you please sit down?"

They'd called me in because they thought I was the circumstances. A lump filled my throat. I couldn't even say they were wrong.

Joselin was dead. Brash, music-loving Joselin who'd tried to turn our missions into an adventure. Who'd believed she deserved to be here as some kind of penance.

She'd deserved better than this. From the Confed—and from me.

The chair squeaked on the floor as I pulled it back. My knees gave, and I sat faster than I meant to. I propped my elbows on the table. "What do you want to know?"

"We have the report from your mission leader," Colonel Alcido said, his knobby hands resting on a file folder in front of him. Was our Dull military representative calling the shots on this subject too? "As he understands it, the target meeting was breaking up peacefully, no one had suspected your squad's presence, and then all at once, you were warning him from outside, just before one of the insurgents raised the alarm. It appears you knew something was wrong ahead of the rest of the squad. How is that?"

I wet my lips, queasiness roiling inside me. "There was… A local girl led us to the building where they were meeting. You know that already. I was waiting with her, watching the guards outside. And when they were leaving…"

I tried to break down why I'd gotten nervous—the way Polina had been talking, the energy I'd picked up from her. I'd been the one who'd encouraged the senior operatives to trust her. I'd been the one who'd encouraged *her* to trust us. No matter what Prisha had been saying the other day, it'd been my responsibility to keep everyone there safe, hadn't it?

But somehow the whole situation had fallen apart with one interrupted casting.

After I finished my story, the three officials took turns asking me questions. Double-checking the details of my conversation with Polina. Confirming the orders I'd received.

"The only time I went against anything Rojanwan told me, it was to go to the building to try to help the squad," I said. "Maybe if I'd done that sooner, we could have gotten Joselin back here sooner…"

One more mistake I suspected was going to haunt me for a long time.

Commander Revett frowned in a way that looked almost

compassionate. "I don't think there was any way she was going to make it after the castings that hit her," she said, and glanced at the other mage official. "I don't see any sign of treason here."

Treason. What might they do to my parents, to Finn, if they decided I'd broken my word to them after all? Wouldn't that be horrifically ridiculous—if I failed the people I cared about not by how I'd defied the Confed but through a total accident that hadn't served the magic or anyone else at all?

The other commander made a rough humming sound. "No, I have to agree."

Colonel Alcido looked from one mage to the other. "It seems to me it's of concern that this is the *second* time you've found issue with Operative Lopez's performance in the last three months. Why was she given a pass before? Her judgment and emotional stability are clearly not sound enough for her to work in the field."

Revett's jaw tightened. "She's met every training standard we have. She hasn't faltered once during the ongoing training sessions."

"A classroom or a gym is a hell of a lot different from active duty." Alcido cut his gaze toward me. "Why don't you wait in the hall while we discuss what we do with you now, Operative Lopez?"

It might have been phrased like a question, but I knew a command when I heard one.

In the hallway, I leaned back against the dingy beige wall with nothing to distract me from the growing ache in my chest.

It didn't take long for the officials to call me back in. All three of the faces waiting for me were solemn.

"Operative Lopez," Commander Revett said. "We've determined that your actions showed no deliberate malice, but a worrisome lack of forethought. For the time being, you are relieved from active duty. You will continue your training and fulfill your debt to the Confederation by assisting with the base cleanup currently underway, until such time as we feel you may be fit to re-enter service in the field."

She set her hands down on the table with a thump of finality that echoed through my core.

CHAPTER TWENTY-FOUR

Finn

I f there was any balm for having suffered a beating and then total ostracization from one's friends, helping another person had to be it. Tucked away in my little cubicle in the Media Outreach office, I left behind the strain of the last few days, if only momentarily. It didn't even matter that the help I was giving was with the most ridiculous things.

"The Records workers are rather strict about access," I said into the phone. "You won't get permission to roam freely. But for a request like yours, I'm sure they'd pull the appropriate files and walk you through whatever data they have. I can even call them up myself to give them a heads-up to expect you."

"Thank you so much," the guy on the other end said. We'd been chatting for almost half an hour, mostly about mages' pet-keeping habits. I gathered he was doing some sort of research on how closely folklore about witches' and wizards' familiars aligned with real-life magical associations with animals. "It's a relief having an idea where to start."

"Just remember I can't say for certain they'll have records on that subject," I said. "But we do seem to keep track of an awful lot of unusual data, so I wouldn't put it past them. If none of those leads get you anywhere, call in again, and we can brainstorm some more. I'm curious to hear what you discover."

"If I get this report written, I'll send an early copy your way," the guy said brightly.

As I hung up, my supervisor for my trial placement stopped by my nook.

"It sounded like that went well," she said. "You really know how to talk to them."

Her voice dipped slightly on the word "them." She meant Dulls. They were people, and I talked to them like I talked to any human being. I supposed her discomfort wasn't much different from the discomfort of the Dulls who were bizarrely comforted by the thought that the mage they were speaking to couldn't actually cast any magic.

"I give it my best," I said, which seemed like a reasonably appropriate way to say, *I really want to continue this placement so please sign off on that.*

"Well, it's almost five. I think you can wrap things up for now. I'm sure we'll have plenty more for you to tackle during your next shift."

I strode out of the building with my spirits still high and then hesitated at the sight of a dark gray Honda sedan parked by the curb outside.

That was definitely Dad's car. That was definitely Dad sitting inside it. Had anyone else noticed him? Being picked up by my parents was hardly going to get me the respect I wanted to cultivate.

I hurried across the sidewalk, deciding that removing myself from the view of my potential future colleagues was a higher priority than protesting his arrival. Dropping into the front passenger seat, I yanked the door shut. "What are you doing here?" I said.

Dad wasn't oblivious to my discomfort. He started the engine immediately and pulled onto the road, away from the office building, before he answered.

"I finished my work for the day a little early," he said. "I thought I might as well save you the cab ride. I was only a few minutes away."

All of those things might very well have been true, but the evaluating look he gave me suggested there was more to his impromptu visit. Even though I was seventeen now, the magimedic who'd seen me when I'd ducked into the Confed's local clinic three days ago had insisted on contacting Dad. She'd checked me over to ensure Ary and her friends' beating hadn't left me with any major internal injuries, but she hadn't healed the marks I'd been hoping to avoid showing off until after he'd arrived. He'd turned up out of breath and pale, so quickly he must have magically teleported part of the way.

The beating itself had done more damage to my looks than anything else, and even that had been temporary. After half an hour of castings, I'd felt essentially normal, other than a sliver of pain that hadn't quite faded around a bruised rib. That hadn't prevented Dad from being in a furor over the situation.

I fell, I'd told him. *Slipped on some stairs and banged my face on the door frame at the bottom. Me and my two left feet!*

He hadn't looked as if he'd believed me, and honestly, I hadn't tried that hard to sell the story. I simply hadn't offered any other one. After several rounds of questions, he'd seemed to accept that if something else had happened, he wasn't finding it out from me.

Nonetheless, he was clearly still feeling rather protective. If he could have held me back from every danger, as Croesus had with Atys, he likely would have—with about as much success.

I forgave him a little when he motioned to a plastic-lidded cup in the holder beside me. "I picked up one of those peppermint hot chocolates for you."

"Thank you," I said, snatching it up. I'd gotten addicted to the stuff ages ago, to the point that ten-year-old me had gone off on something of a rant about how no one carried it in July. I'd endured ribbing about that for quite a while afterward, but it hadn't dampened my enjoyment any.

The heat of the cup soaked into my hands. The liquid would have burned my tongue, so for the moment I simply breathed in the minty sweet scent. A light rain started to patter against the roof as Dad turned the car toward home.

"How's the placement going?" he asked. "Do you think Media Outreach is a track you could settle into?"

"I do," I said, my good spirits returning as I thought about my day. "There's a lot I like about what they do there. If I can gradually have more of a hand in things, I think I could make a real mark."

The Confed's Media division produced and distributed news to the mage community as well as managing public perception of us and our activities among the Dulls. The gap that lingered between magical and nonmagical society, the fears and prejudices that lingered on both sides—we were going to need to get past all of that if anything was really going to change, weren't we?

Naturally, my supervisor hadn't given me any tasks that would help smooth over political relations yet. Today, along with the pet guy's concerns, I'd discussed mage views on gardening with a woman writing an article for a house and home blog and directed a guy doing an indie documentary on mage architecture to some appropriate resources.

I could work my way up, though. My supervisor seemed reasonably pleased with me so far. If I hadn't been a Lockwood— if the higher-ups in the Media division hadn't figured they might be able to call in a favor from my parents or my older siblings after they'd found a spot for me—they might not have accepted me on this trial basis in the first place, so I couldn't really complain.

A pinch of frustration came with that thought. I sipped a little of my peppermint hot chocolate to wash it away. I *was* going to make my own name for myself. I'd earn promotions based on what I could do, not what connections I brought with me, and then I'd be doing work I could take pride in and talk about freely with my family, no matter what else I was up to on the side.

If I didn't, everything Ary and her friends believed about me might as well be true.

"I get to talk to people," I went on. "Half of the job is just being friendly and putting them at ease, which I seem to be decent at. I'd much rather be helping that way than pushing papers around."

After all the time I'd spent with the Freedom of Magic League, by now I probably had more experience at friendly chatting with Dulls than most of Media Outreach's senior staff.

Recalling the League meetings brought a deeper pinch, one no amount of minty cocoa could alleviate. I'd sent a few texts to Luis on my way to the clinic, but Ary had already gotten a hold of him to spill my supposed dark secrets. *We need time to discuss*, he'd written back. *I'll be in touch if we decide in your favor.* Three days seemed like more than long enough for him and the other established members to reach a decision.

I'd heard nothing more. That must have meant I was out, for good—because of the same damned name.

"It sounds like you're off to a good start there," Dad said, drawing me back to the present. "If any stories that need an international perspective come up, you know you can always call on me."

I wasn't planning on making even greater use of my privilege. "Thanks," I said anyway. "I appreciate that."

He turned onto 81st Street, and my gaze slid over the houses before ours, sticking for a moment on the townhouse where Callum lived on the second floor. No doubt *he* was still welcome at the League meetings. Being born into a prominent family had turned out to be a larger crime than attempted murder.

I winced inwardly at my own bitterness. Thinking that way was hardly fair to the League. No one there knew what Callum had been like in the Exam or before it. I supposed they hadn't really known me either. I'd been so careful not to share too much about my identity that I must have looked incredibly guilty in hindsight. I *had* hidden things from them. How would any of my friends vouch for me when they had no idea who I was outside of the image I'd presented, which had clearly been only part of the picture?

The only person there who really knew me was my enemy.

My body went still against my seat as Dad pulled up at our house. Actually, having an enemy vouch for me would be a whole lot more convincing than any friend, wouldn't it?

"There's something I was supposed to drop off for Prisha," I said when we got out. "I'll be back in time for dinner."

Dad's forehead furrowed as if he wasn't entirely sure whether to believe me, but he could hardly insist on escorting me to my best friend's house two blocks down the street. "All right," he said.

I set off toward Pree's house as if I were actually going there, listening for the thump of our door. Then I veered left at the corner and looped back around.

I didn't have Callum's phone number. I'd never had occasion to *want* it. All I could hope was that he wouldn't be too annoyed by my stopping by unexpectedly to hear me out—if he was home at all.

His townhouse had a panel by the door with three names and buttons. I pressed the one labeled *Geary*.

A disgruntled sounding man answered a moment later. "Yes?"

"I'm here to see Callum."

"Callum?" he said, both startled and grim. "Who is this?"

"Finn Lockwood," I said. Here, my name might help me in a way I appreciated.

The lock on the door buzzed open. I ventured into the stairwell.

While Callum's family didn't have the prestige mine did in mage society, this *was* an Upper East Side home. Even the landings boasted crown moldings. Still, it appeared the families who lived here spent all their time working to afford an 81st Street address with none left over for keeping up the place. The hardwood on the stairs was scuffed, and the paint on the walls faded from white to gray. The carpet outside the Geary's apartment door rasped under my shoes with grit that hadn't been vacuumed in who knew how long.

Callum answered the door, his father a boxy shape hovering farther down the front hall. "What the hell are you doing here?" my former classmate said in greeting.

"*Callum*," his father said sharply. Callum's gray eyes turned even flatter than they'd already been.

"I'd be happy to explain if we could talk for a minute or two," I said in my most conciliatory voice. "I promise I won't stick around long."

"Well, I'm not inviting you in," Callum said, ignoring the heart attack he appeared to be inflicting on his father. He stepped forward, forcing me to back up, and closed the door behind him. "What do you want, Lockwood?"

I glanced around, hardly eager to have this conversation right here. I wouldn't have put it past his father to press his ear up to the seam of the door. "Let's..." I motioned to the stairs.

We ended up standing on either side of a dusty window in the landing between the first floor and the second. A faintly musky odor hung in the air, which made me wonder about the pet-keeping habits of the mages who lived here.

Callum propped himself against the wall with his arms crossed over his chest. I cast about for a pose that felt comfortable and determined that such a thing did not exist for this situation. There was nothing to do but launch into my plea however awkwardly it would come out.

"Did you go to the last League meeting?" I asked.

"I did," Callum said. "I noticed you didn't bother to show up. And everyone seemed pretty hush-hush about it. That Ary girl looked ready to blow her top when your name got mentioned, but the leader guy and a couple of the others shut down that subject quickly. How did you screw things up this time?"

I couldn't help making a face at him. "I didn't *do* anything. Ary figured out who I am. Now she's going around telling everyone I'm some sort of mole for my granduncle."

Callum barked out a laugh at that. I was relieved to see he found that idea ridiculous, but his mention of Ary brought back my suspicions about her latest scheme.

"Getting friendly with Ary and her crew, are you?" I added.

Callum gave me a quizzical look. "I'm still figuring out if the dopes at those meetings are worth investing any more time. Maybe not, when they keep a loose cannon like that around. She'd probably punch your granduncle in the face if he was in front of her."

"She punched *me* in the face," I muttered, remembering the throb of the blow.

"Did she really?" Callum grinned. Then he shook his head.

"It's not the right way to get the Circle's attention, that's for sure. You can't bully a bunch of bigger bullies into changing things you don't like."

There was a sneer in his voice, but something had softened in his expression when he mentioned changing things. Could Callum be more invested in the League's fight than he was willing to admit?

He definitely didn't sound as though he'd have trusted Ary to carry out some plan on his behalf. The more time I spent talking to him, the more ridiculous *that* idea was feeling. Callum enjoyed cutting people down a peg when he was there to appreciate the sight. He'd taken a cutthroat approach to the Exam because he'd thought it was his best chance at making Champion. What in Hades's name could he gain from the deaths of half my immediate family? He might be sadistic, but from every observation I'd made of him, he was practical about it.

"That's true," I said. "I was supporting other sorts of tactics— and they were working. They need the kind of access I have."

"Why are you telling me?" Callum said. "Talk to them about it. If you're so important, they'll let you back in."

"They're never going to believe *me* saying I'm innocent. I'd say that whether I was or not."

Callum's eyes widened. "You want me to speak up for you. That's why you're here."

He sounded so disbelieving that my heart started to sink. I spread my hands in appeal. "You know me. You *have* known me for at least the twelve years we spent at the Academy together. You don't like me, fine, but you can't pretend to believe my granduncle would ever trust me to be his lackey. You know I could have walked right into the college, and I gave that up because I thought it was wrong."

"Sure," Callum said. "You're not an evil Confed spy. The question is, what do I get for putting my neck out?"

"How about actual change?" I said. "How about a world where your family isn't ashamed of you simply because you were shortchanged when it comes to magical ability?"

Callum flinched. "Don't you start about my—"

"For Fates' sakes, Callum, do you think I don't mean me too?" I flung my hand toward the window. "Haven't you seen the way my granduncle looks at me, the way he talks to me—or about me? I'm not going to pretend it's as bad as whatever you've had to deal with, but it isn't good either. Do you think I'd have put myself through that wretched Exam otherwise?"

There was a pause. Something shifted in Callum's gaze. "How do you know it was 'wretched'?" he asked.

I blinked, thrown. "What?"

"The Exam," he said. "How do you know it was wretched? I can't—" His voice cut off. He grimaced at the things he couldn't say. "Maybe you spent the whole time eating grapes on a feather pillow."

The laugh that burst out of me was more raw than amused. "Dear Zeus, don't I wish. But that's not the point."

"It's a point to me," Callum said, studying me. "You remember."

He looked both hesitant and hungry. I couldn't imagine what it was like, having that entire experience be a blank. Grappling with the gaps in my recollections had been torturous enough. If I'd had no idea at all...

I wasn't so certain he'd be happy to know the details of his performance, though.

"I can't talk about it," I said. He'd understand that as well as any former examinee would.

"I'm sure you could manage to say *something* if you really wanted to."

I weighed my words. "If all I had to go by was your conduct in there, I wouldn't be here right now."

As I said it, I realized how true it was. The examiners had pushed all of us to our worst. Some of us had resisted and some hadn't, but Callum hadn't set out to be a murderer.

His mouth twisted. "Wonderful."

"That's why we have to stop them."

"And I'm supposed to believe you're the one to do it? Experto credite?" The acid scorn made it clear he didn't believe I was an expert of much of anything.

"No," I said. "Just believe that the League's chances are better if I can contribute. Look, I can admit it was probably stupid of me to think I could see a revolution through without anyone figuring out I had ties to the other side. And it was wrong of me to try. You help me get back in with the League, and I *swear* I'll do everything I can to take down the system we've got now. Even if it means going right at my granduncle. Even if it means I'm not just a disappointment but also a traitor in my family's eyes. You can't ask for more than that."

Callum's jaw worked. His gaze slid to the window and back. "If we break down that system, and certain 'chantments are removed in the process, you'll fill me in on the parts I lost?"

The 'chantment not to speak on certain subjects could be lifted at any time by the mage who'd cast it or anyone else who knew the key. Wiping memories, on the other hand, was essentially permanent. Over time, minor fragments might surface —which had to be why the examiners added the 'chantment as well—but what they'd taken from Callum, he was never getting back.

"All right," I said. "If that's what you want."

I held out my hand. Callum considered it for a second and then grabbed it with one sharp shake.

CHAPTER TWENTY-FIVE

Rocío

The base's underground level stank of mildew and sickly sweet cleaning fluid. The dim fluorescents overhead flickered more often than not. And whichever official had decided my current assignment had scheduled me on the night shift after the regular janitorial staff was done, so it was also lonely.

When I looked up from the wall I'd been scrubbing with a sponge to see four figures ambling toward me, I wished the basement had stayed lonely. Brandt was leading the pack, a couple of the other younger operatives just behind him, and Tonya trailing at the rear as if she wasn't completely sure she wanted to be here, but she didn't want to miss the show either. ¿Y ahora que?

I turned away from them, dipped the sponge into the bucket, and started on the next grimy patch on the wall. You could tell this place hadn't been used in almost thirty years. Every time I finished a shift, I dove straight into the shower.

"Nice setup you've got here," one of Brandt's bunch said.

"No terrorists around throwing magical projectiles or 'chanted grenades at you."

"Maybe she screwed up on purpose so she could get out of the real Champion work," the guy beside her said.

"Too bad Stravos had to go down for her to manage that," Brandt said.

He knew how to land a low blow. I restrained a wince, refusing to give them my attention. That was what they wanted, right? To have a little fun, feel a little powerful by making me uncomfortable before they went off to tackle our real enemies— the ones who'd fight back. I'd gotten plenty of that kind of treatment from my Dull peers back in school.

Keep your head high and don't give them any satisfaction, Javi used to tell me. *We know we're better than those pendejos.*

I didn't feel better than anyone right now. I'd tried so hard, and I *had* screwed up.

The magic should have chosen someone else to champion it, because I didn't seem to be up to the task.

Tonya ran her hand over the tight twists of her hair. "Come on. If you're just going to heckle her, I'm going to bed."

Brandt leaned against the wall I'd just wiped down, his head cocked toward me. "I'm just wondering if she even cares what the assholes upstairs are doing. She always talked such a big game about being out there 'helping the magic' or whatever."

"It wasn't a game," I said quietly. "And I'd rather be out on missions than doing this. If you've got an idea about how to make that happen, feel free to share it."

He shook his head. "Nah, I don't think you're angry enough. No loyalty to anyone but yourself when the chips are down."

My gaze jerked toward him before I could rein my emotions in. "Who are *you* to talk about loyalty?"

Brandt glowered at me. "I'm nothing but loyal, kid. Loyal to this unit, loyal to people stuck here like us, because this is the best family most of us have ever had. I stand up for everyone who stands up for me. We've got the Dulls on one side trying to grind us down, and the insurgents on the other, and we're not getting through it unless we have each other's backs—and you're off doing your stupid crap as if some asshole terrorist's life matters more than ours."

I stared at him. Was that really how he saw the things I'd done, the adaptations I'd tried to make? No wonder he hated me.

"I was trying to do the right thing," I said, though the words sounded feeble now. "For everyone. But for us, most of all. I didn't think—"

"Yeah. You didn't think that risking our lives for your idiotic ideas about the magic was that big a deal. Why should you be angry now either?"

"She probably doesn't even know what we've got to be angry about," Tonya broke in. She sucked her teeth and raised her chin toward me. "The officials got some intel out of the last few missions. They figure they've ID'ed a bunch of facilities that are critical to the Borci *and* the Bonded Worthy. We're supposed to go off on some huge mission to blow them all to smithereens."

"Suicide run, more like it," the younger girl muttered.

My stomach clenched. One huge strike—that was what the officials had been pushing for all along. What the Dull government had been pushing the Confed for. We were actually going through with it.

The magic around me shivered.

"Right now?" I said, my voice strained.

"Within the week," Brandt said. "They're having us follow a few more leads first. Make sure we're hitting everything we can at the best time. As far as they're concerned, we'll bring terrorist networks crashing down or we'll die trying. At least, we will if we go along with the assault. You'd want to stop it from happening, wouldn't you? Too 'destructive' for your tastes?"

"I wouldn't want to try to take them down by blowing up a ton of stuff." I lowered my sponge with a sudden flash of understanding. They had a plan to stop the strike. That was why they'd come down here.

They wanted me to help them with it.

"We all know none of this is what *our* commanders want," Brandt said. "Why the hell are we here at all? The mage insurgents haven't stirred up much trouble back home. But the Dull government is terrified of them, terrified of the Dull groups they associate with, so they make us come out here and risk our lives dealing with problems that started before anyone even knew mages existed. We'd be off at the damned college if it weren't for them."

"There's not a whole lot we can do about that," I said. "So, what's your point?"

A slightly manic gleam lit in his normally stony eyes. "Maybe we've been thinking that way too long. Maybe it's time we went straight to the source and used that power they're so scared of to defend ourselves."

A chill crept over my skin. It sounded like he was talking about some kind of attack on the Dull government. "You can't seriously think that's going to fix our problems," I said.

Brandt's expression shuttered. Whatever response he'd been looking for, mine obviously hadn't been it. "I'm only saying we make a clear case," he said. "But if you're not interested in being part of that, fine. I just thought I'd extend a hand."

He shoved himself off the wall and stalked back the way he'd come, the others falling into step behind him. I watched them go, my fingers curling into the damp sponge.

Had I misread Brandt's tone? Nothing he'd said spelled out what they were hoping to do. I didn't think I'd gotten the gist of it wrong, though. He'd been testing my loyalties, like he'd said.

And when I'd shown the opposite of enthusiasm for doing anything to hurt the Dull leaders, he'd retreated.

Had he really thought I'd be up for it? Maybe he'd figured I might be pissed off enough after this punishment.

Or maybe they weren't sure they could pull off their plan without the skills I could offer, so he'd decided it was worth a shot, no matter how slim the chances.

I started scrubbing the wall more vigorously than before, my thoughts spinning.

Brandt had been with the unit for years longer than me. If I tried to tell Commander Revett or any of the other officials about my suspicions, it'd be my word against his and his three witnesses. He'd have some way of turning it around on me, or he wouldn't have risked saying as much as he had.

What the hell could I do?

I was so lost in that dilemma that I didn't notice I had new visitors until they were halfway down the hall. When I glanced up and saw Sam's face, my back stiffened. Was he also pissed off with me, because I'd messed up the mission—gotten one of the squad killed, nearly gotten him killed too?

But his expression was mild, and he had Prisha and Desmond with him. I relaxed a little when he gave me a nod and bent to grab another sponge out of the open package by the wall.

"Need a little help?" he said.

"I wouldn't turn it down."

The three of them got to work beside me. I didn't know why they'd come down tonight, but I figured Sam would get around to telling me when he thought the time was right—even if I had to keep biting my tongue to avoid demanding an explanation.

"I saw Brandt and a few of the others coming up from here a little while ago," he said eventually. "Were they hassling you?"

"That and some other stuff," I said. "They weren't happy

about this massive assault the commanders are apparently setting up."

Sam grimaced. "I don't think any of us are happy about that. I mean, if I was sure it'd tip the balance in our favor in some significant way, no problem—but we're rushing in so fast. How can they know enough about what we're up against?"

"And we don't know what that kind of casting on that large a scale could do to the magic," I said, bracing myself for disbelief.

All I got was a shrug. "I can't feel it the way you do," Sam said. "But I can see that could be a concern too. Not a big enough one to get us out of this mess, though."

"Not when the commanders don't care, as long as they get the Dull officials off their backs," Prisha said.

"I think..." I hesitated. But, hell, if I didn't trust the three people around me, who could I trust? "Brandt made a couple comments. It sounds like he wants to target the Dull government somehow. Like he figures if they go and, I don't know, blast away the White House, there won't be anyone calling on us to fight their wars anymore."

Desmond's eyebrows jumped up. "Do you really think they'd try to assassinate someone?"

"I don't know. He was being vague. I just... I didn't like the vibe I got at all. Whatever they're thinking of doing, it's going to hurt more people than it helps—I'm willing to bet on that."

Sam let out his breath. "I've seen the four of them and a couple others huddling more than usual. But they'd have a hard time getting anywhere off-base before the assault. None of us has any leave time scheduled between now and Christmas."

"They could make a break for it," Prisha said.

"Yeah," I agreed. "I wondered if that's why they were seeing if they could get me on board. It'd take some casting to sneak out of here, wouldn't it?"

"For sure," Sam said. "If they're willing to talk like that, who knows how far they'd go?"

The three of them glanced at me, and I realized they were waiting to hear what I'd say. Waiting for me to suggest something we could do. Because I'd been the one trying to call the shots since I'd been made Champion.

I paused, leaning my hand against the wall. A wave of hopelessness rolled over me. In the end, I was still just one mage. A mage who'd gotten a friend killed. If Javi'd had any idea this was where I'd end up—if my parents had—

My fingers tensed against the wall's cool surface. This was where all our sacrifices had gotten us. The commanders didn't even trust me to go out in the field. I couldn't turn back an enormous multi-squad assault. I couldn't convince the officials to look into less destructive castings to accomplish the same goals, not in the time we had. I sure as hell wasn't going to talk Brandt and his gang out of anything.

But looking at my hand braced against the mottled plaster, I found myself thinking of Finn. Of Finn at the end of the Exam, grasping the barbs of the metal hedge and shouting to the examiners that he was going to expose them all, even though he must have known he didn't have the power to do it. He'd thrown himself into the attempt anyway. And we had ended the Exam, the two of us, together.

He'd found another point of leverage. He'd maneuvered around the examiners' plans instead of tackling them head on.

He'd always found the bright side, a reason to hope, no matter how desperate our circumstances had been.

"What do we have?" I said abruptly, straightening up. "Anything, even if you don't see how we could use it yet. What do we know or have that matters even a little bit to the commanders, or to Brandt's bunch, or someone else who has some say in what's going to happen?"

Sam frowned. "Brandt isn't the most talkative guy. We haven't even managed to get on a first name basis. I've heard a little about Tonya's family back home—enough to know she isn't on great terms with them. I might have some sway with all of them as a more senior operative, just stepping in and expressing disapproval."

That wasn't going to cut it—and it didn't help us at all with the officials. I glanced at Prisha.

She held up her hands. "If we were back home, I could call in favors, but here... It's possible my family's money could be useful, but I don't see how. Bribe someone into listening?"

"I can get us access to the private server in the magimedic lab," Desmond said.

The three of us gaped at him. "How'd you manage that?" I said.

He smiled a little sheepishly. "After they healed me up, I got kind of bored while the magimedics were going around for hours doing all their tests. It's not that hard to sense what keys someone taps to enter a password if you know the right casting and can do it without looking like you're casting." He wiggled his fingers. "I was actually thinking... Maybe they'd have something in their records about the burning out procedure, since this whole operation is tangled up with the Exam. If you knew how the procedure works, maybe you could switch it around. You'd want to do that for Finn, wouldn't you?"

My face flamed even as excitement shot through me. I'd said a little to him about Finn, but nothing intense. "Why would you — Do I talk that loud when I'm on the phone or something?"

Desmond laughed. "I was there, before," he said, meaning, *in the Exam*. "You're crazy about him. I might be legally blind, but I'm not *blind*, Rocío."

"Right. Right." I willed the flush in my cheeks to recede. "But there could be other information in there too." The way the senior officials' connection to the magic was fraying—the magimedics had to be aware of that, right? "I've noticed things about the commanders that could call into question their competence. If we get our hands on proof of that, we'd have some leverage, wouldn't we?"

The corner of Sam's mouth slanted upward. "Sounds like as good a place to start as any. So, we're doing this?"

For a second, something in me balked. What if I couldn't handle it? What if I just got us into even more trouble?

But Sam and Prisha and Desmond had believed in me enough to reach out. They were standing with me now. From under the grief and shame weighing on me, a flicker of hope had started to shine again.

Maybe I'd tried to take on too much by myself, but I wasn't on my own anymore.

"Count me in," I said.

* * *

"Use that one," Desmond murmured, pointing to a computer terminal on the desk beside one of the operating tables. "That's the one I hearkened them on, so it should definitely work."

We slunk across the unlit medic room to the desk. The magimedics had left for the night after the squads that had been out had returned uninjured. Sam and Prisha were keeping watch in the hall.

The monitor blinked on at a tap of the mouse. A log-in screen came up. Desmond drummed his fingers against his leg as he rattled off the password he'd gleaned earlier, as if he needed the rhythm to jog his memory.

"Thank you," I said. "For thinking of me—of Finn. I know that's not what we're here for right now, but... it was a really nice thought."

He gave me a crooked smile. "It's bad enough having people back home you care about but can hardly see. Knowing they've lost something as important as their connection to magic has to be even worse. Even if there is a way to reverse a burning out, I'm not sure you'd be able to do it without getting arrested for going against the Confed—but at least it'd be good to know."

"There's got to be a way." I scanned the folders on the computer's desktop. "You were burned out. Maybe not the same way, so maybe the techniques they used wouldn't work for someone burned out by the Confed, but the magimedics healed you. You said you haven't noticed anything different with the magic, right?"

Desmond tapped his fingers again, knitting his brow. "No. How do you know that? They didn't mention anything about my magical abilities being affected."

"I don't think they want to spread it around that burning out might be reversible," I said. "Not when that's their favorite way to threaten us into sticking with the special ops unit. But I—I can sense in other people the part of our minds that we use to hearken. Yours had gone dark."

He touched the side of his head. "Damn. I'm glad I was unconscious for that."

I opened a couple files and wrinkled my nose. "A lot of the records are written in magimedical lingo. I don't know all the abbreviations—and Dios mío, they use a lot of Latin. What is it with old-magic mages and their obsession with dead languages?"

"Beats me," Desmond said. "You're not seeing anything we could use?"

"There's a file on Commander Revett and the other senior officials, but I don't see anything there that fits with what I've observed… It could be disguised in the terminology, though. Or maybe they're not keeping track of those factors on the base."

"What exact factors are we looking for?" he asked.

I hesitated, but I couldn't see how it hurt anything to tell him. "You know what I said about being able to sense other people's ability to hearken? Well, I noticed a little while ago that the senior officials... their connection is worn down. Commander Revett's is almost gone—her castings are really weak. I think it might be an accumulating backlash from having used a lot of combative castings over the years."

Desmond whistled softly. "Then we'd end up that way too if we stuck with this job long enough."

"It seems like it."

"You know, it's a weird feeling," he said. "In some ways, I've gotten to do *more* here with my magic than anyone ever gave me the chance to back home. They treat me like I can handle just as much as any other mage. It sucks that the opportunity has to come with so much crap."

My throat tightened. "I'm sure you can find something else like that, somewhere people aren't trying to blow you up on a regular basis."

"If it exists, I aim to find it. Here, let me take over for a minute?"

I slid my chair to the side, and Desmond bent over. The glow of the screen cast a bluish glow over his dark skin as he peered closely at it. He double-clicked on an icon at the top right of the desktop.

"There was another server they logged into at one point. I think this is it. I'd bet it has more records—we could turn something up."

"Maybe if we search for—what do they call it scientifically?" I frowned. "Magical capacity? There might be separate files just on that."

Desmond nodded, his nose just a couple inches from the screen. His fingers clattered over the keyboard. He clicked open a file, enlarged it, dismissed it, and opened another. Then he paused. He scrolled down, stopped, and scrolled a little farther. The furrow in his brow deepened, and then he eased back his chair.

"Rocío, what does this look like to you?"

I scooted closer. At first glance, I could see he'd opened up some kind of database, with a list of names down the left-hand side and columns of other words and numbers stretching out to the right.

"Names, dates, locations," I said. "Both city and... Wait, those are hospitals. *Dull* hospitals."

"That's what I thought."

"All these people are down for the same date, in different places. There's no way all these people have something to do with special ops... They can't even all be mages. What the heck is this?"

I scrolled down and found the point where the records switched to the following date. That list went on and on too. "There've got to be thousands of entries here. All back in the early '80s. Are this many people even *born* on any one day...?"

My voice trailed off as it hit me. That could be exactly what this data was. The Confed tested every new baby in their domain for "magical capacity" within the first few days of birth.

I typed my name into the search field. An entry darted up: Rocío Maria Lopez. April 20, 2002, Brooklyn, New York, Brooklyn Hospital Center. At the far right of the row was a number that didn't mean anything to me: 39.

"Wow," I said. "They have a registry of everyone born since they started testing after the Unveiling."

Desmond leaned over as I typed in his name. Another entry popped up, with a hospital in Chicago.

"Your birthday is February 8th?" I asked.

He inclined his head. "Crazy. But I guess it makes sense that they'd keep track of this stuff."

He had a number at the far right too: 27. I eyed it. "They must keep the Dull kids' records too, or there wouldn't be anywhere near this many."

I skimmed down the list again, this time focusing on the numbers. Most of them were in the single digits, but here and there I'd spot a higher one. None of them, so far, higher than my 39. A strange prickling sensation coiled around my gut.

I typed in Prisha's name. 23. Finn and Leonie weren't there, but then, they were old magic. I'd bet the Confed didn't test those kids. Brandt wasn't in the database either.

Sam came in at 28. Tonya, 16. Javi, 19.

My heart started to thud as I entered the names of some of the Dull kids I'd gone to school with.

3. 7. 1. 5. None of them over 10. I bit my lip.

Desmond had been watching my progress carefully. "That number has something to do with what they found when they tested us," he said.

"Yeah," I said. "I'm starting to think *that's* our magical capacity right there. But the Dulls... They don't have zero. No one has zero." My hands went still over the keyboard. "Desmond, what if they're not really Dull?"

CHAPTER TWENTY-SIX

Finn

I might have been returning to the most dangerous endeavor of my post-Exam life, but only one word could describe the feeling that swept through me as I stepped into the library conference room: *relief.*

The Freedom of Magic League was circulating around the long tables scattered throughout the room, their voices blending together into a wave of chatter. The smell of cheap coffee and close-to-stale pastries reached my nose. The meeting might have been in a new space, but everything was perfectly, wonderfully familiar.

For a second before I'd been allowed in, I'd been gripped by the fear that one of the three pseudo-bouncers who'd looked me over would toss me out by the collar. They certainly hadn't given off the friendliest vibe. Then Luis had spotted me and stepped out, and we'd rehashed most of the conversation we'd had yesterday over the phone. I suspected he'd wanted to watch my face while I explained my motivations for being part of the

League and my disgust with my granduncle's role in the Circle, so he could better judge the veracity of those claims.

My honesty must have been clear, because here I was: meandering through a space three times as large as the church room where I'd attended my first meeting, nodding to the many faces I recognized... and trying not to falter at the tensed expressions and averted eyes I was frequently getting in return.

Luis might have shut down conversation about me as much as possible in the last week, but clearly word had gotten around despite his efforts.

Grabbing a cola from the refreshment table seemed safe enough. On my way over, a head of red hair came into view nearby. I caught Callum's eye and gave him a slight tip of my head. He'd done his bit, at least well enough that Luis had been convinced.

My former classmate's mouth twitched in what looked like a suppressed grimace, which I guessed was about as much friendliness as I could have expected from that quarter. He was still the bully who'd prodded me every chance he could get for our twelve years at the Academy. As the Fates willed it, let him be stewing over what I might know about his performance during the Exam.

The figures around the refreshment table parted at my arrival as if everyone were afraid they might catch some Circle-mage pathogen from me if I passed too near. I managed to shoot a quick smile around me anyway as I took one of the cans. Then I slipped away to a vacant space by the wall, where I could watch the proceedings without intruding on anyone—and possibly lick a few wounds to my ego.

I was reasonably certain I knew what Rocío would have said about this: *You can't blame people for being cautious. Think about how many decisions the Circle has made that've hurt them. It'll take time for them to accept that you're different.*

It'd taken time for her to trust me, even fighting side by side in the Exam. I'd put my foot in it more than once with her, and I probably would again. How could I even complain when this wariness was the trade-off for the huge house and the extensive library and so many favors offered to me over the years?

I hadn't lost everyone's faith. Noemi moved toward me through the crowd with a tight but sympathetic smile.

"How are you doing?" she asked as she joined me.

I shrugged and smiled back more easily this time. "I've had warmer receptions. But I'm glad to be here at all."

Her gaze darted through the room. She dropped her voice. "There's something I need to talk to you about. It's—"

"Okay, people!" Luis called from the table that'd been pushed up against the far wall as a makeshift stage. "It's great to see so many of you here tonight. Let's get this meeting started!"

I turned to Noemi, but she shook her head. "It can wait until after."

Luis raised a fist in the air. "We want this next rally to be our largest yet—at least a thousand people on the street. How many of you are here for the first time?"

Dozens of people waved throughout the crowd.

"All the way from Arkansas!" a guy shouted.

"I made it here from L.A."

"Vancouver."

"Atlanta!"

Next, Tamara climbed up on the "stage" to share tips for finding more concerned people to recruit. A guy got up and talked about making appeals to family members and friends who were full mages. Then Luis took the microphone again.

"We want to get moving with this rally. We've got the people, and our group is growing by the day. Let's make it happen this week. The only thing left to decide is where we'll draw the most attention this time."

Several people near the front tossed out suggestions in a clash of voices. Ary hopped onto the end of the table. Her sharp comment cut through the rest of the cacophony.

"We've got a Lockwood here, don't we? Let's find out what he can tell us with all his inside info."

She stared in my direction with a smile that might have looked encouraging if you didn't know her. It gave me the impression that she was considering how to flay the flesh from my bones.

I hadn't come here planning to act as any kind of leader. After everything, I'd intended to keep my head down and simply show I could be a good follower, the way I'd meant to in the first place.

There wasn't any easy way I could see to refuse Ary's request, though. Luis motioned me forward. Swallowing hard, I wove through the crowd to the edge of the table, but there my legs balked. It didn't feel like my place at all to be getting up there.

"Well, what advice can you give us tonight?" Ary said with an arch of her eyebrows.

I couldn't tell whether she truly wanted to make use of me now that I was here or whether she was hoping I'd make a fool of myself. Either one seemed equally possible—and at this point, equally likely to occur. I tipped my head back as I deliberated.

What would my granduncle absolutely despise? What would make him feel as though we had power that he and the rest of the Circle couldn't simply continue to ignore? The Confederation didn't have any special events in the works that I was aware of until next month. The League wanted to act now.

My thoughts traveled back to that night when Granduncle Raymond had confronted me after one of the early meetings I'd attended, and to the things I'd said to him. Immediately, all the fury I'd been holding in since the Exam stirred up again.

I hadn't been lying to Ary about being angry, no matter what she thought.

"It's the members of the Circle who make the decisions on policy," I said. "They'll look the other way and let their security force deal with us as long as they can. So I'd say we should get right in their way where they can't avoid us. With a thousand people, we could probably surround the Confed's main building, where the Circle's chambers are. Blockade them in there for as long as we can. That's the best idea I have."

Luis was nodding with a dreamy distance in his eyes, as if he were already picturing our victory. "I think we can manage that." He turned to Ary. "Does that sound like a productive plan to you?"

"Sure," she said. "Let's see how far it gets us."

If this plan didn't get us anywhere, she'd use that as one more fact to push the League toward her own approach. This time, she might budge them.

I'd better do everything I could to make it work.

We spent a while discussing logistics for the rally, and then people split off into their own groups to work out details or to drift out the door. Noemi snagged my elbow as I moved away from the "stage."

"Come here," she said.

We crossed the hall to a smaller meeting room on the other side. Noemi shut the door. Her hand was trembling as she raised it between us.

"What's going on?" I said. "Is something wrong? Did Ary get on your case about associating with me, or—"

"Just watch," she said, in a voice so urgent I clamped my mouth shut at once. She unfurled her fingers, her hand palm up. Then she sang in a soft, thin voice a lyric about beaming sunlight.

A glow flickered into being over her palm. It was no larger than a quarter and hazy but undeniably there. My jaw dropped.

The glow disappeared, and Noemi clenched her fingers. She looked at me, her eyes shining. There appeared to be an equal mix of apprehension and excitement in her expression.

My voice tumbled out of my mouth. "How the— You *are* Dull, aren't you? You got your evaluation when you were born?" Everyone who'd been born since the Unveiling had been assessed before leaving the hospital or during their first doctor's visit. If Noemi had any magical potential at all, it should have been identified.

She clearly had that potential—I'd seen the evidence right in front of me—but she was also nodding. "I've even seen the certificate. Believe me, I checked it carefully. There was a while when I was in elementary school when I really hoped my parents had lied to me, that I was secretly a mage underneath. I guess I never totally gave up hope that there was a chance."

She bit her lip. "I wasn't just using those books you lent me from an academic perspective. I've been trying out the exercises. After the first week, I started to see tiny effects, but I wasn't sure if I was just imagining it—wishful thinking or whatever. Then last night I managed to do that." She wiggled her fingers. "It seemed pretty definitive."

"I'll say." My head was still reeling. I set my hand against the wall for balance.

The mage who'd tested her could have made a mistake. The paperwork could have been filed wrong somewhere along the way.

Even as I thought of those possibilities, they didn't ring true. Most mages showed their potential outwardly when they were kids without really trying. At least, most of the mages the Confed counted did…

"Do you have a couple of friends here who are Dull that you trust?" I asked. "I think—I think we need an experiment."

* * *

When the phone rang, I knew it was Rocío before I answered. It was usually Wednesday afternoons that she called—and since my best friend had also been carted off overseas and the rest of my friends had gotten busy with college life, my phone didn't ring a whole lot in general these days.

"Hey," I said, and her simple "Hey" in return was a balm on my nerves. She was still all right. Whatever catastrophe she'd been concerned about hadn't happened—yet.

Perhaps the revelation I was about to share would give her some kind of edge in avoiding it altogether.

I cleared my throat and spoke the words I hadn't imagined needing so soon. "You know, I've been thinking about the dragon you conjured on the Day of Letters."

"Have you?" Rocío said, with a slight shift in her inflection. "Hold on a second." There was a rustling as she must have glanced around. A few rhythmic lines in Spanish spilled out with her breath. "Okay, we should be fine now. What's going on?"

"I found out something that could completely overturn the Confed." I paced from one end of my bedroom to the other. "One of the Dull girls in the group I've been working with—I lent her some of my books with exercises for improving one's magical talent... and it turns out she has one. They labeled her nonmagical, but she can *cast*, Rocío. Just a little, and it took her a while to work up to anything notice-worthy, but— I tried guiding a couple of her friends through it, and both of them were able to get a tiny effect after some coaching. It can't be just a mistake."

Rocío let out a shaky laugh. "I think we've been coming

toward the same place from two different angles. Desmond and I found this file— I can check. What are their full names, the three of them?"

When I told her, she gave me a breathless, "I'll be back in a minute," and the phone went dead in my hand. I stared at it.

A file? Were there records of this happening with other Dulls?

It was closer to fifteen minutes before the phone rang again. "Sorry," Rocío said, breathless. "But I found them. Noemi's a three. Darcy is a seven, and Olivia is an eight."

"Wait," I said. "Three what?"

"I don't know exactly. But there's a database that looks like it covers every baby born to a Dull or new-magic family. I'm in there, and Prisha, and Desmond. You're not. And we've all got a number. Everyone we've checked who was named a mage scored at least a ten. Everyone who's a Dull is lower."

A jolt of understanding raced through me. "You think it's a rating of potential. Noemi's only a three, so that would explain why it took her a long time to produce any definite effects. Her friends harmonized with the magic faster."

"That sounds like the best explanation," Rocío said. "I wasn't sure. It's not like there's any way for us to test any theories here. But knowing what you saw…"

She trailed off as if she didn't quite know how to say the words. I said them for her.

"The Confed's leaders have been lying about *everything*, all along. There aren't mages and Dulls. Someone came up with a cut-off point. A level below which they could be sure nothing magical would show up unless someone experienced took the person through the ropes, I suppose. And when was that likely to happen, the way we guard our texts and stick to our own?"

"Yeah. But that means… if even someone who's marked as a

three could eventually cast a little... Pretty much *anyone* could work with the magic."

We were both silent for a moment as that idea sank in. "How could they have hidden this for so long?" I said. "All those mages doing the tests—wouldn't someone have let it slip?"

"It's not mages doing the tests," Rocío said. "At least, not most of the time, I don't think. There aren't enough—officially— to have a mage in every hospital. I saw one of my cousins get her test. It was just a regular nurse on staff who did it, with a little tool she held up to his eye and his ear. She said the reading was sent off to the Confederation for analysis, and my aunt got the letter saying he wasn't magical a week later."

"Hardly anyone might know what the actual data shows, then," I said.

"I bet they'd rather reveal the truth about the Exam than this." A fraught note rang through Rocío's voice. "My phone time is almost up. I wish we could— Thank you for telling me right away. I think there's something I can do, knowing this, right now."

CHAPTER TWENTY-SEVEN

Rocío

"Are you sure this'll make a big enough difference?" Leonie asked as the five of us hurried down the base's hallway to the dorm rooms. A janitor had come through recently, and the saccharine-sweet smell made me feel like I was back in the basement.

If what we were about to do worked the way I hoped, I wouldn't be down there ever again. I wouldn't be *here* ever again.

"It changes everything," I said, keeping my voice low. "A guy in my tutorial class was only listed as a ten in the database. For all we know, the "Dull" president is a *nine*. Do you really think that smidge should be a reason to cut someone off from the magic? Every supposedly Dull person is closer to that ten than the ten is to me or any of you."

Prisha shuddered. "The last thing I want to think about is my whole family learning to cast."

"They'd probably struggle with it," I pointed out. "It wouldn't come easy, and they wouldn't be able to cast very effectively. But even a small talent… This assault the officials are planning, if it hurts the magic, it hurts *everyone*. All those people who've never cast might never get the chance to. That information has to make the Dull government listen."

They feared the power we could wield. Would they really risk losing the chance to gain the same power themselves?

But we didn't have much time to make our case. Just after I'd gotten off the phone with Finn, Commander Revett had given the word that the special ops unit would launch its strike on twelve different enemy targets with the aim of demolishing the buildings and everything in them, along with anyone who tried to get in the way. The assault was scheduled for tomorrow night.

Thirty-six hours—that was our deadline.

Sam tipped his head to Desmond. "Can you access the database once we're out of the base?"

"I managed to email some of the data to myself," Desmond said. "It's only a small chunk of the total, but there'll be enough for people to verify our story. It'd be better if we had numbers on the people who are actually in the Dull government, though. Too bad that database only covers newborn testing. I doubt there's anyone all that important in the White House who's under forty. The records from the first tests during the Unveiling must be somewhere else."

"There won't be numbers anywhere for people much over fifty," I said. "Even during the Unveiling, I don't think the Confed evaluated anyone older than sixteen." My parents, who'd been in their preteens during the Unveiling, had told me that the Confed had claimed anyone over sixteen who hadn't shown spontaneous signs of talent was almost certainly Dull. Not enough of a chance to bother testing hundreds of millions of people across the continent.

"As far as we know," Prisha muttered.

Desmond nudged me. "I grabbed my medical file too, for

when you have time to check it over. It might have some details about my treatment."

I gave him a grateful smile. Maybe if this plan went off without a hitch, I'd be able to focus on how Finn's connection to the magic might be restored. I wished that didn't seem like such a big maybe.

We drew to a halt outside the dorm room Brandt shared with a few of the other male operatives. Sam rapped on the door. "Brandt? It's Sam. Open up."

Brandt edged open the door. The other guy who'd come down to the basement with him sat on the edge of one of the beds behind him, along with Tonya, the other girl, and a couple guys I hadn't talked to much. They were all braced and tense, as if we'd caught them at something they wanted to hide.

Plotting their own special assault, no doubt.

"We need to talk," Sam said.

He might not have been a senior official, but his status as regular mission leader obviously gave him some clout. Brandt's gaze darted from him to the rest of us in the hall, but he stayed at the door.

"What about?"

"I don't think you want us talking about it out here."

Brandt's mouth flattened. "There's nothing I want to talk about with the rest of them."

"Well, too bad," Sam said. "Because this is a package deal. You can talk with us, or you can have a very interesting conversation with Commander Revett in a few minutes."

With a sigh, Brandt backed up to let us in.

As the door thumped shut behind us, my heart started to thud just as loud. The magic niggled along my arms. I inhaled slowly, gathering myself, trying to tune out how crowded the room felt with eleven of us in here now.

Trusting these people could be the biggest mistake of my life.

I already knew I didn't agree with their tactics, and they didn't agree with mine. I could be setting in motion an even bigger disaster, or at least a different one.

But I couldn't do this on my own. I had to admit that now. I needed them—and they needed me. So I was going to do my best to make this work. That was all the magic or anyone else could ask.

"You've come up with a plan to get off the base, right?" I said. "To make it back home? I want in on it."

Brandt's followers exchanged glances that said enough. Brandt folded his arms over his chest. "*Now* you want a part of this? Not that I'm saying we are planning on doing anything like that."

"I want to get back home too," I said. "I want to take on the Dull government. But not the way you're thinking. I've got something better—something that isn't going to turn them against us."

"You've got no idea what we want to do," Brandt snapped. "But, of course, your plan *has* to be better."

I stopped myself from rolling my eyes at him. "I'm not stupid. You want to attack them. Even forgetting any arguments about valuing life or harming the magic or whatever, how far do you really think the six of you are going to get? Maybe you take down a couple of their officials—maybe you even take down the president—and then the rest of them will declare some kind of national emergency and eradicate every mage in the country."

"Sounds like scare tactics to me," Tonya said, her hands balling at her sides.

"Does it really matter?" Sam said evenly. "I've got the feeling there's no way any of you are making it out of here without Rocío's skills on your side."

"If we have to, we'll make it work," one of the other guys muttered, but none of them looked all that convinced.

"You'll have a better chance if I'm helping, won't you?" I said. "What's more important—stopping that assault tomorrow or doing everything exactly your way?"

"What's your great plan, then?" Brandt asked.

I raised my chin. "If I can talk to the right people in the Dull government, I swear to you I can make them call off the attack. I've got connections I think can get me in there. I've got leverage. I just need to get back into the country."

I didn't see any point in sharing the secret we'd learned about the Dulls. This particular audience might want to shut down that information rather than letting it get out. Being able to use magic allowed them to stay superior to all those supposedly nonmagical people they resented.

Just like it did the whole Confed. Why else would the higher-ups among the mages have made the decisions to set a cut-off point and lie about the results?

The girl next to Tonya made a scoffing sound. Brandt scowled at me. "And we're supposed to just take you at your word, Lopez?"

I stared right back at him, letting every ounce of my conviction color my tone. "You're supposed to believe that I wouldn't risk my magic and the safety of everyone I care about going AWOL unless I was sure I could follow through."

Silence fell over the group. I thought I saw Brandt waver, but not enough for him to back down. I inhaled slowly and played the last card I had, the one I'd hoped I wouldn't have to put on the table.

"You'd be coming with us. All the way to the Dulls who call the shots. If I don't follow through on my promise, then I'll have gotten you into the perfect position to switch back to your plan, won't I?"

Brandt's stance loosened a little. He rubbed his mouth. Had they even come up with a solid strategy for getting at the people they wanted to take down once they were on home soil? I might be handing him up everything he'd wanted on a platter.

Please let me not regret this.

"Okay," he said, sounding suddenly hoarse. "I'm going to hold you to that. If you try to leave me behind or screw me over—"

"I'll be there too," Sam said beside me. "I'll make sure everyone keeps their word. You know I've always been fair, right, Brandt? Rocío gets her turn, and if that doesn't pan out, you can get yours."

Brandt lowered his head in acknowledgment. The others were gaping at us as if they couldn't totally believe that what they'd talked about might actually happen. I didn't want to give them a chance to delay Brandt's agreement.

"All right," I said. "Now how do we get out of here?"

* * *

"Duerme tranquilo, duerme entretanto," I murmured, directing the magic toward the lump under the covers of my bed. The presence I'd conjured shifted with a rise and fall of simulated breath, meant to look as if it were my own body sleeping there where I was supposed to be. The sight made me shiver.

I'd created similar conjured figures in Sam's, Desmond's, and Brandt's beds as well. With our usual schedules, no one would expect us to be up for at least another couple hours. My castings should last long enough.

This was the work Brandt's group had needed me for. They'd worked out how to leave the country but not how to do it before the commanders realized they were gone and raised the alarm. The measures I'd put in place had already brought a sharp ache into my chest, and we had a lot more casting ahead. I could see why they'd been worried about attempting to do this much without help.

The three guys coming with me had joined us in the room while I finished, ready for our escape. As I turned toward the door, Leonie grasped Desmond's arm and pulled him in for a quick kiss. Prisha met my eyes and nodded. The two of them were counting on us to make sure they didn't have to charge out into a potential massacre tomorrow.

I murmured the lyrics I'd chosen as the four of us slipped into the hall. The artificial brightness of the recently replaced lights glared down on us. The strands of magic I was conducting shifted around us with a gentle hum, fading us from view while giving off as little residual energy as possible. If I wasn't careful, the soldiers monitoring the base would catch the signs of a huge casting.

I hadn't been sure I could pull off even that delicate maneuver, but the magic grazed my shoulders with a touch that felt almost affectionate, as if it knew I was doing all this to save it. It had bent to my will more easily than ever before.

We were almost to the stairwell when Colonel Alcido stalked around a corner up ahead. All four of us froze. I whispered my concealing 'chantment, a more powerful adaptation of the one we used when in the field, as he marched toward us. Brandt's jaw worked, his hard gaze fixed on the Dull intruder in our midst.

My pulse stuttered at the naked anger in his eyes. He wasn't going to try some stunt out of revenge *now* and get us caught before we'd even gotten out of the building, was he?

What we were setting off to do seemed to matter at least as much to him as it did to me, I reminded myself. In a tiny gesture of solidarity, I rested my elbow against his with just enough pressure that he'd feel it. Brandt glanced at me and made a face, but a little of his rage dimmed. The four of us stood still and silent until Alcido had ducked into a room down the hall.

We darted into the stairwell and emerged into the yard under thin mid-morning sunlight. A sheen of frost crackled under my feet with each step. Brandt swiped his hand over the short spikes of his hair and reached into his pocket for the key Tonya had been able to "borrow" from a sympathetic pilot friend. We found the jeep parked right where she'd said it would be, just off the main drive that led to the gate.

My voice rose and resonated, expanding the concealing bubble around us. I had barely enough attention left to find my way into the back seat of the jeep. Sam eased me in the right direction with a hand on my arm. As I settled next to Desmond, our former mission leader got into the front seat next to Brandt, who'd insisted on driving.

I propelled even more focus into my words, letting the melody twist and stretch as the engine rumbled. Desmond started murmuring in a similar rhythm. The joint casting took me back to the Exam, when he and I and the rest of our team had worked together to freeze our enemies rather than fight back. I couldn't say that memory was a *good* one, but there was something reassuring about it.

The hardest part lay ahead of us, though. We had to get through that gate without anyone realizing it had been penetrated.

I squared my shoulders and extended my awareness out toward the thick steel door, carried by the hum of the magic. That familiar energy reverberated around me and flowed forward to draw a vast cloak from one side of the wall to the other. Desmond's voice mingled with mine, and then Sam's too. We called more and more magic to us, conducting it into an immense concealing shell that would reflect only what anyone looking would expect to see out here.

Somewhere behind us, a garage door squealed as it opened. My nerves jumped. I sang louder, holding my voice as steady as I could. A pinch of a headache was forming between my eyebrows. I motioned Brandt onward, restraining myself from glancing behind us to see how close we were to being discovered.

Brandt pressed the controls to open the gate and drove slowly up to it. The door swung open. The three of us around him murmured on, all of us rigid in our seats.

The jeep eased past the wall into the sprawling, hilled landscape on the other side. I braced myself for a shout to carry from the base. All I heard was the gate whirring shut behind us. The moment it clinked into place, I released that part of my casting with a ragged exhalation.

Desmond was grinning. "Wow. That was something."

"It was something, all right," Brandt muttered. He gunned the engine. "We've still got to make it to the airport and onto a plane before they catch on. I hope your tricks worked, Lopez."

A slightly hysterical laugh escaped me. "So do I."

"Should we fly as directly as we can into Washington?" Sam asked.

I shook my head. "I mentioned I had connections? We need to get to New York. I've got an in with the Pentagon."

* * *

A thin layer of snow blanketed the grass beyond the park's well-trampled paths. In the fading daylight, icicles glimmered like knives on the bare branches of the trees. I stamped my feet to drive more warmth into them. Ten days until Christmas. ¡Feliz pinche Navidad!

"How long is this going to take?" Brandt said, his shoulders hunched to bring his collar up to his ears. He should've bought a hat when we'd ditched our special-ops-issued clothes for civilian wear.

"He'll be here soon." I glanced again at the prepaid phone I'd bought as soon as we'd gotten to the airport. No new texts, but no reason to believe anything had gone wrong. Yet.

"Don't be such a baby," Sam said to Brandt lightly. "You've made it through five Estonian winters. I think you can handle New York in mid-December."

"If this actually works, I'm never leaving California again," Brandt retorted.

My spirits leapt at the crunch of footsteps in the snow. A tall, lanky figure in a gray wool coat came into view between the trees. He'd said he'd come right away, but he must have dropped everything to get here this fast, simply because I'd said I needed him. The knot of tension in my chest released, even though we were still far from victory, replaced by a rush of warmth and affection.

More than affection, really. Maybe there were other things I should have admitted to myself by now. Like that the boy raising his head with a smile that could rival the sun had captured every bit of my heart.

Finn's smile faltered a little when he took in the company I'd brought with me. I hadn't wanted to risk saying much of anything when I'd asked him to meet me, in case someone was keeping an eye on his phone. He stopped in front of me, close enough to reach for my hand.

"I wasn't expecting you to be back this early," he said. "What's going on?"

I couldn't quite manage to smile in return, not when I was about to lay so much of this mission on him. "I need a favor. We have to talk to your sister."

CHAPTER TWENTY-EIGHT

Finn

I'd once thought of my sister Margo as the Lockwood patron saint of Justice. Today I was simply hoping she'd be a saint of Nearly Lost Causes. We were appearing on her doorstep, a Burnout and a special ops soldier gone AWOL, and I wasn't entirely certain what justice even was anymore.

I'd gone to see her right before the Exam, and she'd helped me then without really wanting to. With a little luck, she'd do the same today. Of course, last time she'd been expecting me.

Margo answered my buzz with a bleary, "Hello?" It was six in the morning, late enough that I didn't feel *too* guilty about waking her but early enough that I knew she wouldn't have left for work.

"It's Finn," I said. "And a friend. Can we come up?"

Margo sounded more alert in an instant. "Finn? What's wrong? Yes, come up, of course."

By the time we made it up the stairs to the door to her loft, she'd pulled back her ash-brown hair into a hasty bun and thrown on a sweater and jeans. Her worried eyes searched mine for a few seconds before her gaze slid to my companion.

"This is Rocío," I said quickly. "We were—" I gritted my teeth at the 'chantment that prevented me from even saying we'd been in the Exam together. All I could offer were the facts on public record. "She just made Champion."

My hand curled around Rocío's, my fingers twining with hers. She offered her other hand to Margo. "I'm sorry we're meeting for the first time like this, but it really is good to meet you."

Margo blinked and accepted the handshake. I could tell our joined fingers hadn't escaped her notice. She motioned us into the warmth of the loft. She'd always liked the heat at least a couple of degrees higher than my parents preferred.

"What's going on?" she said. "What are you two doing here?"

"I'll explain," I said. "Can I get a glass of water? This could take a little while."

"Sure, no problem."

As she hustled to the kitchen at one end of the open-concept space, I let go of Rocío to sit on one of the cushy leather armchairs in the living area. Margo set the sweating glass on the distressed wood coffee table and sank down on the couch across from me. Rocío lingered behind the other armchair as if she didn't feel quite comfortable sitting down.

I picked up the glass, turned it in my hand, and took a sip. The water burned cold down my throat. The scrabble of tiny claws carried from Margo's bedroom where her two rats were darting around in their cage. My stomach twisted with memories of how her former third pet had met its death—memories I *wished* I could wipe from my head.

"Rocío has seen things, heard things, since she was named Champion," I started. In truth, our story wasn't all that long, especially since Rocío wasn't capable of telling me many of the details of her situation beyond her plan for what she did now, but the argument afterward might take some time. "Something's about to happen with National Defense that could deal a real blow to the magic. Weaken it, possibly even destroy it."

Margo's expression had turned puzzled. "Destroy the *magic*?"

"I don't know if that's possible," Rocío said from where she was standing. "But I've hearkened firsthand, many times, how castings that are used to destroy things or to threaten lives affect its energy. The magic turns shaky, almost panicked. Harder to conduct. Sometimes it even lashes out and causes more damage itself. I'm afraid of what could happen if there were a huge impact of a lot of those kinds of castings all at once."

"I've never heard anything about an effect like that."

"I'm sure you can think of a few reasons why people in the Confed might want to keep information like that guarded," I said. "There's only so much we can tell you because there are too many things we can't talk about, as much as we might want to. I know there's a real reason for concern. Rocío's the most sensitive mage I've ever met—she's got a connection to the magic not many could match. If she says there's a danger, it's real. But we can't stop National Defense's operations on our own. You know people who could."

Margo tensed. "You want me to get you access to my boss. Even if I thought bringing you in was a good idea, the Joint Chief of Staff doesn't make military decisions, you know. He can only advise, not change orders already given."

"The Director could help us speak to the people who do make the decisions in the Pentagon, couldn't he?" Rocío said. "I don't think it'd take much for me to get him on board. There's something I can show him that'll make a huge difference. But I have to reach him first."

Margo glanced across the room to where her purse was sitting by the door. Rocío tracked her gaze. It made sense that my sister would keep whatever she needed for accessing her workplace in there.

"Can you show *me*?" she asked, shifting her attention back to Rocío.

Rocío's mouth slanted down. "I can't. But I can say—we've found out that Dulls aren't as nonmagical as we thought. The Confed has been denying hundreds of millions of people the chance to learn how to do what we can do. That's got to make a difference to the Dull leaders."

I'd told her we could trust my sister with that revelation, and I still believed that. My heart still lurched briefly at the shock that stiffened Margo's face.

"You can't be serious," she said.

I coughed. "She is. I've seen *that* part with my own eyes. They've been lying to everyone, Margo."

Margo looked down at her lap and then at me. For a second, her eyes looked almost as haunted as when she'd tried to convince me to back out of the Exam.

"I don't know what's going on here," she said. "And I'll look into it any way I can, I promise you that. But even if people in the Confederation have been keeping secrets—maybe they have good reasons. Maybe it'll put us all at risk to let that information out there."

"I've seen too much to believe their motives are that benevolent," I said quietly.

"Okay. I just can't— I'll look into it, like I said. But my first loyalty has to be to the Confed, not to the Dulls. Finn, you know that. Taking you in so you can tell their government these things —it would be outright treason. If there's something to this conspiracy, something that needs to be said, we'll get there. Veritas numquam perit."

Truth never expires, the quote meant. Nevertheless, it appeared the truth we were carrying was both too much and not enough to get us where we needed to go. I bowed my head. "Are you going out to Washington today?"

She shook her head. "I'm remote this week. But next Tuesday I'm heading over for a couple of days. If I've dug anything up, I'll do whatever I can to resolve this."

"It could be too late then," Rocío said.

"This is the best I can offer."

"If you—" I waved my hand, and my drink slipped from my fingers. It hit the floor with a crackle of glass and a splash of water over the hardwood.

I jumped up. "Damn. I'm sorry."

"It's fine; it's fine." Margo dashed over to the kitchen and grabbed a towel. She handed it to me and ducked into her bedroom to retrieve her broom while I sopped up the water. The wet glass made a horrible gritty sound against the wood when she swept it up. She paused to peer at the boards, searching for stray splinters. I plucked a shard from under the chair, and she gave that space another sweep too.

Rocío came up behind the couch as we finished. She caught my eye and took the towels from me to bring them to the sink. "I guess we should get going, then. It just seemed worth a shot."

Margo straightened up, clutching the dustpan. "You're not going to be spreading these accusations all over the place, are you?"

"I'm not looking to cause a riot," Rocío said. "Right now, all I want is to protect the magic."

"If you can just wait, maybe I can help. I'm not saying no, only not right now, not without checking things out first."

"I understand. And I appreciate that." Rocío offered her a small smile.

As we moved toward the door, Margo touched my arm. "Finn. Since you're here... Have you been involved in these 'Freedom of Magic' protests that've been happening?"

I tried to keep my expression blank, but I wasn't sure if I succeeded. "Would it be a problem if I were?"

"No. I mean, they haven't done anything criminal so far. You should be able to protest if you want to. Just... don't go to the rally today?"

I froze. "How do you know there's a rally today?"

She smiled crookedly. "Do you really think it's that easy to keep a secret once enough people have joined in? I *wouldn't* know, except I heard a couple of my colleagues talking. The Circle found out. They've coordinated with the Dull police forces to take a 'firm stance' on the protesters, to shut things down before the rally even gets started. I'd rather you weren't there. It's not going to get very far anyway."

"Do you think the police are going to hurt the people who *are* there?" I asked.

"I hope not. Not on purpose. But I know how things can turn ugly when tempers are running hot—on both sides."

She might not be wrong. If the police came down on us before we'd even really assembled, some of the League members would be frustrated enough to fight back. We could end up with a riot after all. A trickle of nausea ran through me.

"Thank you for the warning, at least," I said. "And if you change your mind about the other thing—"

"You'll hear from me soon," she said. "Even if I don't."

"You're not going to, like, call Granduncle Raymond on us?"

She made a face. "Should I be thinking I need to?"

"No." I raised my hand as if swearing. "No one else is going to find out anything on this subject from me."

I wasn't making any promises about Rocío, but that statement appeared to satisfy my sister.

We'd walked a couple of blocks down the Tribeca street before I turned to Rocío. "Did you get what you need?"

"I think so," she said. "I found a key card and an ID badge in her purse with the Pentagon symbol on them. I wasn't sure if I could replicate the scan code perfectly in time, so I grabbed them and left conjured replacements. She shouldn't notice anything different if she's not going out there until next week. We can return the real ones before then." She hooked her arm around mine. "You made an excellent distraction."

"My one small contribution to your epic plan." I hadn't really expected Margo to agree to our request, which was why we'd been prepared to take advantage of the visit in other ways. While my sister had been busy with the broken glass, Rocío had surreptitiously riffled through her work things under a casting to deflect attention.

"I wouldn't have gotten in there at all without you." Rocío leaned into me for a second, squeezed my arm, and then released it. "I have to get going. We'll want to catch the first train out to the Pentagon. What are you going to do about the rally?"

That question had been nagging at me from the moment we'd left Margo's loft. "I don't know. I can't just leave everyone else to the wolves, so to speak."

"Of course you can't." She reached for me again, pulling me into a hug. I hugged her back, closing my eyes, soaking in the experience of getting to hold her for just a little longer.

"Promise me you'll stay as safe as you can?" she said when she eased back.

"If you'll promise the same."

"Always." She hesitated, her gaze locked on my face, her mouth tightening. "Finn…"

"What?" I said, my pulse skittering.

"No, don't look like that. I'm just trying—" She drew in a shaky breath and brought her hand to the side of my face. "It still hasn't been very long, and we still haven't gotten to spend all that much time together, but I—I feel what I feel. I want to say it. Just in case. So… I love you."

A rush of emotion socked me in the throat. I couldn't have spoken right then if my life had depended on it. All I could do was cup her face in turn and kiss her with all I had.

When our lips parted, I kept my head near hers. "I love you too," I said, still a little choked up, but in the best possible way. O gods, how could I let go of her now?

I had to, though. I held her close for a moment longer. She bobbed up on her toes to give me one more quick kiss, a teary shimmer in her eyes.

"We'll have lots more time to talk about it after today, right?" she said.

"We will," I said firmly. "We absolutely will."

I forced my hand to drop to my side. Rocío shot me one last smile before she hurried down the street to where her colleagues were waiting.

I ducked into a little coffee shop to catch my breath and recalibrate my thoughts to the task ahead. It took a few minutes and the strongest espresso they offered, between sips of which I may have grinned like a maniac. Eventually, my heartbeat evened out and I focused on the less pleasant situation ahead of me.

The rally was supposed to start at noon. Would the Circle even be in the building if they were aware we were coming?

As soon as the question crossed my mind, I knew the answer. They wouldn't let the other Confed employees see them cowed by a bunch of Dampered mages and Burnouts. That was why they'd called the police to their aid, even though officials like my granduncle hated relying on Dull law enforcement. They wanted to go about their day showing how little we could affect them.

We had to prove them wrong. We had to make this rally work, one way or another.

Stepping back onto the sidewalk, I fished out my phone and tapped Tamara's number. If anyone had an idea, it'd be her. Based on texts I'd gotten in the past, she was usually up by this time in the morning.

"Hi, Finn," she said when she picked up, her voice slightly muffled as if she had the phone tucked into her shoulder while she did something else with her hands. "What's the word? Confirming final plans for the big day?"

"Possibly alternate plans," I said. "I just found out from a source I trust that the Circle knows we're coming. They've got the city's police force on standby to shut us down the moment we start gathering."

Tamara sucked in her breath, and her voice became clearer as she shifted the phone. "Well, I guess that level of pushback had to start sometime."

"What do we *do* about it? We'll look weak if we let them break up the rally before it starts—but I don't want us getting into some sort of street fight. We'd never win that anyway."

"No," she said. "We'll be much better off if we let them fight us while we stand strong. We don't have to stand for very long if there's an audience. It only takes one good photo or video clip to make us the valiant heroes."

"If we get that in time," I said, and an idea hit me with a jolt. "I guess we're a lot more likely to get a key shot if more people are there recording it."

"Absolutely. I know the Dull media didn't care too much before, but I'll put in some tips to the news stations, see if more of them bite this time."

My flare of excitement sputtered out with a clenching of my gut. The regular media reps were hesitant to cover mage news, but there were others who weren't.

"I can make sure they bite," I said slowly. "Lots of them."

"Well, you get to it, then. I'll see you on the street."

My arm sank as I hung up. I picked up my pace despite the

resistance building inside me. On the busy street up ahead, I'd be able to hail a cab.

I wasn't due for a shift at Media Outreach today, but I imagined I could talk my way in. I could linger long enough to get my hands on a list of all the contacts with the local media who were particularly interested in mage affairs. It'd probably be the *last* time I set foot in the building, once it became clear how I'd exploited my new placement.

There would be other placements. Perhaps even ones with as much appeal and promise as that one had offered. If there weren't, well...

It was the least I could do. I'd made my own promises in the last week: to Callum, to Luis. Forcing the Circle to listen was more important than my future job satisfaction. If Rocío was right, if catastrophe was looming and it turned out she couldn't stop it, people were going to need leaders to show them the way through the chaos—better leaders than my granduncle and his accomplices. If we handled this right, we in the League could be the ones guiding everyone toward the future we all deserved.

A taxi was cruising toward me as I reached the street. I could mourn what might have been later. Without a moment's wavering, I raised my hand.

CHAPTER TWENTY-NINE

Rocío

The train sang along the tracks with a high metallic whine as we sped toward our destination. With the magical enhancements that had been developed over the years since the Unveiling, the trip from Manhattan to the capitol took less than three hours. We'd get to the Pentagon not long after the business day started.

But it was already afternoon on the other side of the ocean, where Commander Revett would be preparing Prisha and Leonie and all the other operatives for tonight's assault. How many hours did we have before she sent them out?

"Once we get into the building with the pass you lifted, do you have a plan for how we find this Zacher guy?" Sam asked. We'd spent most of the last couple hours researching the staff at the Pentagon before deciding that John Zacher, Secretary of Defense, was our best bet. He'd made a few pro-mage statements in the past—and he had the authority to call off an attack if we could convince him to.

"We don't need much of a plan," Desmond announced. "I

just found the office number. It's not secret or anything. Third floor, outer ring, near corridor eight. That sounds simple enough."

"As long as no one realizes we don't belong there before we *get* to the office," I said. My hand rose to my face instinctively. My skin felt stiff beneath the layer of foundation I'd applied.

During the breaks I'd taken from researching, I'd been holed up in the little train bathroom with some compacts and a lipstick palette, attempting to make myself look as mature and professional as I could. I was pretty sure I could pass for at least twenty now if I gave off a confident air.

A 'chantment might have done the trick more effectively, but casting an outright illusion felt too risky. The Pentagon had magical security in place alongside the Dull staff. Margo's pass gave off a tingle of energy they must scan along with the bar code. I'd 'chanted her photo to echo my features as subtly as I could, weaving those tiny threads under the existing casting. With luck, no one would detect it.

How much luck were we going to need to get through this?

My fingers shifted to my collar, tugging the sunburst necklace Mom had given me out from under my blouse and squeezing it as I willed myself to stay calm. At least Sam and Brandt were old enough to pass as government staff. Desmond had been practicing his solemn, stressed-out expression—he'd say he was an intern if anyone asked.

Brandt was doing his own research on his phone in the seat kitty-corner to mine. "Zacher has a couple of kids," he said. "One of them's my age, but there's an eleven-year-old daughter." He turned his phone to show a photo of a smiling blond girl next to her father, who was in full uniform. "Could be a point for putting pressure on him. Could you find out where she goes to school?" He nudged Desmond with his knee.

Desmond grimaced at him, and I glared. "We're not threatening someone's *kid*."

"I'm still not convinced you're going to talk him out of this."

"I'm going to do more than talk," I muttered. "I'm just not going to be a terrorist myself."

Brandt shrugged. "I'm not saying I'd hurt her. He doesn't know who else we might have on the ground. I'll keep this information in my pocket for plan B in case yours goes sideways."

"You're going to give Rocío a proper chance," Sam said in a terse voice.

"You're not the mission leader here," the younger guy said, sinking down in his seat. "As far as I can tell, you're handing that over to the sixteen-year-old girl."

Something about that comment prickled deeper than I'd have expected. "What is your problem anyway?" I said. "You talked about seeing the unit as your family—great. Don't you have an *actual* family here? Someone must have sent you to whatever academy taught you to cast in Latin. Don't you care what might happen to them if you go attacking the most powerful Dulls in the country?"

Brandt glowered at me. "Yeah, I've got a family. I've got parents who lost all our money on stupid investments before they drowned when I was five on some vacation they couldn't really afford, and I've got grandparents who never let me forget what an *enormous* favor they were doing by paying my academy tuition and letting me stay in their house—if they bothered to talk to me at all. They already think I'm the worst thing that ever happened to them."

It took me a moment to find my voice, and then all I managed was a strained, "Oh."

"Exactly. Why the hell would I let them stop me from keeping my friends back on the base alive? I'll do what it takes. If

you do what you say you can do, *you* won't have to worry about
my family either, all right?"

I swallowed thickly. "Right. That's the plan."

I yanked my attention back to the article I'd been reading.
Sam had asked about how we'd get to Zacher. The real question
was how I'd make our case once we got there. The more I knew
about him, the better I'd be able to shape my argument. At least,
that's how I imagined someone like Finn would've approached it.
I wished he could've been here to do the talking with that silver
tongue of his.

Zacher looked like a decent enough guy, as much as you
could tell from photographs. He kept his gray-and-white
speckled hair cut military-short on top of a long face with a hint
of jowls. His eyes were warm brown, and in most of the photos
his smile struck me as genuine.

He'd complimented the Confed for their assistance with Dull
military efforts here and overseas, once making a wry comment
about how it pained him to think of how much more effective he
could've been in his early years with a talent like ours at his
disposal. He must have pictured what it'd be like to be magical
once in a while. And he must be keeping track of those National
Defense efforts.

I'd bet everyone in the Pentagon was pretty cautious about
how much we mages took on, even while they were pushing us
for more concrete progress. A couple of Zacher's colleagues were
on record talking about "confirming loyalties" and the need for
central leadership rather than the Confed governing their own.
From the way Colonel Alcido had barged onto the base, I
guessed they were already putting some of those principles into
action, whether the Confed liked it or not.

"Hey!" Desmond said, grinning. "I just thought—there's a
'chantment I can do, probably without anyone noticing, that
might help grease the wheels." His grin turned sheepish. "I used

to cast it on teachers when I got in trouble as a kid. It calms the person down a little, makes them feel more, ah, kindly disposed toward you. Not a huge effect—I wasn't going to risk getting caught—but I think it saved me from suspension a couple times when I couldn't resist pulling a little prank on the Dull kids."

"Anything that helps Zacher stay open-minded sounds good to me," I said.

A digitized voice carried over the speaker, announcing the stop right before ours. We were nearly there. My pulse kicked up a notch.

When the departing passengers had gotten off and the train thrummed into motion again, I walked down the aisle to stretch my legs. The magic seemed to flow with me, tugging at my hair, twining around my wrists. I kept going all the way to the doors, and then I wasn't sure I wanted to turn around and go back. My gut was listing queasily. I stared at the landscape whipping by outside, not sure whether the sight was making my nausea better or worse.

Sam ambled over. He came to a stop beside me and peered out the window with me for a minute. "You okay?" he asked.

I rubbed my arms. The pleated fabric of the blouse I'd bought for this role didn't feel any more *me* than the makeup did. I couldn't wait to get out of all of it.

"Brandt's right," I said. "This is all basically my idea. What if I can't take it far enough? If this plan doesn't work, all those other people in our unit could be out there dying tonight." I'd have failed them. Failed my parents and Finn. Failed the magic. Failed all the people who should be able to reach out to that magic.

"Rocío…" Sam hesitated. He turned to lean against the wall, his mouth going crooked. "I don't know if this is going to help, but—I'm glad you pushed for this. I'm glad to be here supporting your personal mission. There's a hell of a lot that's already screwed up about the unit—about becoming Champion at all and about the Dull government's involvement. I've never liked how it works."

I blinked at him. "Then why have you gone along with it?"

"Well, I— My best friend and I declared for the Exam together, you know? We made Champion together. We went into the field together." He sucked in a breath. "Our second year out, he stumbled onto a magical explosive. There wasn't enough left to even try to save him."

My throat constricted. "I'm so sorry."

He made an almost casual gesture as if to say, *What can you do?*, but his gaze had slid away from me. "I could have stopped it from happening. I hadn't scanned quite that far. I got distracted by one of the locals I was talking to. I didn't consider— And then he was gone. I made sure I was a lot more careful after that, but it was impossible to even consider an idea as huge as challenging the whole Confed when I wasn't sure I could completely trust my own judgment. Like you said, what if I screwed things up even more?"

"So why shouldn't I worry about that?" I said.

He raised his head again. "Because I regret now that I let those worries hold me back for so long. Maybe there are people I could have saved if I'd been willing to speak up, to do *something*, or at least try. I don't know if I can make a good enough case with Zacher, not feeling the magic the way you do, but even if you decide you don't want that responsibility after all, I'll take it on. I'm done with doubt. We've let this system go on too long."

I inhaled slowly and realized that my queasiness had eased off. The responsibility wasn't all on me—I had to keep reminding myself. Maybe I couldn't do everything; maybe I couldn't save everyone. No, almost definitely I couldn't. But I had help to take up the slack where I might falter.

I'd do as much as I could. No one who cared about me would ask more than that.

"Yeah," I said. "Thank you. That did help."

The digitized voice called down again, warning us of our upcoming stop. My chest constricted, but I felt steadier as I walked back to my seat to grab my purse.

Outside the train station, I led the way, veering apart from the tourists heading for the visitor's gate. As we approached the nearest employee entrance, I kept my chin high, my strides brisk, and looped the lanyard for Margo's pass over my neck. The three guys fell into step behind me. I didn't have to get just myself through but them as my visitors too.

I gave Security the quick spiel we'd decided on, and after a few minutes we had the guys' visitor badges. One of the officers checked my pass and waved me on while sending the others through a scanner.

A woman in a loose business suit was standing off to the side of the entrance area, her gaze seemingly distant as her fingers drummed against each other. The quiver of magic that passed over my skin made me suspect she was a mage on staff, checking us all over for 'chantments. We'd done no castings that would catch her attention, gracias a Dios.

Then, just like that, we were in.

We came to a stop in a long hallway. The stark white walls gave me an unwelcome flashback to the Exam buildings. I focused on the directions Desmond had found. We were already in the outer ring, so up to the third floor we'd go.

We passed several employees as we hustled along to the office for the Secretary of Defense, but none of them gave us more than a passing glance. Outside the office door, a young man in a military uniform was poised, a gun gleaming in the holster at his hip. My heart beat even faster. I gave him a quick nod that I hoped said, *Oh, just another normal workday,* as I reached for the door handle. His expression stayed impassive, but he didn't move to stop us.

I'd known we wouldn't be able to march straight in to see Zacher. The clatter of keyboards filled the room on the other side where various members of the administrative staff were working away, this one on her computer, that one on his phone. A woman at the desk closest to the inner door got up.

"Can I help you?" she asked.

"We're here to see Secretary Zacher," I said.

She frowned and tapped her mouse. "I don't believe he has any appointments scheduled at this time."

"It's a last-minute addition," I said, holding my voice as steady as I could. "Not through the usual channels. If you tell him it's about Võru, Estonia, he'll confirm."

She gave me a skeptical look, and I summoned my best haughty air, channeling Prisha. Behind me, Sam crossed his arms and sighed as if impatient with the delay. After another frown at her computer screen, the woman slipped into the inner office.

I wished I could have given a more specific cue, but the silencing 'chantment held me back. I hoped mentioning the town without context would be enough. Võru had been where we'd gotten the recorder from Polina—our first proof, and major proof, that two of the major insurgent groups were moving toward collaboration. If Zacher was paying any attention to mage military affairs, he should recognize the significance.

The secretary emerged a minute later looking even more puzzled. "He says he'll see you."

I'd thought my nerves were jittering before, but that was nothing compared to the lurch of my pulse as I stepped into the inner office. There was no mistaking that this workplace belonged to someone incredibly powerful.

When the door clicked shut, not a sound filtered through from outside. John Zacher stood behind his polished desk, which was so broad it could've supported a queen-size mattress. Velvet curtains hung by the windows, and an

American flag draped from a brass pole beside a stretch of mahogany bookcases. My feet sank into the thick pile of the rug, and for a second, I wasn't sure I could've lifted them if I'd wanted to.

This man's decisions could make the difference between thousands living or dying.

He looked us up and down, his brown eyes a lot less warm without the smile from the photos. "Who are you?" he said. "And what does this have to do with Võru? You'd better give a good answer quickly, or I'll have security here in an instant."

I drew my posture as straight and tall as I could. "Unfortunately, it's difficult for me to talk very plainly," I said. "Because of my position. But we know about Võru. And if I mention Kolomna and Livny and Makat, you know what event I'm referring to, don't you?"

Zacher rested his hands on his desk, but his shoulders had tensed even more. The three locations I'd given him were locations our base had been assigned to strike. No one should have known about those plans except operatives on the base and whoever was in this man's inner circle.

"You're part of the Confederation of Mages' National Defense division," he said.

I gave him a pained smile. "I can't talk about that, sir."

Zacher's gaze slid from me to the three guys behind me. At my left, Sam bobbed his head. Desmond offered a shaky smile of his own. I couldn't see Brandt, but that was probably better for my nerves.

"With all the benefits magic has brought us, it does make everything more complicated at the same time." The Secretary of Defense shook his head. "I assume there's something you *can* tell me about why you're here?"

"We're on the verge of a disaster," I said. "One large enough to make it worth the risk of coming here."

Zacher exhaled sharply. "All right. I'm not going to ignore that. But why are you coming to me and not your own people?"

The idea that the Confed's leaders were any more "my people" than he was, especially after the recent discoveries we'd made, seemed absurd. A slightly hysterical giggle bubbled in my lungs. I managed to will it away.

"They won't listen to me," I said. "I've tried. They..." My commanders and the Circle would probably burn me out for telling him this, but they didn't know, and it was about time someone said it. "They're scared of you. Of the entire nonmagical community. The mages at the top have had so much power for so long, and they're worried that if they don't keep showing off that power by putting it toward the things your government asks for, you'll all turn on us, and then they'll have nothing."

"But *you're* not afraid."

My mouth twitched. "I never expected to have much power in the first place. I've got a lot more to lose if I stay quiet than if I speak up."

Desmond adjusted his hand at his side. I didn't dare look at him directly to see if I could notice him pattering out the subtle casting that he'd said would encourage Zacher's sympathies.

"And what is the nature of this disaster?" the Secretary of Defense asked.

"I've come to realize over the last few months that magic is more than just aimless energy we can conduct," I said. "It has its own intentions. It can get stronger or weaker. It shows distress when it's harmed... and conducting it for destructive purposes harms it. The more it's twisted to those ends, the more it falters. When you take that into account, and what's meant to happen at the places I mentioned earlier, I hope you can see why we're concerned. I don't know if the magic could ever recover from a blow that hard. Is it really worth getting the upper hand for who knows how long if we could lose something so precious?"

I was prepared for the skeptical expression he gave me. At least he didn't laugh in my face. "None of the officials in National Defense have said anything about this to me," he said. "Why is it only a concern now?"

"They don't want you to know," I said. "They don't want to reveal any weaknesses or limitations to your people. And why *wouldn't* it be happening now? Up until a few decades ago, mages only used magic in secret. We weren't out fighting massive wars. In those few decades, we've been warping it in more and more destructive ways. We've pushed it to the breaking point."

"What is it you're asking me to do, then?"

I fixed him with my coolest stare. "After tonight, it might be too late. National Defense answers to you. You can make decisions. You can change your mind."

A sound somewhere between a cough and a laugh escaped Zacher. His jaw worked. "That's a big ask, Miss..."

"Lopez," I said. "Rocío Lopez." It wasn't as if the Confed wouldn't know I'd been here soon enough anyway.

"Now, I haven't been on the ground out there, but I get all the reports. I know that a lot of strategy went into the plan for tonight, and a lot of time and dedicated effort went into gathering the necessary intel to get there in the first place. If what you're saying is true, then I can see why you came here, but I can't reverse a decision that big on one small group's say-so. It could be disastrous if we *don't* act."

I held out my hands in a plea. "I don't know all the answers," I said. "I'm not saying we shouldn't act at all. Just not like this. Hold off and insist on re-strategizing taking what I've told you into consideration. I don't think anyone's aware of any impending action on our enemies' end yet. We have time. If something has to be done... shouldn't we do it as right as we can?"

"We can't trust these people to stay put," Zacher said. "We

can't trust them not to have something up their sleeve we aren't aware of. We've already got a sure thing ready to go. I'm sorry."

He was pulling back from us, retreating into the familiar pattern of warfare and conflict. I hadn't been able to say enough. But I still hadn't done more than talk.

"Look," Brandt started with an edge in his voice.

I cut in before *he* could screw this up. "What if I told you there's more that the Confederation has been hiding from everyone, even from most of us mages—things that affect everyone in this country, including you? What if I could prove it? Would that make a difference?"

Zacher considered me. "It depends on what you're talking about, but proof will always matter."

I braced myself. This would be the first time Brandt heard the news too. "There aren't really magical and nonmagical people. *Everyone* has at least a tiny ability to conduct magic. You could, with the proper training. All of the officers and soldiers under you could. The assessments the Confederation does don't split apart two totally different groups of people; they just have a cut-off line where they decide you don't have enough natural talent that they need to address it. The whole division between mages and 'Dulls' is a lie."

"What?" Brandt snapped behind me, and Sam moved to quiet him. As he yanked the other guy to the side, I tuned out their voices. Zacher was staring at me. The Secretary of Defense was the only one I had to get through to right now.

"That's quite a claim," he said. "How do you intend to prove it?"

His voice held a note I thought I recognized—a lot like the faint thread of longing that colored my parents' tones when they talked about the few years that they'd had full use of their talent, before they'd been Dampered.

I gave him a smile I hoped looked confident. "I can teach *you* to conduct magic right now if you'll let me. You won't be able to produce much of an effect yet, but it should be enough for you to confirm what I said."

The offer was a gamble. If Zacher's innate magical capacity was too low, I might not be able to get him to produce any effect in our limited time. But it was all I had. The hum in the air around us quivered as if in anticipation. As if the magic were eager for the chance to interact with someone new.

Zacher couldn't quite disguise his own eagerness. "What would I have to do?" he asked, transfixed.

I'd spent a good part of last night poring over Finn's instructional books with him, memorizing the exercises he'd said had most helped the Dull friends he'd taught.

"It'll be easier if you sit down," I said. "You'll want to be able to give this all your concentration. The exercises use meditation, music, and patterning, just to learn how to hearken the magic in the first place. It could take a little while before you're ready to try to conduct it."

Zacher paused. He looked at Sam and Brandt, who were still arguing in hushed but harsh voices in the corner.

"Just you," he said. "The others will wait outside."

"Fine with me," I said, shooting a glare Brandt's way.

Brandt started to protest, but Sam cut him off with a light cuff to his head. "If this works, she's saving the whole unit's hide. Isn't that what you wanted?"

Brandt's mouth snapped shut. He scowled, but he left with Sam and Desmond.

When the Secretary of Defense and I were alone in the room, Zacher lowered himself into his immense leather chair.

"I can't say I can give you a *lot* of time," he said. "But let's see where we get with this."

"Okay." I wet my lips, my heart hammering all over again. "Close your eyes. Focus on your breathing to start. There's a particular rhythm: two short breaths in, a long breath out. We can start there."

* * *

My three fellow operatives were waiting just outside the door when I emerged. The secretary shot them another perturbed look, but they seemed oblivious.

"So?" Desmond said quietly. "How did it go?"

"I think he's almost convinced," I said. "He sent me out here so he could make sure he could do it on his own—that I wasn't the one controlling what was happening."

In the last few minutes of our practice session, Zacher had managed to conduct the flow of the magic enough to nudge a piece of paper and to make the surface of the coffee in his mug ripple. I couldn't blame him for wanting to test his apparent skill out without me watching.

The door behind me opened sooner than I'd expected. "Come back in," Zacher said. "All of you."

Inside his grand office, he stopped in front of his desk and turned to face us. A strange light had come into his eyes, a little wild.

"I have a lot more questions," he said. "I understand it'll be difficult for you to answer most of them. But until I can get those answers—I'm putting all major military action on the Confederation's side on hold, as long as there are no significant offensives against us. You can rest a little easier for now."

My shoulders sagged in relief. I could've hugged him if I hadn't been sure that would not go over well.

"Thank you," I said. "So much."

"I don't want to lose track of you four," Zacher added. "I assume your commanders will be looking for you. I can place you in a safe house or similar until we have the issue sorted out."

The thought of being locked up somewhere near the capitol made my stomach twist. "I need to get back to Manhattan," I said. "I have a friend who might need my help." Finn's rally would be starting soon. I couldn't just disappear on him.

"We can arrange a safe house there easily enough," Zacher said. "I'll send a few guards with you. Don't try to slip them, and you'll be free to move around. Wait a moment while I make the necessary calls."

I backed up a step as he picked up his phone. My eyes caught Sam's, and he gave me an encouraging nod. Desmond was beaming. Brandt's expression was clouded, his mouth slanted as if he was torn between relief at our victory and anger at the secret I'd revealed.

Our mission wasn't over. There might still be some way the Confed could screw up the progress we'd made. But for the first time since I'd entered the Exam, maybe the first time since Javi's death, a weight so familiar I'd stopped noticing it lifted from my chest. In that first instant, when the full reality of what I'd just accomplished hit me, I felt as if my feet might float off the ground.

I'd championed the magic and won—this round at least. I could only hope Finn came out of his battle in one piece too.

CHAPTER THIRTY

Finn

I'd never fully appreciated the power of surprise until that crisp mid-December day when Luis, Tamara, Ary, and I huddled in a café near the Confed building to see our con play out.

The decoy rally had been Luis's idea. About two hundred protestors, with Ary's boyfriend and Mark leading them, were converging on Times Square with posters and raised voices around the time we'd originally planned to begin our real protest. As we watched, the police cars stationed near the Confed building roared off—first a few, then another, and another, until just a couple remained.

"*Those dumb mages, getting paranoid about nothing,*" Ary muttered. "That's what the Dull cops will be thinking. That the Circle couldn't even get their intel right."

"Hey," I said. "It works in our favor."

"True," she said, with a cool smile that made it difficult to enjoy her agreement. She'd never apologized for or even acknowledged the beating she and her bunch had given me. No doubt she felt it had been justified by the information she'd had at the time, and therefore there was nothing to apologize for.

Mark called in to report that the police had dispersed the small crowd in Times Square. The four of us waited an hour longer, until the cops should have gotten wrapped up in their regular duties, and then, with a ripple of texts that started with our contacts and ended who-knew-where, we summoned everyone we could reach to the streets around the Confed building. Everyone who'd been ready for the rally had gathered in shops and restaurants within a ten-block radius of the place, ready for their cue.

I wasn't hanging behind or hiding in the background today. This time, I marched at the head of the first rush as we streamed toward the building's main entrance: a pearly white-and-gray marble arch overlooking matching steps. The air was crisp but the sun bright in the clear sky, streaking warmth through the chilly currents of the breeze. Hundreds of feet thundered over the pavement around me.

The heads of the cops in the nearest police car jerked up as we swept around their vehicle. They scrambled out with a few shouts that we ignored. I couldn't see how there was a whole lot they or the two cops farther down the street could do on their own. The guy who'd been in the driver's seat fumbled for his handheld radio. He was calling for reinforcements, I supposed. Well, we were prepared for that.

Other cars were pulling up around the fringes of our crowd. Camera crews and photographers spilled out alongside reporters waving microphones. Every move we made here was about to be recorded.

The flip side was, every move the Circle and their allies made would be too.

Luis strode right up to the steps. Two of the cops hustled past him to block the doors.

The League's leader raised his hand, and most of the crowd hushed so his voice could carry to our audience. "Where's the Circle?" he called out. "They decide our fate, but they can't be bothered to face us? Let them come out here, look us in the eye, and tell us we don't deserve the same magic they have."

A cry went up through the rally. "Come out! Come out! Let's see the Circle!"

The police by the doors stirred restlessly as even more protestors poured into the street. The mass of bodies must have extended all the way around the building by now. I climbed up a couple of steps to stand just below Luis and get a better look at the protest.

Several more police cars were parking as close as they could get to the edge of the crowd. Other cars, gray and black compacts, appeared nearby. The figures who emerged from those wore the uniforms of the Confed's security forces. Even they looked bewildered by our numbers.

There would be more security inside the building, but I imagined they were hanging back behind the doors, setting up defenses to ensure we couldn't burst through.

I raised my voice to join the chanting. Near me, Tamara added a clap of her hands for more volume—and to disrupt any castings the mage security team might attempt. A sharper wave of sound spread through the gathering.

"Come out!" *Clap.* "We want the Circle." *Clap.* "Show your faces." *Clap.* "We want the Circle."

The police and their mage counterparts drifted on the outskirts of the crowd looking a little aimless. An argument appeared to spark between a few of them—each side probably blaming the other for not having controlled the situation.

We hollered our chant over and over. Despite the sun and the closeness of our bodies, the winter chill gradually settled in. My cheeks stung from the breeze and my hands from the clapping. My throat was getting hoarse.

There'd been no sign of anyone from the other side of those doors. The Circle was waiting us out.

Knowing my granduncle, I had to admit it was possible they could out-wait us. They could hole up in there from now through the weekend if they really wanted to show their disdain for us.

A sensation grazed my jaw: a faint tingling like the lightest brush of fingertips, too warm to be the breeze. I turned my head toward it, and my gaze found her in an instant.

Rocío stood down the street at the fringes of the rally. A frowning woman with stiffly straight posture was poised just behind her, as if guarding her, but Rocío smiled the second her eyes met mine. She tipped her head with a little nod, and I knew she'd come to tell me her mission had succeeded.

A smile split my face in return, even though my heart sank slightly, knowing that *my* mission here appeared to be failing right in front of her. Well, it would be what it would be. One victory should be enough for any day.

I couldn't give up yet. The last time I'd made a real difference, it was only because she'd passed on her power to me. This time...

This time I had a sort of power she lacked, didn't I? I hadn't ever really wanted the clout my family's name gave me, but it was still mine. Even Tamara had said my old-magic status was one of the ways I could best help the League. Why in Hades's name wasn't I using it?

I couldn't try to speak for everyone here, but I could make sure we were heard.

With a stutter of my pulse, I swiveled and leapt up the last two steps to the door. Luis dipped his head as if to say, *Go for it.* One of the police officers held out his arm to obstruct me.

"Why can't I go in?" I demanded, pitching my voice as loud as I could. "Don't you know who I am? My granduncle is Raymond Lockwood—he's in there sitting with the rest of his Circle. If he won't come out here and talk to me and my friends, we'll go to him."

The people nearby had quieted as I spoke. The moment I finished, a cheer rose up.

The cops shifted their weight, but they stayed between me and the door. "No one goes in," one said.

"I have a right to enter," I said as the cheer faded so people could listen. "My granduncle and my great-grandfather before him served on the Circle. My father works in there too. Let us in, or bring the Circle out!"

As I hollered those last few words, my chest clenched, but the roar of the crowd behind me loosened it with a wave of exhilaration. A new chant filled the air: "Let us in or bring them out! Let us in or bring them out!"

Cameras were filming and snapping. Reporters were taking their notes. I stared defiantly at the police officer in front of me, and he glared back, his stance tense. It was still a standoff—unless I found a way to push farther.

In one swift movement, I reached for the handle behind him.

I saw the blow coming a split second before it landed. If I'd wanted to, perhaps I could have dodged at least enough to deflect the full impact. I didn't, though. In the instant I registered it, my mind gave over to the moment, to the pain that was about to come—to the story it would present to everyone watching. Anánkāi d'oudè theoì mákhontai.

The cop's baton whacked me across the head. My teeth nicked my tongue as I reeled backward. My feet slipped. Hands caught me, holding me steady on the stairs.

I straightened up slowly, pressing my hand to my temple—

the other side, not the one that had already been marked. A
smear of blood colored my fingers. A coppery flavor was trickling
through my mouth. My head throbbed, but inside I was smiling
again.

Had the reporters out there seen that? The law enforcement
called in by the Circle had struck down an unarmed member of
one of the most prominent families of the Confederation, simply
for trying to access the building where his father worked.

I took a step forward, and the officer tensed. "Don't do this,"
he said.

The chant washed over me as hundreds of voices took it up.
"Let us in or bring them out!"

"I have a right to go in there," I said. "You have no right to
stop me."

The wound on my temple stung with the cold. I took
another step, ready to spring for the entrance. The cop's arm
twitched. Then, like a miracle, the door opened from the
other side.

The first face I saw was Granduncle Raymond's. To say he
looked furious was a grave understatement. Another man and a
woman from the Circle stood beside him. Confed security
flanked them in a semicircle.

"This stops *now*," my granduncle rasped. The man with him
peered out over the crowd, his lips parting as if in amazement.
The protesters erupted into a cacophony of cheers and shouts at
the sight of them.

I swiped at the blood on my forehead with the back of my
hand, holding Granduncle Raymond's gaze. "Come out and talk
to us. Hear us out. We're not going away, no matter how much
you'd prefer to ignore us."

"There might be some room for discussion," the woman said.
"But not like this. Stand down, and we'll see what we can do."

"That's not good enough." I motioned to Luis and Tamara

just behind me. "You come out here and look the people leading this movement in the eye. You commit to discussing policy changes with them where everyone can hear you. We need it on the record."

"You fail to recognize that you have very little bargaining power here," Granduncle Raymond snapped, as if I hadn't already brought him out of his chambers to this doorway.

My mouth slanted into a crooked grin. There was so much he didn't know I had in me.

"I know," I said, letting my voice drop so only the three of them could hear me. "I know the Dulls aren't really Dull. I know the Circle must have been aware of that for at least as long as the Confed has been testing people. If you don't come out here and give us a story you actually mean, I can give them that one. It's your choice."

My granduncle's face turned deathly sallow. The woman looked as if she'd swallowed her tongue. The other man made a sputtering sound, his gaze darting to the edges of the crowd where the cameras were watching.

If I made a statement now, the news would be all over the world within the hour.

"Raymond," the woman choked out.

My granduncle glowered at me, his eyes gone flinty. "Do you have any idea—what chaos you'd cause? The destruction of everything we've worked so hard to build? You wouldn't dare."

I glowered right back at him. "Try me."

For the first time I could remember seeing, something wavered in his expression. The other man grasped his forearm. A silent agreement seemed to pass between the three of them. They moved forward, and I backed up to give them room to cross the threshold.

Luis and Tamara came together to meet them on the front step. I glanced around, expecting Ary to shove her way in too, but she must have gotten caught up elsewhere in the crowd. I eased farther back still, giving all the space to the other two. My part here was done.

Luis raised his hand, and the chanting quieted. "You have something to say to me?" he prompted the Circle members.

"It's clear that the policies we've felt were in the best interests of our societies—both magical and nonmagical—are causing distress to a significant number of people," the woman said in an expansive voice, clearly speaking to the cameras as much as to Luis. "We invite you and four colleagues of your choosing to sit down with us on Monday and discuss the potential changes that might be made."

"*Potential* isn't enough," Luis said. "Are you willing to change the policies or not?"

"We can't say exactly what adaptations we might make without further consideration," the other man said. "But I'm sure there are some accommodations we could implement."

There. We had their agreement in a public statement. The battle wasn't over yet, but we'd won more ground than I suspected any of us had really hoped for even a day ago.

"All right," Luis said. "That's all I ask. We'll leave you in peace for now."

He held his hand up to the crowd again, both in a victory gesture and a motion that the rally was concluded. Whoops and laughter carried through his audience, and bodies began to shift toward the adjoining streets.

"Bloody rabble," Granduncle Raymond muttered sotto voce, turning back toward the doorway without so much as a glance at me. His colleagues moved to join him.

I was just heading down the steps when a streak of magical light split the air overhead.

The conjured bolt struck the marble arch over the doorway.

The stone fragmented in an instant. With a sinister rattling, shards sharp as daggers rained down on the Circle members.

A cry broke from my throat. The woman and the other man stumbled back against the sides of the arch, but one of the slivers pierced Granduncle Raymond's chest.

He crumpled.

Mage security burst through the doorway. Three of the officers dropped down around my granduncle.

"Get those people out of here!" one of them yelled. "We need an ambulance."

The crowd was churning now with murmurs of confusion and distress. "We're done here!" Luis shouted to them. "Head home. Clear the street."

The mage security team hustled past him, urging the mass of bodies into varying streams. They had to be searching for the perpetrator too.

My gaze followed them—and snagged on a head of long, violet-streaked black hair in the crowd. Ary's familiar face sported a wide grin as she turned to be swallowed up in the crowd. My heart stopped.

Her Dampered "friend" with the stone affinity must be here. She'd carried out her plan after all, with an even grander target.

"Move out, move out!" the security officer next to me hollered.

I grabbed Luis's arm. "It was Ary," I said. "She organized this. You've got to tell them—we've got to find her—"

Luis put his hand over mine, his eyes wide. "I'm on it. You look after your family."

As he hurried down the steps, the nearest officer nudged me after him. I whipped around, holding up my hands to show I wasn't looking to fight. The sight of Granduncle Raymond's prone form made my gut wrench.

"He's my granduncle," I protested, and this once today, that fact seemed to matter. The officer brushed past me, and I crouched by Granduncle Raymond's feet while the security team cast their first aid 'chantments.

His face looked even more sallow than when I'd threatened to expose the Confed's greatest secret.

* * *

No one knew what to say. We were gathered there in the hospital's gleaming waiting room—my Grandaunt Phyllis, Dad, Mom, and me—but we stood in a hush, as if our silence would provoke some news out of the room where a team of doctors and magimedics had been working together for the past two hours in a weird sort of harmony, attempting to save Granduncle Raymond's life.

Hugh was on the other side of the country on business. Margo hadn't responded to phone calls—she often had her phone off during the government meetings she facilitated. It was just the four of us.

My gaze roamed from the nurse's desk, where the staff was bustling here and there, to the TV mounted in the corner, to the broad windows that looked over the city. The grand stone structure of the Confed building loomed just a few blocks down the street. Right there—right there we had somehow won and lost at the same time.

I yanked my eyes away just as Rocío slipped through the double doors into the waiting room. The woman who'd appeared to be guarding her before trailed close behind her. My spirits leapt as I turned toward her, but the joy I'd felt in that first glimpse crashed amid the guilt and uncertainty clawing at my innards.

Rocío didn't appear to need me to say anything anyway. She

walked over and wrapped her arms around me, and I bowed my head to her shoulder.

"Any news?" she asked softly.

I shook my head. A lump had clogged my throat. It took me a few moments to dislodge it. "They're still working away in there."

"You couldn't have known it would happen. You were doing what you needed to do. You can't blame yourself for this, okay?"

"Have you stopped blaming yourself for the people we lost?" I said. *In the Exam. The ones who died.*

She swallowed hard. "I'm doing my best."

"I would have been celebrating right now," I said. "But instead..."

Rocío eased back and took my face in her hands. "The attack on the Circle was horrible. But whatever happens, they agreed to that meeting. They agreed that the policies could change. That's still a victory. You don't have to be proud of it right now, but it'll still be there later."

My mouth twitched, but I couldn't quite smile. Rocío raised her hand to my temple. One of the magimedics had sealed the wound from the police officer's blow, but a mark would have lingered.

"That was hard to watch," she said.

"That was the point." Even if, after the way that confrontation had ended, I found it hard to focus on why it had been so important.

Dad cleared his throat. I looked at him, Mom, and my grandaunt in a daze.

Oh. They didn't know who this person comforting me even was.

"This is Rocío," I said. "My girlfriend."

"Hi," she said meekly. "I didn't mean to barge in on a family moment. I just—I was worried about Finn—"

"It's all right," Mom said. "It was good of you to come."

I was about to ask what the situation was with Rocío's new living shadow when a doctor approached our little cluster. The resignation on his face made my back go rigid.

"Unfortunately, we weren't able to stabilize Mr. Lockwood," he said. "The team did everything they could, but there was damage to his heart, and—I'm afraid he has passed on. I'm so sorry."

My grandaunt made a faint wounded sound. Mom caught her arm as she swayed. Dad's face tightened, but he stepped forward to confer about something with the doctor. My own balance seemed to have shifted off-kilter. I wobbled on my feet.

Rocío grasped my hand. I hugged her again with a futile wish that I'd never need to let her go.

She was here now. That was what mattered. She was here and not off fighting some wretched war, and—

Rocío stiffened in my arms. She was staring over my shoulder at the waiting room television. The screen was replaying the fracturing of the Confederation building's archway. I winced and was about to avert my gaze when I noticed the words scrolling along the bottom of the screen.

Terrorist attack confirmed on leading members of the North American Confederation of Magic.

Terrorists? I stalked closer to the TV, Rocío following.

Up close, I could make out the newscaster's spoken commentary. "Two leading Confederation members are injured and one is in critical condition after a vicious attack following a protest rally at their offices this afternoon. The international mage terrorist group known as the Bonded Worthy has claimed responsibility with a taunting video."

The broadcast cut to low-res footage of a figure whose face was nearly completely shrouded by scarlet cloth. Three others, two similarly shrouded and one wearing a ghoulish white mask, stood in the background. A translation appeared on the screen as the first figure spoke in a thick staccato voice.

The people of North America have pushed over those in their way for too long. Now you see how it is to fall. This is only—

"Oh, no," Rocío said in a thread of a voice. She rubbed her arms. "The magic is getting worked up. Something's happening. The Secretary of Defense—he promised he'd keep the peace, but only as long as no one attacked us—"

"No one did," I said. "The terrorists are lying, to scare us I suppose. There was someone in the League who'd been talking about striking back at the Confed like this. I saw her at the rally, right after it happened—I know she set it up."

Rocío's eyes widened. "We have to tell the Dull government that."

She spun and dashed across the room to where her guard had lingered. "I need to speak to Zacher," she said. "Right away. Please."

"Now, wait a second," the woman said.

Rocío clasped her hands by her chest in a praying gesture. Her hair twitched as if a bit of wind had tugged at it, and her shoulders stiffened. Was that the magic pulling at her—hard enough that I could *see* it?

"It's an urgent matter of international security," she said. "*Please*. We have information about the attack the Bonded Worthy are claiming."

The woman's jaw tightened, but she pulled out a phone. After a few quick remarks and a torturous wait, she handed the phone to Rocío. "He's listening."

Rocío paced to the window and back as she spoke to the Secretary of Defense. He must have been the one who'd sent the guard with her. Was the woman Rocío's protector or her jailor?

Rocío's hair quaked against her back in a direction that didn't seem to fit her movements. The hem of her jacket rustled. Fates above, how adamantly was the magic clinging to her, that I could observe its insistence with my own eyes? My stomach knotted. The conversation didn't appear to have gone badly, though. When Rocío handed the phone back to her guard, her expression had relaxed. Nevertheless, she hugged herself before she spoke.

"It's okay. I don't know why the magic is freaking out, but it's not what I was worried about. He said he's sticking to his promise—and they know the video is a lie. Apparently, the Bonded Worthy has a habit of taking credit for any destabilizing events they can to use for their own purposes. There's—"

An eerie crackling that reminded me of Fourth of July fireworks pierced through the window. Beyond the glass, glints of magical light wriggled across the form of the Confed building down the street. With a lurch, its walls crumbled. Tons of stone and steel collapsed in a cloud of debris with a *boom* that shook the ground all the way to the hospital.

My breath snagged in my throat. Screams rang out on the street below us. The dust cloud rising over the fallen building whirled—and a ghoulish mask-like face glowed in its midst, framed by a circle of blazing red script. It was the same visage as I'd seen in the terrorist's video.

They really had attacked us now.

Rocío had dropped into a crouch, her head in her hands, her hair whipping around her. "No, no, *no*," she cried. Then her voice was lost in a warbling sound that rushed up around us, so loud my ears were ringing in an instant.

It sounded almost like magic used to, but I shouldn't have been able to hearken magic. I was hearing this noise the same way any Dull person would. It raged as fierce as a rising storm.

A force walloped the windows in front of us so hard a crack opened in the glass. Everyone in the waiting room scrambled backward with gasps and whimpers. My parents tugged my grandaunt down behind one of the rows of chairs for shelter.

The mirrored face of the building across the street splintered. Car alarms blared. Another stream of smoke streaked up into the sky from somewhere farther away. The force smacked the windows again, and the cracks spread.

The mage insurgents had taken advantage of Ary's gambit in more ways than anyone had anticipated, and now the magic was raging. As I knelt next to Rocío, gripping her shoulder, my memories from the past few months tumbled together into a barbed line.

Mark's skin seared raw. The Exam's vines crushing a girl as she screamed. The bloody mess I'd made of Callum's thigh. My battered face and ribs at Ary's hands, the bash on my temple from the Dull police. Granduncle Raymond's chest split open by a marble shard. The terrorists sending the whole Confed building crashing down.

We'd thought we'd won a victory today, but it hadn't been enough. Not enough to contain all the pain and rage the whole world had been accumulating.

We'd hit out at each other in every direction, over and over, and now we'd broken the glue that had once bound that world together.

The warbling of the magic heightened to a shriek. Rocío trembled and shuddered. I pulled her to me, dipping my head and cupping her cheek so I could catch her gaze. She stared back at me, her face grayed to a sickly shade. Her hand groped for mine and squeezed tight.

"I can't stop it," she said, her voice quaking, as if she honestly believed she should have been able to harness the immense, wild, wounded thing that was thrashing at our city.

"So we just get through it," I said. "Can you—can you cast at all? There might be people down there who need someone to help, to do *something*."

Her chin came up, and the determination I'd always loved her for lit up in her eyes.

"Even if I can't cast, I'll do whatever I can."

Her fingers twined with mine. We pushed to our feet together. Hand in hand, we ran for the stairwell to face the chaos below with everything we were capable of giving.

ACKNOWLEDGMENTS

No book ever comes into being completely on its own. I owe much gratitude to:

Deva Fagan, Amanda Coppedge, and the members of the Toronto Speculative Fiction Writers Group, for their input and encouragement during the early drafts.

Linda Nieves Perez and Elsa Viviana Munoz, for informing the book from a cultural perspective.

Dave Wilton and Alexis Hilgert, for their knowledge of government workings.

My editors at Help Me Edit and Absolute Editing, for polishing my prose.

Jennifer Munswami, for another cover you can't look away from.

My husband, Chris, for his constant love and support.

And as always, the awesome readers who've spread their love for the Conspiracy of Magic series and waited patiently for this second volume. I couldn't do this without you!

ABOUT THE AUTHOR

USA Today bestselling author Megan Crewe lives in Toronto, Canada with her husband and son. She's been making up stories about magic and supernatural conspiracies and other what ifs since before she knew how to write words on paper. These days the stories are just a lot longer. Her other YA novels include the paranormal *Give Up the Ghost*, post-apocalyptic the Fallen World series, the sci fi Earth & Sky trilogy, the contemporary fantasy *A Mortal Song*, and the supernatural thriller *Beast*.

Connect with Megan online:
www.megancrewe.com

9 781989 114063